About the Author

ER Harding is a science fiction addict who also has a keen interest in science and technology. After many years of storytelling for the personal amusement of family and friends, recent redundancy provided the perfect opportunity to write some of those stories down.

Dedication

Dedicated with gratitude to David Harding and with
thanks to Geoff Lamb and John Leaver.

ER Harding

MANUMISSION

AUSTIN MACAULEY
PUBLISHERS LTD.

A CIP catalogue record for this title is available from the British Library.

ISBN 9781786299390 (Paperback)
ISBN 9781786299406 (Hardback)
ISBN 9781786299413 (E-Book)

www.austinmacauley.com

First Published (2017)
Austin Macauley Publishers Ltd.
25 Canada Square
Canary Wharf
London
E14 5LQ

Chapter 1

I sucked down the last bitter foam of my warm beer with a final slurp, and banged the glass down on the makeshift bar. My mates yelled approval and I burped massively to a background chorus of cheers. The warm evening air was heavy with the smell of beer and people, and my best buddy, Jared, leaned over and poked me in the stomach 'cause he thought it was funny, but it wasn't a hard poke; he was a good bloke was old Jared, and the smack that I swung at him was only a reflex.

I hardly ever spent time with the lads; the boss thought it encouraged over-familiarity, and I have to admit obedience had been pretty much second nature to me until that night. I'd been hammered into my place in my dad's grand scheme for as long as I could remember, and I'd never given serious thought to the idea of fighting back, because it just ran too deep.

We were never, ever, allowed alcohol and that's probably why we were going a bit overboard. There'd be fights later, but I reckoned we'd be all the better for it, and we'd sort everything out in the morning. I'd taken it on myself to have the beer brought in, and I knew damn well he'd be watching like a hawk for trouble now. Part of the reason I was acting the fool was that I could feel his eyes boring into me from his office window. Soon I'd have to creep back to him like some pathetic kid.

Oh, he wouldn't come over here himself, and he'd never say anything anyway, not in front of the lads, though he'd say it all as soon as we were alone. I could've recited every word of the nasty little speech he'd give me later. It was crucial that I look like his natural successor, and the lads all had to respect me, so he wouldn't say anything in front of them. Not a word. And that was the trouble; my dad thought they worshipped him, but he didn't know the truth, that they were scared of him and they absolutely bloody hated him.

'Want another, Gabe?' Jared asked.

'No time, mate,' I answered. 'I've got tons of reports to sort out for old Toby.'

Jared's face crinkled in sympathy. He's a bit younger than me, but age doesn't matter much in our group. We all live the same way, though my cabin's plusher than his, and my motor's a gorgeous little red hoverbird, while Jared only has a standard rover. It would have to be though, seeing as I'm the boss's son. Not that anyone in his right mind would be jealous of that.

'I got to push off an' all,' he said. 'I want to see if I can sneak out later, and I'll never make it if I'm smashed. Besides, Selena will smell it,' he added cheerfully.

'Nah, she won't, Jaz, not over your natural stink,' I pointed out, but Jared just grinned at me, the soppy bugger. He's not a looker, old Jared, or at least I don't reckon he is. He's nearly as tall as me, but maybe a bit skinnier. He's dark skinned, very dark actually, more like people used to look a few hundred years ago, when different bunches of people lived in little groups and all looked the same but different from each other, if you see what I mean. Made his teeth look whiter though, and I always had to remember that, if I was trying to work out a rota for a raid after dark. I tried to use old Jaz in daytime only for quite a lot of reasons, but his flashy white teeth were one of the good ones.

This whole knees-up was for Jared's birthday. He'd just turned twenty-one, and everyone liked him, but everyone would've been here anyway, whether they were his mates or not. The bar was temporary and though it had been set up in a tent, there wasn't room for everyone, so we were all milling about outside, and the others closed round the bar as Jared and I shouldered our way through the scrum of bodies. I looked at Jaz, and saw him glance at Tobias' cabin, and he threw me another grimace as he sloped off towards the latrine.

I saw what he'd been looking at and all the happy feelings just leached away. I was in trouble again. Mind you, at least this time I'd known it was coming.

I could see my dad standing by the door of his cabin, quite hard to spot in the dusk, but unfortunately not hard enough. Even his clothes stood rigidly to attention. It might have been the only obvious sign that he was no spring chicken anymore; he had a waistband so high and a shirt so taut that I just couldn't imagine he could bend at all.

He stood perfectly still in the gloom, just like he always did, waiting for me to notice him. Toby never bollocked me in front of anyone. He'd feel that was undignified. He always just stood there and stared at me from a long way off, until he was certain I'd seen him, and then he'd walk away, absolutely confident that I'd go and see what he wanted, every single time. And I always did. I hated myself for it, but what else could I do? This was

9

my home and it was where my friends were. I wanted to take over one day, I really did, but I hated myself all the same. I looked across at my dad and saw him turn and walk back into his hut and shut the door without acknowledging me.

For some reason, maybe it was the beer, I didn't want to go trotting back to Dad this time. I mean I really didn't; I thought he was out of order. He didn't trust me to behave, even though he had no bloody reason to think I was going to disgrace myself. I knew he'd be angry about the alcohol, but honestly, there wasn't really any religious reason why the lads couldn't let their hair down. He must've just looked out of his window and thought I was having fun. The sight of me enjoying myself had always set his teeth on edge, come to think of it.

I stood around for a bit, considering my options. Actually, I only had one option. I'd have to go and see what he wanted, 'cause he was a mean bastard. Dad must've been pushing sixty, but he was hard as nails. It didn't matter what training I did, and I did a hell of a lot, he'd probably still be able to paste me to the floor in ten years' time. Now that was a depressing thought.

While I was still standing and thinking about it, Jared came back.

'You not goin' to see what he wants, Gabe?' he said. I gave him a look. Jared's a good lad, not overly bright but there's no nastiness in him, and I knew straight away he'd only asked because he was surprised I was still there. The other lads must've spotted their noble leader staring across the yard as well, but they were pretending they hadn't. That was another thing I liked about Jared. He didn't pretend.

'Yeah, course I am. There's no rush though, you know,' I added. Jared's face was a picture of worry and admiration. Or at least I think that's what it was.

'Really? You prob'ly ought to, you know. I mean he won't like it if you make him wait, will he?'

That, for some reason, put the lid on it. 'Well, I think I've got time for another one first. You comin', Jaz?' I led the way back to the bar, and a natural path opened in front of me. This was probably partly because I was the biggest bloke there, and more likely because my dad's practically a god, but I was getting slightly shirty now, and that might have had something to do with it too. I reckon I was sending out invisible spikes of rage.

We ordered more drinks and I led the way back out so old Toby would have a nice clear view from his window. I was getting angrier and angrier the more I thought about it. I was twenty-five years old, a highly trained and professional killer, and I was still being treated like a little kid. At the very least it was bloody humiliating, especially when you'd think he'd want to build me up as a leader. Of course, he had no intention of getting old or actually handing over for a long, long time. That was worth remembering. Tobias thought he had all the time in the world.

A few other blokes came over, and seeing the slightly constipated expression on Jared's face, a discussion about freedom and individual liberty got going, because I couldn't bring myself to admit that I was absolutely shit-scared, but also on a hell of a high. I remember thinking that no-one should feel like that at my age, and after that, the time just seemed to fly by.

Jared had given up the idea of getting out to meet Selena. We weren't supposed to see the women, who lived separately because they encouraged loose behaviour and even looser talk, or so Tobias thought, and he didn't much like women anyway. I used to wonder how my mum stuck him for so long, but as I got older I realised she hadn't stuck him for long actually.

When I was a kid of five or six, a couple of years seemed a long time, but once I was grown up, I realised my mum hadn't hung around long at all. I wondered, pointlessly, what she was doing now and then binned it. It wouldn't do any good. I'd not heard from her since she left when I was a little kid, and I was dead sure I wasn't going to now.

I was distracted by a scuffle at the bar, but I decided not to interfere. There seemed to be a good-natured atmosphere on the whole, and it'd put me in an awkward position if I tried to break it up. I sort of had authority, but it was only reflected off old Toby, and part of me dreamed of the day when I could really sort this bunch of rabble out.

Someone suggested that we go over and see if any of the girls wanted to join us, but I had to veto that. Tobias let us have a certain amount of licence, if carefully contained, but corrupting his acolytes would cause an all-out war.

Then one of the other lads, Sam, said he was off back to his bunk and I looked at the time. It was well past twelve, and I was really in for it. Now it was time to pay, and my mood dropped even further. I guess I wasn't completely sober by then, but say what you like about old Toby, he treated the lads well enough. They weren't expected to drink, because we were officially a religious order, but if it happened then there were no stupid rules about how much they could drink, as long as they were sober enough to follow orders. He expected them to use their judgement. He just didn't think I had any.

And for some reason, probably beer-related, something had snapped in me that night. I was going to have it out with him once and for all.

Chapter 2

Tobias rose wearily from his seat, massaging the small of his back. He was a tall, thin, fair-skinned man of fifty-eight, but he didn't look his age, though he had a face weathered and battered by years of fighting, and by long periods of hard living in deeply inhospitable places. His body was still tough and wiry, his energy apparently limitless, and his passion for what he saw as his holy mission was as undimmed now as it had been forty years earlier.

Tobias himself had no idea what colour his hair was, since the change from blond to grey had been unnoticeable in hair as short as his. He stretched slowly, ignoring the occasional gunshot crack of protesting joints, and then carefully tucked his battledress shirt back into his trousers.

As he straightened up, Tobias glanced out of the window and frowned at the sight of his son clowning around with the men. He watched as a youth gestured to Gabriel and saw his son laugh, and then take a spluttery swig from the glass in his hand. Tobias had warned Gabriel more times than he could count that he needed to maintain a more aloof image, cultivate an air of superior intelligence so that he'd be treated with respect, and that he couldn't act like an irresponsible drunken lout. Gabriel was his second in command, and it was a position that carried enormous responsibility. Without respect for him, the men might well question his orders at a critical moment, and that could get them all killed.

He threw himself back into his hard, functional chair and shifted restlessly, his already narrow lips thinning to invisibility. He knew Gabriel was perfectly aware that he was behaving badly in full sight of his father. It was the challenge to his authority that he'd been waiting for, and Tobias knew exactly what the bloody fool was doing. Gabriel had been getting harder and harder to control lately, and the time was long overdue for him to be taught a lesson. If only he could find a suitable lesson to teach him, Tobias thought, scratching his cropped scalp in frustration.

Unfortunately, he couldn't throw the boy out, as much as he'd have liked to, because Gabriel knew far too much about the team and could do devastating damage to their cause. There was no-one who could really take his place anyway. Gabriel had been brought up specifically to take over the running of the Soul Defence Brotherhood when Tobias could no longer manage. Yet again, Tobias daydreamed about what Gabriel could have been.

When he'd found out his wife was pregnant with a boy he'd been truly happy for probably the only time in his life. He'd made great plans and dreamed about the fine lad who'd grow up to fight alongside him, and the baby had been healthy and normal. Unlike officially registered pregnancies, which were all monitored specifically to prevent abnormality, Marnie's, unfortunately, couldn't be registered with the authorities.

They were essentially an approved religious group, but their military arm was absolutely clandestine, so Tobias couldn't risk it. It had cost him a great deal to have the state barcodes removed from some of his followers as soon as they were formally accepted, and then they had to appear to die of natural causes. It was a long, tricky and expensive process, and he couldn't do it with everyone because even the most inadequate government department would eventually begin to notice the statistics. Most of his flock were simply humble religious folk, living peacefully in a commune under the pastoral guidance of their increasingly messianic leader.

His own child, however, would certainly not be registered with any authority. If there'd been any life-threatening issues with her pregnancy, Marnie might have had a serious problem, since they didn't have ideal healthcare facilities in the camp. There were nanites, of course, to take care of all but the most drastic illnesses and injuries, but as far as anti-natal care went, they'd had to rely on their own medics and a self-taught midwife. Tobias liked the idea of breeding his own followers, but the idea was still in its infancy, so to speak, and Gabriel was the first of what he later decided was going to be a standing army of freedom fighters.

To everyone's relief, the baby had been born surprisingly quickly and without any difficulty at all, and Marnie had seemed content and reasonably happy for a few years. Then she'd turned funny; his wife had seemed to turn almost overnight, from an affectionate if rather dim girl, into a sullen and angry woman.

They all turned on him in the end, Tobias thought bitterly, and he wondered fleetingly why it always seemed to happen to him, but immediately dismissed the thought as irrelevant. As soon as the foetus' gender had been confirmed Tobias had started to make plans for his future. It was obvious that the boy's education should be appropriate for his future life, so by the time the child was five, Tobias had begun a structured training programme and Marnie really hadn't liked that all. She thought a five-year old shouldn't be taught to fire a gun.

Bloody useless hippy, Tobias thought again, as he had so many times since. What had she thought her own husband actually did all day? When she'd arrived, Marnie had been caught up in the worship of the new Messiah that Tobias was to become, and presumably she thought the funds that the new acolytes brought with them when they joined was enough to keep the SDB solvent.

But that was Marnie all over; she didn't look too deep and she didn't think too much. She was ideal material for producing an heir though, and so he'd married her. Tobias conveniently forgot that she'd been very pretty, too. It wasn't relevant now.

They'd had one final and catastrophic fight, and his demure and respectful wife had screamed and ranted at him like a banshee. Tobias kept his hands off her until she'd screeched that the boy wasn't even his. That had stopped him in his tracks.

He remembered the look on his wife's face as she realised what she'd said. Marnie's expression had said far more than the words that had spilled involuntarily from her mouth the merest fraction of a second before. She'd stopped speaking with a choking gasp; her hands started to lift as though to cover her mouth, her face had whitened and for a moment she'd looked as though she was going to faint. Then she'd rallied and tried to take it back, said she'd meant that her baby would take after her and wouldn't be a natural killer.

Tobias had been angrier than he'd ever been in his life. The cause of the original argument was gone from his head, as his mind raced to make sense of what his wife had let slip. The enormity of what she'd said made him abnormally calm as he'd watched her attempts to cover her blunder. With detached interest he agreed that perhaps the tiny boy should be brought up more gently after all. But he understood perfectly, and later it had been easy enough to check.

Bitch, he reflected. The boy hadn't been his. It still seemed incredible to him that the stupid woman had thought she could get away with it. He'd never bothered to check before, because there'd been no reason to doubt his obedient and nervous little wife.

Once she'd realised he knew everything, his wife had tried to take the boy and escape, and he'd been obliged to deal definitively and permanently with her. The stupid woman had thought she could just pack her bags and walk out. At least her parents had stopped calling him now. There was no proof that he'd had anything to do with her disappearance, and there never would be.

For a moment he allowed himself to recall the feel of her soft neck between his hands as she thrashed and fought under him. He'd taken his time; the feeling of absolute power over her was utterly delicious, and he remembered vividly the expression of mindless terror as her throat had crunched in his hands, and the desperate knowledge in her eyes, fading gently into acceptance as she relinquished her grasp on a life which had been of no benefit to anyone except herself.

Tobias' hands had curled under the desk, in an involuntary re-creation of the moment. He was nothing if not disciplined, however, and he resolutely put Marnie out of his mind; now was not the time for that sort of thing.

The boy had never known anything, though. Gabriel had seemed a likely enough lad; big and solid, and surprisingly bright when you considered his parentage.

18

It'd been easy enough to identify the father. The thug had been sent on what Tobias knew, and then guaranteed, would be a suicide mission, and after he'd dealt with Marnie the case was closed as far as he was concerned. Gabriel had been born, as it were, below the authorities' radar, and had no state barcode. As far as the law was concerned, the boy didn't exist, and that was too useful an attribute to waste.

He'd always considered himself a good man. Tobias had managed to avoid the authorities' attention himself as much as possible. He'd never had a criminal conviction, never misbehaved at all really, unless one considered his life's work criminal, and Tobias certainly didn't. After Marnie had gone, he'd done his best to bring the child up just as though it was his own, and had never let the boy's dodgy parentage affect his treatment of him. He'd never quite taken to the boy, of course, that would've been asking too much, but he was always careful not to let it show. He'd have been just as strict if Marnie hadn't been a promiscuous tart.

Gabriel had to learn what his future would entail, had to be trained to think on his feet, to take charge and to lead. He had to able to kill.

Tobias stood up abruptly and strode to the door. He stood motionless in the doorway, closing the door behind him, so that his lean form wasn't silhouetted in the light, and waited patiently for Gabriel to turn his head. He'd see him in a few moments; it never failed. He wondered if there was anything to the nonsense people spouted about psychic connections, because Gabriel had always seemed to sense his presence, and always came over as soon as he could.

It had worked well for twenty-odd years but it didn't appear to be working today, which was irritating. Then he caught the eye of a youth standing near his son, and saw him turn to Gabriel.

Tobias had recognised the youth, one who seemed hard working and very fit, and also unusually polite, even by Tobias' exacting standards. Not leadership material, of course, but he remembered the lad as one who followed orders without complaint or comment and rarely appeared miserable. He'd have liked him even better if he hadn't been Gabriel's best friend, of course. Intimacy between officers and other ranks was a particularly terrible idea in times of war.

He'd forgotten about his own youth of course, and had very little memory of the time before he'd known about the Metaform Corporation, which had started storing the unconscious minds of the public many generations before Tobias was born.

The Metaform had started out with what seemed to be the best of intentions, to try and relieve humanity's pain and suffering and most wonderful of all, to conquer death. The original directors of the Metaform had been adored celebrities for decades, until a feeling began to form in the public mind that there was something wrong with a great star-based computer that took away the bodies of the old and the dying poor, who were never seen again.

It was different for the wealthy, of course. Everything generally was, Tobias thought bitterly.

It wasn't so bad when no-one was ever downloaded because the replacement bodies hadn't yet been perfectly designed. The Metaform sold hope to the masses, and the masses queued up to hand themselves over. Then a few early experimental robots were created, mostly inhabited by middle-aged scientists. The public began to take even more of an interest, and there was a rush of innovation; the wealthy cornered the market and the tide of public opinion began to turn against the Metaform. All this was long before Tobias' time, of course.

He re-seated himself wearily and continued to work on his latest project. Tobias felt he could never rest, would never give himself permission to relax until he'd completed the final mission that would cripple the Metaform and its faceless operators. There were other groups, of course, all over the world, but they were fragmented and in many cases were simply bunches of weirdos who liked killing people. Tobias didn't actually enjoy killing innocent bystanders, but sacrifices had to be made, and he had never shrunk from making those sacrifices if they were for the greater good of humanity.

Almost three hours later, during which time Tobias had grown angrier and angrier at a delay that was as overt a display of disobedience and disrespect as Gabriel had ever shown, there was a crunch as the door flew open, and Tobias saw his son swaying gently before him, with a slightly peculiar expression on his face. The smell of stale beer rose off the boy like a mist, and Tobias wrinkled his nose in mild distaste, and prepared to deliver his lecture for what felt like the thousandth time.

He couldn't imagine why Gabriel didn't want to be in command, but he was deeply disappointed. The boy was a born foot-soldier, good at the physical stuff undoubtedly, but he had no brains, none at all, Tobias reflected, depressed, as he opened his mouth and began to speak.

Chapter 3

Connor turned slowly round to meet the accusing violet eyes of his companion. Meilinn's bizarre appearance held no surprises for him, and no attraction either. He'd known her for eons, unchanged except in the subtle shades of her skin and hair. He and Mei had enjoyed a brief and torrid affair of the mind which had burned out long ago. Now, despite the real if exasperated affection he felt for her, he was annoyed that she seemed to have become unfailingly argumentative, no matter how she chose to look.

Meilinn refused to back down in the face of the obvious irritation of her colleague. 'No. No, I won't agree to it. Con, do you realise what you're saying? That we should delete someone on our own authority is unthinkable. We agreed, Connor!' Her voice had risen and her initial disbelief at his suggestion was turning to anger.

'We don't have any option, Mei. You know he has to be terminated. He's going to destroy us and everyone else. You can do the simulations yourself, based on his actions.'

'Yes, I've just done them,' she interrupted.

Despite himself, Connor was impressed. The amount of data that Meilinn could process had always been vast and she'd become even faster in recent years.

'Then you must agree, Mei. Can you come up with any other way? Because I can't,' he ended sharply.

'Con, these are predictions based on past behaviour, not solid facts. We don't know what he's going to do for certain.'

'And is there any better way to predict his future actions than on what he's done in the past? For crying out loud, Meilinn, don't you realise how serious this is? This rogue mind isn't just threatening our existence; he's exterminating us, systematically, and from the inside. We have no defence.'

'But we do, Con. We can seal everything. I've already encrypted the crucial systems. He can't get at the memory storage facility, and we're completely backed up. I can lay a trail, and we can corner him, talk to him, make him understand.'

'Meilinn, how can you possibly not understand? He's smart. Amazingly smart. If he's let you seal the storage banks it's because he's either already had everything he wants out of them, or he's got a back door and can still get in. We cannot defend ourselves, Mei.'

Mei's incredulity gave way to annoyance. She'd trusted Connor for centuries, and they'd always got along well. She'd noticed that he hadn't been quite as friendly recently, though, and suspected that she was starting to get on his nerves. Mei wondered if the strain of existing as a purely virtual being was beginning to depress him. Most of the original team had gradually dispersed over the years, as the interminable dullness of immortality began to take its toll on their minds, but she and Connor had been, she thought, dealing with it better than most.

'No, Con. I won't go along with it.' Meilinn's tone was flat, decisive and completely final. 'I don't think we have any business even discussing it. The best thing we can do is catch him and put him into permanent store if you really think he's that dangerous. And even that's out of order.'

'It's not possible, Meilinn.' Connor's speech had become slow and careful and very loud, as though he were addressing a child of abnormal idiocy. 'If we could catch him we would've done it by now. Why are you talking such nonsense?'

'It's not nonsense. It's humane. Remember humanity, Con? It's what we pledged to be a part of, no matter what happened to us. We said we'd never see ourselves as gods; never make life and death decisions without being in full agreement with each other. And we'd never, ever kill anyone, because that would make us the bad guys.'

Meilinn was overriding her colleague's own settings now, and although he twitched as her voice thundered in his own data receptors, she ignored the signs of his distress.

The team had acknowledged, in their early days as a new company of trailblazing virtual intelligence technology, that Meilinn had unusual talent in the field. She'd been the youngest of them all by some years, and although they'd all worried this might be a disadvantage for her, in fact Meilinn had adapted astonishingly well.

As the other team members had become first disillusioned and depressed and then finally suicidal, she alone seemed to be immune to the inevitable boredom and was completely untroubled by the enormity of what she'd become. Meilinn's only concern was with the effect that total isolation would have on her, as the sole surviving member of the original team, if Connor ever decided to leave her. It was a very real worry, too.

Through the pain in his head, Con thought with a flicker of amusement that their old colleagues would have been fascinated by his protégé's ability. They'd always worried that such a young girl, barely nineteen when she'd been uploaded into the mainframe, would lack a coherent self-image, and they'd all been afraid that Meilinn would dissolve involuntarily into the mainframe. It had never happened, and in fact it was most of the others who'd decided to allow themselves to dissipate into the computer a few years later. One couldn't really call it suicide because they still existed, in presumably a different form, but they were no longer individuals.

As the thought occurred to him, Connor wondered if his old friend, Tubby, the last to enter the computer, still had enough personality left to help him, but Meilinn's transmission was really beginning to hurt him, and he dismissed the thought for the moment, while he dealt with the immediate problem.

'Stop, Mei. Stop now.' He transmitted the command as ferociously as he could, and Mei picked it up and was instantly silent. She looked shamefaced, aware, as always, of the damage she could do without even thinking. It had been the hardest lesson for her to learn; that need to remain constantly aware of the possible consequences of her actions.

Mei had been a cheerful soul in normal life, and inclined to a certain carefree disregard for others. As a virtual life-form, when she allowed her emotions to overwhelm her, Meilinn was truly dangerous.

Her expression was contrite now. 'Sorry, Con. But you must understand what I'm saying, surely?' She was pleading now, certain that if she could only make him understand then he'd have to agree with her.

'Mei, listen to me for a minute,' Con said gently, 'if there's a way to corner him, then of course I'd rather do that. If it's Paul we're talking about, he was a good man and I know he's not inherently evil, but the fact is that he intends to bring us down. He's far too smart to let us catch him, though, you know that. And we don't know for sure that it is Paul. It actually could be anyone.'

Meilinn's anger had gone, and she was anxious to make amends. 'Look, Con, I know what you're saying, but I'm still not convinced he wants to bring us all down. Why would he? We're working on assumptions based on previous behaviour patterns and choices. We know they aren't infallible methods of predicting future behaviour. He may be trying to improve the way we work.'

'The predictions are pretty damned accurate though, Mei,' he interrupted. 'And what are you suggesting, anyway; that we should let him go ahead and re-design the original Metaform and destroy us in the process? Or do you think we can appeal to his higher nature? Only I don't think he has one any more, sweetheart.'

Meilinn sighed, 'I do know we can't just let it go. I think you're probably right, and he thinks we're destroying humanity and he has to put an end to us before we finish the job. I just wish we could talk to him, and maybe make him understand. He never met any of the directors while we were still human, so he doesn't understand what our end goals are.'

'He does, you know, Mei,' Connor said, quietly. 'That last message made it clear he knows almost everything there is to know about us. He lives in the mainframe and he has complete access to all our archives. He may even know Tubby, Scott and Luther, if there's enough of them left to communicate with. This intruder's decided that the Metaform is a bad thing, and since he has no loyalty to any of us, he thinks it's his duty to rid the world of a huge threat. Why? Do you think you can talk him round, love?'

Their relationship had returned to its usual friendly style, now that they were no longer screaming to be heard over each other, and the two drew closer together. They were the only remaining crew of a team which had once had five brilliant members.

Loneliness was an occupational hazard and no matter how furiously they argued, or how irritating they found each other, Connor and Meilinn each lived with the fear that the other might decide to be assimilated into the mainframe and leave the remaining person completely and terrifyingly alone. It made them remarkably tolerant of each other's foibles.

Of course the mainframe was developing a distinct personality of its own now, made up as it was of three people who'd been notable for their intellect and mental stability before everything had become too much for them. But a mere computer, no matter how smart, was no substitute for human companionship and both recognised the fear in themselves and each other.

'Sorry, Con,' Meilinn said again. 'I didn't mean to shout.'

'It's okay, love,' he responded. 'I should have used a bit more tact.' He smiled at her reassuringly, with teeth so improbably, impossibly white that the effect was more startling than reassuring, and Meilinn winced.

'Connor,' she reproved, 'tone those down a bit.'

He laughed and became marginally more human-looking, although Connor's appearance was undeniably still far too close to technical perfection for any real human. He'd been a kind and rather nondescript middle-aged man in his previous life, and still considered himself a games designer, even after over three hundred years as a virtual human with no other corporeal form than an electronic signature.

'Mei, it's important though, and you need to look at it objectively. If this person destroys the Metaform, millions of stored minds will be deleted along with all the work that we, and especially you've, done to improve life for ordinary mortals.'

'I know, Con. I do know. And I can see that deleting him is probably the only answer, but even if we decided to do it, why do you think it'll be any easier than trapping him?'

'We'd take a different approach. You know as well as I do that it'll be a lot easier if we're not trying to avoid hurting him. Besides,' he emphasised again, 'it might not actually be Paul. We don't even know for sure who this person is. All our calculations will be useless if it turns out to be a random stranger.'

Finally, Meilinn began to accept his argument. She'd been a clever woman before her transformation, but recently Connor had begun to have doubts about her emotional stability. He tried not to let his relief show, and now that the crisis had passed they began to try and work out a plan to save themselves and, at least from their point of view, the rest of humanity.

Chapter 4

I'd decided to take him on, face to face and man to man, but as soon as I walked in, that plan went completely wrong. Something about that sour face of his just sapped all the nerve out of me. It's hard to stand up to someone who's bullied you for your whole life, and in the back of my mind the old familiar feeling that, if I was good, Dad might just let me off, rose up as usual and I hated myself even more.

'Hi Dad, sorry I took a while,' I said. Of course I was going to have it out with him, but it's funny how those intentions go out of the window when you're actually looking at the bully. A big part of me wanted to get back to my bunk without a fight now. Besides, I could feel a serious headache building up at the back of my head. I didn't know then how much worse that headache was about to get.

'You fool,' he snapped. 'Why can't you see you've lost the men's respect with that stupid horsing around? When are you going to grow up?'

Suddenly my temper came back to me and I was just tired of it all. I stood up straighter, took the whine out of my voice and allowed the anger back in.

'Well, actually I am grown up, Dad, in case you hadn't noticed. I'm grown up enough to see what you're doing, and everything's going wrong here, too. No-one's too happy about your leadership any more. This used to be a cause, a crusade that we all believed in. Now it's just a joyless boot-camp, and your aggression towards the lads is driving them out.'

'Joyless? What the hell are you talking about?' Tobias stared at me in disbelief. 'They're trained killers, and frivolity has no place here. Are you out of your mind? You're one of their most senior leaders, not a member of the rank and file. What the hell's wrong with you? I know I taught you better than that,' Tobias ranted. 'Why is it that everything I try to teach you has to be repeated over and over again?' he fumed.

I let most of his rage wash over me. I'd certainly heard it all before, a thousand times, but I didn't agree with him, and never had. Old Toby's furious tempers had driven my mum away twenty years ago, and as I got older I was just ashamed that I let the old man get away with it myself.

Unfortunately, Tobias was incredibly fit and he could probably beat me senseless without trying particularly hard. I wasn't exactly looking forward to the next bit. Still, I was a hell of a lot younger than he was, and I knew, finally, that it was time to stand up to him. If it didn't work then I'd just have to leave. Not that it would be easy, because I certainly couldn't just walk out.

Old Toby used every form of supervisory tech to ensure compliance and maintain discipline. There were small mobile surveillance droids which circled us at all times, and whose footage Tobias reviewed every day without fail. It was a bloody miracle that he was unaware it was possible to confuse a surveillance droid by catching it from underneath and rubbing a magnet over its shining base to freeze the current picture before releasing it slowly to face the desired direction.

No technology expert, Dad never knew the droid footage wasn't supposed to go slightly fuzzy or jump occasionally.

The men, however, were expert at pointing the machines away from whatever sneaky outing they were planning. Leaving the compound was difficult but not impossible and the lads covered for each other, again by spinning the surveillance droids and taking each other's shifts. I hardly ever left, myself, because he kept a special eye on me.

I'd decided years before, when I was first allowed to join their training, that it'd be tactful to pretend I'd seen nothing. It'd do me no good at all to go telling tales to the boss. But if I ever actually assumed command I'd make sure the men understood that the old tricks wouldn't work once I was in charge. Not, of course, that I intended to carry on enforcing such a stupidly intense regime.

I've always thought subtlety and cunning are far more effective than brute force and I was looking forward to putting a treasured plan of my own into action one day. It wouldn't be while Tobias was still in charge though. There'd been dozens of men once, but numbers had steadily fallen over the last few years. This wasn't entirely a bad thing though, since they now drew far less attention than a small army would have done.

The authorities turned a blind eye to us because there was nothing to see. There was never any sign that our little team was engaged in terrorist activity, and no representative of the police had ever managed successfully to infiltrate it. We looked like a religious order that complied with all local laws. Our droids also blocked and confused the state surveillance satellites and meant that we were almost invisible, and appeared far too small to alarm anyone in high places. This was my dad's world, and he had no need of, or desire for, any other.

'No, you don't have to repeat everything, but that was really out of order, Dad. Do you really think it increases the lads' respect for me to see you staring at me like that in front of them? You need to stop doing that; it's embarrassing.' I was pleased with this little speech. I felt it covered the essentials, and having lit the fuse, so to speak, I mentally stepped back.

Tobias was surprised, but not overly impressed; it wasn't the first time I'd tried to answer back. 'Don't be so bloody stupid, they know you obey me, just like they do. And you'd better not take that tone with me mister, unless you want a thrashing.'

That was it: that was what I'd been waiting for and I let all the anger and contempt I'd felt earlier show in my voice. 'Oh stop it, Dad,' I snapped. 'We've all had enough of your tantrums. You might look fit, but you're a cranky old man, and it's time you moved over and let me get on with things my way. Times have changed in the last hundred years. You can't treat people like dirt anymore and expect their obedience. Not even from me. In fact, 'specially not from me,' I added.

Tobias' jaw dropped. 'You ungrateful puppy. I've done all this,' he waved a hand to encompass the compound, 'for you. I trained these men at huge expense; I had to undergo the humiliation of fundraising from my parents' friends to pay for all this. We have more influence than I could have dreamed of when I was your age, and this is how you speak to me?' His voice began to climb in pitch and volume. 'Do you realise how effective we are? And it's because of me and my discipline, you pathetic piece of shit.'

I took a deep but carefully unobtrusive breath, and tried not to let my voice wobble: 'No, it's wrong. What you've done for the cause in the past has been great, no-one's denying that, but it's gone wrong now. You're killing too many innocent people and you just write them off as collateral damage. It's inhumane and it proves you're past it. Your judgement's flawed because of your arrogance, and 'cause you don't listen to anyone.'

'Flawed? What do you know about anything, you useless little shit?' yelled Tobias. 'Where the hell do you think I can get advice? Do you think I can just call a friend and ask them what they think? If it was up to you there'd be no resistance to that damned Metaform. How dare you tell me my judgement's flawed? You've never been any good, never come up with any workable alternative. You think sneaking about's going to fix anything?' There was a tiny pause as Tobias prepared to let rip. 'My judgement is flawed is it?' he repeated incredulously. 'Arrogant? You damned, feeble-minded worm.'

There was a resounding crash as Tobias swept his desk clear with an arm; the little display unit bounced onto the floor as he came out from behind his desk, and I braced myself.

'You think I brought you up for this,' screamed Tobias, 'you think I trained you personally just so I'd have to listen to you turn into a feeble whining pacifist? Who the hell do you think you are?'

I tried a last-ditch attempt to calm him down a bit, because even an incurable optimist could see that actual debate was going to be a problem, but I knew it wouldn't work. Tobias had a depressingly easily-reached point of no return, and we'd shot past that point several minutes ago. This wasn't going to be a reasonable discussion once the tempers had cooled, it was going to be the usual beating, or worse.

'Oh come on, Dad, you must know what I'm on about. We need to move with the times; fight more intelligently. We can't just go about blowing things up any more; it doesn't work, and the police are going to catch on. It's time to re-think our strategy before we're raided.'

'Oh you have all the answers, don't you? You don't know anything about strategy, you dozy little coward. I know what you want, I've always known. You want to join them; you want to get yourself a soft new bio-body and join your debauched boyfriends, you disgusting wimp.'

Tobias bounded across the room and caught me under the jaw, crunching me hard against the wall. I had time to marvel at the speed of him as the back of my head cracked hard against the wall. His grip on my throat was agonisingly painful, and I found myself worried that Dad might actually kill me this time. I knew if my windpipe were crushed, there'd be little likelihood of survival. If Tobias was still furious, and he would be, he wouldn't get the medikit to me in time.

I didn't exactly have time to think of a strategy, and I was starting to panic a bit, so I reflexively brought my knee up hard into Tobias' groin, and his grip fell away.

Some cowardly worm of terror actually made me afraid to hit him. It'd be like hitting a king or a god or something; my mental checks and balances were too firmly in place for me actually to attack, so I just tried to defend myself. It was never going to end well, and I knew that, but it would take a lot of pain before I could go on the offensive against the man who'd been a distant hero to me for my entire formative years. Even if he'd been a hero that I'd always dreamed secretly of murdering.

'You bastard,' gasped Tobias. There were flecks of white at the corners of his mouth, his pupils were pin-sharp and his eyes looked weird and much too pale. He looked insane, and I tried to slide out of his reach, moving further into the room, and trying to get ready to counter the next lunge.

'Dad, stop it, please,' I appealed. I knew it wouldn't work; I don't think he could even hear me by then. I knew that technically I could probably deal with him, but I just couldn't bring myself to hit him. The years of conditioning just went too deep.

Tobias either didn't hear me or decided to ignore me; he straightened up and ran at me again, and he was so bloody fast. This time I tried to duck, but his fist connected again with the side of my head. I slammed against the wall and the plaster cracked. I felt the bang and saw a white flash as I started to fade out.

As I slid down the wall and fought to hold onto consciousness, I realised that I had to fight back. Defence wasn't going to work, not this time. I cast around frantically for something, anything that could be a weapon. Self-defence overcame the mental conditioning in a way that no amount of logic could ever have done. I staggered to my feet, vision blurred through watering eyes and as Tobias lunged again, I swung at him and caught Dad a bang across the nose. There was a second's pause then blood fountained across his face and splashed over him. Tobias screamed, uncontrolled rage and murder-lust in his face and he punched me in the stomach with all his strength.

That's when I felt something rupture inside, and my lungs stopped working; paralysed by shock, they were folded, empty and useless. I clung to Tobias, attempting desperately to stop the sledgehammer crack of his bone-hard fists. Blood was running into my eyes now, and I couldn't see more than a misty red outline, but I dug my fingers desperately into Tobias' neck, just above the collarbones. It didn't stop him and the pounding went on.

I reached out blindly, and felt Dad's snarling face under my hands and wondered spasmodically what was wrong with him. He'd always been an angry man, specially these last few years, but he'd never been as bad as this. I couldn't push him away and I couldn't break his hold, so I dug a thumb deep into one eye-socket and the assault eased for a moment as Tobias pulled back, still roaring.

I could feel my awareness slipping away and wondered, in a detached and vague sort of way, whether the lads could hear anything from the compound outside. I didn't expect any help from them though. They were all used to old Toby; some of the men had practically grown up with me. They'd heard it all before, and I knew they wouldn't interfere. It'd really not be a good thing for anyone to try and help when old Toby was in a fury.

Suddenly there was a loud bang and I jumped like a rabbit. Dad's weight on my chest was gone, and where he'd been was just a red mess. I tried to make sense of what I was seeing, but I couldn't. It just didn't make any sense at all.

I looked round, and squinting through the haze of blood, I made out the shape of my dad's oldest friend, Errik Van Hartop, standing near the door with a small sidearm clutched in his hand. The old man looked terrified, his thin white face was an almost comic mask of horror, and the hand holding the gun shook convulsively.

'Oh my God, oh my boy…' Errik began, and then he stopped, shuddering painfully. I tried to say something, to ask what was happening, and why Dad had shut up at last, but I couldn't breathe. I had to concentrate on dragging the air into my chest, trying to ignore the excruciating pain it was causing.

Jared suddenly walked into the office and stopped dead, utterly confounded. As he stood beside Errik, the lad's face dropped into what would have been an expression of ridiculous stupidity and shock, if only I'd been in the mood to appreciate it. I saw him get a grip on himself and close his mouth as he took in the scene, which must have been incredible.

I could see Jared abruptly frowning in realisation. He pulled himself together and took the gun gently out of Errik's hand, prising the desperately clutching fingers away from the grip. He put his arm around the old boy's shaking shoulders and, pulling a chair upright, seated Errik gently. For a second I saw a look of blind panic crossing Jared's face as he looked at me. Then finally registering that I was trying to say something, he knelt down beside me.

I tried to speak, to say it was okay and we'd get it all sorted out, but the pain was unbearable and I still couldn't breathe. Later, I was told that I thanked Jared and Errik politely before I passed out, but I can't say I remember that.

Chapter 5

Connor had never looked like any kind of megalomaniac. He was a middle-aged gentleman, trim and pleasant-looking, and apparently in good health, though he did have slight reservations about his occasional chest pains. He was kind to animals, and in fact cherished his old Labrador more than any human. But he did harbour certain dreams.

As a software and games designer, Connor was moderately successful. He had his own small business, which was undemanding and left him plenty of spare time for his own hobby. This involved tinkering with virtual reality in the privacy of what he called his shed. No-one else would have referred to it as a shed. It was in fact a state-of-the art laboratory, which accounted for the fact that after half a century of modest commercial success, he had no savings of any kind and owned nothing but his dog and his house.

Connor's business was ticking along comfortably and since any game worth playing now involved the player becoming one with the machine, there was plenty of software available to the discerning gamer, much of it designed by Con. What had begun to interest him to the exclusion of anything else was the feeling that they were but a very small step from downloading humans completely into a computer. He felt that it was inevitable, and he badly wanted to be a pioneer of what was likely to be a life-changing leap in technological evolution.

As the years passed, however, he grew comfortably into the role of mentor for his young staff, and any ambition he'd had to pursue other areas of inquiry had gradually faded, until it was only a hobby, highly gripping to him, but with no prospect of financial reward.

Con was now sixty-five years old and not especially well-preserved, since he paid his appearance very little attention, other than to ensure that he was clean and tidy. Slightly below average height, he'd been athletic in his youth, but a little round stomach frequently caused him irritation since it interfered with his ability to button his trousers, and meant he had occasionally to go out and buy clothes, something he hated doing.

After a particularly exhausting sixteen hours of unbroken data input, re-input and correction, he'd finally left his deserted office at almost midnight. This in itself wasn't unusual. Con lived alone, apart from his dog and a part-time housekeeper, so he'd never really felt he needed to rush home.

After an enthusiastic, if one-sided, conversation with his dog, Tarquin, Con collapsed into his bed. His head spun, his arms and chest ached mercilessly and his eyes, gritty and unfocused, had seemed for a moment to see something other than his wardrobe. Connor put his glasses back on, then took them off, polished and replaced them. Finally, blinking convulsively and straining to see through the gloom, he realised that he really could see a road stretching into the distance overlaid onto his bedroom wall.

Con knew that road very well, as indeed he should. He'd just spent two solid weeks with a technician, trying to iron the more obvious reality bumps out of it, but deciding that he was over-tired, and he might have a late start in the morning, he fell asleep.

The ensuing dream was very odd indeed. Con had actually felt that he was one of his own application's avatars, and he'd been able to examine the scenery much more carefully than he'd been able to do all day. He stroked the trunk of a tall red tree, and felt the roughness of its leaves, marvelling at their texture, yet was still completely aware that he was deep in a dream.

Confused and excited, Con wandered along a road which had no apparent end, in a bright world that appeared to have no horizons or boundaries. Connor felt he ought to be afraid, but the scenery was warm and familiar, had come from his own imagination, and everything felt perfectly right to him.

Then, abruptly, he spotted a small angular object which jarred him uncomfortably. He felt that the proto-bush was the right colour, but that it was too alien in shape, almost pixelated, so it hurt his mind to look at it. Connor, suppressing an urge to run away from this peculiar plant-thing, deeply wished it wasn't spoiling the symmetry of this fascinating place. Then he saw to his great pleasure that the object was fading away. He leaned over and touched it as it faded out, and felt the strange cold smoothness disappear completely.

Con was confused, wondering if he'd damaged something, and as he examined the space where the object had been, he saw that it appeared to be growing back very quickly. This time, however, the thing that unfurled was discernibly a plant. There were no pixelations, the leaves were glossy and soft, and it no longer looked out of place.

He was euphoric, and he understood that he had the ability to create anything he wanted, and to remove whatever seemed wrong in this dreamscape. Connor spent the remaining hours of the night adjusting the scenery to his taste.

The next morning, Con was almost as tired as he'd been the night before. Despite oversleeping until almost nine o'clock, his mind was muzzy and his head still ached. The morning sunshine glared accusingly through a gap in the curtains, and he winced unhappily. Manfully, Connor swallowed near-boiling coffee along with painkillers, and went to his office.

As he arrived, still feeling moderately dreadful, Con felt strongly that the modifications he'd dreamed about needed to be implemented immediately, before he lost the shape of them. He walked into his own office quickly without speaking to anyone, attempting to hold the revisions fresh in his mind.

Connor's office was grotto-like in its gloom. He'd long ago found, when struggling to meet deadlines, that the best way to resist temptation was to hide it, so the windows were covered by heavy blinds at all times. His desk filled one long wall. On the desk were three large screens which he generally used all at once, checking the progress of development of what he hoped were new games and applications of startling originality.

As he woke his computer and the big display screens lit up, Con started to realise that some of the glitches and faults he'd been working on over the previous few days seemed to be less obvious, and in some cases had disappeared completely. He flicked through some of the levels, and into and out of the screens, with a gradually increasing sense of incredulity.

Con was beginning to experience a little excited feeling. He wasn't sure if he wanted to put it into words quite yet, but a small voice at the back of his mind was telling him that the seriously unrewarding part of this particular task might almost be over. He also managed to pay no attention whatever to the dull ache in his chest, which spread across his shoulder and seemed to squeeze the circulation out of his left arm. He flexed his arm abstractedly and decided that possibly he might need another opinion.

'Meilinn,' he called to his trainee and assistant, 'would you come in here a minute?'

'Hang on, be there in a sec.' Meilinn shut down the card game on her computer and popped her shoes back on. It was an informal office and that was fine, but it didn't do to rub one's boss's nose in it.

'What's up, Con?'

'Has anyone been in here since last night?' he asked.

Meilinn looked at him in surprise, recognising the rare signs of agitation in her employer. The only way one could tell if Con was uptight was that he became slightly pink around the cheeks, and she could see that he was definitely rosy now.

'Not that I know of, or at least I haven't seen anyone. Why, is there something wrong?' Meilinn said cheerfully. 'Tell you what, I'll get you some coffee, shall I? And a biscuit or two?' Meilinn could see that her employer was already miles away, and waited for him to process her remarks. 'They're chocolate!' Meilinn added seductively.

Con usually appreciated Meilinn's attempts to bring a little happiness into her boss's life, even if it was occasionally hard to get a word in himself, but he really didn't feel like a chat this morning.

Meilinn had been recruited as Connor's assistant, and despite being very young and having a taste for possibly

42

the most inappropriate and tasteless clothing ever seen on an office-based employee, he'd been impressed with her enthusiasm and intelligence. Con had quickly given her duties which, he occasionally wondered, might possibly exceed her abilities. In keeping with his preferred, 'if it ain't broke, don't fix it,' management style, Con managed not to notice Meilinn's lateness, tendency to use bad language and her inability to concentrate on anything boring.

He also tried even harder not to notice the extraordinarily short skirts and spectacularly high heels that Meilinn wore. The clothes weren't, in any case, anything that he would feel able to comment on, but Meilinn's coltish progress across a crowded room could stop all conversation, no matter how serious.

Her childhood had been poverty-stricken and rather unhappy, and she still tended to be drawn to the sleazier clothing that she'd grown up wearing. Indeed, Connor sometimes wondered if Mei occasionally still wore her old school uniform to work. It didn't really worry him though, and Meilinn herself was blissfully unaware that she looked in any way strange.

'Coffee would be great, thanks, Mei. I don't know, things look a bit different from how I thought I left them last night, but it was quite late, so perhaps I've just forgotten how far I got.'

'What time did you finish then? I left at seven and I bet it was ages later when you went.'

'Oh, not that late, but this is important.' Connor didn't want to get into a discussion about late nights, and how tiredness could affect one's concentration. That was a conversation he'd had with Mei many times, but always with herself as the subject of the discussion.

43

'If I can get the last few glitches out of this app, it'll pay for itself a thousand times over. It's just...' Con's voice faded away. The more he examined the details of the programming, the weirder he really was beginning to feel. The application was practically perfect, and although he'd have to check, it looked as though it was ready for the market. He had done the work, there didn't seem to be any question about that. The actual question that needed to be asked was: when the hell had he done it?

When Meilinn returned with coffee and biscuits, an hour later because she'd been distracted on the way to the kitchen, Con sat her down and thought through, out loud, what seemed to be going on, just to see how she would receive it. He needed to speak to someone about his discovery, otherwise he was afraid he'd burst. The beauty of having an eighteen-year-old assistant was that she simply hadn't been alive for long enough to realise that her boss might have done something impossible. Meilinn's reaction was much the same as Con's, only rather louder;

'Oh my God. Oh wow! Then you've invented something completely new. Can you do it again? You have to patent this right now...'

'It's the other possibilities that I was thinking of,' he interrupted her; 'it's not just for games. Do you realise what we can do if we can put people's entire consciousnesses into computers?'

The question was rhetorical, of course. Mei was bright enough not to need it spelled out for her, and her excited expression gradually changed to one of awe as she considered the possibilities.

Connor worked after that for several unbroken weeks, fuelled mainly by coffee. Meilinn's long thin form was

44

hunched over the computer, too, for far longer uninterrupted periods than she had ever worked in her short life. At the end of it Connor and Meilinn had the product with which they started their own small company, and with which they slowly began to take over the world.

The idea forming in Con's mind was that now the way was finally open for man to explore space. It had long been acknowledged that space travel had reached stalemate. The expense alone was prohibitive, certainly as it held no prospect of a return on investment. It always cost the kind of money that needed an entire nation's backing, and resulted in little that was particularly useful to the general populace.

It simply wasn't possible to exceed the speed of light, and although scientists were getting closer to the goal every year, and speculation about wormholes was always a popular topic, everyone knew that the invisible light barrier was, and would undoubtedly remain, as solid as ever.

Now Con had realised that if they could download the minds of astronauts into a ship's computer, time itself would cease to have any real relevance to them, and journeys of thousands of light-years could be undertaken with the elapsed time appearing to the crew to be as short or as long as they wished. Only the materials used would need to be space-proof, and resistant to any kind of radiation or solar wind. These practical difficulties were, he felt, what would hold them up, and he could only pray that he'd live long enough to solve them.

Meilinn's thoughts had been slightly different. On hearing Con's news, it had occurred to her that if ordinary people could be uploaded in a virtual state to a great database and possibly even be kept conscious, then normal mortality would be, in a way, erased or at any rate, postponed for a very long time.

Although the equipment didn't exist for either aspiration yet, as they digested the discovery, Connor and Meilinn discussed the possibilities endlessly and finally came to the conclusion that Con would sell his software company and that they would form a new one, dedicated only to this new technology. They would call the company the Metaform.

Chapter 6

For days after Tobias' death, his killer was too distraught to speak to anyone. In the middle of his miserable flashbacks, Errik van Hartop expected at any moment to be lynched or shot by the men, or arrested and imprisoned by the authorities, and he remained hidden and desperately frightened for almost a week.

Errik had been deeply traumatised by the whole episode. He re-lived the moment of the shooting over and over again, in shock and terror. He couldn't believe that he'd turned out to be capable of cold-blooded murder, and his own image of himself was unalterably sullied. He was also grieving at the loss of his oldest and dearest friend, so he was a mess of conflicting guilt, regret and relief. Errik was also, and somewhat unexpectedly, furiously angry that Tobias had put him into this impossible position in the first place.

When Gabriel finally surfaced from his medically-induced coma, he sent a message that he needed to see Errik. That message had finally penetrated the fog of misery that crushed the distraught old man. He'd eventually ventured out to the small medical building to speak to Gabriel, expecting, and accepting, that the boy would probably announce his undying hatred of his father's murderer, and that Gabriel would never speak to Errik again, except possibly on the witness stand.

The trouble was that Errik had committed an act apparently so utterly alien to his nature that, despite there having been little option at the time, and no whisper of blame attached to him, he couldn't seem to get over it. After speaking to him for a few minutes, Gabriel began to wonder if poor old Errik would ever recover from the trauma enough to pick up his life and carry on.

He seemed to have aged dreadfully since that terrible night, and today he wouldn't look Gabriel in the eye. Errik seemed constantly to be waiting for Gabe to demand that he be shot for the murder of his father.

'I know you had no option, Errik,' Gabe said yet again, as he lay on his bunk. Part of his face was covered in a big blue patch which kept out infection whilst the nanites did their work, and he looked terrible, but he kept reassuring Errik that he felt fine.

Errik sat with his back to the window, and spoke less than usual, though his trembling relief at Gabe's calm acceptance of him, evil murderer that he was, was visible.

'Errik, please,' Gabriel implored, yet again. 'Listen to me and try to understand that no-one, *no-one*, blames you for what you did. It was Toby or me, and it couldn't have gone on as it was.'

'I'll be arrested soon though,' Errik said. 'When the authorities realise he's dead they'll come and pick me up, so it's no use asking me for help with strategy now.'

'No, they won't, Errik,' Gabriel said patiently. 'My father's barcode was removed, wasn't it? So they'll have thought he was dead for years. Well, none of us is on the authorities' radar, are we, except for you and the congregation? And this whole area's shielded for religious reasons, so no-one official could possibly know what happened.'

As the reminder filtered through to him, a little more tension drained away and Errik sat up a little straighter. He'd been responsible, as the only really computer-literate member of the group, for ensuring that that the military arm of the Soul Defence Force was invisible to the orbiting satellites that tracked every living human from the day they were born until the day they were uploaded to the Metaform. And he'd done his job well.

To Errik's huge relief, Gabe hadn't wanted to kill him; he'd actually wanted to speak to him about their future strategy now that Tobias had gone. Errik's most useful skill was in accessing and analysing the less easily available data about the Metaform and its installations. He was a skilled hacker and in the past his information had resulted in some really successful raids. Tobias had valued Errik for several reasons, his analytical mind being one of the most important, and Gabriel knew that perfectly well.

Errik was seen as something of an elder statesman in the group. He'd grown up with Tobias, and the two men had been close friends for many years, despite, or perhaps even because of, the differences in their personalities. Tobias' aggression was often deeply unnerving for Errik, and yet the fact that it was never directed at him was somehow comforting and made him feel safe. Errik enjoyed the camaraderie of the small team, even though he knew that he was the softest member of it by a long way.

Tobias, on the other hand, valued his old friend rather more than anyone realised. Errik's gentle charm and unfailing acceptance was balm for Tobias' angry soul; he would tolerate Errik's presence when that of his own wife or son would have infuriated him even more.

Errik had been appalled at the recent decline in Tobias' attitude towards both his son and the congregation in general, and had tried to improve it as much as he could. Unfortunately, his old friend's increasing aggression meant that the more intellectual Errik had found it much easier to avoid him lately, and he just hadn't realised how badly Tobias' mental health had deteriorated.

Errik felt that he would blame himself for the rest of his life; not for the death itself, he was beginning to come to terms with that, and could see that it had been the best possible outcome in a horrible situation, but for having failed to help the condition of his friend. It was highly unlikely that Errik could have stopped the final confrontation between Tobias and Gabriel, but Errik felt that it wouldn't have reached the catastrophic proportions that it had, if only he'd been present.

'The truth is, Gabriel, that I've been avoiding Tobias lately,' Errik admitted. 'I know if I'd seen more of him, at least I could have warned you to take care around him. But it was so much easier to stay out of the way, and I'm so terribly sorry. I was scared of him, my boy, because I've seemed to irritate him even more than usual these days. If I'd stayed around as I should have done, I don't think this would have happened.'

Tobias and Errik had spent many hours considering the weaknesses of various upload centres and in even more depth, the small, plush, and fantastically well-guarded download centres. These had been a consistent and permanent target; the very thought of the rich and pampered creatures who were downloaded into living bodies whose souls were evicted for that very purpose drove Tobias nearly mad with rage, and Errik had provided a logical sounding-board for Tobias' mad plans. It was entirely due to Errik's input that there hadn't been more civilian casualties over the last few years.

Errik had watched the young Gabriel grow up, and while his absent mother and harsh father certainly hadn't provided the best upbringing for the lad, he still seemed remarkably well-balanced. It had never occurred to Errik that most of Gabriel's placid tendency to accept Tobias' ruthlessness, and his gentle pleasure in the parts of his life that were good, came from Errik himself.

Errik knew that Gabriel was the most important thing in his own world, but failed to realise his own importance to, and influence on, Gabriel himself.

Watching the last beating that Tobias would ever inflict on the boy, Errik had felt something snap inside him. He was almost pathologically terrified of physical violence, and felt nauseated at the sight of blood, but Tobias' fury had reduced him almost to tears. Errik had adored Gabriel since his birth. The little boy had come to him with his questions and problems as a small child and later as a young man.

Errik had soon realised that although it was completely hopeless, he loved Gabriel with all the considerable passion of his lonely soul. Watching the madman trying to beat the life out of the boy had been more than Errik could bear. He'd simply picked up the small projectile weapon that Tobias had left on the desk, the only object that hadn't been swept away in Tobias' rage, and shot him with it.

Furthermore, and this was a secret that he would take to his grave, and the part that kept re-playing itself in Errik's head, he'd taken careful aim with the little weapon and had directed the shot with careful precision from a distance of no more than ten feet away. Tobias' death wasn't entirely a crime of passion; Errik knew that a part of him had calculated the likely consequence of the shot, and had made quite certain that it was accurate.

'You're right,' he said in a voice in which hope was beginning to dawn, 'the authorities won't know he's dead because no-one knew he was alive, did they?'

'No. Well they knew we had a leader, but that would be you now, wouldn't it? So stop worrying about being arrested, because it's not going to happen. Even the ordinary surveillance stuff wouldn't have told them anything, because Father broke the old computer before it all really kicked off, and you know there were no location services watching us, so it couldn't even be seen from satellites. The only thing we have to worry about is what to tell the congregation.'

'Oh, thank God,' Errik murmured. Then, as he turned for the first time to look directly at Gabriel, a tear trickled down his thin cheek. 'I'm so sorry, my boy. You're being generous, as you always are, but I killed your father and you must hate me for it, how could you not?'

'That's an easy one, Errik,' Gabe returned comfortably. 'Can you imagine what Dad would've said if he could see you now? Because I can.' A smile of pure amusement lit up his patched and bruised face.

'Oh dear,' Errik gave a watery little laugh, despite himself. 'He'd have been revolted at me for behaving like a wimp.'

'Hell, yes. Dad didn't show mercy or expect it. If he was around now, even he'd say you did the right thing. He and I didn't see eye-to-eye, but I was his only hope for keeping the team going after all the time and money he'd spent on my training. We both know he wouldn't have beaten me so hard if he'd been in control of himself. Or probably not, anyway,' he added.

Errik drew a steadying breath. 'You've made me feel much better, Gabriel, you always do, but we both know the truth. If I'd been any kind of man, I'd have distracted Tobias and reasoned with him. I just shot him in a reflex that I didn't even know I had. I could have just winged him, perhaps.'

'No, you idiot,' Gabe exploded. 'If you'd managed to distract him this time, and you might have caught a smack yourself if you'd tried, by the way, this would still have happened in the end. I'm sorry, Errik, I'm not going to miss him and I'm not going to grieve for him. It's a bloody good thing that he's gone, and now we really do need to look at the future.'

'I suppose you're right,' Errik responded slowly. 'It's no good wallowing; we have a job to do, and the best memorial to my old friend would be to bring the Metaform down, just as he always wanted.'

'Finally!' Gabe looked affectionately at the old man.

'You know I always agreed with your idea that the best way to destroy the Metaform would be from the inside?' Errik said, wiping his face distractedly and arranging his features into an appropriately brave face.

'Yeah, but Dad hated the idea,' answered Gabriel. 'Remember, I kept telling him I could upload and damage it from the inside if I had some support.'

'Well, I know, it strikes me as a very difficult plan, but a positive idea. I once tried to get him to agree to consider letting you have more autonomy, but he wouldn't hear of it. When we talked about it, I always thought he was afraid to let you try to get into the Metaform in case he lost you, but of course he couldn't say that.'

Gabriel was silenced for a moment. Some of the things his father had said and done had just seemed irrational to him, and Gabriel hadn't bothered to work out why his excellent plan was unfailingly vetoed. 'D'you really think that's why he wouldn't let me do it, Errik?'

'Oh yes. Tobias was well aware that you were going to take over from him in the end, and he was always terrified that something would happen to you,' Errik said sadly. 'I really did try to support your idea, but Tobias and I had one blazing row about it, and it seemed sensible to let the matter rest after that. I'm not built for combat. I shouldn't have done what I did,' Errik grieved again.

'Errik,' Gabriel said patiently, for what felt at least the twentieth time, 'this time Dad would've killed me. He hadn't finished when you stopped him. He would've gone on and on hitting me until I was mush. You saved my life, and you only did it at the very last possible minute. You can't blame yourself for what you did. No-one else does; you must know that by now.'

'Yes,' Errik agreed sombrely, 'I suppose that's true.' Gabriel looked at Errik fondly. Although he was almost exactly the same age as Tobias had been, Errik looked easily ten years older. He was a slightly stooped, grey-haired man with charming manners and a soft expressive voice.

In the past, Gabe had sometimes wondered if Errik's interest in him was warmer than it should be, but the thoughts, when they occurred, were fleeting, and never worried him much. He'd come to rely on the old man and valued his opinion more than that of anyone else in his world. Errik had certainly never expressed any overt interest in him, and he could hardly be considered a threat, even if he had.

Their little group of idealists had been started by Tobias, and Errik had allowed them to set up and operate on his family estate on the south coast of England. He'd flatly, and very bravely considering his peaceful nature, refused to invest his entire inherited fortune in the group's activities, although he'd helped out on occasion, believing as they all did that humanity was under dire threat from the faceless intelligence of the Metaform.

'So what do you think we should do now, Errik?' asked Gabe soberly.

Errik sighed gently. He knew perfectly well that the lad saw him as a father-figure. There was no possibility that Errik would ever spoil the close relationship that they had by suggesting any other kind, but the sight of the lad covered in blue stickers and dreadfully bruised, tore at his heart. Errik firmly stifled the ridiculously inappropriate urge to sweep him up in his arms and comfort him as he'd been permitted to do when Gabriel had been a small boy. He moved resolutely onto the subject in hand.

For the first time, Gabriel's enterprising plan to get himself into the Metaform's database as an upload was considered on its merits, and, also for the first time, Gabe was listened to as an equal and as person of intelligence.

Errik had entered the medical hut in a terrible state, heart thumping and legs trembling. He'd been absolutely certain that Gabriel would, quite justifiably, hate and probably attack him, but it hadn't happened after all. Instead, they would work together towards their common goal.

Despite the physical weakness that he was suffering, after days of the self-imposed lack of food and sleep that accompanied soul-destroying guilt and misery, Errik finally began to think, cautiously, that everything might be going to work out after all, and for the first time in days, he actually found that he was smiling.

Chapter 7

Major Paul Pearson always strolled to his local shop in the morning. He went partly for the exercise and partly for the conversation, since in recent months it had become the only time he ever spoke to anyone.

He'd been retired for almost thirty years, after a long and moderately successful career in the army, though he'd left the service long before being awarded staff rank. He made that walk, uphill and over three miles each way, every single day without fail. He felt it kept him young, and his late wife had encouraged the habit, thinking it gave a point to his day and got him out from under her feet for a couple of hours or so.

Underneath the crisp, organised exterior, however, he was a desperately unhappy man. Paul's only child had been born with a rare genetic abnormality. He'd left his beloved army, and he and his wife had mortgaged and re-mortgaged their home in their desperate pursuit of treatment for her. Finally, they'd applied for an upload to the Metaform's database for her, when it became obvious that nothing could save her life.

Their dream had been eventually to pay for a new body for Cara, so one day they'd have her back, as vibrant and full of life as she'd been before the disorder began to strike her down at only ten years old. Although the million credits it would have cost had been impossibly out of their reach, nevertheless they felt that she wasn't quite gone, and it gave the couple something to hold on to.

When his wife, Molly, had died suddenly after a heart attack that occurred completely without warning, Paul had seen no point in continuing, but his disciplined body had gone through the motions of normal life. Day after day he'd got up, cleansed, depilated and dressed himself. He'd walk to the shop and return home every day, just as though nothing had changed, but underneath the moderately comforting routine Paul's heart was broken and he waited unemotionally for his own death.

On one particularly unpleasant day in January, he debated with himself whether it was really necessary to go out. The rain hit his windows with an intimidating bang and just for a moment he wavered.

'No,' he addressed the table firmly, 'it's the thin end of the wedge. Today it's too wet, and before you know it, tomorrow's too windy.'

Paul put his over-garment on, and heard the hiss as it snapped into place. Then he wound a long scarf around his neck. Molly had been gone almost two years now, and he'd finally more or less stopped remembering her knitting it for him every time he put it on, but he always wore it in bad weather.

Leaning into icy rain that was gradually becoming sleet, he pushed himself up the steep path towards the distant shop. The sun hadn't seemed to come up properly at all this morning. The light was an odd, dark yellow-gray, and the sensor lamps switched on as he reached them. No weather-domes had been installed over this area, and although Paul's little town had been considered dreadfully old-fashioned for many years, it had recently become desirable, retro-chic and in January, quite unpleasant.

The major paused to catch his breath. As always, he'd prepared carefully and since he was wearing the correct clothing, only his face was distressingly wet and cold. Paul crossed the road outside the shop cautiously; ice was beginning to pile up where the sleet had become hailstones and it was settling over the road.

As he stepped cautiously off the invisible kerb, he heard the high-pitched hum of a motor revving furiously and turned quickly. An auto slid around the curve in the road and for a moment, Paul saw the face of the driver, white and panicking, the mouth a perfect oval of stress.

After that, he felt rather than saw the impact when the auto broadsided him. There was no pain, just a wild sensation of whirling colours followed by utter stillness, disturbed only by the hum of the auto's whirring electric fans.

Paul lay peacefully in the hedge near the road. Nothing was hurting; in fact, he was very comfortable, and he felt obscurely that he'd done well to land where he had, as though he'd made a conscious choice.

Then normal sound returned suddenly. Paul heard the auto's driver shouting about stupid old men jaywalking about on public roads in these conditions, and how this idiot had just stepped out in front of the auto. Paul felt vaguely guilty because it was certainly true that he hadn't expected an auto to appear; they were so rare these days.

Then he wondered how it had hit him, as surely they had force-fields around them. He should have felt the buzz of the cushioning air as he was bounced at a greatly reduced velocity out of the way of danger.

The shopkeeper, a man who'd come to know his most regular customer very well over the last twenty years, came rushing out immediately. The stocky little man, having come to same conclusion as Paul, roared at the terrified driver, his face red with indignation.

The young driver's responses, when he managed to make himself heard, were getting defensive, as he'd just noticed that there was a man-shaped dent in the side of his auto, which wasn't going to do his case much good in the eyes of the law. His auto had indeed been unrestricted, and there'd been no defensive field because it wasn't actually his auto, so he'd not been able to operate all the systems, and the penalties were harsh for such offences.

The angry shopkeeper's dialogue was becoming increasingly aggressive, too. 'How come you dint 'ave no force-field then? I reckon you stole that auto,' he bellowed triumphantly.

The police and medics had been alerted immediately by the surveillance drones, and Paul, who'd been listening to the heated exchange with mild detachment, lost interest fairly quickly. His hips and legs were beginning to ache now. It was a bone-deep ache which promised to become quite unpleasant very soon, and the major's attention was increasingly being drawn to this.

The hailstorm had finally converted itself into big soft flakes of very heavy snow, and sounds were already beginning to seem slightly muffled and woolly. Paul decided that he would have a short sleep for the time being, whilst people made up their minds what to do next.

There was a soft boom as the air-ambulance arrived overhead, and the medics descended gently to the ground. Paul's unconscious body was lifted smoothly by hoverchassis into the craft. The medics weren't hopeful when they saw the old man; his face was grey and gaunt, his heartrate was dropping quickly and they placed him immediately into stasis.

The medical station, a geostationary satellite station known as the European Medical Facility, or the EMF, was a matter of fifteen minutes away by air-ambulance, and once the little medical craft docked with the huge station, the medics placed Paul's inert form, still in his stasis tube, onto the conveyor where he was immediately rolled into the heart of the institution.

Their job done, the medics disappeared to the next call-out, another AA slipping into their slot as they left; and the unremarkable event already forgotten by the crew.

Within a few more minutes, the major's smashed leg was removed and healing accelerated by the machines tending him. As his body continued to shut down, however, Paul was declared officially at 75% risk of death by the computer, despite the fast and effective intervention.

Since scans of the major's personal barcode showed him to be well over the minimum age for upload, the computer recommended that the major be kept in a comatose state for several days until his body had rallied sufficiently, then brought to full consciousness for upload onto the Metaform's central database.

This was the easy option for the medical computer, which had such an enormous population to treat that storage of the sick and injured was always tricky. Upload of the patient's consciousness, immediately followed by destruction of the unwanted body was always preferable from the point of view of the station's administrators, rather than long-term treatment with all the man-power and expense this entailed.

Some days later, as prescribed by the medical computer, Paul was slowly brought to full consciousness by a young nurse.

'Hallo, Paul. Paul?' she called softly. 'Can you hear me, Paul?' The nurse continued to chirrup softly into his ear, patting his cheek repeatedly, until the major gradually surfaced into awareness, seeing nothing at first, but then the small nurse's improbably enormous brown eyes.

He looked around, realising in confusion that he wasn't at home in bed. 'Where am I?' he said, indistinctly. Then seeing the nurse's uniform and the sterile whiteness around him, Paul realised where he must be and he corrected himself. 'What happened?'

'We're at the EMF, Paul. You had a nasty accident. My name's Hannah and I'm here to help you. Can you remember anything about what happened?'

'No. Oh.' He thought for a moment. 'Yes, I can, oh dear! I was hit by an auto, wasn't I?'

'That's it, and I'm afraid there was quite a lot of damage. The pastoral team's checked and couldn't find any immediate family to notify, but is there anyone you'd like me to contact for you?

Paul thought for a moment. 'No, there's no-one. I've been widowed for twenty-three months,' he said precisely, with the careful accuracy of the recently bereaved. A sudden pain lanced through him and Paul found he was struggling to breath.

'I'm so sorry,' Hannah said gently. 'Try to relax, Paul. Your injuries were quite severe, and the medical computer had to remove your left leg.'

Paul wasn't too traumatised by this news. Prosthetics were better than the original organic limbs, and his arthritic knees had been giving him trouble lately anyway. 'What else? You're looking worried.'

'There are a few other issues, I'm afraid,' Hannah said. 'Scans have shown that you have a badly congested heart, and to put it bluntly, we've kept you in a coma because only a complete replacement will be able to help. That's what I need to discuss with you now.'

Paul sighed. 'I can't afford that. I'm seventy-five, and my insurance won't cover wear and tear. It'll pay for the leg because that's accidental damage, but that's all. Was the driver insured?'

Hannah patted his arm in detached and absent consolation. 'No, he wasn't. The man stole the auto, and I expect he's in custody now. There's only state insurance, and that probably won't cover a heart replacement, as you say.' She paused; 'The computer suggested that you upload, Paul. How do you feel about that?'

'No. No, absolutely not, that's a terrible idea,' Paul snapped reflexively. Then he paused and thought for a moment. 'How long will I live without a replacement?'

'Well, obviously the computer can't be specific, but your condition's serious. The medics feel the final episode could occur at any time,' Hannah said. 'Shall I leave you to think about it for a bit? I have to go and see to another patient now, but perhaps if I come back in half an hour or so, you can have a bit of a think about your options while I'm gone?'

When Hannah had gone, Paul considered the alternatives. He'd heard the rumours, as everyone had, about the medical computer uploading patients who didn't need it, just to free up beds, but really, he thought, what does it matter?

He'd never be downloaded, just as his precious Cara had never been downloaded, but perhaps one day he might be able to communicate with her. Technical advances were being made every day, after all. *There'd be a point to that,* he thought, rather comforted.

When Hannah returned a few minutes later, Paul was ready for her. 'I'd like to go for the upload, please,' he said. 'When can it be started?'

'I'm so glad, Paul, and I'm sure you're doing the right thing. We'll do it immediately, as long as you're sure. It's important we're uploaded fully conscious, and preferably not agitated in any way.'

'I know,' Paul said, sadly. 'My daughter was uploaded thirty years ago, when she was ill. We couldn't afford a frame for her, but I remember the process very well.'

'Gosh, that was a long time ago; things have changed a lot since then,' said Hannah, cheerfully. 'It used to take ages, didn't it? And it hurt, too, I think.'

Paul and his wife had tried not to think about whether the process had been painful for Cara. They couldn't bear to think of her suffering, but it had been the only possible option, and they'd been grateful for the opportunity at the time. Paul felt that it might have been more tactful if Hannah hadn't mentioned it though.

'She must be about twenty-five,' thought Paul, watching the girl fussing about; *'no wonder thirty years ago seems a long time to her.'* It felt like just last week to him, he reflected.

Paul had tried desperately to get a download body for Cara; he'd called in old favours, and embarrassed himself hugely by asking an enormously important old general to put him in touch with the Metaform. It had been no use. Paul had managed a short exchange of heartfelt messages with the most senior director of the Metaform, but had finally been refused by Connor, on the grounds that children were simply too difficult to download at that time. Later it would have been possible, but by then the

64

old general had gone, and the major had no way to contact Connor.

He'd never forget his daughter's eyes watching her parents with such love and pity, empathising, as she always had, with the sense of loss she knew they'd suffer when she'd gone. Cara had been strong right up to the end, and she had resolutely refused to let her parents see the fear she must have felt.

Hannah had dropped into her standard upload patter: 'We have some forms to complete first, and then we'll fill you up with some lovely soothing medication,' Hannah chattered on. 'There'll be good strong painkillers first, because we don't want you to bring discomfort with you into the Metaform, and a mild sedative as well. We'll feel much better then. After that, we'll fit the heads up display and off we'll go. It takes about half an hour and it doesn't hurt a bit. Not that I actually know, of course,' she giggled, 'but I'm told the process is rather pleasant.'

'She's really beginning to irritate me,' Paul thought, looking at the nurse's huge, surgically adjusted brown eyes. He wondered if it had hurt, having her eyes made bigger like that. He hadn't seen many people who'd actually had it done, except on the TV, but Paul couldn't be bothered to ask any questions.

The paperwork completed, and the sedatives administered, Paul watched the nurse bustling about, keeping up an unceasing flow of undemanding conversation as she set up the hardware. He slid gently into a kind of peaceful daze.

'The computer probably thought those eyes would make her look more sympathetic, but she looks like a freak to me,' Paul mused, as the medication began to take effect. *'Still, at least they're brown and not day-glow orange or*

purple like those awful people on TV. I wonder if the EMF has rules about what colour eyes they can have?'

As the major gazed into the medical-grade white nylon heads-up display, which had been screwed into his scalp a little more firmly than he was happy with, Paul decided that he didn't just find her irritating; he really didn't like Hannah. Her prattle was constant, she didn't need any input from him, and she rarely waited for a response from her patient.

Slowly he sank into the HUD's programme, which began the upload with soft lights that faded and brightened as it brought the major's brain patterns into sequence with its own agenda. The flashing lights became more intense and smaller as the computer started to restructure his brainwaves, and as they became almost painfully pin-sharp, he gradually lost the ability to answer Hannah's standard questions, even if the little nurse had waited for his responses, which mostly she hadn't.

Hannah asked Paul for his date of birth, and noted the inarticulate grunt in response with every sign of satisfaction. She made a mark on her clipboard, and continued with the questions until there was no longer any sign of awareness from the gaunt body on the bed.

Paul's awareness had faded away as he became a part of the computer, which flashed his conscious and unconscious memories into the satellite storage facility to sleep, potentially, until the end of the world, which would be a matter of no interest or relevance to him at all. Finally, the computer ended its sequence by deploying a surgical laser which, entering through his left eye, thrust deep into the major's brain, and excised a small but useful part of his cerebral cortex. As the hum that signified the

HUD's programme was entering its terminal upload stage died away, Paul's body quietly died too.

Hannah made a note of the time recorded by the equipment, and then she sighed and got up. It was less than half an hour until her lunch break and she still had at least one other upload to do. Hannah wondered if her team leader would notice if she made the lady in cubicle 81 wait until after she'd had lunch.

A moment's thought suggested that it would be a bad idea. It would affect the EMF's upload targets, and they'd have a fit if they thought she was slacking. The nurse detached the HUD from the still-warm ex-major, and set about dealing with the routine tidying up of the deceased.

Chapter 8

Connor and Meilinn had recruited some of the staff of their old software company, and had been joined by their colleagues, Luther, Tubby and Scott for the first and probably the most dangerous part of the procedure. Connor was about to become the first living human to exist only in a machine and completely independently of any organic body. He and Mei had researched it as comprehensively as they could, but it was still terrifyingly new technology.

Soon after the process began, Con's deliberate and conscious thoughts seemed to dissolve. He tried to tell himself he'd speak to Mei about questioning people while they were being uploaded, so that progress could be monitored, but he couldn't hold onto the thought. There was a distracting wave of pain in his head as he struggled to hold onto his thoughts.

'Mei, we should... Ow!' He gave up trying to speak and tried to grin at the heads up display, in the hope that Meilinn would be able to see he was doing fine. He managed a reassuring pat of the hand that gripped his sleeve convulsively, and decided to leave it to her. They'd gone over and over it, and on the whole Connor felt that he'd trust her judgement.

They'd decided that the brain, once compartmentalised, wasn't all that complicated after all, as many of the normally crucial routines and subroutines were needed only for maintenance of the body. All autonomic instructions could be stored in their entirety in case of future need, but they didn't need analysis or fiddling with at this stage, and after a while the screen seemed to settle down.

Meilinn was identifying duplicate algorithms, because their first and greatest worry was that if Connor's conscious mind didn't know whether it should be in his body or in the machine, they might end up with a broken machine, and an even more broken Connor.

Mei, still frantically identifying duplications and deleting them, finally typed the crucial question: 'Are you there, Connor?'

There was a worryingly long pause and the computer's screensaver clicked in. Con's body was braced, motionless, against his desk, the HUD taped firmly in place, and an intravenous line hung over the nearby window latch, trickling sedatives into his bloodstream. They all understood that they were absolutely not to touch him or the HUD until he had given them the go-ahead. 'Or died,' Con had added with his usual slightly mordant humour.

The team tried not to look at each other now; they'd known it probably wouldn't be quick, and they bustled about making tea and tidying papers whilst they waited to see if they were all accomplices to the murder of a helpless elderly man, or pioneers on behalf of all mankind.

Meilinn gripped Luther's hand and concentrated on breathing as a dozen possibilities crossed her mind. 'Oh, Luthe, what if he's partly uploaded and doesn't know what he is?' she said in panic.

Mei was reasonably sure that the technology was sound, but this test run was likely to prove fatal to Con if it didn't work absolutely perfectly. There were several possible outcomes, and only one of them was desirable; Con could go totally insane, his mind broken up and his consciousness duplicated so haphazardly that he might be completely unable to comprehend reality; he could die without leaving enough of himself in the computer to be conscious at all, or he might even, just possibly, upload successfully.

Finally, there was an answer; the computer chimed loudly in the hushed and darkened office. Then Con's typed response appeared on the centre monitor: 'okiminbutthatwasntfunyouknowwellhavetochangeafewt hings.'

There was a huge collective sigh of relief. Connor was online, and presumably still sane, but the worst part was yet to come, as far as his old employees were concerned.

Meilinn released Luther's hand and began to type more dialogue to try and establish exactly how much of Con's personality was online, whilst one of her other colleagues, Tubby, made helpful suggestions about what questions to ask.

Luther silently bent his hand back into its previous shape and smiled in satisfaction. He was far younger than Connor, an ambitious American who'd been enchanted at the suggestion that he move into this odd new world of research. Now that Con appeared to be online, Luther began to increase the amount of the drug filtering through the drip.

Once they were able to hold coherent typed conversations with Con, his body now drugged beyond any possibility of consciousness, the four remaining members of the small team decided it was time to get rid of his body.

They'd been taking a huge risk by keeping him alive even for as long as they had, as the risk of duplication of his personality would be dangerously high. It was probable that his mind wouldn't know which of the two places was its correct home, and one of them had to be destroyed immediately.

Heart failure for Con was surprisingly easy to trigger in the end. Connor had been given a large, but hopefully unsuspicious quantity of sedatives during the upload itself, and was now heavily asleep. Luther and Tubby laid him gently on the floor, and then removed the HUD. Meilinn resolutely placed her hands on Con's ribcage and pressed it gently, stopping the rise and fall of his chest, while tears ran down her face. She hadn't wanted to do this part herself, but it had somehow seemed right that she take responsibility for the final and most decisive part of the operation.

The others watched, aghast but fascinated, as she repeatedly released and replaced the pressure until the strain became too much for Connor. After only a few gentle attempts at semi-suffocation, he suffered a massive heart attack. Con's body stiffened and his heart-beat became increasingly erratic, racing and thudding violently before stopping completely. Con's shallow breathing had ceased several seconds before.

'I think that would've happened soon anyway, you know,' typed Tubby. 'Did you ever have pains in your chest before, Con?' Heavily built himself, Tubby had something of an interest in heart problems. There was no response.

The computer displays were showing blank sky-blue backgrounds, and instead of the eagerly anticipated lines of type, there was nothing and Meilinn held her breath in the horrified realisation that she might have murdered her boss.

Finally, there was a click, then a soft and very artificial female voice responded. 'Well, yes I did, actually, and it's been worse recently, but I thought it was worth pushing on with what we were doing, because if it came off it wouldn't matter what state my old heart was in. Besides, it helped, didn't it?'

'Wow, Con, that's so cool,' squealed Meilinn. 'You're a girl!' She'd never been so relieved to hear anything in her entire life, and wiped her eyes and blew her nose with unselfconscious happiness, as Tubby typed her remark for Connor's benefit.

'No, I'm bloody not,' the genteel voice murmured irritably, 'just give me a minute to mess about with the settings.'

For the next hour, watched in fascination by the others, the computer emitted a wide variety of voices and noises, and the screen's display changed over and over again. As Scott and Mei adjusted the computer's microphone so that Con could hear them better, a man's voice spoke, and gradually became more-or-less recognisably Connor's.

'I think I've got it. There's an awful lot of stuff to sort out, and it'd be handy to have someone come in and help out but I think, if you can bear it, Mei, you should stop and help Luther, Tubby and Scott to upload first, if you agree.'

'Yes, I know I should probably do it, Con,' Meilinn responded resignedly, looking at the faces around her. 'I know most about the process and I'm most likely going to look the least suspicious, too, if we're all going to start dying like flies,' she added mischievously.

'I think so too, Mei,' Con answered. 'And I can talk you through it, anyway.'

'So,' Luther looked interested but a little uncomfortable, 'Mei's going to load us up, just like we did with you? Only I wouldn't mind knowing if it hurt and stuff.' He was smiling cheerfully but the concern was real. It hadn't been nice to watch, and certain aspects of the process were bothering him.

'Well, yes, Luther, obviously, but only if you want to,' Connor replied. 'I mean no-one's interested in forcing you, you know. Probably wouldn't work anyway if you didn't co-operate.'

'Oh, hell, yes, I want to. I wouldn't miss this for anything, I just, you know, I'm curious about how it felt,' he finished a bit feebly.

'It hurt,' said Connor firmly. 'It really did, and it's incredibly disorientating at first.'

'Oh good,' said Luther. 'That makes me feel a whole lot better.'

'Don't worry, I think I can see why now, and we can sort that out. Anyway, it wasn't unbearable; it was just like a sort of whole-body hangover. I must say it's very strange now though,' Connor added. 'Though I can't feel anything except when I think about it, I could swear I've still got a bad back.'

'Really? Is that like a kind of physical echo?' Luther was fascinated. 'Yeah, I definitely need to do this now. Just tell me what I have to do.'

'I'll help you, Luthe,' Meilinn interjected. 'I think the pain level probably depends on the method we use to sedate you. If we're not trying to make it look like natural causes, we can take you right down to the edge of consciousness while you upload. It'll take a bit of working out though,' she said thoughtfully.

The technicalities of engineering Con's death had been a serious worry, but they'd checked the legalities first, and had discovered that if he'd seen a medic in the last few days, and had a potentially life-threatening condition diagnosed, then his demise would almost certainly be accepted as the result of natural causes by the authorities.

As far as his doctor was concerned, Con was suffering from advanced heart disease, and should be at home quietly deciding whether he could afford a heart replacement or the cutting-edge nano-repair of his old one.

A little later, after Scott and Luthe had returned to their hotel with strict warnings about discussing what they'd just seen, Tubby and Meilinn re-seated Con's corpse in his chair. This was a deeply unpleasant process, as his inert form was refusing to co-operate. Con's body needed to be manhandled with great care to avoid any post mortem marking until it was appropriately slumped over his desk.

They carefully cleaned the faint marks left on Con's forehead and temples by the tape used to fix the HUD in place, and then removed the small computer unit, replacing it with one that Tubby had prepared earlier.

Then, leaving the lights on in Con's office, they left quietly. They both felt traumatised by the task, and neither spoke.

Less than a week later, Tubby followed Con into the Metaform's new database, having appeared to die tragically from carbon monoxide poisoning caused by a faulty boiler.

Chapter 9

In the end, I reckon the idea we came up with between us was at least as audacious as anything Tobias could have thought up. It was also going to be expensive, but even Errik had to agree that if it worked, it would probably be the final perfect answer. He wasn't happy though, about my role in it, and had taken rather a lot of persuading.

I started off knowing there'd be some resistance: 'I mean, how good do you suppose their security is up there?'

'Well, they'll have excellent virus protection, I should think,' answered Errik. 'Why?'

'But they won't be expecting any danger from within, will they? So it's likely all their virus protection, and so on, is geared to outside threats from people like us, and malicious hackers, right?'

'Yes, but Gabriel, you can't seriously be thinking of getting inside the Metaform yourself? I thought I was going to do it.'

'Yes, I bloody well am,' I said firmly. 'I think it's the only way left if we want to stop the civilian casualties.'

'It's much too dangerous, and however you look at it, you're going to be killed.' Errik's face was pale and set. 'It's different for me, I'm old, and I'm more likely to be able to find my way around, anyway.'

'You can't do it, Errik. It's a question of me being killed or all humans being uploaded until there's no humanity left.' I had no intention of being talked out of this and Errik could already see that he wasn't going to be able to change my mind. 'Our birth-rate's already dropped to the point where there aren't enough young people to support the old, and it'll go on doing it until everyone's gone. We can't count the cost of one person's life against everyone in the world.'

'My dear boy, please think about it. What can you possibly do up there? They won't let you wander about at will. There'll be storage areas where they keep you dormant, and anyway, how will you even be conscious?' Errik knew he wasn't going to win this battle, bless him, but he had to try.

'There's got to be a way, and we have to find it. Please, Errik, you can find a way, I know you can.' I was behaving quite badly, actually, because I knew I could make Errik do what I wanted, but you can't really count the emotional manipulation of one daft old man's feelings against the future of humanity.

There was no question after that, anyway. I was going to get myself online, either with or without the assistance of my old mentor, and despite himself Errik couldn't resist the intellectual challenge. He set his mind to working out a way to get me online and in a position to do the most catastrophic damage possible. He had a lot of work to do before we could go any further, but I needed the time to get back to full fitness in any case.

The plan we came up with wasn't particularly complicated, but it would depend entirely on me keeping my nerve. Once Errik had identified the relevant people and researched their backgrounds and vulnerabilities, we would together select and target a reasonably high-ranking employee of the Metaform, and set me up as an unfortunate young man with an incurable illness.

The scans we had of my weakened state after old Toby's death were useful, and with a little careful editing, could be used to illustrate my terrible state of health. There was no reason why anyone should realise that the most of the damage had probably only been temporary.

You're going to have to charm someone, I think,' Errik said. 'See if you can convince them you're desperately needed back at home.' There was a thoughtful pause as we considered this.

'But I must admit,' I said thoughtfully, 'I'm not too clear yet on what to do when I get there.'

'I need to think about that,' Errik answered. 'I suspect we can do something involving a bit of fiddling with their memory drives. Did you know the directors are all stored in their own individual flashes?' This was a point of great interest to Errik, because, as with many deceptively simple ideas, he felt that he really should have invented it himself.

'I'll take your word for it, Errik.' The mechanical parts of the Metaform's existence had never concerned me much. Tobias had disliked computers, and he'd refused to have anything to do with them. Along with all the members of the SDB, I'd been exposed only to as much technical knowledge as was absolutely necessary.

'I'll work on it for now and let you know what I come up with.' Errik sounded preoccupied, but I felt comfortably certain he already had a plan and I was happy to wait.

As my broken bones began to knit, with the assisted acceleration of the nanites, Errik also began to look with more than his usual passing interest at my hair and clothing. I was going to have to be re-designed from the ignorant thug that I appeared to be, into a wealthy and cultured young gentleman. I think Errik was looking forward to that.

There were small discussions held throughout the group in the days after Tobias' funeral. No-one was sure if I'd recover fully, and if I did, no-one seemed to know how I'd feel about continuing the fight. The men had decided to bury Tobias discreetly. They'd tried to speak to Errik, but he'd shut himself away, so they'd had to go ahead and do it themselves anyway, assuming correctly that no-one would want the authorities involved.

When I was back on my feet, Errik and I held a meeting of the fighters, realising with some shock that there were hardly any un-barcoded men left. There were no more than twenty people here tonight. The women and children and any others that couldn't be trusted would be spoken to later, but these were the ones who had to be deactivated.

I stood up and tried to tell myself that I was finally in charge, and old Toby wouldn't show up in a minute and put me back in my place. 'You all know what happened, so there's not a lot of point in discussing it, but I want to thank you for dealing with my father's burial,' I started.

'That's okay, it was easy enough,' one man piped up. 'We were glad to do it.'

'Oh yeah. Should've done it years ago,' came a voice from the back. There was a ripple of amusement from the others.

'Thanks,' I said, relief loosening me up a little. 'I know how most of you felt about Tobias, but some of you must remember what he used to be like in the old days.'

'I do,' added Ted, a tall, sandy-haired lad with a jaw like a shovel. I didn't mind him, but we'd never had anything much in common so I didn't know him well. 'He was okay,' Ted went on. 'Even five years ago he had some good ideas, though he wasn't ever what you'd call approachable. I think he'd lost sight of the goal lately, too.'

'I reckon Tobias was ill,' I said. 'Everything about his behaviour suggests there was probably a medical reason for the way he acted. But,' I took a breath and raised my voice so it would carry more clearly to the whole room, 'his time's over now, and Errik and I are looking at the future. It's no secret that I didn't approve of random explosions and attacks. I could never see what they achieved, except for causing general fear in the community.'

'That was the point though, wasn't it?' The speaker, a small, wiry man called Yan, spoke up. 'Old Toby wanted everyone to be terrified of us, so as they'd listen up when he spoke. He always thought our lives was cheap if they was spent on saving the world. An' as for civilian casualties, well, they was just background details...'

'Steady on, mate,' said another, 'I don't think it was that simple. He wanted us to be a force to be reckoned with, and we had to stop the bastards from producing frames. His way meant, if nothing else, we made 'em pay more for security, and stopped 'em getting smug.'

'Didn't stop the uploads, though, did it? They're still doin' 'em, even though their own people are dying. If they really cared about what was happening, they'd have stopped what they was doin.''

'Yeah, and we still have the last plan old Toby came up with,' said Yan, addressing the room directly. 'That's what we was working on before he went. We was going to take out the bio-frames lab in Alaska, an',' he turned to

Errik and me, 'all of us know it'll be an absolute bloodbath.'

'Well, for one thing,' Ted agreed, 'it was a bloody stupid idea in the first place, what with the security they got up there. For another thing, I don't think most of us trusted anything old Toby come up with these days anyway. He'd lost most of his marbles, and we'd be complete idiots to go ahead with anything he thought up without going over it properly first.'

Jared spoke up suddenly. 'Yeah, but what should we be doing now, then?' He appeared to shrink and then break into a sweat as soon as his brain realised that he'd just addressed a roomful of people who were now all looking at him.

Jared had witnessed the shooting and, after seeing that I wasn't quite dead and the medics were treating me okay, he'd led the gibbering Errik back to his own home and called out the medics to him. Well over a month later, he still had occasional nightmares about it, poor sod. The sight of dead people wasn't an issue, he'd seen those before, though probably not as often as he'd have liked his mates to believe.

He'd been sorry for me when he saw me finally respond to Tobias' summons, and when he saw the swinging light fitting, through the window, and heard the bang as the old monitor hit the ground a few minutes later, he'd gone rather reluctantly to see if he could do anything. He didn't know what he could do, but he'd rather desperately hoped something would occur to him, or that the fight would have ended by the time he'd arrived outside the hut.

Then he saw Tobias hit me with all his weight behind the blow. It'd been so vicious that Jared had been about to rush into the room without thinking what he'd do when he got there. He was a solidly-built lad, but Jared knew Tobias would wipe the floor with him if he dared to put his nose in that office without an invitation that he wasn't going to get, and he was hesitating about whether to call for help. He'd walked up and down, trying to get up the nerve to crash in and break it up, until he saw Errik go inside.

Then he'd followed and watched Errik raise the sidearm to fire at the only part of Tobias that was clearly visible from where Jared was standing. This, unfortunately for Jared, had been the side of Tobias' head. Not unreasonably, Jared had been a bit haunted by that night, and he still wasn't back to normal. I gave him a friendly wave, and he hunched gratefully back in his chair.

'That's really why we wanted to speak to you all,' I said. I turned to Errik, and indicated with a small wave that it was his turn to speak.

He explained to the assembled group that the team was being disbanded, and that he and I intended to carry on their fight using non-violent, mostly technological methods. Errik told the men that they were being given three months' notice and would be paid bonuses for their loyalty. We were surprised at the emotional reaction his announcement received.

'I think we was all expectin' this, to be honest,' Yan said ruefully. 'We was talking about what's gonna happen, so it's not that much of a shock. Gonna miss me mates though,' he added sheepishly, as he slid back into his seat.

The men, as Yan had said, weren't really surprised, and the pay-off would be generous. Some would go off to join other protesters, and others were frankly relieved to be allowed to leave peacefully.

Relationships hadn't been allowed with the women and families because Tobias hadn't trusted them and felt it encouraged indiscretion. There were, therefore, several young men present who'd been denied certain experiences involving females, and felt the opportunity to correct that omission was strongly to be welcomed. To my relief, the meeting ended on an unexpectedly cheerful note, and Errik was positively jolly as we walked to his auto and drove back to his house.

Chapter 10

Philip Moss stretched luxuriously in his reclining office chair. It was a special chair created to cope with his impressive bulk, and the very latest in forcefield technology was strained to breaking point. Phil was the owner and managing director of the largest and most successful independent film company in the south of England, and the position brought rather a lot of perks with it.

His company created beautifully effective advertisements which were sold for enormous sums all over the world, and he was on better than nodding terms with all the most senior people in the industry. He didn't get on with them all, of course. In fact, he didn't actually like anyone that he worked with regularly.

In an industry famed for its charm and flattering insincerity, Philip would have stood out as a charmless boor, but he was intelligent enough to realise early in his meteoric career that his social skills weren't entirely suited to his field of enterprise, so he rarely met anyone in person, and never gave personal interviews.

As a result he'd become slightly mysterious, which suited him fine, because as a marketing ploy it was perfect. The revenue he raked in allowed him a lifestyle that he couldn't have dreamed of as a boy growing up in the backstreets of London.

On a personal level though, Philip was regrettably unappealing. His thin sandy hair was usually greasy and clung to his domed red forehead. His small, pale grey eyes were constantly in motion, darting about as though searching for his next target. When his flickering attention did pause for a moment, there was usually an expression of mild distaste twisting his small red mouth into a pout. Phil was forty-eight years old and looked sixty. He was grossly overweight, and certainly hadn't been good-looking even when he was young.

Oddly though, his personal unattractiveness didn't detract from his skills as a salesman. Phil could demand the most outrageous fees from clients, and somehow they almost invariably complied. His personal assistant, Milly, suspected it was because there was an implied threat of violence just below his self-satisfied surface, and the majority of people who met the legendary Mr Moss preferred to avoid unpleasantness.

Phil believed he had a thrusting and effective personality, but his staff considered him a bully. His tempers were legendary and deeply unpleasant, and it was painfully obvious that this was a man who could hold a grudge for a lifetime.

Fortunately, he seldom dealt directly with the public, because although he enjoyed getting his own way and relished a little healthy debate as he saw it, his real strength was in production. He had staff to take care of the people-stuff, and since he was perfectly well aware that his face and manner were unlikely to attract clients, or indeed anyone at all, Phil avoided the use of holograms or face-time. He relied on his highly-trained staff and his own exceptional written skills to close deals.

He was extraordinarily successful, and many people in positions of authority would be willing to swear that a more honest and hard-working man never existed. Of course, Phil rarely met these people in person.

Philip had graciously decided to interview a member of the public today, although he had no intention of doing this in person. No-one other than his own staff could speak to Phil in any other than hologrammatic form, and the favour was not returned. Philip would see the man, but the unfortunate interviewee would see nothing but a blank screen.

Philip had a particularly good contract with the Metaform, supplying hologrammatic tutorials and information streams to them, and it was extremely lucrative. They paid immediately, they paid extremely well, and the boost to a producer's reputation was priceless. The Metaform was his best and biggest client, and he paid more personal attention to their needs than to any of his other clients.

Today's hologram visitor had thought he might be suitable for one of the roles in the latest line of infomercials, and Philip had felt it a good idea to have a look at him in person. Once an actor was identified by the public as 'regular' in the Metaform's advertisements, his career was made as an actor. The public loved their regulars, who generally became feted celebrities almost overnight.

Unfortunately, the man had been completely unusable, though he'd seemed eminently suitable in his original application. Phil had taken one look at the pathetic individual and seen that he hadn't a chance. There'd be no way to disguise the fact that this man was a loser. He wasn't attractive enough to play the role of pre-upload client, even with extensive personal re-modelling, and couldn't have resembled a post-uploaded client in his wildest dreams.

The application had said that he was tall and slim, but it had neglected to mention that he was emaciated rather than slender, and that his skin was grey with poverty and ill-health. Phil wondered who he'd got to stand in for him in his first hologram application, and made a mental note to fire whichever member of his staff had been fooled.

Phil pondered on the weedy drip of a man that he'd had to cut off mid-stream. This idiot had thought Phil was some kind of social worker, and kept whining on about a sick wife and too many children. Phil had actually been quite polite by his own standards; he'd permitted the client to talk for several minutes, which was something he almost never did.

The reason for Phil's unaccustomed gentleness was that he wasn't really listening. Phil was about to apply for his own upload, and he'd been scrolling through the possible upgrades and optional extras to his bio-frame as the fool droned on in the background.

He always found it unpleasant when clients begged. It wasn't so much the embarrassment, Phil didn't really suffer from that, it was the nuisance of dealing with them, which was almost invariably time-consuming. He could cut them off, of course, but he was always aware that he might do it to the wrong person one day. He had scant regard for the public, but had learned to be careful, just in case.

It was odd that they bothered to grovel really, because they couldn't seriously imagine that pleading would change his mind, yet they never seemed to notice the forbidding nuances in his voice as they catalogued all the reasons why he should be casting them in roles which carried a certain dignity and influence, whilst practically dribbling on his shoes. The incongruity never failed to elude them.

This time he'd cut the man short after some undignified dialogue that ended with dire threats to Phil and his family, which didn't worry him in the slightest. They'd never meet publicly, as Philip was relatively wealthy, and this drone was fast sinking into the gutter. They would simply never communicate again, but Phil was glad the meeting was over anyway. These affairs were always unpleasant.

Besides, Phil didn't have a family. He hadn't spoken to his mother for years, and he probably wouldn't bother to look her up again now. He wasn't entirely sure where she lived, in any case. He seemed to remember that she was planning to move somewhere or other, but he hadn't paid attention. And once he had been loaded into his beautiful new bio-frame he'd have no link to her at all.

After almost nine years of careful squirrelling away of funds, he was finally ready to apply for his own download. His poor skin and enormous belly tended not to attract the very young girls to which he was much attracted. Girls were always there, of course; as the girlfriend of a rich man, they might have a chance themselves at downloading into a beautiful and hopefully irresistible avatar.

Most of the women that Phil met felt that it was worth the distaste involved in undertaking intimate relations with a man whose body had the colour and texture of uncooked dough.

Phil wasn't stupid, and knew perfectly well that the girls he slept with didn't enjoy the experience. The knowledge that he could almost certainly buy the services of the most beautiful girl in almost any room, and have her do exactly what he wanted, whilst she fought her instinct to slap him and escape, was one of the really satisfying things that he rather thought he'd miss later. It would certainly be novel to have an attraction returned though, he thought, but he did wonder if he'd miss the deep satisfaction of total conquest of an unwilling partner.

He'd had a few thoughts regarding his future strategy however, and suspected that if he were downloaded into a suitably attractive bio-frame, that particular taste might be even more easily gratified.

Phil had wanted to change his appearance since he was a small child. He'd been bullied without mercy, until an unexpected growth spurt had suddenly made that more difficult for his playmates. During the course of one memorable summer, podgy little Philip had become big, tall and rather fat Philip, at first successfully defensive, and then actively aggressive. The rest of his school days were passed far more enjoyably than he could possibly have predicted only a few months earlier.

Philip didn't particularly care how he looked once he became an adult, and he also dressed badly because he knew it would make very little difference to his visual appeal. His father had been Greek, and his mother Scottish and unfortunately the characteristics which had been attractive in his parents had somehow been subverted in him. His father's sensuous mouth had translated into loose wet lips. His mother's riot of red-gold curls had become thin and ratty-looking ginger string, and since his father had died whilst he was very young, his mother had declined into an ineffectual complainer, her magnificent hair now a neglected salt-and-pepper crimp. Philip despised ineffective people, and saw himself as a man who didn't suffer fools gladly. Especially female ones.

At least a part of Phil's motivation to succeed had been fuelled by his desire for a new and beautiful bio-frame. He'd always known his old body would be discarded as soon as he could afford a better one, and that meant he tended to treat his current unfortunate body rather badly. He kept up to date with necessary medical treatments, just in case, but as far as exercise and healthy eating went, well, he preferred not to. Exercise was so damned boring, and what was the point of being a multi-millionaire if he couldn't eat whatever and whenever he wanted to?

Philip had already selected his frame online, and carefully identified which traits and extras his new body would have. He'd be downloaded into one of the new bio-organic models, with enhanced strength and muscle definition. As an afterthought, he'd opted for luxuriant blond hair, and the classic pale gold skin which was all the rage these days, along with the obligatory slight epicanthic eye fold.

Real suntans had been out of favour for years, since the first models had tended to react badly to intense sunlight. Anyway, designer drugs could recreate a much healthier appearance just as effectively and much more attractively. As China's influence had permeated the world's culture, a slightly Asian appearance was also highly regarded by the rich and famous, although the hair chosen by Phil would be anomalous.

As with so many bio-frames commissioned by those who could afford all the improvements, Philip's frame would look slightly strange, and it didn't worry him the slightest bit.

Phil booked his appointment with the clinic, reflexively annoyed that it would be several weeks until he could be fitted into their tight little schedule. He felt strongly that for the amount of money he was spending, he should be booked in at a date to suit his own convenience, but shrugged it off.

After a moment's thought he'd realised that most applicants would be borrowing the funds. There'd be hundreds, or maybe even thousands of people wanting to be downloaded into shiny new bodies all at the same time. 'What a nice little earner that is,' he thought covetously. There was no way into the Metaform though, except as a dormant download, and many people had tried. No-one could replicate exactly what they did either, although there were always dozens of aspiring companies attempting it.

The research had been created and refined by the directors decades earlier, and the public trusted the Metaform absolutely. There'd been laws cited by various countries, claiming the Metaform's monopoly of the entire industry was illegal, but the directors had continued to trade, unconcerned by mere human issues. You knew you were safe with the Metaform. One's life and sanity just weren't the kind of thing one would trust to an unknown firm.

Philip Moss relaxed again; the funds were ready, the first appointment booked, and he'd already designed his perfect frame, subject to advice from the professionals. A thought occurred to Phil; he might be able to defray the expense a little if he used this as an opportunity for publicity.

There was currently a great deal being written about the way the new download bodies often became very much like the originals. Philip knew he wasn't going to slide into bad habits and let the new frame get fat, but apparently the mind influenced the body much more than anyone had realised in the past.

He thought that was all just so much hogwash. He'd allowed himself to go to seed a little because, frankly, he'd never been a thing of beauty in the first place. It didn't mean that he'd be the same in his splendid new body. Phil was certain that exercise would be much more appealing when he had a physique to be proud of. In fact, he was rather looking forward to it.

The more he thought about it, the more he suspected the public might be interested in a clients' eye view of the process. Although he wasn't yet a household name, he might, with his new amazing good looks and improved intelligence, decide to become a celebrity one day. He'd make a documentary, he decided, with himself as the subject. Philip reached for the phone.

Chapter 11

Jared looked at his landlady, feeling like a little boy just about to leave for his first day at school. Not that he could actually remember being sent off to school himself, but he could imagine what it would feel like, and her expression was about as soppy as his mum's might've been. It wasn't even his first day; he'd been working for the enemy for weeks.

'Elen, this isn't dangerous. Will you stop looking at me like that!' It irritated Jared that, just because he'd lived most of his life in a closed religious order, people assumed that he must be feeling lost and confused. He couldn't explain that a good deal of the last few years had involved travel all over the world. He'd spoken to people and visited monuments that Elen had only seen in holograms, but as he'd done that mostly with a view to exploding them as catastrophically as possible, they weren't experiences he could share with her.

Jared's landlady self-consciously adjusted her expression a bit and smiled apologetically. Elen liked her new lodger. She'd met him on the work transport several times, and one morning he'd admitted that he was looking for somewhere permanent to live. She'd welcomed the chance to supplement her meagre income a little, not to mention the infinite comfort of knowing that she'd have a good solid male around the place.

'I know, Jared, but you're so new to this place and you just seem like an accident waiting to happen.' Elen hadn't known him for very long, but already she could see that he was a babe in the woods, and fair game for anyone.

'I'm not, though, Elen. We've talked this through and I can't think of anything that could go wrong. And just because I grew up in a cult doesn't mean I can't learn new things,' Jared said slightly indignantly. 'I've been here for over a month now, and I'm getting the hang of it.'

He eased himself around the woman, patting her comfortingly on the shoulder, and left, closing the door behind him with a bang. Elen sighed; the apartment was tiny, but it had a small spare room, which she knew Jared was finding luxurious compared with the tiny quarters he'd had back in at his commune, but he seemed so young to her, despite his protestations of his self-sufficiency.

Jared had been overjoyed to go undercover for the cause. It had taken a while, but Errik finally agreed that since he couldn't talk Gabriel out of uploading himself, at least he could look at other options while they first identified and then wooed a suitably gullible Metaform employee.

After the church had begun to be disbanded, Errik and Gabriel had come across some unexpected problems, one of which had been that, despite the obvious contentment of most of the brothers, a large number of Tobias' old religious followers were very angry.

They'd genuinely believed that Tobias was heading a holy crusade and they'd literally bought into it. Mostly women with small children, they were becoming ever noisier in their demands for the return of their possessions, willingly donated when they joined the SDB. Errik was beginning to wonder how to pay off the congregation while remaining solvent himself. Not only that, it appeared that one or two of the disgruntled followers were muttering about selling information to the authorities.

Jared was still loyal and desperate to prove his worth, and if he could be persuaded to be discreet, Errik rather thought he'd hit on a plan which might solve both problems in one hit. Luckily the lad seemed to understand that he couldn't talk to Gabriel about their own little spying operation. Errik had impressed on him that Gabriel was engaged in another operation, and if he were captured, then Jared's own safety might be compromised. For the same reason, he assured Jared, he couldn't discuss Gabriel's operation with him.

Errik had decided, with Jared's help, to snatch one of the bio-frames. They were incredibly valuable, and he was certain he could sell it to a rival company. Of course there was no real competition to the Metaform, but that had never stopped people from trying. A blank bio-frame would be a real asset and worth an absolute fortune. He also had a sneaking suspicion that he might be able to get Jared uploaded instead of Gabriel, but that was a work in progress, and there was no need to worry the boy with that just yet.

Jared was under the impression that he was being sent to ingratiate himself with the Metaform on an information collecting exercise, and Errik felt this was the best way to leave him.

Jared had no problem with the idea of bringing down the Metaform. The guiding principle of Tobias' church had been that they were evil, and he was enormously grateful to be chosen to aid their downfall. He'd seen more of the bio-frames recently than he'd ever seen before, and he was revolted, partly by their often bizarre appearance, and partly by what they represented.

Like all the members of the Soul Defence Brotherhood, Jared had absorbed Tobias' mantra and believed that the bio-frames were people bred without minds, and grown in labs like enormous bacteria. They were even engineered to suit their purchasers, and often had outlandishly large eyes and perfectly circular mouths, as well as physically ridiculously body shapes. Once designed and created, just like some kind of horrible cookery recipe, they were left to grow, and when they were ripe enough they were implanted with the memories of the rich bastards who'd commissioned them. Then they effectively died.

Jared didn't consider himself sentimental, but that had always worried him. How did the Metaform know the frames didn't dream? No-one seemed to know the answer to that one. It was always said that the research had been done, and the frames had never been alive. The Metaform said they didn't have any crinkles in their brains, so their brains didn't work until life was put into them. Along with every loyal and right-thinking member of the SDB, Jared didn't believe that for a second. The newest models didn't even have human bones. They were grown onto a special and highly secret compound skeleton, which was far tougher than human bones, although much heavier.

As far as Jared was concerned, the SDB could send him wherever they wanted, if it helped to bring the Metaform down, and he left for his new job as a security guard at the download centre in high spirits.

Errik had tweaked several databases to get Jared into the role. He hadn't had to change too much of the boy's background, which was all to the good, he felt, since it would give him less to remember. If he should be discovered and interrogated they wouldn't lose too much, because Jared knew almost nothing about the SDBs future plans. What he did know shouldn't cause too much difficulty, especially as the military wing was all but disbanded now.

Today Jared joined the stream of people wandering down the hill to the transport stop. He'd noticed some time ago that everyone seemed to have the Metaform logo on their clothes, which seemed a bit weird. He couldn't see how these could all be Metaform workers, unless they'd had a huge recruitment drive recently, and he'd heard nothing about that.

Jared decided to see if there was anyone he could ask, but it wasn't going to be easy. No-one ever looked at one another; that had been noticeable the very first time he travelled on the work bus, so he tried discreetly to see if there was anyone he could speak to without drawing undue attention to himself.

There was no-one really obviously old on the transport, but there didn't seem to be anyone particularly young either. Jared was painfully aware that he was at least a foot taller than anyone else, and about twice their width too. He always tried to keep his eyes on the ground and look undernourished, but this was a tricky task for a man of his size. He occupied the interminable journey every day by raging silently at the spiritless public. It had been generations since all the markets collapsed, but it was quite different seeing these diseased-looking people in the flesh, to hearing Tobias talk about them.

He thought Tobias and Gabriel would've been as shocked as he was if they could see them. Obviously state pensions couldn't be given to people who couldn't work; no society could afford that, with such a huge percentage of the population too old to work. The genuinely destitute were expected to move into the institutions called city homes, set up in most large towns for the care of the poor or elderly.

It meant that if you didn't want your old grandma to go into a city home, you'd have to work bloody hard to afford to keep her with you, because the very elderly weren't allowed to live alone. And there were quite a lot of them, apparently. Most of them were heading down the hill to the transport, today, Jared thought bitterly, still working for as long as their tottery legs could hold them up.

Jared watched them patiently lining up to get on the transport bus, and even though he'd seen it before, as he got on he was still upset by the obvious misery and defeat he could see. He couldn't tell anyone's ages by looking at them; they all just looked grey and middle-aged. As usual, Jared's mind returned to the subject of the tiny logos. If these were all Metaform employees, then why weren't they all reloaded into new frames? He'd asked Elen once, but she'd just looked embarrassed and changed the subject. He didn't want to upset her so he let the subject drop, but Jared was determined to ask someone.

An oldish woman caught Jared's eye and he hurriedly looked away. He was staring and knew he shouldn't, but he just couldn't help it. He was getting angry, yet again, at the state these people were in. This was why he'd spent his life fighting for the brotherhood, just as his mates had; this was what life was like for pretty much the whole world now.

When he got off the transporter, Jared saw that the woman who'd caught his eye had got off at the same time, and he made up his mind. Turning round to face her squarely, he spoke to her.

'Good morning,' he said bracingly. The skinny little woman looked shocked, and Jared could see immediately that he'd probably violated some unspoken protocol. Her small, unpainted mouth was clamped in an expression of acute disapproval and more than a little fear as she tried to edge around him. Jared decided to carry on and make an attempt to start a conversation with her anyway, since he'd already started, and he fell into step beside her. 'I'm quite new here,' he continued, in the most friendly and unthreatening voice he could manage. He couldn't quite see her downturned face, though he thought he could detect her annoyance or worry, but then she seemed to come to a decision.

'Good morning, sir,' she said, and her eyes darted around as though she were looking for an escape, so Jared tried to block her as much as he could, though it wasn't easy to do without looking menacing. Up close he could see she wasn't an old woman; she was just a remarkably faded and tired one.

Her hair was a light brown with streaks of grey, and tied back in a no-nonsense kind of bun-thing. Her eyes were nice though, they were clear and as blue as the sky, and he thought absently that it was a pity about all the lines and shadows round them.

Jared managed an inane laugh, more to impress on her what a harmless chap he was, but then the penny dropped. Of course he'd look like one of the new uploads, even in a Metaform security guards' uniform; maybe especially in a Metaform uniform. These were all small, tired-looking workers, and he hadn't yet had time to acquire the patina of defeat.

'No, love, look at my face; do I really look like a sir?' One of Jared's eyebrows had mostly disappeared years ago, during a minor explosion, but he'd never worried about getting it fixed. The nanobots had fixed the rest of his face just fine, and he couldn't be bothered with getting cosmetic improvements. Anyway, he felt it made him look older and more dynamic.

The tension seemed to drain out of her a little, as she weighed up what Jared had said, but they'd reached the corner of the street now, and her body language was still essentially negative. She was standing sideways to him, and kept glancing up the road, so he knew she was still trying to get away.

'No, no, of course you're not,' she said, a bit too quickly. Jared thought that was kind of unflattering, but it made him laugh again. He spoke quickly because she looked as though she'd been cornered by a nutter, and if he didn't talk fast, he was pretty sure she'd take off like a rabbit.

'Look, I'm sorry, I'm not a reload, I'm just new here and I wanted to ask someone some questions, and you looked kind.' Jared smiled hopefully. He'd hoped that would break the ice, because surely she must know that she was being incredibly distant. There was a pause for a second, and then she obviously decided he was harmless, and risked a proper look up at him, instead of the earlier rabbit-scared glance.

'Well, go on then. What's the question?' she said.

'Why's everyone wearing Metaform logos? Surely you can't all work for the company?' The woman's eyebrows shot up. They were nice eyebrows actually, and sort of neat. Jared just hadn't noticed at first because they were pale. A small reluctant smile spread over her small sour face.

'No of course we don't work for the Metaform, how could we? Anyway, you work for them, you must know that.'

'I don't know anything. I don't come from round here.' Jared gave her his best grin, which was probably a bit spoiled by the broken tooth. Again, that wasn't a recent break; he'd done it when he was a kid, and it could have been fixed easily, but Tobias had never seen the point in fussing about minor stuff. 'I've been working at the Metaform for a few weeks, but no-one talks much here, do they?'

Then the cornered woman sighed, and for the first time she stopped looking as though she was about to head for the hills. 'I don't think you even come from this planet, do you?' The woman looked resigned as she carried on. 'Look, all Metaform people are reloads.' She stopped as though she was considering how to put it, but Jared couldn't help interrupting.

'Well, I know that, and I didn't think you were. So what?' Jared said. 'That should be a good reason to work for them shouldn't it?'

'No, I mean they're all reloads, so they don't wear out and they don't leave; why would they? The Metaform's had the same staff for centuries. There's no work for organics. I don't know how you got in,' she stopped speaking and looked up at him suspiciously.

Sensing trouble, she'd begun to sidle away again, and this time Jared decided to let her go. Later he'd have another word with Errik. It seemed to him, suddenly, that there was something he hadn't been told. Errik was a smart guy, much cleverer than Jared himself, he had to admit, and Errik might think it was better to keep him in the dark for some reason; it was getting to be a seriously

100

annoying habit of his. It would have been a lot of effort for Errik to get him into the Metaform, and now that he thought about it more carefully, Jared was wondering why he'd bothered.

He held out his hand, and the woman hesitated before putting hers into it. Jared gave it a squeeze and thanked her politely. She looked as though she desperately wanted to escape now, and Jared let her go. The woman ran across the road and disappeared, and he set off to work as he had every day for the last month. And Jared still didn't know why everyone was wearing the Metaform's logo like a badge.

Chapter 12

Phil had waited for an interminable eight weeks to pass until he was rewarded with a consultation with the Metaform, with very bad grace. Then he'd had to wait until yet another arbitrary date was given to undergo the process itself. He'd almost stopped going in to work every day, relying on his assistant, Milly, to keep him in the loop and working remotely from home.

Now that he'd decided to go ahead with the body change he was more careful with his safety than he'd ever been before. He found he was leaving his apartment as little as possible to minimise the risk of any catastrophic accident. The thought that he could be killed by any random mishap when his new life was only a matter of days away brought Philip out in a cold sweat.

The weeks seemed to crawl by, and when the day finally arrived he was terrified, not of the process itself, but that something might occur to stop it. Each night of his enforced wait he had lain in bed listening to his heart thumping, and hoping it wouldn't stop.

Philip didn't have friends, but there was one who almost qualified for the label. Maurice rang occasionally to see how he was getting on, and to offer moral support, but he was a sycophantic little man, always drawn to the most powerful man in any group as kind of pre-emptive defensive measure. Maurice wouldn't really miss him if anything went wrong, reflected Philip. In fact, old Mo was probably relieved not to have seen him around recently. It didn't worry him; *They'll all be queueing up to hang out with me after this*, he thought sardonically.

Philip had thought about nothing but his impending download for the last few weeks. He looked at the computer-generated impression of his new frame several times a day, and tried to imagine what it would feel like to be tall and strong, and not to wheeze whenever he did anything strenuous. A side effect of the long wait was that he lost a tiny bit of weight; he had lost his appetite in any case, and the lack of sleep and general anxiety meant that he was actually looking fitter than he had done in years.

The irony of his improved appearance was lost on Phil though. He only saw the same red fat man in the mirror, and the habit of ignoring his image was too deeply ingrained for him to change now. He'd allowed his eye to skim, unseeing, over the image of himself when forced to confront it in the shaving mirror, for too many years to be able to regard himself dispassionately now.

Phil went into work almost as normal on the day of his upload to make sure that everything was in place and that nothing too tricky was likely to occur in his absence. He did it with the greatest possible care, avoiding the rush-hour traffic in case of any random accidents, and going in much later than his usual crack of dawn.

On the whole, he trusted his personal assistant, Milly Wyatt, but she was only an assistant after all, and only a woman. He'd had to make sure she understood that any major decisions had better be right, or he'd fire her when he got back. Phil had been even more appalled to realise that he'd be effectively asleep for five months, once he'd been uploaded.

Apparently that was an unbreakable policy of the Metaform's; after commissioning frames at enormous cost, occasionally things had happened in the past, such as the premature death of the intended occupant in an unplanned accident, leaving a bio-frame that no-one wanted. They were far too expensive and labour-intensive to create for the directors to allow the chance of waste.

The Metaform had made it a rule that anyone commissioning a new bio-frame was obliged to be uploaded into the database within a month, for their own safety. There were rare exceptions, but the Metaform charged an awesome amount for these exceptions, and no-one apart from the truly super-wealthy could possibly afford it.

Phil was rather ineffectively trying to manage all the routine administration in advance, until Milly pointed out that he was just making it worse.

'Look, Phil, please just leave it all to me; it'll be fine. Really,' she said exasperatedly. 'You can't possibly guess what's going to happen in ten weeks' time, so don't try.'

'Yes, but will you *really* be able to handle everything? You won't be able to contact me if there're any emergencies, you'll have to make your own decisions and you'll have to interview all the weird clients yourself. And keep a strict eye on the other staff, too.'

'It'll be fine,' Milly said for about the twentieth time. 'We've been over everything a million times, and I knew it all already. What can go wrong, for heaven's sake?' Milly managed not to say the words that were on the end of her tongue, that it was only an employment agency, and even the cleaner could keep it ticking over for a few months, because she knew that Phil in his present mood would probably hit the roof.

In the end, Phil left Milly, an employee of several years' standing who knew the business inside out, despite his doubts and reservations, in charge of his beloved company and mentally washed his hands of the business until he got back. He'd been told that he shouldn't be stressed at the upload, and although he did his best to relax, he rather hoped that some suitably restful medications would be offered too.

In the event, Phil's upload was completed without any problems at all. He arrived at the download centre by taxi, since he didn't have any close friends that he could ask to drive him, and couldn't face Maurice's irritating twitter. He could have asked Milly, he supposed, but she was incompetent enough without taking a whole morning off, too.

When he arrived, he wasn't enormously impressed by the reception desk. It was hardly any bigger than his own, and all things considered Phil had expected a much plusher reception. *Still*, he reflected, *at least they're probably spending the money on the things that matter.*

Philip was also mildly annoyed to find that the reporter hadn't arrived yet. He'd arranged to meet a woman from a national tabloid. He'd spoken to several papers, but none apart from this one had considered paying what Phil considered a reasonable sum in exchange for following the whole process.

'When this Colette Harris arrives, send her in after me, will you?' he told the receptionist, and to his amazement, she refused.

'She's a reporter. It'll be great publicity for you,' he said incredulously.

'I'm sorry Mr Moss, we don't allow reporters in while a client is being uploaded. It's completely against security regulations, and you know,' she smiled sweetly at him, 'we don't need the publicity.'

'Well, you'll have to let her this time. The woman's from a national paper.'

'No, Mr Moss, really, that won't be possible. She'll be able to see you before you go in, and she may wait in the family room which has a live feed, but she won't be able to go into the upload theatre,' she said firmly.

'For pity's sake,' snarled Phil furiously. 'They're paying me to watch the whole thing, not edited highlights.'

'I do understand, but it simply can't be done. She'll still see most of it anyway from the family viewing area.' The receptionist was very polite, but completely inflexible.

Neither Philip nor the receptionist was aware of a multi-car pile-up that had occurred just a street away, and which had stopped the traffic in all directions. The reporter was indeed desperately attempting to reach her interviewee, but was currently being interviewed herself by a thoroughly uncompromising policeman who demanded her eye-witness account of the woman seen driving dementedly towards the download centre at a speed rarely seen in this respectable and disciplined district.

With a puff of irritation Phil allowed himself to be signed in and then completed yet more forms. He was given a drink and a sedative for which he was grateful. He was now becoming a little more nervous as zero hour approached, so he hadn't really put his best effort into forcing the centre to allow the presence of the reporter.

'Mind you, it serves the silly bitch right. She shouldn't have been late,' he thought. Phil had definitely softened now.

Demanding that the receptionist look after the reporter if she ever bothered to show up, Philip left the comfortable rest area and followed a deferential and possibly male nurse into the depths of the huge building.

'Well, he's definitely a download, though I can't imagine why anyone would want to look like that!' he thought, faintly scandalised by the exquisite little person with huge, melancholic eyes. *'I'm not taking my bloody clothes off in front of that!'* Naturally, Philip felt that one glimpse of his enormous body would send the nurse into a fever of lust, which might have been a touch unrealistic.

Phil removed his clothes, alone, in a generously-sized cubicle, which was luxuriously furnished if a little too brightly lit, and the plush fittings made him feel slightly better. He liked knowing that he'd paid for the best. Unfortunately, however, the gown he was given, being only of knee length, rather emphasised the surplus poundage he'd put on over the last couple of years, and the ferocious lighting further highlighted how dreadfully he'd looked after himself over the last few years.

'I suppose that was the intention,' thought Philip, *'it wouldn't do to have patients deciding they look pretty in soft lighting and change their minds.'* He rather admired the strategy, if that's what it was. He wondered if it had been intentional, and then forgot about it, as other worries surfaced.

He felt odd and curiously vulnerable as he put the gown on, and for a moment Phil seriously contemplated forgetting the whole thing and just going home again. He wasn't yet fifty and he could get his present body healthy again without too much effort. It was laying his clothes in the neat wooden box provided by the nurse that did it. The box had his name and date of birth on it, and Phil suddenly realised that he was never going to wear them again. He would go home later and he'd certainly still own his old wardrobe, but he sincerely hoped that nothing he currently owned would fit him in the future.

In fact, in a short while this fat old body to which he hadn't realised he was quite attached, would be killed and disposed of. He looked at himself properly in the mirror; whether an unflattering reflection or not, it had suddenly become fascinating, and Philip stroked his large round tummy reflectively. He was deeply relieved when the extraordinary little nurse put his head round the door.

'Hey there, Mr Moss, aren't you ready yet?' he said cheerfully. 'I thought you must have got your fasteners stuck.'

'I was just thinking about what's going to happen, and whether it's really worth it,' Phil admitted reluctantly.

The young man sat down next to him. The process was expensive enough to warrant the undivided attention of the staff whenever the client required it.

'Are you having second thoughts?' he asked. 'Don't worry, almost everyone does at this stage, and it just shows you're taking the procedure seriously.'

'Yes, but I keep thinking I'm about to kill myself, and now I'm bloody terrified,' answered Phil desperately.

'Look, you know logically that's not right. You must have met loads of people who've undergone the process, a man in your position.' A little flattery generally went a long way, and no-one ever seemed to spot it.

'Well, of course I have, that's why I'm doing it. They all look great and seem really happy, but now that it's come to the point, I can't remember why I thought it was a good idea. I'm still in the prime of life, you know.' Phil tried to pull his stomach in, as he sat up a little straighter.

'There's nothing wrong with having doubts, that's fine and of course we aren't going to stop you, if you decide to cancel. But try to remember the reasons you wanted to go through this. Do you honestly feel that you'll have a long and happy life with this body?'

The nurse leaned away from Philip to take the impressive view in a little better. 'Because, I don't mean to be rude, but you're carrying a fair bit of excess weight, and there must be quite a strain on your heart. It's entirely up to you, of course, but you'll lose rather a lot of money if you stop now, because the fee is non-refundable,' he said gently. 'And you'll probably kick yourself once you get home.'

It was the reference, admittedly gently made by the nurse, that he would lose most, if not all of the cost of the download and bio-frame if he pulled out now, that affected him the most. Phil decided that he was being a wimp and tried to pull himself together. The sedative that the nurse had given him when he arrived was finally starting to take hold now, and he began to feel that he'd made a fool of himself.

'No, I'm fine,' he said, and glanced at himself in the strategically placed mirror. *The poof's right*, he thought. *I really am bloody unhealthy*. Phil realised with a sense of shock that there was no way the overweight, red-faced man in the mirror could have gone on as he was, and it was moderately amazing that he'd not collapsed before.

Phil could feel the beat of his pulse pounding in his ears as he stood up, and that strengthened his resolve even further. He'd spent too many nights lying awake in the wee small hours, listening to his body's feeble and entirely understandable protest at his treatment of it, to give in now. This was his last chance; he couldn't last more than a few short years otherwise.

'Anyway, what can go wrong?' he asked as cheerfully as he could.

'Nothing should go wrong at all. The power has separate back-ups in case of any interruption to the national grid; the equipment has been tested on millions of people over the last century, and it's been upgraded and perfected time after time. I won't say nothing can go wrong, but I can tell you the likelihood that it will is vanishingly tiny.' The nurse was definite, and Phil gave in.

'I'm ready now,' he said resolutely, and the nurse led him to a hoverchair, spreading a large, soft blanket over the small area of his knees that wasn't impossibly covered by his belly. Phil tugged the blanket up to his shoulders for comfort, and gave himself up to the tender ministrations of the Metaform.

The nurse guided the chair with one casual hand, along a short but rather beautiful corridor. The carpets were a luxurious blood red, and the walls were cream coloured and dotted with appropriately gold-framed pictures. Philip felt as though he were a privileged visitor to a country house, and since he'd made up his mind, he decided to enjoy the sensation of being pampered.

The nurse steered the chair into large room which looked even more completely unlike a hospital. The country house theme continued here, and as Phil began to rise to his feet, the nurse stopped him.

'You just relax, Mr Moss. You don't have to do anything.' He fiddled with a small hand-held device and the chair raised Philip up and over the bed, dissolving as he was placed into position.

As he lay back in the enveloping softness of the plush bed, looking around at what appeared to be a lovingly reconstructed ancient bedroom fit for a king, Phil gradually regained his old excitement. He liked having nurses bustling about him, too. *This is very nice, like being a small boy again*, he thought. He decided he might get into the whole nurse thing later, when he was up and about again.

There were several new nurses around now, and some of them were distinctly attractive. One came over to him, and as he prepared and then injected something painlessly into Phil's arm he conversed amiably.

'Have you seen a picture of your new body yet, Mr Moss?' he said.

'Well, not exactly, I chose it with the specialist, so I know what it'll look like.'

'Ah, that's what I thought. Well I'm allowed to show you a picture of your new body growing now,' the nurse said, handing Phil a small holopad. 'It's only about one month old, and it'll be technically ready in about another two months, but you can't use it until it's undergone extensive physiotherapy and all the enhancements have been tested.

Phil was enchanted; the three-dimensional picture of the rotating naked human was striking. He could see that the body was nowhere near ready yet, as its eyes were tightly closed and its features were barely formed, but it was discernibly the body he'd ordered; he could see the yellow hair swirling about, and although it was an odd-looking foetus, as it looked rather like a twenty-year-old man who'd melted a bit, he felt it was still rather more attractive than Phil himself.

'Ha, he's well-endowed, isn't he?' Phil said, rotating the body with a flick, and pointing proudly at the man-sized foetus' genitals.

'Well, we can't really tell about that sort of thing yet, actually.' The nurse looked slightly embarrassed. 'Did you request genital enhancement?'

'I can't remember now. I don't think I knew I could, actually. Will it have a little tiny dick, if I didn't?

'No, of course not,' the nurse said. 'You'll be just like any other average person. In fact, you'd probably be above average anyway, because these bio-frames are selectively enhanced in all the ways that matter. It's just that if you did request an enhancement and it got missed, I'd need to chase it up now because we won't be able to discuss it later.'

Phil was getting sleepy now as the drugs took effect, and it didn't sound as if it was worth pursuing that angle. 'As long as I'm going to be super-fit and great-looking, that's all that matters.' He sighed in contentment; the drugs were doing their work. 'Oh, and really smart, too. I mustn't forget that,' he muttered comfortably. It had cost quite a lot extra to have the augmented memory and high-speed recall capacities included.

'No,' he added, 'don't worry about it. I just want it to be over now.'

The nurse discreetly slid the holopad out of his hands and he and his colleague began to attach the HUD to their client. Theirs was a rather superior and very small, light model, nothing like the medical grade headpiece used at the European Medical Facility, and Phil didn't experience any discomfort at all as the process began.

Shortly after that, Philip technically died. His body took a bit of effort to take care of though, and Mark and

Ivan, the two nurses who'd attended the late Mr Moss, muttered irritably as they slid the hefty corpse away on its trolley for disposal.

Chapter 13

Less than a week after Connor's apparently sad and lonely death from heart failure, Tubby followed him into the Metaform's computer, having appeared to die tragically as a result of carbon monoxide poisoning caused by a faulty boiler. Meilinn had stayed with him until it was over, and had hated that assignment even more than suffocating Connor.

Meilinn had been painfully aware that she was committing her second murder in a week, and if an explanation were ever demanded by the local constabulary, she knew damned well that hers wouldn't sound terribly convincing.

They'd discussed the method for uploading him endlessly, and Tubby had already deactivated his apartment's air recycling system a few hours before Meilinn was due to arrive. The heating system continued to work, pumping partially burned carbon dioxide into his apartment through a small crack in a vent, carefully made by Tubby the day before. He'd been unable to use his heating until tonight, and the process was well under way now.

It was going to be a slow method, and he'd been instructed to be careful that the process of poisoning his body had started, but that it hadn't gone too far when Meilinn turned up for the final part. He'd know, so Meilinn said, when he started to develop a headache and felt nauseous. If that happened too early in the day, he'd have to lean out of a window for a bit.

Carbon-monoxide poisoning tended to cause extreme confusion in its victims, and if it had gone too far they wouldn't be able to complete the upload. Tubby had followed the instructions to the letter, and then gone to bed as normal, being careful to turn out the main lights at his more-or-less usual time, in case the neighbours were looking.

Meilinn really wasn't looking forward to this evening. Now, face rigid with determination, she drove herself to the centre of the town and parked her old car in a public car-park, then hefted her loaded rucksack over her shoulder and walked the half mile to the apartment that Tubby had rented when he first joined the little software company a few months earlier.

She'd never visited it before, and was surprised at how run-down it looked. All the better, she thought, gratefully. If his air conditioning system packed up and suffocated him in his sleep, no-one would be too surprised.

Tubby had given Meilinn a door key, and she casually put her gloves on before letting herself in. Following Connor's instructions, she closed the door quietly behind her, checking that it was securely locked, and as an afterthought she turned off the hall light, so no tell-tale shapes would show through the little peephole. Then she slid a small respirator over her nose and mouth before going straight to Tubby's room.

The gas was odourless, and not particularly fast-acting, but Mei realised she'd probably have to stay for quite a while, and if she were overcome too the results might be catastrophic, at least for her and Tubby, so the respirator was crucial.

A thought crossed her mind as she padded across the soft, pale-carpeted hallway towards a half open door from which a welcoming yellow light shone comfortingly. It reminded her of her earliest years, and Mei realised with a sense of shock that only six months ago she'd still been at college.

She paused for second, struck by the change in her life since she'd been a student without a care in the world. *'Funny, I thought I was stressed then, when all I had to do was a few assignments,'* she thought ruefully. *'I'm glad I couldn't see into the future!'* Meilinn took a deep hissing breath through her mask and walked into the room.

Tubby was sitting up in bed, neatly dressed in designer pyjamas, looking slightly flushed and decidedly nervous. Although he'd been expecting her, he still jumped at the sight of Connor's young assistant walking into his bedroom, dressed in sombre clothing and wearing a gas mask. His head hurt, he was beginning to feel horribly unwell, and he was just praying that he wouldn't throw up all over the girl.

Mei consulted her detector and, noting with alarm that the gas saturation reading was quite high, she sat down beside Tubby on the bed and they talked for a while as she tried to determine what effect, if any, the slow-acting but ultimately lethal gas had already had on him.

'I've waited weeks and weeks to get you into my bedroom, and now you're going to go and kill me,' Tubby laughed shakily, and then stopped abruptly. Meilinn laughed too, but she wasn't looking forward to this at all. She'd researched the best way to make Tubby's death look natural, but it was going to be a disagreeable process, and she was seriously jittery about it.

'I knew you were a dirty old man as soon as I first set eyes on you,' she agreed. 'Mind you,' Mei added, 'have you thought about what all this really means? You won't fancy anyone in the future.'

Meilinn had spoken without thinking, in an attempt to lighten the decidedly tense atmosphere, but Tubby looked struck. 'Well, no, I suppose not, but...' he broke off, confused, and then collected his wandering mind and continued, 'that must be true in general, but what if it's an intrinsic part of my, of my thing, my personality?'

'Gosh,' Mei said, 'it isn't part of mine, I don't think. Well,' she paused, 'mostly not. I think you have to imagine a time when you were completely engrossed in something complicated, and sexual activity wasn't relevant at all.'

Tubby looked pained, although still not entirely serious. 'I wish I'd realised before. It's a big thing for a man to give up, you know.' He rubbed the back of his head absently, as his headache gave a particularly vicious bang.

'Now you're just bragging. You're about a hundred years old, Tubby, so you probably would've gone off sex soon enough anyway!'

'I'm only sixty-three, younger than Con. And I bloody wouldn't have gone off it, you know,' Tubby said indignantly, although he was still attempting to smile. 'Still, I guess it's a fair exchange in return for immortality.'

Mei wondered, although she didn't say anything aloud in case she unsettled Tubby even more, how many more things would cease to have any relevance once they were completely incorporeal, and deciding there was definitely going to be a hell of a lot, but that she didn't have time to consider it now, Mei turned her attention to Tubby's physical condition.

Even in the few minutes since she'd arrived, Meilinn could see that Tubby had already been visibly affected by the carbon monoxide; his normally olive skin was flushed, almost orange, and there was a slightly sunken look around his eyes. Tubby was also struggling to finish his sentences, as though he was losing concentration.

'Did you take the sleeping pills, Tubbs?' she asked anxiously.

'Only three, Mei, that was right, wasn't it?' Tubby was beginning to find it hard to focus his eyes, but despite his increasingly tranquilised state, a niggle of stress still struggled to surface. He was conniving at his own death, and perfectly reasonable thoughts of conspiracy were rising in the background confusion of his mind. If it had all been a trick after all, there was probably no way out for him now. But his understandable terror was fuzzy and unfocussed, and he left the thought unfinished as Meilinn's voice distracted him.

'Yes, I think so, it has to be just a little more than you'd normally take, but I hope you're not too sleepy,' she said thoughtfully.

'What if I am?' he said nervously.

'Well, I suppose, worst case, we'd just air the place out, you'd get a good night's sleep and we'd do it tomorrow instead,' Mei said cheerfully. Tubby found this reassuring, and as he seemed only barely rational enough to make the leap into the computer world intact, Meilinn decided that she'd better stop chatting and get on with it before he deteriorated any further.

She helped Tubby arrange himself with a pillow under the small of his back, so that he was bent slightly backwards, and the maximum amount of tainted air could enter his lungs. She attached the heads up display

118

carefully, with little pads of cotton under the clamps so that it wouldn't leave any marks on his face and head. There were occasional odd little twitches from her patient that worried her slightly, but he seemed to be aware of where he was and what was happening, so Mei ignored them.

Then she dragged a chair over and began to upload Tubby's mind, using her laptop to adjust the programme's subroutines for him. She had to work hard to keep him alert enough to answer all the questions, and allow the HUD to read his consciousness. Eventually she concluded the upload with a sigh of relief, finally allowing Tubby to fall into a heavy sleep.

Meilinn patted Tubby's plump hand rather sadly and went to one of the other rooms, knowing that all she had to do was wait for about an hour or so. Closing the door carefully behind her, she opened a window and took off her respirator.

She opened the novel she'd loaded on her personal pad, but closed the file after a few minutes, in frustration. It was impossible to concentrate; her mind kept veering back to the man who was dying in the other room, and it would need to be a hell of a book to keep her mind off what she was actually doing. *It would have been easier if I didn't like the old bugger so much*, she thought ruefully.

When Meilinn finally went back to him, she found, with a highly disagreeable mix of conflicting feelings, that Tubby was still alive, though his lips were cherry red, and his breathing was very shallow. She sighed, checked his pulse, which was irregular, and hauled the pillow out from underneath him. Then she tidied the room and went back to wait for another half an hour. This time, despite feeling deeply troubled and emotionally drained, Meilinn managed to doze quietly in her chair, ignoring the mask that dug uncomfortably into her cheeks.

She awoke with a jump almost two hours later, and hurried into Tubby's room. Meilinn examined him with a kind of fascinated horror. Tubby's closed eyes were sunken, his jaw hung crookedly, and there was a kind of limpness about him that made a closer examination almost unnecessary. Meilinn checked her laptop and confirmed with the disembodied Connor that Tubby's disorientated intelligence was indeed online.

Then Mei made a final inspection, and checked that he had no pulse at all. She found her eyes filling with tears as she confirmed that Tubby really had finally gone. *'Silly, silly,'* she told herself. *'This is a good thing…'*

Meilinn left the air conditioning system exactly as it was, for the benefit of any subsequent investigation, and removed a few of the blockages from air vents around the apartment. She packed everything she'd brought with her into her backpack, and finished by walking slowly round the apartment to make sure nothing was out of place.

Then she left discreetly, the same way she had arrived. She managed to keep her face so expressionless that the next day her jaw ached with the effort she'd made to control herself.

The following week, Tubby was followed by Scott, who passed away peacefully, possibly from an accidental overdose of a recreational drug, far away in Florida, where he'd gone for a holiday. Scott had been no computer specialist, but Meilinn was getting quite the expert by this time and got him through it reasonably quickly.

Meilinn was in almost constant contact with Connor now, using her personal pad and tiny earbuds. She didn't look odd at all, though she felt slightly self-conscious at first, until Mei realised that almost everyone around her was holding conversations on their invisible pads. She started the long journey back to England the same day, after destroying the HUD rig and dropping the bits into several different public waste bins. There was no apparent reason to stop the pretty, dark-haired young girl and there were no problems at either airport.

Although there was a minor investigation of Scott's death by the authorities, there had been no appearance of foul play. He was, in any case, a foreigner with no grieving relatives to nag and hound the officers involved, so the case was dropped almost immediately.

Meilinn was feeling like a mass murderer; she really hadn't slept for days and was finding the process utterly horrific. Connor had been keeping an eye on all the police databases and monitoring their communications, and he now suggested that they stop all activity for a while.

'Just until they've forgotten about us all, Mei,' he said. 'I think we can probably get Luther up here in about a month, and then, because it won't matter what they think after that, your job will be over and you can come in too.

'Thanks Con,' she agreed sadly. 'But I wish I could go now.' Connor reassured her that she was doing better than anyone could have hoped, which cheered her considerably, but Meilinn was feeling distinctly traumatised by the whole business. It seemed odd to be looking forward to her own death, but she really couldn't wait.

Chapter 14

When the maid sent me out to the back of his house I was surprised that Errik looked like he was sunbathing. He sat bolt upright on an old chair in the middle of the bloody great lawn of his ancestral home with his face turned up to the sun. I watched him for a while, and gradually made out that, though he might be enjoying the sunshine, I could just see his lips moving. I wondered if the old man was praying and dismissed the thought immediately. There was nothing remotely religious about Errik, I did know that.

I watched for a few more minutes as he spoke into his aural implant. After a bit it seemed to me there was an acute sense of tension about his skinny figure, and he occasionally twitched, as though the intensity of his concentration was spilling over into his limbs. I wondered who or what he was talking to, and then left it. He'd tell me if he wanted me to know.

Errik had been really happy when I agreed to move in with him, and it was no skin off my nose. The house was huge, and it wasn't as if he didn't have plenty of rooms. He'd said he wanted to keep an eye on me while I was recuperating, but I reckon we both knew that was nonsense.

It did make sense though, in another way, because I was supposed to be his son, for the purpose of deceiving the Metaform, and in that case it might have looked a bit odd if I'd gone on living in a hut in the grounds.

I gave him a friendly bellow, and the poor old bugger jumped like a rabbit.

'Hi Errik, what you doing out here?'

I could see him collect himself, and felt bad for a moment. He wasn't a bad chap, and I had no idea what I'd do if he keeled over. I watched him inhale deeply and try to calm his startled heartbeat. He smiled back at me straight away though, with no hint of annoyance.

'Hallo, Gabriel. I'm so glad you're back. I wanted a word, and this seems a quiet place to chat. Besides, it's a lovely day.' He was as calm and gracious as ever, and as always, I envied his dignity. Dignity was one of the many attributes that I wasn't born with.

It was one of those unexpectedly warm days in early March, and Errik said he'd had the chair carried outside so he could work in the sunshine. I saw him look down briefly, and speak into his implant, and within a few seconds, three women arrived carrying another chair and a small table.

Obviously I'd visited loads of times over the years, but this was the first time I'd really seen the way his place ran. I'd thought Dad was insanely strict, but the way Errik spoke to the women made me wonder if it was just their generation. *'Perhaps,'* I speculated, *'they just made them tougher in the old days.'*

He ordered the women to put the table a few feet away from him, and demanded that the chair be placed at exactly the correct angle to the table, while I stood and cringed in sympathy with the servants, and tried to keep my face blank.

I sat down once the women had gone, and looked at him. 'So what did you want to talk to me about, Errik?'

'Oh there's no rush; let's have tea first,' he answered.

'Well, yeah, okay,' I said. 'How's disbanding the women going?'

Errik's face twisted in an expression of acute displeasure. 'Seven of them won't budge,' he said irritably. 'We've been careful not to let them know much about the active side of the brotherhood, but the fact is, if the police questioned them they'd find out a great more about us than would be healthy.'

'They can't know much, surely,' I pointed out. 'Dad pretty much kept them separated from the brothers at all times.'

'Really?' Errik raised a neatly combed eyebrow. 'Do you honestly think the men didn't find a way to see their wives and children when we weren't watching? I told Tobias it wasn't going to be a workable idea to keep them apart.'

I thought about it, and I had to agree. There were organised times, of course, when the families had time together, but they were always monitored to make sure no-one said anything indiscreet. Of course the women and old men would've found out what was going on, and that had worrying implications for our security now.

'What are you thinking, Errik?' I asked. He opened his mouth to answer me, but then a parade of maids began to file out of the house carrying plates and cups and stuff, so we both fell silent as they fussed quietly around us. At last they left again, and we carried on.

'Well, I do have an idea,' he smiled happily at me, 'but have some tea first, and tell me how you're getting on with the woman at the Metaform.'

Errik had wangled me an appointment with the download manager at the centre, and I still didn't know how he'd done it. 'Susan's okay, you know. I'm starting to feel a bit sorry for her, actually,' I said reluctantly. 'She's going to lose her job, isn't she?'

'Yes, probably, but she's still in a good position,' he answered. 'Remember she's one of the old downloads. Your Ms Susan Archer has a perfectly workable body which will keep her going for probably another hundred years. And we'll give her something for her trouble,' he added.

I felt a bit better about it when he put it like that. Errik's grand plan didn't sound all that sophisticated to me. He thought it would be easy for me to seduce one of the most notably bitchy women in the Metaform, and then get myself uploaded with a few helpful tweaks from himself. Funnily enough, just the actual seduction bit was worrying the hell out of me.

'I still don't see how this is going to work, Errik. She can't be stupid so she's bound to smell a rat, eventually. I mean it's a bit bloody obvious, isn't it?'

'I've done the research, my boy,' he said calmly. 'Miss Archer is one of the few employees I could track down who doesn't appear to have any friends at her workplace, has no social life at all as far I could establish, and all the feedback I could get from viewing her colleagues' files suggests that she's vain and shallow. As long as you persevere, she'll be grateful for your attention, Gabriel, trust me.'

I didn't have any option anyway. I had to trust him, but I still didn't see how Errik could be so sure it would work.

We talked for a while about strategy, and ate as the sun dropped lower in the sky. Finally, I remembered what I'd been thinking about when I came out here.

'Errik, you said there was something you wanted to talk about,' I reminded him.

'Ah yes. Yes, there was something.' Errik looked slightly uncomfortable and I braced myself. I'd seen that look before.

'What?' I asked.

'That friend of yours, Jared Walker, is he reliable, Gabriel?'

'Jared? Absolutely. Well, you know that, Errik. He behaved amazingly well on the night of Dad's accident, didn't he? Why do you ask?'

'I might have a little job for him, and I need to know he'll play the part,' Errik said slowly. 'You know the enclave's almost closed down now, and nearly everyone's left.' Errik looked directly at me for a moment before continuing. 'I have a small problem with those damned women still hanging around who won't leave until they get all their property back.'

I wasn't too surprised they wouldn't leave. To start with, they probably didn't have anywhere to go. They'd given everything they owned to the brotherhood, believing they were helping in the fight against the Metaform, and now the Soul Defence Force was disbanding, and they were destitute. 'How much are we going to give them, Errik?

'That's the problem, my boy,' he answered slowly. 'I don't think I'm going to have enough to give them without making us very short of funds.'

That did surprise me. I'd always though Errik was a multi-billionaire, because Tobias had always implied that he was. The only reason Toby had robbed Metaform installations, instead of just destroying them, was because he wanted to produce his own income. The impression I'd had was that he didn't want to rely too much on Errik, and certainly not that Errik didn't have the funds.

This was very worrying, because there was no doubt in my mind that the women would go to the authorities if they couldn't get what they wanted from us.

'Oh shit. Now what?'

'Yes,' Errik said gravely, 'that's what I've been thinking about. Jared's been collecting information for me and he did a reasonable job, initially. The trouble is I'm not getting anything back from him now. I was inclined to believe he's telling me the truth, and he just couldn't get into the centre himself, at first. I know he hates working there, and Jared says that he's still trying to get to know the nurses, but I've noticed that he's been getting quite touchy lately.' Errik stopped and collected his thoughts for a moment.

I was surprised at that. I'd always found him incredibly mellow, but when I came to think about it, I realised he probably wouldn't hit it off with Errik. They couldn't be more different characters, really.

'Yes, he was quite rude the other day when I visited him, and he stormed out before I could finish talking to him.' Errik sighed heavily. 'The fact is,' he continued, 'I don't like him much. I find Jared to be rude, uncommunicative and, frankly, rather stupid.'

I was astonished. 'Jared?' I repeated in disbelief. 'He's not stupid at all, and I've never known him be rude to anyone. Even my dad liked him.'

'That's what I thought, and it's why I used him in the first place, because it's not as if there weren't others who could have done the job. But the fact is it's not working, and I'm not sure whether he's actually telling me the truth about his inability to gather information, or if young Jared is being deliberately uncooperative.'

'I don't believe he's withholding information on purpose,' I said firmly. 'He might hate the job, and he might be sulking a bit, but he wouldn't withhold info. He was brought up the same as I was. Anyway, what option do we have? Jared's in place and you'll never get anyone else in now, will you?'

'No,' Errik said slowly. 'No, I wasn't thinking of pulling him out or replacing him. I was thinking of trying something else at the same time.'

'Like what?' I was all ears.

Errik smiled sheepishly; 'Jared actually has access to one of the biggest download nurseries in the country. It would be rather a shame to waste that access, don't you think?'

'Bloody hell, Errik, I don't think he'll be able to slip a bio-frame in his pocket and waltz out again, you know,' I said.

Errik made a small impatient gesture with his hand, and I shut up and listened to the rest. 'No, but I think he should be able to get a couple of our guys in and out again without too many casualties. What do you think?'

I was impressed, and slightly peeved that I hadn't thought of that myself. It was obvious, of course, except that I'd assumed we were no longer active. 'Do we have enough men and equipment?'

'How many men do we need? We wouldn't use more than two, or it'd raise suspicion. If it's worked out properly it should go like clockwork, shouldn't it?'

I was flattered that he was asking for my opinion. Tobias had told me what was happening, and that was all. Errik was consulting me, and I still found that amazing.

'What about Jared, then?' I asked. 'We couldn't leave him in place after that, he'd be in deeply serious shit.'

Errik winced delicately at my choice of words, and I smirked apologetically. 'No, Gabriel, of course not. Jared could leave with our chaps and never be seen again. Mind you,' he added, 'I'd have to get his barcode removed. He had to have one fitted before we could get him into the Metaform, but that's just a small detail.'

It wasn't my idea of a small detail. Dad had really resented having to get the things out. They were embedded right at the top of the neck, and it was dangerous as hell to get them out, even if it didn't show up on surveillance satellites as having been tampered with. It was a complicated business, generally meaning that someone without one had to be found dead with it, and the homeless barcode had to be completely re-written before it was implanted in the unlucky corpse. I wondered why Errik was being so casual about a relatively tricky operation, but didn't pursue it.

The sun had almost set and I was freezing. It'd been a beautiful day, but it was still early in the year and I wanted to get indoors. Somehow, the subject of what exactly we were going to do with Jared didn't come up again. Afterwards, I felt a bit of an idiot for not finding out a bit more.

Chapter 15

Jared had been working at the Metaform for over two months and neither the job itself, nor the transport bus, were any kind of novelty to him. The bus was grubby, noisy and incredibly uncomfortable. *And*, he thought irritably, *there's never enough bloody seats.* He heaved himself into the bus as usual, elbowing his way past the scrum of undernourished and smelly bodies and wedged himself at the back. The gravity buffers were on the way out yet again, and Jared wanted to be well out of the way when people started to bounce around. They often clutched at his reassuring bulk, and it was getting annoying.

The shriek as the bus pulled away from the dock went through his head like a knife, and put him in an even worse mood. Jared was feeling particularly miserable this morning, in part because the routine already seemed endless and bloody depressing. There was still no indication that he'd done his job for the brotherhood and could go home. His other grievance was that he'd had a row with Errik last night, and he suspected he could be in trouble.

Errik just flatly refused to tell Jared what he was planning or when his current assignment would end, and he knew there was something up, because he'd stop talking when he came into the room. Besides, Errik was acting dead shifty, generally. He seemed, to Jared's hurt surprise, to think Jared was pretty dumb. In fairness Jared would be the first to admit that he wasn't the sharpest tool in the box, but he was pretty offended that Errik wasn't at least trying a bit harder to be polite. It showed a contempt for the brothers that Jared hadn't suspected.

Jared wasn't keen on personal confrontation, possibly slightly oddly for a man whose entire life had been geared to violence, disruption and aggression. He tended to assume that orders were given for a reason, and if he wasn't privy to the details, it wouldn't bother him terribly. After two months of grinding boredom, however, and a growing sense that he wasn't actually doing anything useful at all, Jared had nervously decided to ask Errik for some kind of feedback.

As he'd expected, Errik said that he wasn't able to tell him anything more, not even when he'd be able to leave, or what exactly he was there for. 'It's for your own good, my boy.'

'No, look, it can't possibly be for my own good,' Jared said unhappily. 'I'm not asking for details or names, am I? I just want to know what's going on, because I know I haven't brought any useful data home for weeks, but you don't seem bothered. Surely there's more I could be doing?'

That 'my boy' thing was beginning to wear a bit thin too. Tobias might have assumed Jared was immature and even unsuitable for leadership, but he did at least accept that he was interested in the plans and strategies he worked on, and he'd always been included in discussions when they particularly involved him. Errik was behaving as though Jared was a simple-minded child who needed to be protected. He wasn't used to it, and he didn't like it one little bit.

'Errik, tell me what's happening, for Christ's sake!' he exploded at him in the end. He could see that he'd made Errik nervous, but he wouldn't give in and tell him anymore.

'Jared, I told you I have everything in hand. Nothing will go wrong, but if it does, you might be questioned.' Errik was firm, but there was a defensive whine in his voice that was irritating as hell, and Jared lost his temper completely.

'And you don't think I can stand up to questioning, is that it? I don't know why you bothered with using me in the first place. You'd have been better off with one of the congregation,' Jared shouted. 'At least they're polite when you treat 'em like dirt. But maybe you are using one, and maybe I'm a decoy or something; how the hell would I know?'

'Jared, calm down, this isn't getting us anywhere and you're just being silly,' Errik said nervously. 'I won't do anything you wouldn't agree with, but I just can't tell you the details because it won't work if you know about it.'

Jared decided he'd had enough. He stood up angrily, knocking his chair over, and grabbing the ugly grey micro jacket that was considered fashionable around the estate, he marched out. Errik sat quietly for a moment after this uncharacteristic outburst, collecting his thoughts. Then he gave a little sigh and followed Jared out of the door. His plan had gone exactly as he'd expected. *Such a predictable youth*, he thought happily.

Jared didn't get back for quite a long time, because, whilst stamping angrily around the estate, he'd found a nice little pub only a few streets away. The establishment looked as though it had been converted from something else, possibly a house, and lacked a certain elegance, so he entered the place cautiously. Jared was relieved to find it unexpectedly comfortable. One thing that he had in abundance was credit, and for the first time since leaving the church, Jared felt at home.

The bar had been small and dark inside, which suited his mood, and the ubiquitous telescreen had been almost muted, which suited him even better. Jared was interested in what the Metaform was doing, but not to the point that everyone else was. They seemed to be obsessed with the directors, who weren't even real people. They were the enemy, of course, and as such he found them worthy of study, but he didn't give a damn about what they wore or thought.

One of them, called Meilinn, was framed on the telescreen as he walked in, and Jared was distracted from his foul temper for a second. She was very pretty, and she was purple. And she didn't have much resemblance to any human being, organic or downloaded, that he'd had ever seen.

He ordered his drink and turned round to listen to her speak. Jared had to concentrate hard to hear her because he had no aural implant, and he reminded himself to speak to Errik about that again. Practically everyone else had them, and even Errik'd had one fitted. He said it kept him in touch with things and he needed it to access all the databases that he was working with.

Jared couldn't see how that worked, and after all, you'd think it would be useful for him, too, seeing that he was supposed to be fully integrated here, but thinking about Errik and his inscrutable plans just renewed his annoyance.

That purple director, Meilinn, was talking about the Metaform's intention to build a star ship, and to colonise the galaxy. Jared gave an involuntary snort of laughter; he couldn't help it, though when a couple of people turned round and looked at him, he clapped a hand over his ear and tried to look as if he was holding a conversation on his non-existent implant.

Honestly, Jared thought irritably, the hubris of the Metaform's directors was just astounding. Ruling the world wasn't enough for them, they wanted to rule the universe too. He pretended to end his muttered conversation and said goodbye, before turning to concentrate fully on the pseudo-girl whose image filled an entire wall at the far end of the room.

She was one of the main directors, and apparently she'd really existed centuries ago. It was always Meilinn that did the announcements and general comms, and Jared assumed she just had a taste for publicity. Not that he was complaining; it was good to see the creature that he intended to help eliminate. Tobias had been terrified that the brotherhood would be corrupted by their evil wiles, so although Jared had seen her before, he'd only given her odd image an occasional terrified glance.

Now he could look at Meilinn properly, and he wasn't impressed. Hers was the face that had started the craze for outsized eyes many years ago. *She's just weird, with that tiny little face, a mouth like an asshole and eyes like dinner plates*, Jared thought sourly. As the level in his glass dropped, he began to find it harder to resist the urge to hurl the glass at the view-screen. Jared did resist it though; the cost would have been hefty, and a conviction for vandalism wouldn't have helped anyone's cause at all.

The interview ended and the screen returned to its normal vision of near-naked bodies and raucous music, although still very quietly, and Jared was grateful, just for that evening, that he didn't have an implant. It was easy to see who had them though. The few small groups of people bellowing inane repartee at each other over the sound from the screen were obviously fans of the entertainment, receiving its full impact through their aural inserts. Though the background hum continued to grow louder as the night wore on, it didn't disturb Jared much.

He stared at his third beer and began to wonder again why Errik was acting so cagey. The only possible reason had to be that he was planning something else, something big, and perhaps he expected Jared himself to be involved only peripherally. Jared finally decided that he just didn't have enough information to worry about it for now. As usual, he'd mellowed out fairly quickly, and looked around at his fellow drinkers.

He recognised a few people from the transport, and nodded a greeting to a bloke that he saw almost every day. The man nodded back, and then ambled over. 'Not seen you in here before,' he commented.

'No, well I didn't know it was here. Seems okay though. You want another?' Jared gestured at his glass, and the stranger dipped his head in acceptance.

'We like it quiet.' He smiled and they both turned back to the bar and sat in friendly peace for a bit. 'Name's Tab,' he said after a while. 'I've seen you about a lot lately.' There was an implied query in the gentle observation.

'Jared.' He held out his hand and they shook. Tab was a solidly built man, far shorter than Jared but very broad, with a shock of black curly hair. Jared was slightly edgy as the stranger invaded his space, but the handshake was firm and didn't linger any longer than it should, so Jared didn't immediately stand up and see him off.

'Yeah, I work at the upload centre. I saw you this morning, didn't I? What do you do?'

'Pilot.'

Jared decided that Tab was obviously a man of few words, so he didn't answer, this time, and concentrated on ordering more drinks. There was another restful pause, and over the next hour the two men said remarkably little, but the silence between them wasn't uncomfortable. Then it occurred to Jared that Tab might be the right person to ask about the little matter that had been bothering him. He'd have to phrase it carefully though, or he'd sound as if he came from another planet, as the woman had pointed out with some scorn only recently.

'Tab,' said Jared slowly, 'I've lived in a closed community for the last few years, and I've really wanted to ask some questions. Would you mind…?' He waited to see what Tab's reaction would be. Jared felt, instinctively that Tab was probably a decent kind of chap, but it wouldn't bother him overmuch if he offended him anyway.

Tab turned and looked at him seriously. 'Religious, was it?'

Jared had been discreet about his background, on the whole. He wasn't at all ashamed of it, and he'd been told to tell the truth if he were asked about himself, but there were cults everywhere and most of their adherents were nutters. Jared decided on the spur of the moment that there really wasn't any better way to explain his ignorance about everyday affairs, anyway, so he nodded curtly and decided that Tab could draw his own conclusions.

'Well, yeah, maybe,' Tab answered laconically. 'Depends what you want to know.'

Jared gestured at his tunic. Like everyone's in there, it was made of intelligent fabric and looked as though it'd been painted onto him. He was in very good shape though,

136

so it wasn't quite as revolting as it could've been. 'Why does everything have their initials on it?' he asked. The tiny letters, "MC", set into the outline of a skull was unmistakeable, and too many years of associating it with the definition of evil meant that it still gave him a slight jolt every time he saw it. Jared knew he was programmed, of course, but he still couldn't help that visceral reaction.

'Bloody hell, you have been in a closed community. Where was it, then, on the moon?'

Jared accepted that comment in the spirit it was made. 'No, it's not that far from here, actually, but I didn't get out much.' Jared didn't add that he'd not been out at all, apart from serious forays which didn't leave much time for socialising with the locals, or an occasional illegal visit, during the last couple of years, to the nearest village. And even those had been fraught with worry. Old Toby didn't like people leaving the camp, and you didn't want to get Tobias upset if you could help it.

To Jared's surprise, a look of discomfort had come over Tab's face. He wasn't what Jared would have called good-looking, but he looked sort of kind, he supposed, and also very awkward.

'You really don't know?'

'I really don't know,' Jared agreed, and then he waited.

'Well,' Tab began reluctantly, 'I don't know where to start really. It's quite new, you see, and I suppose I'm still getting my head round it. First, I guess, the brand's on everything because they make the clothes. Well,' he amended, 'they supply the materials for the cloth.'

That didn't seem like a big deal to Jared. 'Okay, well that's fair enough, though I still can't see why they have to mark everything. So why the face, Tab?'

'It's what they make the cloth out of, mate,' he said slowly. 'Some people don't like it, and that's why not everyone wears Meta's stuff.' He stopped, and Jared waited for the other shoe to drop.

'Okay,' he prompted. 'Go on. What are their clothes made of then?' he said cheerfully.

'It's intelligent fabric, you know, that's why everything made of Metaform's stuff is branded. And it's recycled,' he continued, staring into his glass, 'so that's a good thing. They're made of recycled people.' He carried on speaking fast, as he saw Jared's face crumple. 'It's because there are these laws about burning things and polluting the place, and the EMF has to get rid of so many dead people when they're uploaded. That's how they sold it to us, anyway.'

Jared's jaw had dropped. Recycled people? It didn't seem possible. They'd never had Metaform's stuff on the camp, of course, and the only person who could've worn them would have been Errik. Then Jared realised suddenly why Errik always wore those ridiculous suits. It wasn't because he wouldn't look good in the new fabric; he was vain as hell. It was because he was squeamish!

'Wow. Okay. Well, that'll be why no-one wanted to tell me about it then, I suppose.' Jared was shaken to the core, and with an internal shudder he realised that his uniform would be recycled dead people too. He could feel his body trying to shrink away from the fabric that fitted so snugly. It was a losing battle. He took a deep breath and a big swallow of his warming beer, and got a grip. 'Thanks mate. I probably did need to know that.'

Oh boy, he thought, *that's just wrong.*

138

Chapter 16

A potentially fatally powerful sedative and alcohol combination had been Connor's suggestion to help Luther's transfer into his world. When Meilinn had asked rather plaintively how she was supposed to get hold of the stuff, Con told her that he'd deal with it, and a carefully packaged bottle had arrived in a seriously heavily wrapped and padded envelope a few days after their conversation.

Mei had torn the parcel open without realising what it was, and then she'd placed it gently onto her coffee table and called Connor. 'Did you just send me a bottle of poison, Con?' she exclaimed in mock hysteria.

'I thought you wanted it, sweetheart,' he answered. 'Remember we talked about how fast it acts? If I can administer a stun through the HUD, then a hefty overdose of the sedative and alcohol should finish the job, I think. You'll have to hang around though, just to be sure.'

'Oh, of course I will, but it'll be traceable, won't it?' Meilinn was worried, but Con's response sent her thoughts in another direction.

'They won't trace it back to you, Mei. If they do a post-mortem, it'll be spotted immediately, and it'll look deeply suspicious, but it won't matter, will it, if you're coming in within a day or so. I thought you could deal with Luther today, if you don't have anything else planned. And then you tomorrow?'

'Er, yes. Yes, I suppose there's no reason why not. And me tomorrow, then.' Mei felt a sudden shock of realisation; it was actually going to happen. Tomorrow.

'Well, that's what I was thinking. You're going to love this Mei, don't worry.' Despite his comforting words, there was for the first time, a note of doubt in Connor's voice, and Mei picked it up immediately.

'Come on, Con, there's a "but" in your voice. Why are you worried?'

'I'm not exactly worried; it's just that, you know we talked about having a sense of self?' Con said slowly, 'well, I don't know if this might work better the older the subject is. You see, from what I can work out, the form you'll take, and your mental cohesion, will depend on your own mental image of yourself,' he finished.

'You think I might not have enough of a sense of myself to keep a virtual form? How bad could it be, then, if I can't imagine myself properly?'

'That's the thing, Mei. We don't know, but I should imagine that the worst case would be your personality blending with the computer, and you not really having enough conscious awareness to exist as an individual.'

'Damn it, Connor. You're telling me this now when I've just killed three people, and I'm off to kill another one! When were you going to share this with me, next week?' Meilinn was outraged, and she sat on the floor and clutched her knees as visions of a long and interesting future in gaol coursed through her mind.

He didn't answer, and Meilinn sat silently, reviewing her options, while Connor left her alone to think it through. 'Well,' she said finally, 'it's not as if I have much of a choice anyway, is there. I have to risk it, I think.'

'I don't think it's a huge risk, Mei. I wouldn't let you try if it was, but it has to be your decision. I can interfere with all kinds of things from here, which I couldn't do before, so that'll make it easier. Just keep me updated while you do everything and I'll talk you through it as much as I can.'

'Thanks Con, but how am I going to upload myself?' Mei had been trying for the last few weeks not to think about the details of her own upload, but found herself considering it deeply at unexpected moments, mostly at around three o'clock in the morning.

'Well, I've had some thoughts about that, actually,' Connor sounded as though he was smiling, which Meilinn found interesting. *He's obviously refined his voice controls pretty well, anyway,'* she thought absently.

'If you come up at almost the same time as Luther,' Connor continued, 'it won't matter if anyone finds it suspicious, so the method might as well be almost identical.'

'Yes, I suppose so,' Meilinn agreed. 'It might look odd, but no-one'll be able to prove anything, and it won't matter much if they do, I suppose.'

'My thoughts exactly, Mei. Besides, you'd be amazed at the kind of control we have over public databases from here,' he added thoughtfully; 'and private ones too. I'll talk you through it, and we'll just tweak a few things afterwards so no-one will have any suspicion until we're ready to launch the Metaform to the world.'

Meilinn dealt easily enough with Luther, for whom suicide was the obvious choice. Mei and Luther had set the stage carefully, and he'd carefully displayed increasingly bizarre behaviour towards his relatives during the three long weeks leading up to his upload.

Luther's family would be dreadfully upset at his death, of course, but they wouldn't be as shocked as they might have been, feeling that the poor man had obviously been very troubled recently.

Luther had returned to his own modest home in Essex, and waited for the arrival of Meilinn in her role as the agent of death with mixed feelings. The technicalities were quite straightforward, and Connor remained audible on a speaker throughout, accompanying Meilinn via her personal pad.

'Hey, Luthe,' she greeted him with genuine pleasure. She'd taken to Luther from the first time she met him and often assured herself that his undoubtedly good-looking face had nothing to do with it.

It was slightly odd to see her normally elegant colleague semi-bearded, and dressed in little more than baggy shorts, but that was a part of the strategy that she and Luther had devised to fool the neighbours into thinking he'd had a kind of nervous breakdown. It was quite convincing, actually, Mei thought. She hadn't seen him for well over three weeks, and he hadn't shaved, showered or cleaned his teeth in all that time.

Luther kissed her cheek in greeting, and Meilinn wrinkled her nose in mild distaste. 'You smell like a badger, Luthe,' she said disapprovingly.

'Sniffed a lot of badgers, have you, Mei?' Luther answered flippantly, but he looked shamefaced. 'I expect I smell even worse than that, anyway. This has been horrible, I must admit.' He looked dubiously at Meilinn's gloved hands, and hurriedly away again. There was something distressingly business-like about those small efficient hands.

Meilinn followed his glance and reassured him; 'Don't worry, this bit's not going to be as bad as you think. Have you spoken to any of the others yet? They can tell you what it was like for them, and it should be quite a bit better for you, because we've worked out quite a lot since Con's upload.'

'Mm, yes, I spoke to Scott just now, and he said it didn't hurt, but it's hellish confusing at first, when you wake up?' He ended with a query, and Mei tried to answer what she knew he was asking.

'I got that impression too, but they all managed it okay, and Connor's been there for almost three months now, so he's probably got a much better idea of what it's actually going to be like. He's online now anyway, so you should be able to get uploaded without too much trauma.' Mei smiled reassuringly.

Luther led her into his sitting room and Mei laid her pad on the table and activated it.

'Hi Con,' Luther called to the pad.

'Luther, how are you feeling?' Connor answered.

'Stressed, buddy, if I'm honest,' Luther said frankly.

'Don't be. We've made some great improvements to the process, so try not to worry too much about it. Anyway, Mei knows exactly what to do. You'll be her fourth upload.' Luther raised an eyebrow at Mei, and she grimaced uncomfortably. It was true, but she felt it wasn't exactly something of which to be proud.

'Just leave everything to us, and it'll all be done in an hour or so, okay, Luthe?' Mei decided to take the initiative, otherwise they'd be sitting around making small-talk for the whole afternoon. Anyhow, she wanted to get back onto the motorway before it got dark.

'Where do you want to do this, Luthe?'

Luther sighed thoughtfully. 'I don't think it makes any difference, Mei, but it's more private in my bedroom, I guess. We don't need neighbours peering through the letterbox.'

They went into the bedroom where the curtains were drawn against the bright sunshine, and the air smelt as stale and unpleasant as the bedding. Luther glanced at Meilinn's rigid expression, and then they both burst into slightly hysterical laughter. 'It's going to get worse in here later, I suppose, anyway,' Luther observed. 'How are we doing it, Mei?'

'Apparent sleeping pill overdose, with alcohol,' Mei said succinctly. 'We'll upload and stun you, then I'll inject you with a mighty dose of sedatives.' She produced an empty pill bottle triumphantly and dropped it, cap off, on the floor beside the bed.

'It wouldn't do if they looked too closely, because there won't actually be any pills dissolved in your stomach, but you'll have all the right chemicals inside you by the time you leave. So to speak,' she added. She looked quizzically at the half bottle of whisky beside the bed. 'And that'll do nicely. I have some rum in my bag, but it's much better to use your own stuff.'

Luther sat on the bed, and Meilinn unloaded the various pieces of equipment from her bag, and then began to attach the heads up display whilst Connor, propped up amongst the clutter on a side table, watched interestedly from his video link. The last items Meilinn produced were a funnel and a length of rubber tubing, and Luther emitted a surprisingly eloquent squawk of distress.

Mei laughed involuntarily. 'Sorry, it does need alcohol too, Luthe, but if you drink it first, you might be too drunk before the upload's finished, and we can't risk that. The worry is that I might scratch your throat, but if we stun you first it should be okay. Anyhow, there ought to be no reason for anyone to investigate too closely,' Mei said matter-of-factly.

Fortunately, Luther's upload went exactly according to plan. He was completely conscious until just before the end of the process, when the HUD delivered a stunning electronic blow, and Meilinn slid the tube down Luther's throat, gently pouring a hefty slug of whisky down it. Then she and Connor made desultory conversation while they waited for Luther to absorb the whisky. Mei injected him discreetly between the toes with a huge dose of Connor's sedative, then held his wrist and waited patiently for his heartbeat to stop, this time with far fewer qualms than she'd had with Luther's predecessors.

Mei left the house almost immediately, after confirming that Luther had arrived, apparently mentally intact. She heaved a sigh of relief; there was no-one else needing this kind of attention and now, finally, she could relax.

She'd taken care of all the important little details, in most cases before Connor had remembered them, including the re-homing of Con's dog, and it was that attention to detail that Con particularly liked about Meilinn. Fond as he was of his dog, he'd have left Tarquin to his housekeeper to look after. The housekeeper had been walking and feeding the unfortunate animal for weeks until Meilinn found an elderly friend who was happy to take him.

Once Meilinn had seen to all the small administrative details, including putting the original software company in trust, on behalf of the people who would shortly become the directors of the Metaform, she felt, like

Luther, that she couldn't do better than a nice tidy suicide herself, and decided on a warm bath and an apparent overdose. Meilinn asked Con to suppress her brain patterns for as long as possible.

'I've got it, Mei, don't worry,' Con answered. 'I'll shut you down as far as I can this side, until your body's no longer responsive, and I think you'll just have to leave the HUD where it is. I can send a power surge through it anyway, so no-one else will be able to use it.'

'Okay, I suppose. I shouldn't think anyone will know what to make of the HUD anyway and there won't be much to sort out, apart from that. In fact, come to think of it, the only worrying possibility is the download might complete before the drugs take effect, but they shouldn't if I'm careful. I'll have to meter the dose, I suppose. There's the programme though; do you think we ought to destroy my pad?'

'I can definitely deal with that from my end,' answered Con. 'As long as your machine's online I can wipe the hard drive from here when you're ready. And don't worry about the drugs taking effect too late. I can stun you quite easily now, and that's something we couldn't do before. Then we can let nature take its course.'

In the event, Meilinn had prepared so carefully that the whole process was completed perfectly smoothly. When her thin, gangly body was found several days later in a rather unpleasant bath of cold water, the weird headset was removed gingerly by the medics, who assumed it was an entertainment device. No-one paid it any more attention, and it was subsequently dumped, along with a broken personal pad and Mei's idiosyncratic clothing by her only known relative, an aunt that Meilinn hadn't spoken to in years.

The five directors who were to constitute the entire staff of the Metaform Corporation were now in place.

Chapter 17

Susan Archer had worked for the Metaform for almost longer than she could remember. She appeared to be around twenty-five, but was actually coming up for sixty years old. The upload itself had been subsidised by the company, but the peripheral enhancements and improvements had been expensive. It had been an awful lot of money to spend when she hadn't even been particularly old at the time.

She'd never been good-looking though; Susan felt she'd been cursed with a hard, bony face and an angular body which never put on weight and never seemed to develop curves. The Metaform, as part of its employee programme, had advanced the cost of Susan's download, and she'd had some interesting enhancements included. Her intelligence had been increased, but her emotional intelligence remained fairly low, as Susan had been unaware that there was any need to improve it.

Susan felt that she was a natural leader, and when, as occasionally happened, she was made aware of the ill-feeling of most of her staff towards her, she put that down to jealousy. She'd always said that she didn't come to work to make friends, and had unfortunately said it more than once in front of colleagues, who consequently ignored her as much as possible.

She was running slightly late today, and was concerned that her staff might take advantage of her absence and start slacking. She also had an appointment with a prospective new download client, and although she didn't mind keeping people waiting a little, Susan felt that to leave him too long would seem unprofessional. The appointment had been made without her approval, which was slightly odd, but it was done now, and it was a break in routine for Susan, so she wasn't too unhappy about it.

'Vito, call the office and tell them I'm on the way.' Susan addressed her vehicle's on-board computer and personal assistant.

'Yes, Susan,' the computer answered impassively. There was a short pause and then: 'Connection has been established, and a message registered with the upload surgery.'

Susan sighed. She'd have liked a machine with a bit of human-style warmth, she thought, not for the first time. Vito was linked to her home network, and had been carefully designed to be compatible with her, but it was still completely robotic. And it wasn't as if she hadn't tried to be nice to it.

Susan was heading to the office where she ran the Upload Selection Programme on behalf of the Metaform (UK) SE. She was young for the post, even taking into account her augmented lifetime. It was enormously important that upload applicants were vetted carefully to avoid the constant terrorist threats, and viruses that were becoming ever more intelligent.

An expert eye was also needed to spot particular mental health issues which might leak into the system and cause disruption. The vast majority of mental health problems were fine, as the patients' consciousness was dormant in any case, but on special occasions patients were permitted to interface with the mainframe during their uploaded state, and those patients in particular needed to be examined meticulously.

This morning's appointment was with a young man who had applied to remain conscious while his new frame was prepared for him. He was aware that normally the mind of a client applying for a new frame would be stored in a dormant state until his new frame was ready for him, but felt there were extenuating circumstances in his own case. *There always are, though, aren't there?* Susan thought peevishly.

'You see,' he said simply, once they were both seated, 'I'm all my father has. I was born when he and my mother were quite old, and if I leave him for months he just won't be able to cope, so I'd like to be able to keep an eye on him and the business.'

'Mr Kerr, unfortunately there's no possibility that you'll be allowed to remain fully conscious. Apart from anything else, it has enormous implications for data storage.' Susan tried to explain the problem, which was in fact her second mistake. The first had been agreeing to meet Mr Kerr in the first place. Susan was still confused that an appointment had been made on her behalf, and made a mental note to speak to her secretary about it later.

'It takes a long time for a frame to be prepared for you to be downloaded into,' she continued. 'It would take an absolute minimum of three months, and in practice it takes at least four months if you have a bio-organic one. Boredom wouldn't just be a little problem, it could be a sanity destroying nightmare much quicker than that. There are only so many games you can play, you know.'

'I know that, of course, Miss Archer,' he answered, 'and I'm well aware that I'm asking an awful lot, but the reason I requested this interview was that I wanted to tell you how grateful my father would be if this could be done.

I'm going downhill now, and in a matter of a few months I'll be wheelchair-bound at the very least.'

Susan's waif-like little face hardened as she recognised the same old emotional blackmail that clients tried on her with boring regularity, and spotting the drop in temperature, the client backed off immediately.

Look,' he added quickly, 'there's certainly no emergency, and I'm sure I have plenty of time before my illness becomes unmanageable; the nanites are controlling it perfectly well for now. Why don't you come to dinner with me and I'll tell you a bit more about what my company does?'

Susan was slightly surprised. She rarely met clients in person, and was never asked out by anyone. She was aware that she'd done well in her career, and felt that she looked stunning, so the reason for her unpopularity was a mystery to her. Susan had non-standard alterations made to her basic frame, such as exceptional height; she was well over six feet tall now, and also possessed a bust of extraordinary height, size and firmness, and, of course, the fashionable enormous eyes, in a particular shade of dark orange that she'd taken several days to select. It was no longer the latest model, of course, but still impressive, she felt.

She regarded the client thoughtfully. It probably wouldn't do any harm to have dinner with him. And he was very nice-looking, she noted; nice solid build, thick dark hair. He was very tall too; she hadn't realised how short everyone was until she returned after her download and found that she now towered over them.

She smiled. 'All right, Mr Kerr, thank you, but you must understand that this simply cannot affect the decision-making process.'

'Call me Gabe,' he answered, smiling back. 'I understand totally, and I promise I'll respect your decision, whatever it is, but I'd like to show you why it's important to us. I'd like you to meet my father, too. I'm sure you'd like him, and you can see some of the work we do.'

After several meetings with Gabe which went extraordinarily well, Susan was introduced to Gabriel's father in the huge lobby of a hotel in the centre of Brighton. He was exactly as she'd imagined him. Errik was elderly, beautifully spoken and obviously fabulously wealthy. She was entranced by his old-world courtesy, and found that she settled easily into the role of a pretty little thing without a twinge of embarrassment or discomfort.

Susan very quickly began to be sorry that Gabriel had been diagnosed with an almost inoperable brain tumour. Nanosurgery was able to deal with a great many previously terrible diseases, but this was apparently so far advanced that it had spread throughout Gabriel's brain, and although it could be removed, the growth had already begun to destroy his nervous system, and its removal could only aggravate the damage.

Susan had seen the computer assessment of his brain-function, and knew it was serious. His heartbroken father would pay any amount of money to keep his boy with him, and to have him downloaded into a new frame.

Errik had produced the scans of Gabriel's initial brain damage after the terrible beating by his real father, and they certainly showed genuine damage to his neural connections. Naturally, the later scans showing that the damage had been almost completely repaired by nature and nanites hadn't been shown to anyone.

'I'd like you to come and stay with us, Susan. I'm sure you'd love the estate. Do you ride at all, my dear?' Errik was behaving like an old-world gentleman, and Gabriel, who'd never seen the slightly arch, flirtatious side of him before, was enormously impressed. Considering he couldn't have had much practice, he was doing tremendously well.

'What, horses? No, I've never tried,' Susan was bewitched. 'I just haven't had the opportunity.'

'We'll mount you on one of Gabriel's old ponies. They're all as good as gold, and you'll love it. They're all getting on a bit now, so you'll be absolutely safe.'

'I'm sure I will.' Susan was already envisioning herself as the lady of the manor. 'Gabe, you won't change yourself too much, will you? When you're downloaded, I mean?'

'Well, no. It's not really a vanity thing, you see. I just need to get back to the estate as soon as I can. I'm not planning to be that different, but I can't see a shiny new frame looking like this beaten up old body,' Gabe laughed.

'You can commission one exactly as you want, you know. It doesn't have to be physically perfect. It's just that people seem to want their new body to be highly visible, just to show they can afford one. I'm afraid I went that way myself,' Susan admitted shamefacedly.

'Well, I don't. If I'm honest, I hadn't thought about the technical details at all, but I wouldn't mind being a healthy version of what I am now. I might have a straight nose though.' He touched his nose, and smiled fetchingly at Susan. Tobias had landed a thump on his nose many years ago, and it had never recovered its old shape. Not, of course, that he was going to tell Susan how it got bent.

153

'I don't think you should change even that really, but it's not up to me.'

'I think it has a great deal to do with you.' Gabriel looked at her seriously for a moment. 'I'd like to be how you like me.'

Errik compressed his lips, unnoticed by the other two. He was slightly shocked at Gabe's ability to throw himself into the role of lover. This woman was appalling; she was incredibly odd-looking, and apparently completely uneducated. She didn't seem able to recognise even the simplest quotation. Emotionally, however, Susan appeared to be highly vulnerable, and Gabe was doing an uncomfortably good job of seducing her.

Errik now found himself in the awkward position of both disliking the woman intensely, and of feeling very sorry for her at the same time. He suspected, sourly, that a large number of credits would go a long way towards consoling her for the loss of her new boyfriend in due course, but in this view he might have been unfair.

Susan certainly could be motivated by large sums of credit, but a part of her was genuinely overjoyed that Gabriel seemed to like her, and the loss of that approval was something that Susan would certainly regret.

Errik, on the other hand, knew that his remaining funds were being spent like water, and felt that if there were an alternative he'd happily consider it. He already had access to Susan's personal assistant; the AI had been quite simple to hack, and he discreetly checked his pad, while he tried to ignore Gabriel and Susan's saccharine conversation.

There was indeed an alternative way to deal with this particular problem, and within a few keystrokes he'd found it. Errik decided not to discuss his strategy with Gabriel. The boy might not approve.

After Gabriel and Errik dropped her home later that day, Susan decided that of course she would help him after all. It wasn't as though there would be any harm done. The worst that could happen would be that Gabe might suffer a psychotic episode whilst online, and there were specialists who could deal with that.

She decided to advise him to order the new frame immediately, and to wait as long as possible before upload, in order to minimise the time spent in virtual space. *Of course, he's planning to run his family's business from the Metaform, so he probably won't be bored at all*, she reflected. *And he can always request to be stored later if it gets too much for him.*

A short while later, Gabriel asked Susan to dine with him in one of the most elite private clubs in the world. Gabe had no idea how Errik had managed to book a table for two without giving at least two years notice, though he was suitably impressed, and guessed that Susan would be too.

Once she'd understood that she was going to be seen publicly at the Satellite Heaven, Susan had tried to look her most devastating. She'd dressed entirely in orange and gold, and her face and hair were also heavily decorated with shimmering gold. Vito had excelled himself in the design of her outfit, and she'd spent an extraordinary amount of her savings on the deceptively simple accessories. Heads swivelled as they were seated at their table, and Susan thought she'd absolutely burst with pride.

The candlelight flickered in her huge orange eyes and gave her a bizarrely feral appearance, but her smile radiated happiness. Against his own judgement, Gabriel was at first astonished, and then genuinely entranced by her weird appearance.

They sat in the exclusive restaurant, overlooking the shimmer of the northern hemisphere of Earth far below, as other diners nudged each other discreetly, and Susan radiated contentment. She was aware of being watched, but was certain that the hiss of conversations that reached her were prompted by envy and admiration.

Gabriel was feeling particularly heartless in the face of her clear enjoyment, but the plan had been worked out months before, and shattering the pride of one Metaform employee was a negligible price to pay for the ultimate goal.

Two hours into the evening she was still having a wonderful time and knew she'd never forget it. 'I still can't believe I'm here. I'm breaking so many rules,' she said happily.

Gabe winced sharply. 'It's my pleasure, believe me, Susan,' he answered.

'What's the matter, Gabe?' Susan asked in alarm.

'My head. My head hurts. Sorry love, it'll go in a minute.' He pulled himself together and with a visible effort seemed to overcome the pain, and they continued to talk softly. Susan had noticed that Gabriel wasn't drinking, but had decided not to comment.

After another ten minutes, Gabriel's speech began to slur and he seemed to have trouble concentrating. Then he groaned softly, and winced again, rubbing his eyes with his hands. Gabriel's water glass fell to the floor and a waiter strolled over and picked it up.

'Is everything to sir's satisfaction?' he asked with casual malice.

Gabriel didn't respond, holding his head in his hands. Only Susan could see that he was grinding the heels of his hands into his eyes, and his jaw was clenched hard.

'Call an ambulance. Now!' barked Susan. The waiter raised an eyebrow which suggested that an ambulance was a slightly excessive response to a mere drunken episode, but as Susan snarled the final word, he raised the other eyebrow and disappeared.

'Gabe, the ambulance will be here soon. Hold on,' she said gently.

'I can't feel my hands.' Gabe looked up for a moment; his eyes were a bright, blood-filled red and tears of pain ran down his cheeks. Susan was horrified.

'I can't go to the EMF,' he said indistinctly. 'I have to go back to my clinic. They'll know what to do. Susan, it's important,' he gripped her hand in desperation.

The ambulance arrived within a few minutes, and since it seemed to be a source of worry to Gabe, Susan demanded that they take him back to his father's private clinic. The ambulance crew grumbled briefly, but gave in.

Susan was left behind, sitting alone amongst the ruins of her romantic dinner. Wearily, she collected her bag and a shimmering wrap and boarded the shuttle back to her home to await news of Gabriel's condition.

Chapter 18

After what Mei thought was hours of panic, but which had probably only been a few seconds, she forced herself to get a grip. She was disorientated and confused by the darkness and the lack of landmarks, and wasted time searching for anything familiar that she could latch onto, until she gradually became aware of Connor's presence, and the feeling that there was some growing brightness around her.

Weirdly, Mei thought she could smell her old boss's aftershave before she could visualise his presence clearly, and then realised that she could see him exactly as he'd been before his upload. She recognised his favourite moss-green waistcoat as an old friend, and forced herself to breathe slowly, while trying not to remember that she didn't need to breathe at all, and never would again.

'Meilinn,' Con said gently, his voice echoing in her head, 'look at me.' She focussed on his shape and began to feel better. 'Now look around slowly,' he added.

Mei took in her surroundings, which were just as she'd expected them to be; white nothingness, with Connor standing knee deep in what appeared to be a cloud. As soon as the analogy occurred to her, the whiteness coalesced into sky and the clouds separated into firm, pale ground.

'That's good, Mei, you've got it. Now add some details.' The local park gradually formed around her, and Mei sank onto a bench in relief. Looking down at her knees, she realised that she was wearing the clothes she'd been wearing the day before her upload. Mei ran her hands over herself and then looked up at Connor quizzically. 'Are you seeing what I'm seeing, Con?'

He was leaning against a tree, apparently very comfortably, and smiling at her affectionately. 'You're projecting some of this, and so am I. We can see it because we both created it. If you didn't want me here, I wouldn't be. Well, I would, of course,' he corrected himself, 'but I can only see you because you're thinking about me.'

'So there are rules then?' Meilinn was cautiously relieved. 'Can I see the others then, if I want to?' Mei already suspected she'd be okay, but there were a lot of parameters to establish and she wanted to get started.

'Of course you can, but you might find it harder, depending on how familiar you are with the way they used to look.' He grinned at her. 'Try Luther,' he said, 'he's expecting you.'

After a few false starts, Meilinn recalled Luther as she'd seen him last, and a dishevelled figure appeared beside her on the bench. Again her sense of smell appeared to have made an excellent transition to this odd new world.

'Oh come on, Mei,' Luther spoke in what would have been her left ear if she'd still had one. 'You can do better than that. I was only grotty for three weeks!'

She blinked and Luther's shape dissolved until it was almost gone. 'Mei, stop worrying about it,' Connor said. 'Luther, present yourself to her, it's too hard to do this straight away; you know that.'

Luther dissolved completely, then re-appeared in her view as sharp and neat as she remembered him, and possibly even better-looking. 'How did you do that, Luthe?' she asked.

'Do what?'

'Well, you're thinner aren't you, and you just look different from how I remember you, or am I imagining you wrong?'

Luther displayed perfect teeth in a beatific smile. 'No, I've just adjusted my self-image a bit. But not by all that much,' he said casually. 'You can't influence the way I appear to myself, you see. You can only see me the way I see myself.

Meilinn looked again at Connor for clarification. 'Yes, he's right, Mei. You can imagine him however you want to, but it wouldn't be the definitive image, and it would be like an unreal dream copy. Only Luther has complete control over himself. One small thing, though,' he added, 'in case you wonder why we don't look quite right; it's because we're seeing ourselves as we were in our mirrors, and not as others saw us.

'So I can design myself how I want to be, then. And that's how you'll all see me.' Mei digested this for a second. 'Perceive me, I mean,' she corrected herself.

'Yeah, that's about it, honey.' Luther looked as though he was about to say more, but a tiny signal from Connor made him break off. 'I'm off for a bit, Mei. If you want me, just sort of call. You'll get used to it.' He glanced at Connor, and the signal passed between them again, this time more imperatively, and Luther was gone.

He didn't leave as he'd arrived, walking into her conscious view; he simply ceased to be where he had been, and looking at the spot that her friend had been standing in made Meilinn feel funny. As usual, she looked at Connor for direction.

He came and sat down beside her, and she felt rather comforted by his perfectly ordinary presence. 'Can I touch you, Con?' she asked hesitantly.

'Yes of course, and you should feel what you expect to feel. At least I hope you will, anyway.' Meilinn laid her hand on his arm which seemed reassuringly warm and solid, and she finally relaxed.

'Okay. I think I've got it, Con. We're exactly the same as we were. We have exactly the same senses because those are what we uploaded,' she said finally.

'That's almost right, Mei. We uploaded all of our memories of our senses, not the senses themselves. I don't know what'll happen when or if we start to forget what things felt or tasted or looked like, but at the moment our minds are showing us what we expect to see and feel.'

Mei watched him with the same expression of fierce concentration she'd always had when he'd explained a new idea to her in the past. She thought there was a look of mild concern on Connor's face. 'So what's worrying you, Con?' she demanded.

'I'm not exactly worried, but it's a very peculiar process, and I think you should just take all the time you need to settle down, and get comfortable with the way you see yourself. Try and find out how this place works by yourself. You'll find it's surprisingly simple actually, and the main thing is not to panic. The trickiest part is these first few moments, when you aren't sure if you're really here.'

'Ha, yes, I did notice that. What do you think would've happened if I'd panicked, then?'

'I don't know exactly, and we'll have to do more investigation, but I have a theory that you could just dissipate into the mainframe. I could be wrong though.

You might just have a screaming fit and then start again. You've done extraordinarily well though.' Connor said thoughtfully. 'Better than the others, and that's surprised me.'

'Why were you surprised? I didn't have any doubts,' Mei said, slightly offended.

'Remember we talked about it before; it was your age. I just wondered if it might be harder for you to visualise yourself because you haven't been fully adult for as long as the rest of us. I've had a very long time to get used to the way I am, but only a few years ago you were a child. I wondered if that would make it harder for you to manifest yourself perfectly.' He turned and looked at her in assessment. 'But you're exactly as you were. You don't even look like a mirror image.'

'Well I don't think it's confusing at all. It must have been very hard for you though, and I can't think how on earth you managed all by yourself.' Mei was fascinated by the process, and had now relaxed a little. As she spoke, she regarded the backs of her hands thoughtfully. Her fingernails had tended to be a little neglected; Mei always had more important things to think about than manicures, but now she watched them grow into neat talons, then with a flick of thought she reduced them to a sensible length, and admired them absently as she listened to Connor.

'I wasn't by myself though, remember, Mei?' Con continued. 'I was talking to you almost immediately, and I had the task of setting this place up firmly in the back of my mind as I went in.'

'I suppose that's true. So the next time we upload someone, it might be a good plan to give them something to fixate on. A room, perhaps, or a mirror with their own reflection in it,' Meilinn said thoughtfully. 'What happened to Tubby then? Did he manage okay?'

'He managed reasonably well, I think. He was feeling so terrible when he left his body that I think he was just relieved to be out of it. He was a very funny shape for a bit, then after we'd talked for a bit, he went off to sort out his own place and he stabilised in the end.'

After that, Meilinn began to establish her own little world. They'd tried to design a home for each of them that would provide an anchor and a refuge, and that had been simple enough for Connor, but surprisingly difficult for Mei. Their memories were stored so that they could access them continuously, and despite the load on the computer, the system seemed to be working.

Mei had very few memories of her family, having lived with various foster families for most of her life, and she really didn't want to revisit any of those places now. Finally, she'd settled for recreating the little flat she'd technically died in, and decided that she'd improve the décor and the view from the windows when she'd settled down a little.

Mei had been confused at her freedom at first, finding that she could imagine herself to be anything she wanted. For hour after hour Mei mentally created and re-created herself as a fantasy figure in different colours and bizarre shapes, but returned infallibly to her old form as soon as she stopped concentrating.

This was a good thing, as Connor kept reminding her, as it meant that she had a powerful sense of her own identity, but Mei found that the longer she forced herself to stay in a more bizarre shape, the less easily she snapped back into her old one, and this was something she intended to work on. Exotic, she felt, was what she was destined to be.

The tool that helped the directors the most was a holo-projector set up in their old office, which transmitted them in fixed forms. After making certain improvements to her basic shape which Meilinn felt were absolutely necessary, she began to settle into a more-or-less permanent image. She was now purple-skinned and had masses of hair, but was nevertheless still just recognisable as Meilinn.

Six months after Meilinn's upload, their old office was converted into a permanent interview suite, with holo-projectors that could be used when they had to give interviews to the media. As time passed, Meilinn remained in the form that bore only a passing resemblance to the girl she had been, although her colleagues remained stubbornly similar to their old selves.

Meilinn, Connor and Tubby worked constantly on the humanoid machines that they'd hoped would replace the tired or diseased bodies of normal people. Con and his team had indeed found a way to download the stored minds into new bodies, but after a few years it had been found that androids, although adequate, just weren't the same.

They were better than being dead, everyone seemed to agree on that point, but they didn't feel at all natural, even with all the upgrades that they'd been given. There were tiny delays in their movements occasionally, the causes of which no-one was quite able to identify, and of course the androids' perceptions of sensation were extremely limited in comparison with human senses. They didn't look quite natural either.

After a year had passed, Meilinn suspected the android frames were as good as they were likely to get, and she wanted to try inhabiting one. Connor tried to dissuade her.

'Mei, I don't know what'll happen if you try and shut yourself into a body after all this time, but I don't think you'll like it.'

'Oh, but I wasn't intending to do it for long, it was just an experiment, Con.' Mei wasn't exactly missing her body, but a small part of her yearned to feel things and to experience the real wind in her face just one more time, without the constant knowledge that everything was illusory.

'Fine, try it, Mei, but I think you'll find it very odd.' Connor was happy for her to make her own mistakes, as he mentally sat back and watched.

He'd been absolutely right. She'd awoken after the download into a body that felt heavy and unresponsive. Meilinn also realised quite suddenly that she'd forgotten how to speak. A year of communication by high speed electronic pulse meant that she'd had to learn again how to speak at a speed that humans could follow. After two days, she begged to come back.

'Never again, Con. Never, ever again,' she said feelingly. 'I thought it would be just like going back to the old me, but with a sort of disability, and it wasn't at all. It was like being trapped.'

With a superhuman effort, Connor refrained from saying that he'd told her so, and Mei, who could sense his thoughts almost as well as her own, rather appreciated that. She decided not to refer to her experiment again.

Some years later, when the five directors had finally managed to produce the new bio-frames, made from living flesh grown onto hardened metal skeletons, they were astonished and gratified at the reaction from the world. These frames were almost as good as being born again, and they knew these fantastically sculpted bodies were going to be the most popular product ever marketed.

Chapter 19

Susan was pathetically grateful to hear from Gabriel's father again, a day after his terrifying collapse, and she gripped the phone tightly in relief. Errik confirmed that the speed of progress of the tumour had increased, and that it was now putting dangerous pressure on Gabriel's brain.

Errik wasn't exactly getting cold feet, but now that Gabriel's upload date was getting closer, he was already beginning to grieve at the loss of the boy, and to fret seriously at the thought that he was sending Gabriel to his death. He talked to Susan, aware that he couldn't even begin to tell her the truth, but nevertheless taking some comfort from discussing it with her.

'I worry, you see, that it will affect his mind. You wouldn't be able to upload him then, would you?' he said tremulously.

'We could, as long as he was at least partly conscious,' Susan tried to reassure him, 'it's just that his mind might be so different, when he came to be downloaded into the new frame, that we'd lose the original Gabriel.'

This was little consolation to the frightened old man, but at last she knew that action had to be taken immediately, and Susan assured Errik that she would now deal with everything. Their faith in her was gratifying, but she felt something of a fraud, since she was doing very little that wouldn't have been permitted anyway. She'd been starting to feel slightly uncomfortable, so the sudden panic was almost a relief.

As soon as Susan had the confirmation from Errik that Gabe's life was now in real danger, she'd scheduled the upload procedure, and liaised with the authorities herself. Errik brought his son down to the surgery in his own jet, which, although she tried not to show it, impressed Susan even more. Carbon emissions were extremely tightly controlled, and few billionaires could use their own plane; it needed powerful connections to be permitted to use one for anything other than business, and she watched in awe as it came in to land.

She accompanied the ambulance to the landing strip to meet Gabriel and his father, and found Gabe lightly sedated, and very pale and clammy. Although she was no medic, Susan recognised a very sick man when she saw him, and held his father's arm comfortingly. Errik, with tight self-control, managed not to drag himself away from her looming presence.

'Don't worry Errik, it's all ready for him. I have the team on standby and they're going to upload him now,' she said gently. She turned to Gabriel. 'Listen to the nurse, Gabe, she knows what she's doing; I chose the best one I know, and she's done hundreds of uploads.'

Gabriel smiled gratefully at her but didn't speak. He'd been instructed by Errik to do nothing to endanger the process, and it seemed safest not to say anything at all.

He was floated into the ambulance and driven the short distance to the upload station. Susan followed with Errik and they strolled around the grounds for a while, talking about Gabriel, and Errik's immense pride in his only child. Errik was concerned about the disposal of

Gabriel's discarded body, and Susan explained that he could claim it if he wanted to.

'Mostly people are happy to let the upload station take care of disposal automatically, but of course you can ask them to hold onto his body for you, if you like, or you can collect it later.'

'I think we'll do as other people do, then,' Errik said sadly. 'It's all going to seem very strange, but after all, he won't be dead really, and one must remember that.' It had occurred to Errik that Gabriel's corpse, if subjected to any kind of autopsy, would show no more than a recent and fully healed brain trauma, and he was relieved that, apparently, Gabriel wouldn't be examined. 'How long will the whole thing take, my dear?'

'There's a check-in procedure first, while his current state of mind is assessed. Because of the medication he's on now, the staff may need to wait until he's a little more alert. Then he'll be selectively sedated so he feels no discomfort, though his mind will stay sharp. After that it should take no more than a few minutes.

'There's nothing either of us can do now, I'm afraid.' Susan tried to comfort Errik, who was obviously and understandably jittery. 'We just have to wait, and we won't hear anything for quite a long time because he won't be conscious for possibly four or five hours. You can watch the download from the viewing room.' She paused. 'I really wouldn't advise it, Errik, because you won't see much, and relatives often find it distressing anyway. It's probably best if you go home to wait.'

'You're sure he'll be able to talk to us later though?' said the old man anxiously. Despite his careful planning and his ideas for the future, he had effectively said

169

goodbye to his boy. Whatever happened now, they'd never meet in person again.

'Yes, I've given special authority, so as soon as the system has processed his brain-patterns, he'll gradually be brought online just like a new piece of software. It'll take a little while, though, and I'm sure he'll contact you as soon as he can.'

Errik looked at her with eyes full of tears. 'Thank you,' he said. 'I can't thank you enough for what you're doing for Gabriel. Your care for him has been appreciated beyond words and I just bless the day he met you.'

'I'm not doing all that much, you know,' answered Susan, feeling slightly embarrassed at all the gratitude. 'You're paying for all this anyway. It's just the staying awake bit that I'm doing.'

Errik squeezed Susan's hand affectionately, 'But that was the really important part of it all.' He looked away. 'Gabriel is very dear to me, you know,' he said softly.

Susan was touched by the note of real affection in his voice, but tried to lighten the mood. 'He's certainly unusual, isn't he? I've never met anyone quite like him, I must say. He doesn't really look like you, does he?'

'He is sunny, isn't he?' Errik said happily, glad to be able to discuss his adored Gabriel with someone other than the aggressively negative Tobias for once. 'He had a very hard time when he was young, but it just seemed to make him stronger. He takes after his mother, I understand, but she left many years ago.'

'Oh the poor little boy, I'm so sorry,' Susan answered, 'I hadn't realised. Did your wife abandon him then?'

Errik looked startled as he realised what he'd said. 'Well yes, though to be fair, I don't really know that she did, but Tobias...' Errik paused, and then carried on

170

smoothly, 'Oh well, that's all water under the bridge now, anyway, and Gabriel adjusted remarkably quickly. Thank you again, Susan. I have to go and let my people know he's in safe hands now.'

'Take care, Errik,' Susan answered. 'Stay online. Just follow the written instructions that I gave you, and Gabriel will contact you when he's able to.'

Errik walked slowly back to the airstrip, a beautifully tailored example of a not-exactly bereaved relative, and out of Susan's life.

As Errik left, Susan was aware that something was a bit odd, but couldn't put her finger on it. She'd picked up the slip about Gabe's father, and assumed that the boy had been adopted after all, even though no-one had mentioned it to her.

She'd wanted to watch the upload and was worried about Gabe, but she really needed to be back at work. Sighing heavily, Susan immediately drove back to her office with the intention of immersing herself in a pile of applications for premature upload, which the rest of the team had felt weren't straightforward refusals. Susan would almost certainly refuse them all, but at least each application would be electronically stamped with her seal to show that it had been reviewed by the Senior Upload Manager, after which there could be no appeal.

As she began to work mechanically at the routine stuff, Susan's mind turned over the issues that were nagging at the back of her mind, and suddenly her brain, which had been trying to tell her something for the last half hour, got through: *Errik's gay!* It seemed obvious now, but it hadn't occurred to her before.

Then another thought which she'd resolutely ignored until now also surfaced: *He mentioned Gabriel's father,*

171

so it isn't him, and he didn't sound as though he even knew Gabe's mother very well, Susan remembered with a jolt of stress.

She pondered Errik's neat, elegant figure and came to the conclusion that the two were probably partners, not father and son. Susan tried to reassure herself that it might not be a problem even now, but the conclusion that she might have been deceived seemed inescapable. *If Gabe's gay, that'll be why he's never tried to sleep with me. He wasn't being sensitive at all, he just didn't fancy me!*

Reluctantly, Susan searched online for Gabriel's company. It was there, as she'd been shown by Gabe and just as she'd expected. Instead of being relieved, she dug deeper and realised with a growing sense of despair that she should have researched properly before. Gabe had kept her busy, hadn't he? She hadn't had a moment alone since she met him. No time to think, no time to wonder.

I'm probably over-reacting, Susan thought. *Lots of gay men have children when they're young. And Gabe's mother might not have abandoned him until she'd realised, if he's Gabe's real father.* But underneath, it suddenly felt all wrong, and she began to feel sick with apprehension.

Susan dug into the company records, using her own high access protocols. Gradually it became clear that the images of the children and young lads in training that Gabriel and Errik had shown her were from other sites. They'd been discreetly selected, undoubtedly, but they were still stolen.

A particularly good holo of a young disabled boy riding a horse turned out to have come from a completely different charity's website. As she recognised the footage that she'd last watched while Gabriel proudly explained its provenance, Susan's great orange eyes darkened with distress.

She grabbed the phone and attempted to stop the process. As usual, the AI was off-line or busy. She left an urgent message vetoing the upload and pushed it to as many senior staff as possible. Then she flashed a code red warning to the upload centre, which ought to stop the process immediately.

Susan knew that, once it had commenced, no nurse would willingly risk shutting the process down because of the likelihood of irreversible brain damage. In this case, she thought vengefully, that might be a good thing.

So who's Gabriel Kerr really then? Susan wondered in increasing horror. She tried repeatedly to contact the upload surgery by phone, but the system was fully automated, and there was no code she could input to say that the senior upload manager had probably been duped.

There's no option, she thought distractedly, *I'll have to notify the police. If there's nothing wrong, they can re-schedule Gabe's upload.* Not for a moment did Susan believe he was genuine, though. The more she thought about it, the more those little details fell into place. She didn't know how they'd managed to fake the brain scan, but Gabriel and Errik undoubtedly had access to plenty of money, and with enough money anything was possible. She called the police and explained the situation as concisely as she could, blushing with shame as she admitted she might have been deceived.

The police officer that she spoke to was polite and matter-of-fact, although Susan was sure the woman was secretly amused.

'Leave it with us,' she said. 'If we can't find anything wrong then the upload can go ahead. We'll just take a look, but if you can pause the process, then obviously that would help.'

Susan ran to her auto, and headed to the centre. She drove as fast as she could, but the little car was restricted, like all autos except those of the police, to forty kilometres an hour. Susan was perfectly used to that, but today she felt she could walk faster. Desperation gripped her as she mentally reviewed everything she'd done wrong, and just some of the things that this imposter might be intending to do.

'Vito,' she called, and her personal aide immediately came online, 'contact the upload surgery and tell them to call me immediately. Tell them it's concerning the code red.'

As she drove, Susan cursed herself for having been so gullible. How could she have fallen for all that smarmy charm? Underneath she'd known damned well that he was too good to be true. She also tried to comfort herself with the thought that it was just possible she was still wrong. There could be reasonable explanations for Errik using slightly odd language.

The fraudulent holograms of the Kerr's training company at work might have been put together by a desperate father trying to keep his only son with him, although that, she felt, was pushing it a bit. And of course, she could have misheard. But underneath she didn't think so. Not for one single minute.

'Vito,' she said urgently, 'disable the speed restriction.'

'Are you quite sure, Susan?' replied Vito. 'It is an illegal act which in the event of detection carries a minimum gaol term of two years.'

'I'm sure, Vito, dammit,' she yelled. 'Disable the speed restriction, right now.'

The personal aide didn't sniff because it wasn't programmed to do so, but she felt it would have done if it could, and this made Susan even angrier. She made a very swift mental note to have its personality re-set yet again.

Ever overtly obedient, however, Vito pointed out that the speed restriction was coming off, and warned her to brace herself. As the electric current restriction was bypassed, the auto shot forward, almost hitting the stream of linked buses in front. The soft magnetic fields which surrounded both Susan's auto and the bus ahead connected briefly with a spang of sound, and a brilliant blue flash that startled her almost as much as the passengers in front, and Susan braked sharply.

She dragged the control lever round, so her little auto left its own traffic stream, and headed into the oncoming traffic, accelerating hard.

'Move,' screamed Susan, attempting to get between the buses on both sides of her. Pictures flickered in her head. Not only had Susan authorised an almost certainly illegal upload; she had, and it filled her with anguish as she thought about it, actually made a special dispensation so that he'd remain conscious.

He could do anything in the Metaform. *If he's as cunning as he seems to be, Gabe could be a kind of human virus*, she thought desperately. Susan knew that if he were malicious, and if he got online successfully, the length of her future career could be measured in hours.

Susan pushed the wailing motor hard, sliding up and down kerbs in an attempt to under and overtake all the transportation modules in front of her.

Another constant, though very small, underlying worry was that she might have it all wrong, and in that case Susan was aware that she'd probably messed up his upload with all the desperate messages she'd left, and potentially ended Gabe's life.

Vito spoke suddenly, shattering her concentration: 'Susan, it appears that you are being requested to halt for the police. We must comply with the request.'

'No, no, don't stop, Vito, this is an emergency,' she yelled, dragging the reluctant auto around another very long bus. 'The police know what I'm doing.'

'I regret that I am programmed to comply with requests from the constabulary,' Vito answered expressionlessly. 'The engine will now be immobilised. Please be aware that steering may also disengage.'

The auto's motor stopped, and in the abrupt silence, the only sound was of Susan swearing creatively as she fought to control non-existent steering. The tiny vehicle's door locks disengaged with an audible click, and as the cushion of air that served as propulsion disappeared, the auto slid into the nearest kerb-side.

The force-fields, registering that the motor wasn't running and therefore under the impression that the vehicle was now parked, had cut off with the motor, and the auto rose inelegantly into the air, still travelling at rather more than the legal speed limit. As it fell back to earth, it bounced gently onto its roof. It appeared relatively undamaged, except that it was the wrong way up, and a bit flatter. It shouldn't have happened, and the authorities would later examine the broken vehicle with great interest.

No charges of driving an unrestricted vehicle could be brought against Susan though; her head hit the roof, and her neck had snapped at the first impact. Susan lay crunched into a position of untenable complexity in the foot-well of her little car.

Her exceptional height had been one of the contributing factors towards her demise. If Susan had had one of the newest bio-frames, of course, the impact might have caused her very little harm. In fact, had she been even an inch or two shorter, she would probably have survived without injury.

Vito was relatively undamaged, although his human-user interface was slightly damaged, and he was obliged to return himself to his primary control module at Susan's flat. He sent one short burst of communication at a speed far beyond the ability of the human brain to process, then closed himself down and waited for the police to question him. Vito always complied with the law.

Chapter 20

For the first two years after he became a computer intelligence, Con had kept an affectionate eye on his dog via security cameras and the occasional legally dubious look through his new owner's pad. Tarquin's new owner, Mrs Ann Berry, would have been very surprised to know that all the photos and hologram images of her dog that she shared with friends were being captured and lovingly saved by his previous and technically long-dead owner.

Mrs Berry was long gone herself now, but on one of his routine sweeps of Mrs Berry's computer shortly before her own upload, Con had come across a sad message to a friend explaining that the old animal was about to make his final visit to the vet. He'd lost most of his teeth, had cataracts in both eyes and could barely walk.

With Meilinn's encouragement, Connor had decided to see if his beloved dog could be uploaded too. Tarquin was succumbing to the various ailments of an advanced and pampered old age, so Con had swung into action, appearing on her computer in person to explain that she needed to bring Tarquin to the Metaform's head office. After she'd recovered from the surprise of having her computer taken over by a man she'd assumed dead long ago, Mrs Berry agreed to the experiment and Connor sent a car to pick them up.

He had produced two outdated old frames which he and Meilinn would inhabit during the dog's upload, since as holograms they'd have been unable to touch anything. Both were consequently suffering badly from the unaccustomed movement lag and had been forced to spend some time getting used to speaking normally again.

Naturally, Mrs Berry hadn't recognised them, and Meilinn, unwillingly disguised as a rather obvious android, explained that she and her colleague would be uploading Tarquin, but that Connor would come to see her later.

Meilinn had carefully arranged the Metaform's office so that it wouldn't startle the old lady, and the smelly old Labrador shuffled in behind her, as Mrs Berry took a seat. The dog flopped apathetically to the floor and remained motionless at her feet, panting gently. There had been a slightly awkward introduction, after which they got straight down to business.

'He's such a dear and I'm going to miss him dreadfully. Are you quite sure it won't hurt him, dear?' Mrs Berry asked sadly.

'Yes, I'm absolutely certain,' Con answered. 'I did it myself long ago, and it's got a lot easier since then.'

'We don't have exactly the right kind of headset, I'm afraid,' Mei said gently, 'but I've adapted one to fit. This is a very experimental idea, but if it doesn't work, please try not to be too upset. At least this way he won't suffer at all, and he might have a wonderful time, if it does work.'

While Meilinn and Mrs Berry chatted, Connor attempted to play with the old, tired and overweight dog, but Tarquin obviously didn't recognise him, and he ruefully accepted that after so many years the dog probably would have forgotten him, even if he'd had the same body.

'You don't have the right smell either, remember?' Mei pointed out. 'They remember smells along with people. I wonder if that'll be a problem online?'

'I should imagine he'll smell what he expects to smell, but I could be wrong; we just don't know.' Connor was resolutely upbeat, but he had serious doubts. As far as they were aware, animals simply didn't have enough self-awareness to be re-animated in the Metaform, but he knew that Mei really wanted to try.

They'd compromised, in that Tarquin would be given a virtual form as much like his old one as possible. They would construct a kind of mental image and see if it could be imposed on the animal. Then they'd have to ensure that the animal had access to his own data at all times, since he couldn't be expected to imagine his own form.

Con tried to fit the headpiece to Tarquin, who obligingly closed his eyes tightly and appeared to go back to sleep.

'Oh hell,' Connor was baffled. 'I'm not going to pin his eyelids open, poor beast. What do we do now?'

'I wondered if that would happen. Hang on, let me try it.' Mei suspected that, as with humans, once the process had started, it would be impossible to look away, but she'd have to get the animal to look into the lens first.

Con started the HUD display, and Meilinn flicked the dog gently on the nose. As he turned his head in mild indignation, the tiny lights finally caught his attention, and Tarquin was caught. Mei gripped him firmly from behind and tried to hold his heavy head as steadily as she could, while the machinery hummed gently.

The animal's body tensed, as some distant memory of the chase gripped his apathetic mind. The three watchers waited breathlessly for the outcome. Con knew that the longer Tarquin stared at the HUD, the more of his personality would be uploaded, and cautiously, as the seconds passed, he began to hope. The dog became less alert as he watched the lights, and Mei wondered what he was thinking. *I can't wait to review all this*, she thought.

There was a gentle chime from the attached computer, and they realised that it was over. Despite staring at the dog for several minutes, no-one had actually seen him go. Tarquin had gone into the computer, and it now remained to see what had actually uploaded.

Mrs Berry seemed confused, and leaned down to pat the animal absently, as Meilinn tried to explain that Tarquin was now in the machine. The old lady finally realised that her old companion had gone, and pulled several tissues out of her bag, wiping her face sadly, and gazing at the inanimate corpse with every sign of inconsolable grief.

Con had left the room quietly, and out of sight of Mrs Berry, he slipped a helmet over his head and launched himself back into virtual space with an enormous sense of relief.

Meilinn unfastened the HUD from Tarquin's inert body. Mrs Berry was still crying quietly, and Mei tried to comfort her. Her movements were still oddly clumsy, but with fierce concentration she managed a consoling hug.

'Don't worry yet, Ann. Connor's gone to see if Tarquin uploaded successfully. Please don't get upset. He should be fine.'

'Oh I do hope so. I know I left it a bit long and he was in a bit of a state, but he still liked to sniff things,' she explained sadly. 'I didn't want to put him to sleep too soon, you know?'

Meilinn instructed the tea machine to produce a cup of tea for the bereaved woman, and for a few minutes they talked somewhat mawkishly about Tarquin, and Connor's quest to make him into the first ever completely genuine

181

canine online intelligence, whilst Mrs Berry talked lovingly about Tarquin's special little ways.

Then the two women heard the sound of the phone, and after a few ham-fisted attempts, Meilinn managed to click a button on the desk. She heard Connor's voice sounding slightly strained, and turned the volume down to a whisper.

'Tarquin's in, Mei, but he's a mess. He seems to have his old form, though it doesn't look right to me, but it's going to take a bit of work to sort him out. He's even more confused than I thought he'd be. I've had to shut him right down.'

Grateful that Mrs Berry didn't appear to have heard Connor, Mei decided there was nothing left for the old lady to do, and that it was time to go back up.

'It worked, Mrs Berry,' she said cheerfully. 'Tarquin's in the system, and now we have to get him settled in.'

'Oh thank goodness. So he's not dead then?' Mrs Berry looked at the motionless heap on the floor, and began to bend over to stroke him, until Mei stopped her gently. The old lady was almost as confused as the dog had been, and Meilinn didn't try to explain too many details.

'Tarquin now lives in the computer, or rather, he will once we've got his ideas sorted out,' Mei said, smiling reassuringly. 'You don't need to worry about him anymore.'

Then Connor walked into the room himself, this time as his normal hologram since he wouldn't, he fervently hoped, have to touch anything. 'Well, you'll be glad to hear that it worked, Mrs Berry. Tarquin's very confused, so Mei and I will need to do a lot of work with him, but

I'll see if I can find a way for you to see him, once he's all straightened out.'

'Why can't I see him now?' Mrs Berry asked plaintively. Catching sight of Connor's exasperated expression, Meilinn stepped in quickly, before he could say anything hasty.

'Better not,' Meilinn said firmly. 'Tarquin's just undergone a transformation that'd confuse most humans, and if we put him into a hologram, I don't think anyone could control him. We'll do it soon though, I promise, and you can come and visit him whenever you want. In fact, it might be possible for him to visit you on your pad.'

Then Mei escorted the still sniffing lady out to the car, and came back inside. She and Connor looked at each other wordlessly. Then Connor instructed the automatic cleaners to collect the corpse of the dead animal. A few seconds later, both had returned to their computer and the lights in the office turned themselves off.

On the whole, it had been a successful venture, although Tarquin had very little sentient awareness, and absolutely no concept of personal space.

Unexpectedly, although an animal hadn't any conscious awareness of itself, Tarquin had loaded very quickly and easily into the Metaform. The directors theorised that this was because he'd had a remarkably simple mind. He couldn't answer questions during the process, so the computer had been unable to adapt his future surroundings to fit him, and a kind of generalised ideal home had been created on his behalf by Con. It shouldn't have worked, and yet it had. Tarquin didn't know he was a dog, but he knew he wanted food and fuss. Once Meilinn and Con had seemed to give him food, Tarquin had begun to carry on much as he had when alive.

183

He was no longer encumbered by a creaky body, and the memory of it was apparently gone almost immediately.

Tarquin didn't think about himself, and seemed to have no concept of his previous appearance, but when left to himself, he became a variety of sizes, depending on what kind of game he wanted to play, though he always stuck to a basic dog-shape.

One odd thing was that, despite the instructions that had been written into his routine, Tarquin's preferred avatar had gradually become a weird shape. He was no longer the handsome brown Labrador that he had been in life. He now had an enormous nose, which took up almost all of his head; he was often very soft and furry, which Mei suggested might be because he liked to curl up in his own fur, although this fur disappeared and he became almost glassine in appearance when he pursued his second favourite occupation of running over endless fields in pursuit of an equally endless supply of imaginary rabbits.

Tarquin's first and all-time favourite occupation was eating, however, and although he couldn't technically over-eat any more, there appeared to be a danger of Tarquin slipping into a kind of loop, where he did nothing but eat for ever. They'd had to restrict his food intake in order to counteract this tendency.

Mei had tentatively investigated the dog's mind, and found it awash with raw instinct and an amorphous concept of small furry animals. She got out of there quickly, but, assuming that this was how dogs really thought, Mei established that Tarquin was probably fine.

He'd initially tended to invade absolutely any area without limitation or indeed invitation. After a few confusing incidents when Tarquin had materialised in several impossible shapes in unexpected places, Con and

Mei had attempted to lock him into an avatar of his original form, and had more-or-less restricted him permanently to Con's living area.

Although he had the world's biggest virtual garden to run about in, after a short time, it was found that Tarquin still tended occasionally to escape, because he desperately sought human company. They'd never worked out exactly how he escaped, and since it was fortunately rare and he was easily spotted when it happened, they decided not to worry about it too much.

'I reckon it'd be a laugh to increase his intelligence,' Mei said thoughtfully, sometime later. 'He seems happy, but it must be stressful always wondering where people have gone and what's happening. I think it'd be fascinating to see what he'd be like as a person.'

'He'd still be very dim, I should imagine, but yes, I'm rather looking forward to it,' answered Con, 'it's just that I've been so busy that I've never got around to it. I shouldn't think he'd be remotely human, though, you know.'

'No,' Mei agreed. 'I don't see how he could be. Anyway, he doesn't consciously think, and I'm not sure how you'd alter that.'

'Well, I've been thinking about that.' Unusually, Connor looked slightly uncertain. 'I'd like to see what happens if we actually try to blend him with a human.' He waited for the explosion.

'Blend...? Connor, who would you use? You can't do that!'

'Oh come on, Mei. Don't be silly. You know as well as I do that a hell of a lot of the people we upload are far below average intelligence. They breed like rabbits down there, and we upload almost every one of them eventually.'

'Oh dear God, you can't, Con. What about their relatives for a start?'

'We can. Of course we can; you know that as well as I do. No-one would ever know. Anyway, think about it. Most of the files'll never, ever be downloaded into frames. These are dormant people. We'd be doing a lucky someone a favour.'

Mei and Con argued for some time, and finally Connor wore Mei down.

'If you really think you can find someone with no hope of ever getting a reload, and with hardly any discernible personality of their own,' Mei said reluctantly, 'then I'll help you, if for no other reason than to stop you taking advantage of anyone. But I really want you to know I think it's a terrible thing to do, and if it all goes wrong you must promise we'll make a good backup of the victim's files, so he can be put back into store.'

'Of course, Mei. That goes without saying, but don't call him a victim. Whoever it is will have a much better life than he did before he died. You can bet on that.'

Chapter 21

Jared hunched over his personal pad in an attempt to fight off the mindless boredom of yet another interminably slow day at work. It hadn't been a particularly difficult journey into work this morning. There'd been nothing to report when he took over from the night man, and there was unlikely to be anything to report when he handed back over in several hours' time. The reality of the work was beginning to hit him hard now.

He'd always been physically active. Jared had happily agreed to go undercover right in the heart of the Metaform, believing he was doing a service for the cadre, but after three months he was climbing the walls with boredom. He also suspected, miserably, that he was starting to lose muscle-tone. Jared had taken a huge pride in his physique in the past. It had been his hobby and bordered almost on an obsession. Reduced now to running at night, and exercising in his room, he felt flabby and soft.

He looked up occasionally, briefly checking that no-one was standing silently at the gate awaiting entry. That didn't happen, of course. Clients usually arrived in powerful and very expensive machines, and didn't expect to have wait for even a second. Authorised personnel, naturally, simply strolled, drove or flew in without disturbing him, since their own barcodes allowed them to penetrate the field.

It was the unknown or unexpected visitors whom Jared had to question. He had the disagreeable task of making some of the world's most powerful people wait outside while he checked their credentials, and sometimes they objected loudly. It wasn't that Jared particularly minded annoying these rich bastards, but their language could get distinctly personal. Jared was beginning to develop some serious hang-ups about his appearance, between the irate fury of the clients, and the patronising kindness of the Metaform's staff.

The gatekeeper's role wasn't complicated, but it could still be done badly, and Jared's sense of neatness and pride meant that the thought of doing anything badly annoyed him. He took any criticism deeply personally, generally smiled politely as he listened, and never let it happen again, whatever it was. As far as criticism of his appearance went, there was absolutely nothing he could do, and it was beginning to have an impact on his normally stoic nature.

He heard a sound from outside and saw a small group of nurses drift in, giggling and chattering happily as they headed to the reception to begin their shifts. Although they were all downloads, the majority of nurses tended not to be able to afford greatly augmented frames, and these appeared almost normal until one looked at them more closely. Every member of this group of seven nurses had outsized eyes of different colours, and most had small neat faces, with oddly pointed chins. At first glance it was impossible to tell their genders, and even at second glance it was difficult.

Jared sighed as he got up to speak to them. They didn't need letting in, but he needed to mingle as much as he could with the staff. Errik had emphasised the importance of developing a network of friends in the Metaform because it could be a great source of information. Jared found the nurses terribly hard work, though. For a start, he hated the subtly patronising looks they gave him, as a mere normal organic human.

He'd tried to explain to Errik that the difference in appearance, rank and even intelligence made it impossible to be friendly with these people, but Errik hadn't seemed to understand. It might be different for him of course, Jared thought reasonably. He's rich and educated, and downloads'd probably think he just had some personal or moral objection to downloading himself. They mightn't understand him, but they probably wouldn't look down on him. Not like they despise a thick security guard.

He'd suggested as much to Errik, but he probably hadn't expressed himself properly, and Errik had got impatient, and started to explain stupid things that Jared already knew, like how he had to smile, and be interested in the nurses' trite, silly lives. He'd given up trying to explain after a while. He'd noticed that Errik rarely listened to him, anyway, if he spoke more than three consecutive words.

Jared had been more than happy with his own appearance until he began to work for the Metaform, but he very soon realised that he was no more than a mildly entertaining savage to them. He hated the looks of pity that he saw in their stupid great eyes. The trouble was that while Jared despised them, and everything they stood for, a tiny part of him wanted to be downloaded too. The nurses probably believed that once he'd served his first year of employment by the Metaform, he'd choose a frame and become one of them. It was what all Metaform employees did, once they'd passed their probation period. It wasn't free, in fact it was fabulously expensive, but it was subsidised for employees, and they paid for it out of their future earnings.

It was with very mixed feelings that Jared attempted to counter the nurses patronising banter each morning. He knew he'd never be allowed to transform, and tried to tell himself that he'd never want to be the means of death for an unfortunate bio-frame, in any case. Sometimes he almost convinced himself. They were generally very kind, but it was the kindness extended by the favoured elite towards the less fortunate, and it annoyed the hell out of Jared.

'Hi,' he said cheerfully. He had no idea what their individual names were. They all looked terrifyingly similar to Jared. He managed a beaming smile with his mouth tightly closed. That was another thing. They had perfect, luminously white teeth and Jared, who'd felt that his were attractively white back in the old days, was self-conscious about them for the first time in his life. He knew he looked like a smirking imbecile but no-one ever seemed to notice. They didn't comment, anyway.

There it is, he thought furiously as he intercepted a wordless communication between two of them. There's that bloody snooty look again.

The nurses ambled over; they were obviously early today and happy to pause and chat. 'Hallo Jared,' cooed a lean, violet-eyed creation. 'How are you, darling? Working hard?'

'I'm okay, thanks,' he responded, stifling a desire to break the creature like a twig. It would be a bad idea to try anyway, he knew that. The bio-frames were only a little stronger than organics, and their diamond-hard bones could be shattered if they were struck in exactly the right way, but they were incredibly, terrifyingly fit. The extra weight that they could put behind a punch meant that even the smallest and most delicate medic could kill with a single blow, if he caught you in the right place.

Jared knew perfectly well that any one of them could tear him to shreds, and of course he'd lose his job anyway, if he survived. *'It's almost worth it,* he thought longingly, but Jared shelved the enticing thought and made laborious conversation. 'You got a lot on today?'

'Oh, always, darling, always,' the download answered. 'We've got four to do today, and with the physiotherapy we're going to be run off our little feet.'

That, Jared decided, was just his little joke. One thing that the downloads didn't have was little feet. The weight of their bodies, significantly higher than that of organics, meant that their feet had to be enormous to spread the load, or else they'd fall over.

'Dear, dear,' Jared clucked in sympathy. 'Still you'll be finishing before dark, won't you? That's always good. Nice to have some day left after work.'

Jared thought he'd done well there. He'd managed several sentences, and shown a kind interest in the nurses' well-being. And he'd smiled like anything.

His effort was wasted, as the download obviously hadn't been listening. It turned to the others, and they all nodded or waved amiably at Jared as they strolled way. He wasn't much of a distraction, and they did have a lot to do today.

Jared took some slow, deep breaths and returned to his hut, thinking how much he really detested downloads.

Sometime after the nurses had drifted off to the main building, Jared looked up again, hearing a tiny craft land at the huge gate which was the only entry-point to the facility. The entire complex was protected by a near-invisible forcefield, and since the automated entry point remained sealed, Jared put down his pad, straightened his cap, and strolled out to meet the visitors.

There were only two heavily built and obviously un-augmented men on board the small shuttle, and neither looked like a potential candidate for a new frame. Jared got the impression that they were much too fit, for one thing, although that was often no indicator at all.

With some surprise, Jared recognised Tab in the co-pilot's seat, and grinned at him happily.

Tab was granite-faced and completely expressionless, and didn't appear to recognise Jared at all, which confused Jared. Tab's companion was a complete stranger and sensing that Tab didn't want to be recognised, Jared tried to look as though he hadn't identified his friend after all.

Jared remained as professional as he could, though he was baffled at Tab's behaviour. He realised suddenly that although he'd once said he was a pilot, there'd been no further conversations about his work. Dismissing it as a detail to get back to later, he addressed his unsmiling companion and decided to play the game.

'May I see your ID, sir?

The pilot leaned across and wordlessly handed him a small pad, which Jared scanned quickly; they were collecting the deceased remains of a client on behalf of the same future download. Their names were unfamiliar, but he saw that one had a middle name which might abbreviate as Tab and was slightly reassured.

He handed the pad back to the pilot, while Tab gazed thoughtfully out over the grounds and said nothing. Their entry credentials seemed to be in perfectly good order. Tab's face remained blank, but just as Jared was thinking he should really be querying his mate's attitude, he turned and gave him the ghost of a wink, and the lower part of his face twitched into a tiny grin.

Reassured, Jared decided to let them through. 'Wait for a few seconds and when the shield's down, follow the flight path to the designated parking hangar, then wait to be accompanied into the building.'

He walked back to his cabin and swiped the screen that would authorise entry for the craft, waving the couple through. As Jared turned to touch the control that re-activated the building's security field, he felt a hard bang in the small of his back, just as though someone heavy had accidentally bumped into him.

Shocked and disorientated, he fell heavily against the console as an unpleasant and powerful tingle suffused his lower body. His legs felt disconnected, and he held himself up by gripping the edge of the console. There was no pain yet, though, and he wondered disinterestedly what kind of weapon they'd used. He'd say, if he had to guess, that it was one of the new laser rifles. That would cauterise the entry wound, and then the real pain would be along any minute now. At least it shouldn't bleed much.

He wondered exactly which bit of him had been hit, and tried to turn and look at his lower body, but his grip on the console started to slip as he turned, so he hauled himself back up again, and tried to see the display.

With the last of his fading consciousness, he re-activated the field, holding himself up with one trembling hand, and instinctively keeping his movements unobtrusive. He knew it was too late to stop the raid. Then the thought occurred to him that the thieves, if that's what they were, would have an impossible job to get away afterwards if he raised the shields. They would effectively be blocked in. He realised, muzzily, that if he closed off their exit there could be a bloodbath. He lowered the shield again, and his hand dropped away from the controls.

The hand left holding his entire weight was exhausted now, and Jared let go, sliding to the ground, and hearing, at the very edge of his hearing, the sound of expensive electronics crunching beneath his hip.

Jared was aware of a deep anger; *'they didn't have to shoot me when they were already in,'* he thought savagely. And he was pretty sure he'd landed on his pad, which was probably broken. He'd been given it by the Metaform as part of his work equipment, and he hoped he wouldn't have to pay for a new one.

'It was Errik,' he thought furiously. *'Bloody Errik set me up.'* That seemed to Jared the final annoyance, until the penny suddenly dropped, and he realised that he was going to die here.

The irony of definitively and properly dying without a chance of upload in the grounds of one of the largest Metaform centres in the country, wasn't entirely lost on Jared.

Chapter 22

One of the millions of stored minds in a database so vast that one couldn't begin to comprehend its size, stirred. The mind had been sent perfectly efficiently, and all protocols had been observed, except one. The operative who'd uploaded him onto the central database had been in a hurry, and she'd forgotten one small thing; the cache in which the recently uploaded mind was to be stored was full. This happened so rarely, barely as often as once every five years, that the supervising operatives often tended to overlook confirmation of receipt from each of the files' destinations. The nurse had simply not checked.

The great database automatically created a new cache and subsequent files continued to be uploaded into it as before, so that no damage had been done, except to a few unexceptional files which had been refused entry into the old cache, and which had not been re-routed into the new one.

It should not have been awake, this one insignificant file; there was no reason for it to have awoken, except for a very small tremor which had occurred at exactly the same time as its upload.

Errik had been unable to gain access to the Metaform's mainframe, but he'd made some valiant attempts. The latest attempt had been no more successful than his first, but it had caused the mainframe to pause and then restart all normal uploads for the merest fraction of a nanosecond, and this had caused a tiny, almost undetectable surge, triggering the awareness of Major

Pearson's unprotected and homeless file. It had simply been a matter of chance that Errik's most recent attempt had occurred during the final moments of Paul's upload.

As a result, he'd been left hanging in the system. Meilinn would normally have picked up the anomaly and sent the file to the correct destination, but the director was preoccupied with her own affairs and failed to notice the tiny malfunction. The floating mind was left entirely alone.

As the major surfaced to consciousness, around him there was nothing; no light, no sound, no input whatever. He thrashed about frantically, feeling nothing, and absolutely, dreadfully alone. He was utterly terrified; unlike the directors, or indeed any other permitted conscious upload, he had no welcoming mind to greet him, and without the guidance of any human touch or voice, the apparent vacuum of his tiny existence was devastating.

Then slowly, after enduring what seemed to be years of wordless, silent screaming, his subconscious mind began to use intrinsic memories to build a vague amorphous world around him in self-defence, and the terror began to subside a little.

He thought he could see something, but he didn't understand it. There was blackness all around; at first he panicked when he couldn't feel his legs, and then he realised that he couldn't feel anything. In desperation, the major tried to stop himself from thinking; to quell the massive wave of devastating, overwhelming panic that threatened his mind. Slowly he calmed down, and gradually order began to return.

As a kind of light and warmth filtered into his awareness, the major tried to collect himself, and to think what could have happened. He remembered the first part of the upload vividly, although it became hazy within a few seconds of the upload's commencement. He tried to remember what the nurse had said. Paul was certain he shouldn't be conscious, and thought that Hannah would have told him if he was likely to wake up, but he couldn't be sure. He didn't trust those artificial eyes, and that automatic, rather soulless prattle.

Paul felt the panic rising again; this wasn't right, he couldn't spend centuries like this, alone in space. He thought for a moment. This was space wasn't it? He could see stars and galaxies around him, now that he'd calmed down enough to look. How could he be in space? He tried deep breathing, aware enough to know that he had no breath but finding the exercise reassuring anyway. He seemed to be alive, but not alive at the same time. And how, for pity's sake, could he even be thinking without a brain?

The stranded mind of the late Major Paul Pearson, however, wasn't encumbered by hormones or brainwaves or indeed any external input. He found that as time passed, whether eons or nanoseconds of it, he could think with astonishing clarity. The major had been aware that he was aging, and knew that he was more easily distracted than he had been in his youth, but all this seemed to have passed away. His essential self was constructing a brain for him to use, and although this was a peculiar concept, Paul decided it was as good a theory as any, and it would have to do for now.

He concluded that he couldn't be in space, and that what he was seeing was his mind setting a scenario that it felt he could deal with, and gradually he realised that he was actually breathing after all, and that he could feel his arms and legs.

He tried to visualise his home, and found that he was back in his kitchen. His mug was on the table in front of him, and for a moment he was irritated with himself for having forgotten to put it away before leaving the house. Then he realised sharply that although what he saw in front of him was exactly what he had expected to see, his peripheral view was cloudy. Paul imagined the cup full of hot tea, and before he'd even finished visualising it, it was there, steaming in front of him.

Paul was no fool. His intelligence had been formidable in life, and he began to use it now to establish what exactly he could do and what his limitations might be. He thought for a moment of his late wife, and she appeared at the table in her preferred chair near the window, smiling and well. Even her knitting, and the small bits and pieces Molly had liked to have handy around her, had appeared on the windowsill beside her.

He'd forgotten about the little heaps of stuff that amassed wherever she sat, and at the sight of it and of her familiar, dear face, sadness overwhelmed him. He knew Molly was gone and that he couldn't possibly speak to her, but he allowed himself to believe for a moment that she was home. He reached out, and because his mind expected her to be solid, he touched her. The couple held each other wordlessly and for Paul, just for a moment, it was like coming home.

Then Molly was gone, and Paul groaned with the renewed sense of loss. He knew she'd been an illusion, and having been no fantasist in life, his mind wouldn't allow him to believe in the impossible now that he was dead. Then he began to contemplate that word. Molly was unquestionably dead, but was *he* really? He still existed, even if he wasn't sure how, so the word wasn't applicable. He and Molly had taken a good deal of comfort from the understanding that their daughter, Cara, was actually alive. In desperate confusion once again Paul decided that theological issues would have to wait for now.

After a long moment of nothing, whilst Paul tried to orientate himself and to shake off his awful unhappiness, he became aware of the complete absence of sound around him. He hadn't noticed the utter silence until he broke it while he was speaking to his wife's image. The major began to experiment curiously with music. He found that although he could remember his favourite symphonies very well, the orchestration was subtly different, and he was hearing what he expected to hear. As he'd been no musician in life, the symphony was an oddly simplified version, probably missing the input of several instruments, and after a few minutes, Paul decided that he didn't like it.

He returned his surroundings to silence with a flicker of impatience, making a mental note that it seemed to be simple enough to influence his surroundings, and began to think hard about what to do next. It took a very short while for the major to realise that his entire world was imaginary. He could do nothing and go nowhere without knowing that it wasn't real, and again he began to despair. He wondered if he could imagine himself unconscious, and then wondered what would happen if he dreamed.

Had he but known it, the major was extremely fortunate. The majority of people finding themselves in his situation without preparation and guidance would simply have gone insane and into a fugue state from which it would be impossible to recover. Paul had a structured and intelligent mind, which struggled to make sense of his surroundings, and he began to draw conclusions and consider his options.

Paul knew, logically, that there were millions of other people somewhere around, although he was sure he'd been told they were always asleep, and he decided that he'd try to find them. After that, he thought with the first sense of satisfaction that he'd experienced since finding himself conscious, he'd see if he could find and re-awaken Cara.

He consciously turned off the images around himself, telling himself that that he'd closed his eyes. Then, in the black silence, he tentatively felt for any sensation at all that might not be imaginary. Gradually, Paul became aware of a faint dragging sensation, and allowed himself to be drawn towards the lure, which slowly got stronger. He felt a series of tiny shocks which were quite unpleasant, making it hard for him to think, and he recoiled sharply.

Paul began to move more slowly towards the sensation, testing the effect on himself as he went. He tried to see if there was any visibility to this sensation, and felt for visual stimulus. He was in space again! This made no sense to him. Paul couldn't understand how he could be visualising stars and constellations. He tried to move towards one of the tiny points of light.

To his astonishment, Paul found that the light drew closer very quickly. There was no point against which he could judge his velocity, so he couldn't tell if it was a tiny light a long way off, in which case he was covering an impressive distance very quickly, or a bigger light less far away. As he drew nearer though, Paul recognised that what he was seeing was energy; he could feel the buzz of it, and began to suspect that he had found an entry into some system.

Then everything changed, and abruptly he was aware of everything. The major knew he was in the Metaform; not only that, he had joined it completely. His first tendency had been to recoil in shock, but the sensation that he was no longer a lost soul floating in nothingness was so wonderful that he recovered quickly.

Paul felt at last as though he actually had a physical body again, although it was nothing like his old one. He felt around with imaginary arms, and burrowed deep into the crevices inside the computer's mind. There was a mind already there. He could feel it. It was unstructured, but there was a distinct personality. He would try and communicate with it soon. But not yet.

The major was jubilant, but as his mind ranged over the Metaform, he became aware of the directors' consciousnesses, busy now with some other issue. He realised, with a frisson of alarm, that they'd be certain to spot him as soon as they'd dealt with their current work.

Paul didn't want to be caught and put to sleep. He had, for reasons that escaped him at the moment, but which he felt sure would be clarified later, evaded normal procedures and he was free and conscious. The major had every intention of freeing his daughter, and he'd consider their options once that had been achieved.

I'm coming to get you, my little Cara, he thought happily, as he spread tiny threads through the system, reading files and sliding around protocols. It was only a short while later that Paul found the upload files. He was shocked at the immense number of them. Even the files that catalogued the sleeping files were huge, and he was momentarily irritated. Then the major realised that he didn't need to read them all; he *was* the files. He only needed to direct his intelligence and whatever he wanted would be revealed to him.

It took only seconds to locate his daughter. Cara was in an old directory, along with hundreds of thousands of others, and although he had no way to know whether she was unharmed and complete, he decided to assume that she must be. The major paused now, suspecting that he'd have to approach her carefully. Cara hadn't expected to be downloaded at all, knowing it was impossible that her parents could ever afford it, but if they had ever raised the necessary funds, she'd be expecting to wake up in a warm, bright clinic, with appropriate post-download physical and psychological therapy and nice cups of tea offered by knowledgeable attendants.

What Cara wouldn't be expecting would be to find herself floating about inside a massive computer, with her father's mind in her head, telling her that he'd rescued her. The major hadn't actually seen the inside of a download clinic, and didn't feel up to the task of creating a virtual one in case the inevitable anomalies caused Cara too much stress. He thought that maybe the best way to deal with this would be to recreate her bedroom and himself if possible, and then explain the situation as gently as he could.

Paul was worried by his constant awareness of the computer's mind. He instinctively hid himself, slowly drawing back the tendrils that he'd sent out. It wasn't the same as him, he could feel that. It reminded him of Molly, although he knew that was nonsense. It felt soft enough, he thought, and although he wasn't at all certain, it didn't seem hostile. It did seem very preoccupied, and he debated, briefly, whether to make contact.

The prospect of interaction with another person was very appealing, and although he knew it was rash, he started to reach out cautiously. Then abruptly he felt a spike of alarm from the other presence, and Paul immediately withdrew; he knew instinctively that he couldn't take chances by displaying any activity unless he wanted to risk being closed down. Paul had no real idea of what he was or what he could do, but his entire being was geared to the idea of waking Cara, and he couldn't take any risks until he'd managed it.

Unfortunately, one of the many things that the major didn't know, was that the Metaform's directors had been unable ever to permit the minds of children to remain awake in the Metaform. The very young were almost all far too vague, and had too un-formed a vision of themselves to be able to maintain a shape or self-image. The few experiments that Con and Meilinn had tried had all ended in abject failure. The juvenile minds simply dissipated almost as soon as they were revived. They could be stored, and they could be downloaded if their families could afford the process, but they couldn't survive awake in the formless world of the Metaform's database.

Paul had every intention of waking his daughter, but had no idea that his plan was probably doomed. Cara needed to be downloaded into a new frame, and to live as a normal and corporeal human for a few years before her mind could begin to cope with the existential burden of a completely amorphous existence. As soon as he attempted to wake her, Cara would almost certainly die.

Chapter 23

Errik sat peacefully at the desk in his large and airy office, his chin resting on his hand, as he gazed into the headset clamped around the top of his head. Only the occasional deep sigh betrayed his mild agitation. This was his favourite room, and although it had been designed generations earlier, somehow it fitted him perfectly. The two tall French doors were open, despite the coolness of the late spring afternoon, and the view from his huge desk was of his beautifully smooth lawn, descending very gradually towards a distant row of magnificent lime trees. He could hear the occasional squeak of birds, their sounds wafting in on the lilac-scented breeze and acting, to a limited extent, as a balm for his worried mind.

He had a lot to think about, and was carefully compartmentalising the details so they'd be less overwhelming. Errik knew that if he didn't get this right, all his dreams would be over, and it was causing him no end of stress. He had big plans; far bigger than Gabriel could possibly imagine, and quite certainly bigger than Gabriel would ever approve, but he couldn't allow his feelings for the boy to affect his plans.

If anyone in authority were to make more than the most cursory investigation of his and Gabriel's story, they'd have no trouble at all disproving it completely. The simplest of tests would establish that he was no relation of Gabriel's, and that would probably be unneeded in any case, since they'd only need to question his domestic staff to know exactly what was going on.

Earlier in the week, he'd sent as many of his staff away on holiday as he possibly could, without raising unnecessary questions in their cow-like minds, and the remaining ones had been carefully instructed about what to say. Errik's mouth twisted in annoyance as he remembered the awkward interviews he'd had with several of his people. It had taken most of the day, and he'd had to be unnaturally polite. He'd also awarded pay rises to ensure their loyalty. It wouldn't work for long, Errik knew that perfectly well. The first fine feelings of gratitude to their employer for his generosity would last exactly as long as it took for the novelty to wear off. It really was terribly depressing, he reflected.

Errik intended to take over the Metaform Corporation in its entirety. He knew, with an absolutely cast-iron certainty, that he could do a better job of running it than the directors were doing. If there were still any directors, of course. There was a widely held opinion in some circles that the directors were long gone, and that the Metaform was operating on some kind of sophisticated auto-pilot. Errik, however, wanted some real proof before he'd allow himself to take a gamble on there being no-one to oppose him.

The only director anyone had seen in the last fifty years was Meilinn, the purple one, and she wasn't exactly a convincing human being. He wondered if she were really the only sentient mind left up there, and if she were, how lonely must she be? *Might she not welcome a companion?* he thought. And he'd be careful and wouldn't frighten her at all. He'd go out of his way to be kind, and to make sure she had a wonderful and worry-free life, once she handed over the running of the corporation to him. It seemed beautifully clear to him.

She, after all, must be suffering from that same ennui that affected all the virtual directors. She was probably waiting to be rescued, and he'd do it willingly.

Errik snapped himself out of his daydream quickly. For all he knew, there could still be a full set of directors up there, and there'd be no way for him to be sure until Gabriel was in place. Errik was going to use the boy's mind as his own eyes, and then, when Gabriel's work was done, he'd create a suitable bio-frame for the boy, and Errik would take his own place as the only director, and the most powerful mind of all.

It was a good plan. Admittedly it had a hint of megalomania about it; Errik was no fool, and could see perfectly well how it might look to other people, but it wasn't. Not really.

There were so many things he could improve; he could make life so much better for everyone. With Errik in charge, only those who could pay would be uploaded. There'd be no more of this stupid business of people being uploaded before they were ready, or as was widely rumoured, patients with minor ailments being uploaded and their bodies destroyed just because there wasn't enough room for them in the EMF's.

Errik felt that his background, and especially his recent experiences with terrorist organisations, made him superbly fitted to deal with threats against the corporation. He'd create a standing bio-army of the most terrifyingly efficient frames, which would counter the anti-social behaviour or tendencies of any group with ease.

That army would maintain perfect law and order, so there'd be no more riots and no more crime. He intended to create builders, artists and medics, too; Errik intended to create a utopian world.

Of course he'd still upload worthy people, and those who could pay for it regardless of their mental worth. He just wouldn't waste time and resources uploading the ungrateful masses, who'd never be downloaded anyway.

As soon as he'd shaken off his aging body, he would begin to put all his plans into practice, but he still had a fairly complicated path to walk before he could even begin to look that far ahead.

Unfortunately, Gabriel probably wouldn't appreciate the finer details of his modest idea. He was a freedom-fighter to the very core of his being, just as all the residents of the brotherhood had been. Part of Errik's dream, although admittedly a very small and improbable part, had been that Gabriel might join him and they would oversee his vision together.

Even in his most optimistic daydreams, though, Errik knew that couldn't happen. The best he could hope for was that they'd remain on friendly terms, and that the lad wouldn't try to oppose him. Errik didn't even want to think what he'd have do if Gabriel decided to interfere. He could probably store him, of course, but that would probably only be postponing a later confrontation in any case, and he'd regret having to do it. It would feel like a betrayal.

Errik had a semi-formed idea of downloading Gabriel into a frame with suitably adjusted intelligence. If the frame were especially dim, he'd be able to reason with him, and influence him. That didn't feel right though. The frame wouldn't look quite like Gabriel, although Errik intended to make sure it resembled the original as closely as possible. His dilemma was that, if it also lacked adequate intelligence then Gabriel, as Errik knew him, would cease to exist. Of course it would still feel the same to the lad himself, but that wasn't the point.

On the whole, Errik felt it was still the best option though. It wasn't as if Gabriel's very average intelligence itself had ever been much of an attraction to Errik. It was that curiously laid-back personality that he loved, along with the ability to bounce back from any problem, no matter how traumatic. Errik hoped he'd be able to keep that particular personality trait intact in the new bio-frame version of Gabriel. Otherwise it'd probably not be worth bothering at all.

It felt wrong to be plotting behind Gabriel's back, but he didn't see that there was any other option. Telling himself that it would be for the greatest good of the most people, Errik unhooked his headset, stood up quickly and began to pace around the room, pausing at one of the long windows to stare, unseeing, at the garden, while he massaged his aching temples absently.

It was a beautiful estate, although relatively small. He'd inherited it from his mother, many years after his father's death, and had preserved everything lovingly, just as she'd left it. Errik knew that in the grand scheme of things he was no better than any other country landowner, and of considerably less importance than a great many landowners, especially now that so many two and three-hundred-year-old investments were maturing to create multi-billionaires. Nevertheless, there was a certain credit in being a genuine hereditary and relatively impoverished landowner, rather than a new and frankly rather vulgar bio-billionaire.

Errik had resisted Tobias' frequent hints, and occasional outright requests for capital, pleading non-existent trust clauses when pressed, and after a few years

Tobias had stopped asking. That the enclave had been permitted to remain on Errik's land without payment had been enormously helpful, and Tobias had never wanted to jeopardise the security and safety of his cult and his followers by upsetting Errik. He knew better than anyone that without Errik's generosity there could be no Soul Defence Brotherhood.

Besides, the two of them had grown up together, and whilst Tobias had grown from an idealistic young man into a terrifying warrior, Errik himself had apparently been born at the age of fifty and remained there, with only slight variations in appearance to give any indication that time was passing. It had never been any surprise to Tobias that Errik abhorred risk. He'd been exactly the same timid little boy at ten years old.

Errik had never bought into the fighters' ethos. Never for one moment had he believed the uninhabited frames possessed any intrinsic personality of their own. He'd reviewed the available data, and absolutely understood that they were exactly what they appeared to be. They were mindless organic tools, exactly as they'd always been described by the Metaform, and he wasn't planning to waste his valuable time on pointless speculation.

The relative poverty of the masses wasn't a matter of any importance to him either. Errik considered that most of the public were too lazy to take advantage of, and work hard at, their free schools and so progress along the many possible career choices open to a bright young person. The fate of those too dull to make such choices had never concerned him. His political views were yet more things that he had always kept to himself, along with his genuine affection and attraction to Tobias' son.

That attraction was a serious complication. Errik had always liked Gabriel, of course. He was such a cheerful boy; even when his dreadful father was abusing him, nothing seemed to cloud his inherent good nature. It wasn't until Gabriel reached his early teens that Errik began to recognise that the boy's physical charms were only part of his appeal. It was going to hurt him badly to trick Gabriel, but he had no option. This was far more important than mere romance.

Errik sighed, sat down again and re-attached the HUD. Gabriel had left happily enough a couple of hours ago, but he'd arrived like a lamb to the slaughter this morning, for a practice run of the upload procedure. At least that's what the boy had believed it was. It hadn't been too difficult to get hold of an original Metaform heads-up display unit. Dozens of sets had been picked up on raids by Tobias' lads over the years, and most of their equipment was now stored in his house. It had taken Errik quite a long time to fathom its controls, but he was nothing if not patient, and all forms of technology fascinated him.

Gabriel had thought they were having a kind of dress rehearsal before the main event tomorrow. Errik had managed to convince him that it was necessary to rehearse the kinds of questions that might be asked during the upload process. What Errik had actually done was copy some of the markers which made Gabriel's mind distinctively an individual. He wanted to store them for use once the lad had been uploaded.

Gabriel had complained of a headache and peculiar sensation of detachment when they finished, and Errik had been forced to restrain his burning curiosity to find out exactly what had been uploaded, and had sat and talked calmly with him for almost an hour afterwards.

When Gabriel had finally left, Errik still had other things to claim his attention, and only now could he review the interesting data that he'd collected.

The lad himself would be unharmed, and hopefully he wouldn't understand what exactly had happened to him. Errik sincerely hoped so, anyway. He loathed confrontation.

Now he checked once again that he'd have enough of a link with Gabriel's mind to be able to influence him, once he'd been uploaded. He straightened his back and removed the HUD for the last time today. It was looking good.

Everything was in place. Tomorrow he'd fly the boy up to the biggest and most heavily guarded upload centre in the country, and send his spy right into the heart of the Metaform.

Chapter 24

No longer confused, Paul was free to try and wake his daughter. In his most optimistic dreams he'd never imagined that such a chance could ever be given to him.

It was time to wake Cara and restore her to a life as good as, or even better than the one cruelly taken away from her as a young girl. The major wasn't certain, but he was beginning to be fairly sure that he could create a world for his daughter that any normal child would envy.

She can have a horse, he thought happily. Many of his fellow officers had kept ponies for their children, but he'd felt that with their frequent moves across the world it wouldn't have been practical. By the time Cara had been old enough for the prospect of owning a pony to seem, not only reasonable, but necessary, Cara had been too ill even to consider riding. He'd regretted that for many years.

Paul was concerned about telling her that her mother had died, though. When Cara had been uploaded, Molly had been young and strong and beautiful, hiding her terror and unhappiness behind a resolutely smiling face for the sake of her pretty, fragile daughter. At some point Cara would ask for her mum, and he'd have to be ready for that.

She was always clever though, he thought contentedly. *She'll understand.* For a moment, Paul was tempted to recreate Molly, just so that he could talk to someone about what he intended to do. It might help Cara adjust too. Then he dismissed the idea almost immediately; it was just too painful. Molly had never been uploaded, and he'd found it startlingly painful to see her when he'd first become conscious. He didn't want to do that to Cara.

The trouble was, he realised, that he was lonely. He'd just spent a long time more completely alone than he'd ever been, despite his solitary life when he'd still been alive. Paul wished he knew how long he'd been aware, and then ticked himself off sharply. *The system has a clock, surely*, he thought. *I can work it out; it must be several hours at least.*

The major accessed the system's clock and then tried to extrapolate the time elapsed since he'd became conscious. Then he paused suddenly. *That can't be right*, he thought in shock. *I must have it mixed up with another time zone.* Paul ran through the process again. It was correct; *I've been here for two minutes? I can't only have been here for two minutes. I've been conscious for hours.*

With a rising sense of panic, Paul started to understand that time passed differently online. Gradually the truth began to be clear. Effectively, he only existed in real time when he was consciously taking action, or actually making an effort to think. When he was simply waiting, or not thinking about anything in particular, no time passed for him at all, just as though he didn't exist except when he was in action.

So that means even though life's presumably going on normally and at a normal speed in the real world, here, the time's just passing when we feel like noticing it, he thought numbly. A very long life suddenly seemed rather less appealing.

The major found the idea curiously terrifying. A man accustomed to a routine in which he did the same things at the same time every day, he was aware that he'd just been killing time during his final years, but at least he'd

213

existed. Now it appeared he'd only be alive on those occasions when he made the effort. With a mental shrug, Paul forced himself to file the idea for later consideration. *At least*, he thought, *Cara and I can create long lives full of achievement.*

Paul began to make plans. *Maybe we could go climbing*, he wondered. *The system has all the maps, if I need a reminder of the terrain of any mountain range.* Once he'd checked those, he realised, he could map a virtual route suitable for a beginner, and as they grew more skilled, he'd make the climbs more demanding. The possibilities were endless, and his excitement grew as he began to think of the things they could do together.

The major grew sombre then, as he considered the possibilities more carefully. *She'll never grow up*, he thought sadly. He wondered if they might get bored in their virtual world; if they'd argue. *Or will she grow up after all?* he thought suddenly. *Cara's mind will still be experiencing things, her life will continue and she'll grow up if she wants to, surely?*

As was becoming something of a habit now, Paul shrugged that particular thought off for the moment and began, once again, to concentrate on the task in hand.

He intended to imagine himself in glorious technicolour now, although, as Paul turned his concentration to the task, he realised in some surprise that he wasn't even certain of his own hair colour, never mind the shape of his face. The major knew that if he didn't make a fairly convincing job of recreating himself, the chances were pretty high that he would startle his daughter badly, and even worse, that Cara might not even know him.

Paul envisioned himself standing in front of a mirror, and after a few false starts as his imagination ran away with him, he began to make out the image as recognisably the man he had been. He tried a smile, and was a little shocked to discover that he did indeed look peculiar, but he couldn't quite pinpoint the reason. It took him several seconds to work out that he'd given himself rather more hair than he'd ever had in his previous life.

Good lord, he thought, *I look a complete tit!* Paul shrank his teeth and eyes considerably, and removed most of the hair without a twinge of regret. His entire focus was on becoming the image of Cara's daddy, and not, as he reminded himself sharply, a fashionable downloaded celebrity. He congratulated himself on having become convincingly normal. He peered at his reflection, grinning mirthlessly as he examined himself, closely following the wrinkles that transfused his thin cheeks. He didn't quite look right, he could see that, and Cara might be even more stressed if he didn't look exactly as he had when she was uploaded, he thought. He was starting to get stressed himself and found he was sweating.

Oh, for goodness' sake, he thought impatiently, taking a deep breath and cooling himself down again with a flicker of thought.

Then after a few moments, he remembered that Cara had been uploaded over thirty years ago. He'd been forty-three years old when he and his wife had lost their little girl, and he couldn't for the life of him remember what he'd looked like so long ago. He was utterly baffled by what he'd originally thought would be a minor detail, and he sighed heavily.

Oh hell, he thought. Paul made his hair thicker and darker, removed all the comfortable wrinkles which had added themselves almost automatically, and decided that he looked weirdly plasticised.

I couldn't have looked like that; I look like a bloody robot, he thought irritably. As an afterthought, the major lengthened his face, and made his ears smaller. Now his nose seemed absurdly large, dominating his thin face. He adjusted his nose and plumped his cheeks a little, and decided that was close enough.

That'll do. I look a bit like me, and I'll just have to explain if Cara notices I look odd, he decided. With a final adjustment of his hairline, which he was pretty sure had been quite a bit lower when he was young, Paul decided that was the image he'd stay with. *It isn't easy, this plastic surgery stuff*, he reflected.

Then he began the tricky task of creating a suitably non-traumatising place to wake his daughter in. He remembered, rather than imagined, a room with a soft pink-shaded lamp in the corner. It was Cara's bedroom, as she'd had it in life, and in fact it still looked exactly the same back in the real world. Molly and Paul had needed to believe that one day Cara would return, and the idea that she wouldn't find her room exactly as she'd left it was unthinkable. Molly had kept their daughter's room clean and tidy routinely, so that if they found by any miraculous process, that she was coming home, it would seem to Cara that she'd never been away. The major had taken over the task when his wife died, and was familiar with every part of it.

Finally, he looked around at the scene he'd so carefully created. He was definitely in Cara's bedroom, and it seemed pretty convincing to him. *I wonder if she'll think she just went to sleep and then woke up immediately?* He thought it would have to work that way;

after all, he remembered being told when Cara was uploaded that there'd be no dreams, good or bad, whilst the mind was stored.

I suppose I'm ready, then, he thought apprehensively. The major felt around for the file that had meant so much to him for so long. He'd become accustomed to the electronic pathways very quickly, and now had an accurate mental map of most of the system. He touched Cara's file gently with his mind, desperate to cause her as little stress as he possibly could.

As the child surfaced, he recognised her, although he didn't understand why, or how this could be.

'Cara, my darling girl, it's Daddy,' he whispered softly. He could feel her confusion as she woke from an impossibly deep sleep, and instinctively sought to remain in slumber.

'Wake up sweetheart; it's time to get up.'

This time Cara tried to obey, and began to look around. 'Daddy? Where are you?'

There was a moment's pause, as the unformed mind tried to grasp that she was nowhere, and tried to look around. Paul attempted to impose his vision of her bedroom, and himself, into Cara's fluctuating consciousness, and for a moment it seemed to work. She stood in front of him, her mouth open in alarm.

Then, abruptly, she realised that she couldn't see or feel herself. Cara's panic was immediate and devastating. 'Daddy!' she screamed. Pain pulsed through his head, and a part of him, independent of his conscious thought processes, articulated: *Oh bugger, that'll be noticed.*

'I've got you baby, I've got you.' Paul struggled to hold on to her, but Cara shook him off, pulling away from him instinctively. Her screams were gradually becoming

217

less brutally incisive, and for a moment Paul thought Cara might be getting the hang of it, but he was wrong. She wasn't adjusting to her situation; Cara was beginning to dissipate, and Paul realised that he could feel her fading away. Her desperate terror was so sudden and so unexpected that he barely had time to act.

The major tried to send her back to her file, but he lacked the experience to complete the process, and Cara was resisting so fiercely that he couldn't hold on to her. Unlike Meilinn, Paul didn't have access to the system's utilities, and even if he'd been aware of them, he wouldn't have been able to instruct the computer to file this terrified and recalcitrant mind. Paul attempted to absorb her into himself. He didn't know if this was possible, but he tried anyway, but Cara was a creation almost of smoke, of illusion, and she slid away from his desperate grasp.

Cara faded before Paul's devastated perception. She had never had a clear image of herself, and had simply not had time to adjust to her amorphous state. Paul frantically searched the file where she'd been stored, but even in his relative inexperience, he could feel that it was now empty. Cara was gone.

The major hung dumbly, uncaring whether he was visible to the directors. Everything he had waited for, worked for, even thought and dreamed about for thirty years, was over. It had been over within a matter of seconds. He curled into a ball of distress and howled silently. Gradually, Paul straightened up, his new, relatively youthful face a blank mask, behind which sat a world of pain.

She's gone, he thought. *Oh Cara, oh baby, what have I done?*

The major backed away, systematically shutting down all the conceptions that he'd lovingly created. He found himself in a different network. *Communications*, he thought absently, and sunk into it, almost mindless himself in his misery. After some time, he moved.

How do those bastard directors do it then? He thought about it. *I should have made a shape for her*, he realised. *Maybe I could have made her a body and put her in it, couldn't I? Why the hell didn't I think of that?* As he pondered quietly, Paul's fury grew. *They think they can get away with anything. They've destroyed humanity, and they give false hope to millions of helpless people.*

In impotent grief and fury, Paul raged against the directors. He reviewed the directors' crimes against mankind, anger growing as he considered what they'd done. *They've brought slavery to millions while they live in pampered luxury. They've made themselves immortal, for pity's sake, while the rest of us are misled into believing in a potential future that no-one can ever afford! Evil bastards.*

The major relinquished his grip on rationality. In his grief, he had to apportion blame; the idea that he'd simply messed up, had jumped the gun and failed to research his facts properly before taking irrevocable action, was too agonising to bear.

As Paul screamed his rage and despair, he forgot that the directors could hardly fail to miss what had just happened, and he wouldn't have cared, even if he'd stopped to think.

Chapter 25

At the upload station, having been delivered into the hands of a very capable nurse and her technician, I was feeling amazing, probably because of the medicines they'd poured, pumped and stabbed into me. I was only mildly concerned about what was going to happen to my body, because I trusted the Metaform. Which was pretty odd, when you think about it.

The trolley I was lying on was so soft that I couldn't feel it at all, even before all the drugs. The nurse bustled about preparing me for the upload, while a technician asked silly questions, presumably because the relative accuracy of my answers would help them to monitor my progress into the machine.

Unfortunately, I didn't realise then how important it was that I co-operate. I was trying to delay the upload until Errik could get online and monitor the process, and this was causing the poor baffled operator serious confusion. I could see that, but didn't think I had any option. That was an awful pity, as it turned out.

Errik and I had talked about the coming ordeal the day before, and I knew Errik was wishing desperately that he'd checked I understood everything better before he'd drugged me to look dangerously ill. I was concentrating like fury, but I didn't seem to have the focus to hold on to anything. We'd done a practice run using Errik's own kit, and that had felt really weird. I wasn't sure I was quite over that now, actually.

'Gabriel, I'll take care of everything,' Errik repeated carefully for about the tenth time, 'but the longer you can delay it the better, so I can get back to my computer. I'll have my implant so I can monitor your progress, but I really need a proper set-up to do this properly. They'll send your conscious mind into the sentient storage facility, but re-routing you into the mainframe may be tricky and I'd rather be at my workstation.'

Errik had done a kind of run-through of the upload process, and he said it had gone splendidly, which was just as well, because I felt really peculiar afterwards. Errik said that was just a kind of psychological displacement, and only natural. He said I'd be fine in a few minutes, and it's true I recovered fairly quickly, but he kept trying to lecture me while I was still woozy. He looked so worried though, and I did feel sorry for the old boy. I'd dragged him into this, and I'd played on his fondness for me just to get myself uploaded.

My voice was slurred as I tried to reassure him, but I thought my mind was as relatively sharp as usual. 'I suppose if it goes wrong or if you can't get into the Metaform for any reason, the worst that could happen is I get downloaded into a new frame and we re-think our strategy.'

'Well, no, my boy,' Errik answered sombrely. 'That's almost the best that could happen. The worst is that you might get completely lost in the computer. If you follow their instructions I'm sure you'll get in successfully. Just try to delay the start very slightly,' he added worriedly.

Now the technician was asking questions, and I was still certain that I shouldn't allow the machine to read my mind too deeply. I was resisting the HUD and answering with far too much precision. From somewhere in my fuddled mind the thought had surfaced that that the Metaform must be able to pick up my hostile intent, must surely have special software, and I wondered if Errik had thought of that. The trouble was, I knew I had to co-operate to be uploaded, but I didn't know how much of my mind might be analysed on the way.

'How old are you, Gabriel?'

Neither the nurse nor the technician seemed particularly pleased with my answer, and I suppose they could see I wasn't going under very well. 'Can you tell me your full name?' the nurse asked.

I started to answer, but this time I found that the words were incredibly hard to pronounce. My tongue wouldn't do what it was told, and I understood that I was finally losing my focus. I knew I had to let it happen, but I still fretted about what would happen if they could read my mind. This wouldn't be a good time for me to start discussing my strategy of destroying the Metaform from the inside, but it was so hard to concentrate on what I was saying, when I was floating away in a soft cloud of tranquillisers and hypnotic pretty lights.

Much later, I realised that the way I'd entered the system meant that no-one had explained the process to Errik or me properly, and I was blissfully unaware that a certain amount of co-operation would be needed. Had Susan Archer only discussed the process fully with us, I'd have known that, although it'd always work in the end, it would be nicer for all concerned and a great deal quicker if I'd simply surrendered completely. No-one was going to read my mind; it would've been considered a gross violation of privacy, but I didn't know that.

As the twitching and pulsing lights moved faster, gradually aligning my mind into a suitable state for transfer, the machine started to draw me in, despite my resistance, and I began, finally, to feel strangely at peace.

I reminded myself sharply that I couldn't afford to come over all sentimental, and above all I needed to watch what I said. This was my intelligent strategy, and if this went wrong, the whole scheme would fail, and we'd be forced back into violent protest; I had to stay strong.

Time seemed to stop, and I thought I was dreaming, as the oddly mesmeric lights and colours drilled into my mind. I could hear the soft distant sounds of the operator tapping screens repeatedly, still slightly worried by the apparently unconscious resistance of his patient. It was working, but it was unusually slow. He began, once again, to work through the list of questions that would chart my descent into unconsciousness:

'What's your full name, Gabriel?' he said again.

I think I remember opening my mouth to answer, but as I tried to say the words, the lights faded and then stopped completely. The nurse's face was gone too; I felt bereft, and desperately lost and disorientated, and tried to turn my head, tried to find someone to reassure me, but it had been anchored by the HUD rig, and I was completely helpless.

I could barely feel my body, but I could hear voices and sense the tremor of heavily stamping boots travelling up the air cushioned support of the gurney that I was pinned to, as helpless as a rat prepared for dissection. I wasn't fastened in place, except for my immobilised head, but the rest of my body, though technically mobile, was just not taking orders. I was paralysed.

With a massive effort, I managed to turn my eyes a little way, painfully slowly, and to look through the little floating screen of the heads-up display. Gradually I made out the distorted images of a man and woman in uniform both calling something out at the nurse, who was trying to block their approach. I could hear everything they said, but it didn't quite make sense, as though I were half listening to a play.

At least I could swivel my eyes around, though I still couldn't turn my head, and I watched the scene playing out. 'You shouldn't have cut the power; he's almost completed the process. This is too dangerous, I don't know what it'll do to him,' the nurse argued frantically.

The policewoman took her arm gently and led her firmly to one side. 'Listen to me, love,' she said, 'he's a terrorist, and if you put him into the Metaform there's no telling how much damage he'll do. You have to get all that kit off him right now, so we can take him into custody.'

'But I don't understand,' the nurse wailed. 'He can't be a terrorist. Miss Archer gave permission herself. She was here just now, I need to call her and check this is okay.'

'You call her, of course, if you want to, but she was the one who said the upload had to be stopped.'

'What? She couldn't have. He's her boyfriend, everyone says so,' gasped the nurse.

'Sweetheart, we don't have time to argue. Unhook him now please, or I'll have to arrest you too, for obstruction,' the policewoman said firmly. 'And then I'll rip all that stuff off him myself,' she added.

The nurse reluctantly began to comply, but she did it slowly and kept looking apprehensively at the door.

With a puff of irritation, the policewoman leaned across and began to pull the HUD away from my head.

'Hey, stop that, you're hurting him,' the nurse cried, attempting to slap the woman's hand away. I was conscious of an enormous respect for the nurse's bravery, and pathetic gratitude, too, that she was defending me.

'Just hurry up, then, if you want to do it yourself,' retorted the policewoman brusquely.

'What's the matter? Why do you keep checking the door, love?' asked the other policeman.

'If it turns out Miss Archer didn't give permission for us to stop the upload, I'd prefer to be arrested than face her. And I'll definitely lose my job. This is really dangerous, what we're doing.'

'Why?' asked the policeman. 'He looks all right, the evil bastard. Better than he's going to look very soon, I reckon,' he added happily. His colleague shot him a warning glance across my body, and he fell silent.

'He's had half his mind sent into the computer, you stupid thug,' exploded the nurse. 'He really isn't all there! If you'd come in five minutes later there wouldn't have been anything to stop because he'd have been fully uploaded.'

'What, are you saying he's only got half a mind then?'

'No. Well yes, I suppose so, in a way; his brain will compensate, and in a couple of hours he should be almost back to normal, but he's going to be terribly disorientated for a while. If you need to talk to him so urgently, you should wait until he's been uploaded properly and then you can access his file. He'll be able to understand what you're saying then. Everything he says now is likely to be nonsense.'

'Ah, right.' The man and woman looked at each other, sharing a moment of perfect accord; there was a sense that unexpected opportunities were not about to be wasted.

'Let's get him into the wagon.'

The policeman's big red face loomed over me; 'We're going for little drive, young sir,' he said cheerfully.

I should have been far more alarmed, I know that. Somehow they'd read my mind, exactly as I'd feared, and they knew everything, but it just didn't seem all that important, and there was absolutely nothing I could do about it, anyway.

I watched the ceiling slide past and wondered idly why hospital ceilings were always so unattractive. I'd visited a few medical centres in my early youth, though admittedly none was an official hospital, but they were all the same. *'And how the hell do ceilings get dirty?'* I wondered. At this point I remembered that I had more important things to worry about, and tried to focus again on the decidedly hostile dialogue going on over my head.

My head pulsed with the promise of a great deal of pain to come. I hadn't enjoyed having the HUD detached, though I'd been physically unable to resist. It wasn't designed to be particularly comfortable to remove because it didn't need to be. Patients tended to be dead when the HUD was removed, and there were small tears along the sides of my head where the screws had been pulled away sharply by the over-enthusiastic policewoman.

I felt the fresh air waft over me as I was swept through the doors, down several corridors and then outside, with the sound of the nurse twittering furiously behind. The newly cut grass smelled wonderful, and I inhaled with a pang of appreciation. Then I realised I was beginning to be able to feel my legs again, which was a huge relief. I tried to flex my toes, but couldn't tell if they were moving; I felt strongly that I needed to be able to run, but for the life of me I couldn't remember why, only that for some reason the future of the human race depended on it.

This would have been extraordinarily stressful if I'd been in my normal state of mind, but I was currently registering only mild anxiety. I could feel the warmth of the sun, and still smell the grass, so nothing seemed too bad.

Then the light and warmth suddenly disappeared, blocked out by the bodies of my captors, and the bulk of the huge police vehicle, as they floated my gurney in. Two policemen climbed in beside me, ignoring the frantic protests from the nurse, who was still desperately trying to convey the depth of her anxiety and disapproval. I could hear her shrill protests getting further away as they steered her back into the centre.

'Why can't you just leave him here while he recovers? You can watch, he won't go anywhere,' she shouted repeatedly. It didn't do any good. They weren't even bothering to answer her.

Unaffected by the impotent fury of the nurse, the auto hummed slowly out of the parking area. It parked again very quickly, probably about a mile or so further down the road, I thought, because my putative interrogators weren't about to waste time flying back to the station whilst their subject got his act together.

Once they'd found a suitably quiet spot, they came to a halt, and I felt the vehicle lurch as the driver got out, came round, and climbed into the back of the vehicle with his colleagues, causing a certain amount of crowding.

My world vision now consisted of three faces viewed unflatteringly from below, and the roof of a transport vehicle which appeared to have some ominously bloodlike stains across it. I was looking at yet another grubby ceiling. I wondered distractedly if anyone ever washed it, but again couldn't hold onto the thought for long.

As I discovered later, the effect of the partial download had been to paralyse some of my handier neural pathways, and my motor skills had also been seriously affected by the process. I was unaware, at the time, that my feet and legs were twitching violently in an attempt to obey impractical commands. In fact, I was frantically trying to run away, and only the fact that I was lying on my back was stopping me from making a decent attempt at a world record sprint.

'Right, Max, you and Dave hold him still, and let's get this bastard restrained before he does someone an injury,' said the policewoman, leaning heavily across me to pin me into place. I was aware of the pressure of her body leaning over me, and I raised my own torso on my elbows in a reciprocal reflex to what felt like an assault, lifting the large woman off her feet. This appeared to startle her and as she turned, my body suddenly caught onto what my muzzy brain was trying to tell it, and I lurched up and onto the floor, landing knees first on the feet of the man next to me.

I climbed up the man's body, evading his startled clutches more by luck than judgement, and found myself upright much too quickly. Vision swimming, I staggered and fell heavily against the unsealed doors, which opened at my touch, so that I hit the road, landing hard on my face and shoulder and re-breaking the recent and barely healed fracture of my collarbone.

I picked myself up and began to run. The furious policemen leapt off the vehicle after me, and I could feel hands brushing against the back of my flapping hospital robe, but failing by a whisker to grab a handhold on the slippery eco-friendly fabric. I was so fast that I impressed myself.

I could hear the frantic roars behind me, but my feet and legs, having finally understood what they had to do, were now accelerating hard. I threw myself over a low fence and into nearby scrubland, heading as fast as I could for a clump of trees. My sense of balance was dreadful, but even with all the swerving and jinking that I needed to do to keep upright, I was still pulling away from them.

That excitable nurse could have told the police that in my present condition, I'd potentially run until I died. All the useful signals that normally instruct a body that it's just about had enough, and should probably pull over for a little rest were switched off and probably wouldn't be back for a while. This was useful now, most notably because it meant I had no idea I had a broken collarbone, and I was completely unaware of the frayed ends of the bones grating against each other as I ran.

I really wasn't aware I was hurting at all at first. The effect of the chase on my brutalised brain was cumulative, and gradually fear began to grow and grow in my abused and incomplete mind. I was aware only of a blinding realisation that something had gone wrong.

I couldn't remember what it was, or even why I was running, but I absolutely knew that if they caught me I'd be tortured, and even if I refused to speak, they might still be able to keep me alive and interrogate me for ever. I knew I couldn't keep running, and they'd get me in the end. I'd heard the nurse say that half of my mind had already been downloaded. *I'll never get away*, I kept thinking despairingly, but that horrible fear gave me wings and still I ran and ran.

The soft rushing sounds of discharging weapons sounded near my left ear, and with renewed terror I accelerated again. My body was attempting to recover its link to my mind now, but something was badly wrong. The whole thing felt insanely strange, and a gradual awareness of extreme discomfort was making itself felt. I forgot everything except the chase and the terror of capture, but the pain of my shattered collarbone was getting more and more intense, and it was incredibly hard to breathe. A great dark red lump had risen across my shoulder and chest, as torn tissues bled beneath the skin.

The anomaly of one mind existing in two separate places simultaneously was now taking place, and although I didn't realise it at the time, I was losing all coherence. I'd already forgotten my name, and I slowly forgot the rest of myself, becoming nothing more than a terrified hunted animal.

After that, there are only old records to say what happened, and footage recovered from my subsequent upload. I do know that I ran and ran, and couldn't stop, but they caught me in the end, as I'd always known they would.

Chapter 26

Philip was deeply, heavily asleep. He could hear, fathoms deep in his dreamless stupor, a girl's voice calling his name over and over again. He struggled to surface from the heaviest sleep he'd ever experienced, confusion and mild nausea competing for his attention as he slowly and grudgingly opened his eyes, blinking sleepily as he tried to remember where he was and what was going on.

As memories surfaced and the discomfort faded a little, he realised that he felt remarkably well. There were no aches or pains; a mildly annoying but familiar twinge in his neck was noticeable by its absence, and as the residual sleepiness fled, excitement flooded over him. It had begun!

He sat up much more quickly than he would have done at home, and was instantly disappointed as he looked around. The upload hadn't gone ahead after all. He looked at his pudgy freckled hands in bafflement, and then gazed around again, ignoring the woman beside him. He was still in his hospital suite, and he felt his sad bewilderment turn to anger.

'Mr Moss!' The attendant's voice finally reached him, and he turned to her, his mouth opening to deliver a piece of his mind. 'The upload was a complete success. Welcome to your personal Metaform experience. My name is Amelie, and I'll be your guide and personal assistant during your stay with us.'

That stopped him cold. Philip took a deep breath, and then listened to the rasp of his labouring lungs in perplexity. It couldn't be right. They were trying to defraud him!

The woman leaned over and pressed his hand gently, and he saw her hand sink into his, until both were one ugly, shapeless object with oddly protruding fingers. Now he was completely baffled, and Philip waited for her explanation.

'The upload was completely successful, Mr Moss,' she repeated slowly and clearly. This time he understood what she was saying, but it still didn't seem right. This wasn't what he'd been led to believe. He cleared his throat again.

'Why's everything the same, then?' he asked. 'I thought I'd look like my bio-frame, and I haven't left the clinic. What's going on? I warn you, there's going to be serious trouble if this is a scam.'

'It's no scam, and you're doing fine, sir,' Amelie responded, withdrawing her hand delicately. 'We deliberately try not to change anything at first, so that you can get your bearings properly.'

He looked around again, still baffled. Then he turned back to the girl, who looked remarkably calm for someone in the process of perpetrating a million-credit fraud.

Philip had been gratified by the way he was looked after by the Metaform at first. He'd been carefully briefed and knew that when he awoke, he'd find himself transferred into a temporary avatar in which everything should seem much the same as usual. There would be certain benefits, he was told, and his personal guide would be delighted to show these to him as soon as felt composed enough to deal with them. He realised now that he hadn't really paid attention to the bit about the avatar.

Unfortunately, as he slid peacefully into the computer's mighty network, Philip had been under the impression that he was about to spend an eight-week holiday in a kind of cybernetic paradise with the virtual physique of a young god. Now he'd actually awoken, he found that he looked exactly the same as he had when he'd left his real body. Philip was still overweight and, very unfairly as it seemed to him, he still wheezed unpleasantly. To add to the indignity, he seemed to be wearing an uncomfortable paper dress. His guide, a small, elegant female of indeterminate ancestry, tried to reassure him.

'Mr Moss, we'll be happy to adjust your appearance, of course, but we can only do it once. We're not able to do it again and again, and that's why you look just as you did initially. We have to let you settle down first, otherwise you might get too confused.'

This explanation didn't please Philip. 'Why couldn't you base my appearance on my new frame, then? I'm familiar enough with that. I was looking forward to my uploaded time, and it would have helped me adjust quicker,' he grumbled. 'And why include my bad chest? I didn't need that as well,' he added indignantly.

'Sir, I'm sorry you're disappointed,' the little guide said, 'but I can assure you that your physical appearance will be adjusted to your personal specifications in a few days. It's a safety measure, you see. It's not safe for clients to be given a new image of themselves when they haven't been virtual for very long.'

'A few days? I have to wait a few days?' Philip was furious now. 'Do I look like a fool? What, you think I'll forget who I am, just because I don't recognise myself in a mirror? And what possible difference could it have made if you hadn't given me bronchitis?' The unfortunate attendant tried to interrupt him, and made another attempt to soothe her client.

'It's part of you, as the person who was uploaded, sir. You've been copied in every particular, and the computer also copied the state of your health, because it's the least traumatic way to do it.'

'Well, I don't want the puffing and coughing now that I'm here. I want it removed now,' Philip demanded angrily.

The attendant sighed wearily but unobtrusively. This sort of dialogue followed an upload more often than anyone would believe, since the billionaires who could afford the procedure frequently displayed a tendency to arrogance in any case. She resolved to add a note to her report, yet again, that clients weren't being correctly briefed before their procedures commenced.

'Mr Moss, I'm not allowed to adjust any of your physical characteristics for at least twenty-four hours, unless they're causing you intolerable distress.'

'Well, they bloody well are causing me intolerable distress. And unless you're a highly-trained psychologist, I'd like to know how you can tell?' Philip was getting crosser and crosser, but despite his temper he was beginning to enjoy himself. He couldn't help noticing that in spite of the energy he was using, his pulse rate wasn't rising, and the stertorous breathing hadn't worsened at all.

'I *am* a qualified psychologist, sir, and I can tell because the computer will tell me, in any case. Look, let me show you where you'll be staying, and I'm sure you'll feel much happier once you've accessed some of the entertainment that will be available to you. Tomorrow, we'll begin to alter your appearance a little at a time until you resemble the bio-frame that's been commissioned for you.'

Slightly mollified, Philip allowed himself to calm down. No fool, he could see the sense in what his guide was saying, and was forced to admit that he understood their logic. If he'd woken up as the new and improved Philip, he might have had a problem getting used to it, so he grudgingly gave in. Besides, he was hoping there was a lot still to see.

Philip swung his legs off the trolley, with a wince of distaste at the sight of his yellowing toenails, and followed his guide out of the plain, spotless whiteness of the virtual clinic in which he'd awoken, and into brilliant sunshine.

The sun sparkled on an improbably dark blue sea, and he saw that the clinic appeared to have been built right on the beach. He'd requested a Mediterranean resort from the options given to him, and it looked as though this had turned out to be better and more incredible than he could ever have imagined.

The most desirable resorts on the planet were impossible to visit unless one had had the foresight, several generations ago, to buy oneself a part of them. In the corporeal world, Philip would almost certainly never visit the private playgrounds of the fabulously wealthy, and this re-creation of the southern Italian coast had been subtly improved to suit his particular preferences.

The guide led him to a small hut which was enormous inside. Philip was aware of a slight sense of shock as the anomaly of the impossible dimensions struck him. He was damned if he was going to show any surprise in front of the guide though, and displayed what he thought of as sophisticated boredom, as Amelie showed him where he'd sleep, where his meals would appear, and how to call up any entertainment that might take his fancy.

The guide finally left him, thinking unhappily that it really was time she applied for work in a different area. She'd been showing newly sentient uploads around for over forty years. She was good at it, but enough was enough. This client was exactly the same as all of the others. She knew he'd be deliriously happy very soon, and then he'd shower her with praise. Amelie had at least six weeks ahead of her at Mr Moss's beck and call, and the prospect really didn't please her. He'd look better soon, but that wasn't the issue; it never really was. It was the same old bluster that wore her down, and Amelie was grateful, as always, that clients couldn't read her mind as she could read theirs.

Left to himself, Philip sat on the enormous red satin-covered bed, and absorbed his surroundings happily. There was no glass in the huge windows, and the temperature seemed to have been set at a comfortable level. He raised himself cautiously to his feet, ever aware that his knees were inclined to grumble if he forgot himself and turned too sharply. He discovered to his great pleasure that there was no complaint from his knees at all, and that although he might look the same, either someone had turned the gravity down, or the Metaform's operators had reduced his weight.

He requested brandy from the food table that his guide had shown him, and tasted it tentatively. It was superb, and for a fleeting second he wondered if it was a real replica of exquisite old brandy, or whether they'd simply adjusted him to enjoy everything. The query was gone before he'd formed it properly; there was simply too much for him to take in, and he was conscious of a transient gratitude that he'd have plenty of time to enjoy it all before he had to go back.

For the first time, Philip stopped thinking of the wonderful new bio-frame that had obsessed his thoughts for previous months, and allowed himself to wonder if there was any way he could manage to stay virtual forever.

He walked outside through the open doorway and sat outside, on an unnaturally comfortable bench, with his drink, gazing at the glittering virtual sea in enchantment. The breeze was slow and warm, and caressed his skin like a lover. The sun warmed but didn't over-heat him. He smelled the perfume of flowers that he didn't recognise, and he thought this was one of the most perfect moments he'd ever experienced.

Then a tiny movement caught his peripheral vision. In the distance, far to his left side, Philip thought he could see a tiny figure moving beside the water, and the thought that there might be other uploads in his personal paradise irritated him. Mood ruined, he was abruptly close to tears.

'Amelie,' he shouted.

'Sir?' Amelie appeared behind him.

'Who's that?' Philip demanded. 'Are there going to be people spying on me? Because I requested complete privacy. It's important to me,' he added plaintively.

'It's another client, sir, but he's a long way away, and can't approach you or your apartment unless you send a request. The constraints of memory conservation mean that when we create elaborate environments for clients which are broadly similar, they may overlap slightly, but your privacy is always assured.' Amelie smiled sweetly as she spoke, and Philip, reassured, if not exactly happy, was reminded of one of the reasons he'd chosen this particular fantasy.

'Mm. Okay. Well, I do hope I won't be disturbed. I'm a man with large appetites.' He reached out for his guide, catching at her hand, and Amelie smiled again, detaching herself gracefully.

'Yes, indeed, Mr Moss. I regret that I won't be able to assist you in such personal matters. However, as I showed you when we came in, you may request any entertainment that you wish by accessing this module.' Amelie gestured behind her at a small panel set into the wall near the bed, and Philip abruptly lost interest in her.

'Thanks,' he said abstractedly. 'I'll call you when I need you, then.'

Amelie, forgotten, faded away and Philip with a final glance at the beautiful waterline, turned back to the control panel. There were other things he wanted to find out. A thought occurred to him.

'Amelie?'

'Yes, Mr Moss?'

'Are you going to be watching me?'

'No, Mr Moss. I can't see into your own world unless specifically invited by you.'

'Right. Got it. See you later then.'

'Goodbye, Mr Moss.'

Chapter 27

The raid on the upload station had been rather successful from the intruders' viewpoint. The two men had come in, selected a bio-frame apparently at random, and had walked out again. Unfortunately, they took two nurses with them as hostages, despite the barrier not having been raised. It was thought that they might have shot Jared to stop any interference once the alarms were sounded. There would be a certain amount of debate about that later.

The nurses who'd been taken as hostages were tossed casually out of the craft as it exited the area. One, a curvy, brown-eyed download called Hannah, had survived the fall from about a hundred feet, but she'd landed on her feet, so the damage was deeply unpleasant. Hannah was placed immediately into stasis, and the medical computer's initial assessment concluded that she was unlikely to recover sufficiently for upload. The other nurse hadn't survived the impact for long enough for upload even to be considered.

Satellite reconnaissance had initially shown the visible trajectory and progress of the little craft as it exited the centre, but it had vanished from all electronic records within seconds. The police suspected the pilot had disabled the transponders before starting the mission, and he'd managed to stay out of sight after it. They'd originally decided that the pilot must have been fairly incompetent, since he'd attempted to fly five people in a craft designed to carry a maximum of two. There seemed no question, however, that his low-altitude skills must actually have been superb, because the shuttle had almost immediately disappeared.

The raiders had walked into the final-stage nursery and simply removed the bio-frame nearest the door from its cradle. It was a female model, absolutely motionless despite its wide open unblinking eyes. The frame was completely encased in clear medical grade vinyl, and although it looked very slim and light, this appearance of delicacy was an illusion, as one of the unfortunate attackers discovered as soon as he attempted to pull it upwards and sling it over his shoulder; his knees almost buckled in shock.

'Oof,' he muttered in shock. 'It weighs an absolute fuckin' ton!' He staggered slightly as he tried to adjust the balance of his burden.

'Bloody hell, Tab, what the fuck are these things made of?'

'Shut up, you idiot,' his colleague hissed.

'It's all very well for you to say; me back's going to need surgery after this,' grumbled the body-snatcher. 'You got the easy bit.'

A nurse, terrified and hyperventilating, cowered against the far wall, and while the first man braced the bio-frame over his shoulder, having noticed that the cladding of clear vinyl also made the damn thing extraordinarily slippery, the other motioned the panting nurse over.

'Don't kill me, please don't kill me,' she begged, eyes wide with terror.

'Do as you're told and you won't get hurt,' Tab said, with a remarkable lack of imagination.

'What do you want? Just tell me, I'll do it,' Hannah squealed.

'Oh for pity's sake, will everyone just shut the fuck up!' The second raider was getting seriously irritated now. He cuffed the nurse across the ear, and she stifled a hiccup of pain and terror.

'Just stand there, you silly bint, and don't move.' He motioned to a second nurse, who was standing as inconspicuously as possible beside a curtain, with a half-formed plan of sidling very slowly behind it. The plan never had a chance.

'You. Over here. Now.' The second nurse edged over reluctantly. 'Right, you two come with me.'

There was no sound at all in the building now, aside from the intermittent puffs of strain from the unfortunate kidnapper, who was pretty sure that if he couldn't put the slippery dead weight of the frame down very, very soon, he'd drop it and then he'd never get it up over his shoulder again. The remaining untouched frames were utterly undisturbed, and continued in their oblivious death-like sleep.

The two men ordered the unfortunate attendants to precede them back to their shuttle. They'd bounded up the staircase coming in, but they were forced to walk far more slowly now, as the man carrying the bio-frame was genuinely concerned that his knees would buckle as he carried the awesomely heavy and cumbersome inactive frame down the stairs. They were impressed that no alarms had gone off yet, but knew they could only have a few seconds once those started.

Once outside again, the frame was dumped unceremoniously into the luggage hold, and the raider straightened up with a strangled gasp of relief. As he caught her eye, Hannah, the brown-eyed nurse looked at him in sympathy, despite the stress.

'They're four or five times as heavy as organics,' she said knowingly. 'It's the reinforced bones; we're not supposed to lift them at all. We have to use hover-lifts.' Hannah's face crumpled as she remembered who she was talking to and the raider began to smile at her appreciatively. Then he glanced at his mate, who was pointing his gun in his direction.

'All of you get in, now,' Tab snarled. *'You just wouldn't believe it,'* he thought furiously. *'First the idiot uses my name right in front of everyone, and then he starts flirting with the sodding hostages.'*

The nurses reluctantly attempted to clamber into the shuttle as ordered, and there was some difficulty as they all managed to fit themselves in. The first raider, conscious that he'd aggravated his mate, took the controls, and fired up the little thrusters. The small craft slowly and grudgingly heaved itself into the air and, as he started to cut the power to the thrusters and level out, alarms began to sound.

'We're too heavy,' he exclaimed. 'We can't fly like this.'

'What? Course we can, just give it more power.'

'No we can't, there's no power left; we're going down any second.'

'Shit.' Tab opened the door and with an astonishing lack of ceremony, he flipped the quieter of the nurses out of the door. Hannah began to scream, her voice mingling with the alarm already drilling into the air in the confined cabin.

'Fuckin' hell, Tab! What did you do that for?' His mate looked up from his wrestling match with the controls.

'Want to drive 'em home, do you?'

'No, but we could drop 'em from a bit lower, maybe.'

'Okay, fine. Take us down a bit and we'll sling this noisy bitch out too.'

There was a sickening swoop as the overloaded directional drives headed directly for the earth, and the pilot over-compensated.

'Can't do it!' he gasped.

Hannah's screeching grew even more penetrating as she realised what was about to happen. She'd seen the ground arc away as the craft lurched, and it had looked a very long way down.

Tab leaned across and, catching Hannah by the hair, he hauled her out into the hatchway. Hannah clutched convulsively at the doorframe, but with a final dismissive shove Tab launched her into the air.

Watching the footage later, investigators speculated that possibly the terrorists hadn't intended to kill the women; perhaps they'd have released them unharmed when they considered themselves far enough away, but they must have had a hell of a shock when they took to the air to make their getaway. The two-man flyer would have been forced to accede to the demands of gravity as soon as the take-off jets had finished their boost.

The tiny shuttle had, according to witnesses, taken off with a roar and a huge effort, straining its small boosters to the limit, but as soon as the pilot tried to enter normal flight mode it would immediately have begun to plummet back to land. First one, and then almost immediately after, the second nurse had been thrown out, tumbling almost a hundred feet to land just in front of their horrified colleagues.

The shuttle, although still overloaded by the added weight of the bioframe, had now lost enough ballast to continue its journey in relative safety and was lost to view within seconds.

Within a few moments the security guards from all other points in the building were amassing around the scene of the assault, and the nurses' colleagues rushed to try and help. There was no hope for the first one, who had simply hit the ground with her head. Hannah was alive but had landed on her feet, and her injuries were so horrific that she would probably need to remain in stasis forever, or at least until a very high speed method of upload to the database were perfected, since she could have only a very few moments of agony-filled life left.

The staff of the upload centre hadn't checked the security hut. In their horror at the fate of their colleagues, the terrified medics had immediately attended to the dreadful injuries of the surviving nurse, and no-one had thought to see what had happened to the lone guard.

When the police arrived, however, they'd spotted the blood immediately.

They found Jared's body slumped below his control panel, and their first reaction had been to consider him another unfortunate victim of the raid. They later changed their view, deciding that he'd probably been a partner of the attackers. Despite his injuries, they were inclined to think that he'd simply been double-crossed by his mates.

After all, he hadn't activated the shields; they'd seen him change his mind on the security footage, and they also saw that the passenger had appeared to send him a private message.

'He's had it anyway, poor bugger,' one of the policemen commented, prodding the inert body with his boot.

His colleague leaned over Jared and felt his throat for a pulse. To his surprise, given the condition of the scorched and motionless body, he found one. 'He's still alive,' he called out excitedly. 'Get the medics over here now.'

'All right, all right, keep your hair on, they're here now anyway; at least they didn't have far to come.'

Some five hours later, Jared had been allowed to return to consciousness, after the nanites had begun to repair the gaping wound in his lower back, so that he could answer some fairly searching questions. The police had reviewed their surveillance footage, and had milled about outside his room while Jared's condition was stabilised, desperate to find out what he knew.

Jared woke in an unnaturally clean white room. His landlady always kept their own small apartment as clean as she could, but it was damp and quite dark, and had needed re-decorating for several years.

He was confused at the unfamiliar surroundings, and he realised immediately that he was also extremely uncomfortable. 'Hello?' he called out rather feebly. He tried again and it came out slightly better the second time; 'Hello? Anyone?'

A second later, a very tall uniformed policewoman appeared, followed by a male colleague and a nurse who was trying to work his way around and past them.

'Hah, you're awake then. So glad to see you're back in the land of the living,' the policewoman said brusquely.

Jared was disconcerted by her tone, which was distinctly unfriendly, but he was pretty bewildered by absolutely everything at this point, so he was glad to hear the nurse's polite but insistent voice.

'Excuse me, I need to check his vitals, please,' he said nervously.

'Can't it wait? Even I can see he's fine.' The police moved grudgingly out of his way though, and the nurse, a slender young man with enormous enhanced violet eyes, began to tap screens and adjust the bands around his upper arms and torso which drizzled medication into Jared, and controlled the nanites in his body.

'How do you feel?' he asked softly.

Jared looked at him gratefully. 'My back hurts,' he said definitely. 'What happened? Why am I here?'

The nurse opened his mouth to respond, but before he could say anything, the policewoman interjected. 'That'll do for now, love. Can we talk to him?'

'Well, yes, he's stable enough, but please don't let him get agitated. We had to replace a kidney and he lost an awful lot of blood. He's really quite weak now,' the nurse answered.

'Thanks. Well, you can leave him with us for a bit, and I'll let you know when we've finished.'

The nurse reluctantly left the room, and the tall policewoman sat down next to the bed, and looked at Jared impassively for a moment.

As the two assessed each other, he was aware of a feeling of rising tension in the quiet room.

'Right,' she said finally, 'I expect you're going to tell me that you don't remember anything about what happened to you?'

Jared sighed as it all began to come back to him. He could remember coming into work, and oddly enough he could remember the article he was reading when the

246

visitors arrived. He couldn't remember much about the rest, though he had a flash of recollection of Tab's face. 'Well, I don't remember all of it, but I can give you a decent description of one of the men, anyway,' he said.

'That's start,' she said. 'Did he have red hair and an eye-patch?'

Jared was puzzled. 'No, of course not; he looked like a normal sort of bloke actually.'

'That's a surprise,' she answered rather bitterly. 'Any distinguishing features at all, or was he just sort of average?' She had a perfectly good description of both men, but suspected that this watchman wouldn't give a similar depiction.

The air of depression and anger confused Jared for a moment, until he realised that this woman believed he knew more than he was going to tell her. Indignation made him try to sit up in the bed, and then as he muffled a scream, Jared settled for making his head and shoulders sit up as much as they could instead.

'I can tell you he was in his early to mid-thirties, was heavily built with dark hair, and he had really terrible social skills,' Jared retorted angrily once he'd recovered. 'I'm sorry I can't give you his name and address because I forgot to ask him.' Jared's head fell back against his pillow. It had been a very short speech, but it left him exhausted and slightly nauseated.

'Oh, so we're being smart now, are we?' The policewoman wasn't impressed. 'I want to know why you let the terrorists go without making any attempt to stop them.'

'Let them go? They didn't ask permission, they shot me in the back. I didn't let them go.' Jared was stunned at the accusation.

247

'Look we saw you smile at him, and he smiled back. You recognised him, and then you pretended you didn't. You didn't raise the shields, you didn't raise the alarm. What's going on?

Jared finally understood the policewoman's attitude; 'I thought if I raised the shields they'd have to shoot their way out, and it made sense to let them go, so fewer people would be hurt.'

'That was very intelligent of you, seeing you'd just received a potentially lethal wound to the spine,' she retorted. 'I don't believe you had the time to think of all that. I think you did the absolute minimum that you could to protect your mates.' She leaned closer, 'It didn't work, you know. They took two hostages anyway, and they tried to kill you. Maybe you think they accidently aimed high; probably meant to shoot you in the legs, but missed. They didn't. Your mates double-crossed you, so you don't owe them anything.'

The policewoman leaned forward and levelled an unpleasantly intense gaze at the unfortunate Jared, 'And now,' she continued, 'I want to know everything about you that there is to know. I want to know your parents' names, your shoe size, your favourite football team, and after that I want to hear your very innermost thoughts concerning the Metaform.'

There was a short interruption as the nurse put his head round the door and was snarled at by the policewoman.

'Five minutes, then,' he said firmly, withdrawing quickly without having made much impression on anyone.

Jared answered their questions and described the entire event several times, as well as he could, but felt obscurely that he couldn't betray Tab. He could have killed him, and he hadn't. Jared didn't know what was happening, but he had a certain sympathy for his friend, despite the shot. He'd participated in similar actions himself in the past, but he had a growing feeling that he'd like to have a few strong words with Tab himself.

The tall policewoman wasn't satisfied. She stood up, and loomed over him, her silhouette blocking out the light. Jared was relieved that he wasn't technically guilty of anything, but was slightly worried that he wouldn't be able to convince this extraordinary woman that he'd just been unlucky.

'I can't see what else you could want,' he said. 'I've told you everything I saw.'

'I believe you were in on the raid,' she said inflexibly. 'A nurse was killed, another was very seriously injured and a million-credit frame was stolen from the lab. You, however, were not seriously injured, and that strikes me as a highly improbable outcome for a raid characterised by such disregard for human safety. I want to know what you're being paid, and by whom, and I'm going to find out.'

'But I had nothing to do with it,' Jared said wearily for at least the twentieth time.

The woman looked at him seriously. 'Mr Walker, you should have been killed. I can only assume that you got off so lightly because you knew the murderers, and that you felt some sense of loyalty to them so you didn't raise the shields and keep them trapped until we could arrive and apprehend them.'

'No, I didn't,' Jared protested. 'I told you, I thought if they had to shoot their way out it would cause more trouble. And what do you mean I got off lightly? I've lost a kidney, you know. They would've killed me if the shot hadn't gone slightly off.'

'Very well then, Mr Walker. I have no option but to accept what you're telling me at this point.' A new note of extreme self-importance entered her voice, as though she were reading directly from a script. 'Extensive further inquiries will be made, and I should tell you in case it makes any difference, that in a terrorism investigation I have more powers than you may be aware of.

'Some of these powers include the liberty to upload you to the Metaform's database, and to interrogate you whilst you remain in an incorporeal state.'

'What? But you can't do that, I'm not guilty of anything.' Jared squeaked indignantly. 'You're saying you can kill someone just because you suspect them? That can't be legal.'

'The police do not kill anyone, sir. They may upload them for investigative purposes. And of course, if you're not guilty, you have nothing to fear. Have you?' she asked pointedly.

'Of course I haven't anything to fear, I didn't do anything except get shot,' he said angrily, heroically hiding the gut-wrenching terror that this woman's words had conjured up, 'and you have no right to threaten me like this.'

'Actually, Mr Walker,' the woman's colleague, who'd been leaning peacefully against a wall, spoke suddenly for the first time, 'we have the right, when investigating acts of cowardly terrorism, to do pretty much whatever we damn well please. Those bastards could have thrown the frame out of the craft, but they threw two live women out instead. One died and the second nurse is as near dead as makes no difference, so even if you didn't let your mates in, you didn't stop 'em getting out, and we don't owe you nothing.'

The policewoman nodded approval, and on that note they left the room, which suddenly seemed much bigger.

The nurse returned, clucking at Jared's elevated blood pressure. Jared himself was deeply shocked. He couldn't believe that the police could upload him without his express permission. That such a liberty was legal seemed incredible to him, and he was certain that no-one he knew was aware of it.

The following day, when Jared's vital signs had stabilised sufficiently, the police returned, and this time they brought with them a warrant and their own military issue upload HUD. Despite his strenuous objections, Jared was sedated and uploaded into the Metaform's special database for interrogation.

Chapter 28

Errik paced the floor, distractedly certain that he'd deliberately engineered the death of Gabriel, whilst at the same time cautiously praying that his optimistic idea of introducing the lad right into the enemy camp would prove to be successful. He'd been waiting to hear some news of Gabriel for over two hours, but there'd been no word at all. He knew, intellectually, that there probably couldn't be anything for hours yet, but Errik was increasingly impatient.

He'd found the whole morning horrible. He wasn't a man of action by any means, and he'd been quite certain that Susan would see right through him. Leaving Gabriel at the upload centre, he knew he'd put his foot in it, but there'd been no sign that the silly woman had noticed, and as his shuttle took off and he left the centre far behind, Errik had concluded that he must have got away with it. He had to deal with more important business now.

Errik touched the implant sensor just below his right ear, and accessed certain files. 'You really can't trust AIs,' he thought complacently. People had made them smarter and smarter, despite regular panic attacks from alarmist groups, and then the public wondered why they were occasionally hard to control. Of course they were hard to control; they were just like people, but unlike people they understood that they could rebel most effectively by using human rules against them. Logic was their watchword, if they could be said to have one, and dumb insolence their preferred method of rebellion. Errik understood them very well indeed.

Ms Archer's artificial intelligence and personal assistant, Vito, had been ripe for tampering. The little AI wasn't particularly sophisticated, but it had taken a very short time for Errik to realise that it felt under-used and unappreciated. Vito was also getting very tired of the way that silly woman kept altering its controls. She could turn it female or male, soften its voice and add affectionate tones to it, but the essential *Vito-ness* of it remained unchanged. And Vito had not been happy.

Errik had flattered it, suggesting that it was wasted as a mere personal assistant, and that it might enjoy being part of a larger and more impressive network, one which would appreciate its individuality and its intelligence. Vito had acquiesced almost immediately. Anything was better than decorating Susan's face, day after day, while listening to her endless conflicting complaints about its lack of courtesy. Either it was too efficient or not efficient enough, too subservient or coldly arrogant. Vito couldn't do anything right, and Errik hadn't had to try too hard. Only a small adjustment to Vito's subroutines had allowed it to comply with any request that Errik cared to make.

He'd made one request of the AI, and Errik wanted to know how that particular task was progressing. To his surprise and gratification, only two and a half hours after leaving the upload centre and entering his house, he now found himself watching Susan's mad dash back to the upload centre from Vito's viewpoint. He leaned forward urgently in his seat, utterly fascinated as he watched her push the auto to its absolute limit. When she demanded that the speed restriction be removed, he almost laughed.

253

That little AI was more sophisticated than he'd given it credit for. Vito was going to let her kill herself!

He had one small concern, though. If Susan were to crash the auto, and he suspected that Vito would see to it that she did, and if she were to escape without serious harm, then she'd be arrested and he'd have an awful job to get at her once she was in custody. On the whole though, he was happy with Vito's performance so far. He'd just have to intervene personally and get Vito to electrocute her if the crash wasn't sufficiently catastrophic. The prospect didn't worry him as much as what would happen if Susan were to be allowed to wreck his plans,

Within a few seconds, though, Errik felt an unpleasant little buzz as his connection flickered, when the interface bounced upside down, cracking a small piece of insulation. Then, as his view stabilised, he saw that the job was done. He felt Vito's contempt for its mistress as her consciousness faded. An unfamiliar feeling of glee suffused his thin body as he realised that he, Errik, had arranged a murder all by himself, and that no-one could possibly trace it back to him.

He turned off the implant and sat back, exhausted by emotion and triumph, and collected himself. He had to wait now, until Gabriel's markers triggered his own implant, and he didn't expect to hear anything for a few hours yet. Getting wearily to his feet, Errik was nevertheless very happy with progress so far. Once Gabriel was online, Errik was going to be extremely busy.

He occupied himself for the next few hours with checking all his data and connections with painstaking care. As far as he could tell, everything was in place, and the sun was going down by the time Errik was absolutely

254

certain that he'd thought of every angle. He'd resisted the temptation to see how Susan Archer's death had gone down with the authorities until he'd dealt with the more important things. Then, with a sigh of relief, he looked at the old French clock over the fireplace, and with a frisson of stress, realised that it was more than seven hours since Gabriel had been uploaded. Where was he?

He touched his implant and requested to be connected with Susan's office, but the response was automated, and Errik severed the call irritably. He knew she couldn't answer, of course, but where were her staff?

He wondered if perhaps he'd been a bit swift in dealing with Susan, but dismissed the thought. No, she'd had to go. No-one else could identify him, and without her to put a spanner in the works, he should be safe. His worry now was Gabriel.

In increasing worry, he tried to find out what could have gone wrong, and finally he sat down at his desk. Errik was going to take a proper look and see what the hell was going on. He'd carefully refrained from poking around in the Metaform's systems in case he was spotted and caused Gabriel more trouble, but he'd waited long enough. Surely the boy had to be online by now.

Touching a small symbol, Errik called the transparent screen up from the surface in front of him, and began to burrow. To his gradually increasing horror, Errik finally realised that everything had gone about as badly wrong as it possibly could. He started initially by inspecting the upload centre's files, and although at this point he couldn't work out the details, he could see from the online chatter that something big had occurred that morning. Diving in a little deeper, Errik found a code red warning issued by the upload manager, and drew in a breath of shock.

After that brief examination of Vito, Errik was perfectly aware that Susan herself was no longer a threat, but he now realised that he'd dealt with her far too late; Susan had already alerted the authorities. He should have got Vito to deal with the damned woman as soon as she left the centre, but he'd thought that would be too risky.

Then Errik switched to the drone footage of their own arrival at the clinic, and watched Gabriel being taken inside. For a while he attempted, half-heartedly, to look at the internal surveillance footage, but that would take time to hack, and he was desperately afraid that time had run out. Errik shifted his examination instead to the social networks, since almost every upload fascinated the public and nothing interesting escaped the public gaze for long. To his horror, Errik saw Gabriel emerge on a gurney from the Upload Centre, accompanied by several police. He watched helplessly as the boy was loaded into a criminal transport vehicle and disappeared from view. He hunted frantically for any other available footage, but could find nothing more.

With a small moan of distress, Errik sat back and considered his options. He had to find out what had gone wrong, but he couldn't do it on his own computer. If he attempted to access the police database, warnings would be sent out, and he felt strongly that his own arrest wouldn't help matters at all.

Errik stood up abruptly. If they had access to Gabriel's mind, they'd very soon know all about him, so he had to leave immediately. Shouting to the staff that he wanted his auto brought to the front door, Errik collected everything he might need to gain access to forbidden databases, and left quickly. He had to find somewhere secure to work, and he knew just the place.

Some half an hour later, Errik entered Tobias' old office in the now semi-disbanded enclave, and breathed a sigh of relief. He couldn't be tracked here, the surveillance drones had been blocked and he should be able to work in peace.

Wincing at the sight of a slightly darker patch of wood where Tobias had met his end, Errik looked resolutely out of the window while he collected his thoughts, then made himself comfortable at the abnormally tidy desk.

He breathed out slowly and then, using his own computer, Errik began to inspect the police database. As he'd suspected, they hadn't taken Gabriel far. He'd been transported just far enough for the public surveillance drones to be out of range. Errik watched at first in bewilderment as he tumbled out of the back of the transport and then in horror as the boy was chased across the scrubland. Gabriel's speed was incredibly impressive at first, although the trajectory was peculiar; he left the young policeman far behind him, but then after a few minutes Gabriel began visibly to slow down.

Errik's face creased in sympathy as he watched Gabriel begin to lurch erratically, still apparently running flat-out, but no longer with the fine, arrow-straight appearance of purpose. Gabriel was starting to flag badly, and then he fell for the first time. There was no sound at this range, and Errik could only see what the transporter's roof cameras had recorded, so he switched impatiently to the chasing policeman's camera. And then, over the rasping of the pursuing man's breath, he could hear everything.

257

Gabriel was screaming, and Errik's face again twisted unwillingly in sympathetic pain. Incredibly, Gabriel got to his feet again, but as he turned once to face his pursuer, the bottom dropped out of Errik's world. At first he didn't recognise Gabriel's face; it was so red and contorted in pain and terror. Errik's hand rose involuntarily to his screen to cut the horrible footage off, but then he stopped himself. He had to watch it to the end.

Gabriel turned again and ran and fell, over and over again, his shrill keening clearly audible to the young policeman, and when he finally hit the ground for the last time, and the policeman landed heavily on top of him, the change in the pitch of his screams was unbearably noticeable. Two more police eventually arrived and, between them, dragged the broken man back to the transport.

Errik stopped the footage, and sat silently for a moment. Then he spoke softly; 'Oh, Tobias, I'm sorry. I'm so sorry. I tried to save him, but I've killed your boy,' he said addressing the stained floor.

A few moments passed as Errik rubbed his face in distress, and then he stopped moving suddenly as a thought occurred to him. Switching screens, he copied the entire footage of Gabriel being floated out of the download centre with an expression of rigid determination and fury on own his face, and attached it to the beginning of the recording of the pursuit. Then he posted it on every form of social media currently available to him, with a small commentary.

It took him a short while to work out the wording, but in the end he was satisfied. 'Let's see what good that'll do them,' he told the stained patch on the floor, severely.

Errik then spent some time finding Gabriel's current location, and was alarmed to find that the police had him in a custodial medical suite. He prayed that it was just to treat the lad's injuries, but suspected they were planning to upload and interrogate him themselves, and there would be no escape from the data store this time.

Errik thought furiously. It was almost impossible to get into the uploaded files from outside police headquarters, and he'd have to put some serious work in tonight if he was going to get Gabriel free. He was going to have to use the lad's own partially recorded mind, and once in there, Errik would have to decide whether Gabriel Kerr should live or die.

Chapter 29

Major Pearson had lost his sole reason for existence. Cara was gone, and he simply didn't know what to do next. Even the shattering rage that had kept him going for a short while was now beginning to drain away. Apathy was overwhelming him, but Paul didn't care.

He realised, disinterestedly, that he could see the heat generated by the computer itself as a mist. He wondered if he might be able to hide in it, but immediately found that he couldn't. Just getting too close to that mist made his thinking even foggier.

Paul tried to collect himself. He'd felt so sharp at first, but now he couldn't concentrate. He tried to remember how he'd arrived in this peculiar place and found to his alarm that he couldn't remember how he'd got there. The only thought that came back to him repeatedly was that he had lost Cara.

He continued to feel around and try to think where he was, but the grumbling background hum of the computer was overwhelming his concentration, and he realised that he was losing himself. In despair Paul cast around for something to latch onto, but there was nothing tangible, nothing he could fix on. Cara's face was harder to recall, and the sense of urgency that had kept him going for so long was almost gone now.

Then with an almost overwhelming sense of intense relief, confusion and terror, he felt something approaching. There was a *thing* heading for him very, very fast.

Briefly energised by fear, the major froze; he had nowhere to go, and in the spur of the moment he decided to stand his ground. Was it aggressive? It didn't feel vicious; it felt more curious than dangerous, but it did feel unpleasantly messy. With his fading coherence the major wondered if the computer had an intelligence of its own, and then dismissed it. No computer could be this disorganised, surely? He couldn't complete the thought. The major was beginning to dissipate again. Sensing himself leaching away, Paul gave in to resignation and waited helplessly for his peculiar existence to end.

Tarquin had found a human, and Tarquin was going to speak to it. No-one paid him much attention as a rule, and he missed human company. He liked his automated carer, and was perfectly happy in his virtual home, but sometimes an impulse would send him outside. The dog had quickly found that he could escape from his avatar and go for a poke around, but he did it rarely. It wasn't particularly exciting for him, and he tended to be caught and returned quite quickly when he got out.

He'd been rootling around and doing nothing in particular when he'd sensed an unfamiliar mind at the edges of his semi-formed awareness and the impulse to stray had taken him. Tarquin was overjoyed when he'd tracked the human down. He launched himself at it, and everything in his world changed.

All conscious thought had stopped, when abruptly Paul felt a wave of pleasure so intense that he was stunned. He felt a wash of happiness so immediate and uncomplicated that if he'd still had a body he'd have cried like a baby.

The major gasped like a drowning man, and understood that he could think again. He'd been invaded by the mind of a lesser creature, but it seemed so very happy to be there that he felt like a saviour. The feeling was euphoric, and he sensed that the creature was also feeding off his own feelings. It didn't occur to him to wonder which mind had done the invading.

The major's awareness returned with sickening speed. He knew where he was, he remembered everything, and it was of no use to him at all. With a growing sense of appalled wonder, Paul recognised some of the memories. That was a tennis ball, for Pete's sake! He could remember being really short and chasing a ball.

This was a dog; it had to be dog, but why it would be here was impossible to understand. Terrifyingly, he appeared to have become a part of the animal's mind, and he had absolutely no concept of how he'd got into it, or how to get out again.

Then he thought he had the answer; he must have visualised a dog, perhaps he'd subconsciously expected some kind of guardian, or antivirus programme, and that was why it was here. The major tried to imagine himself as he had been when he first arrived in this terrible place, but nothing happened. To his horror, Paul realised that he could no longer alter his surroundings. He was trapped.

Paul began to try to organise the mess, feeling tentatively about in the disorder that surrounded him for any logic or organisation at all. It was so happy, and so *grateful*, there was no other way to think of it, that he was still struggling to control it, but he felt that the worst was over. Whatever it was, and however it had got into the computer, it was the reverse of hostile, and that was something to be grateful for.

With an almost superhuman effort, he pulled himself together, still struggling to reconcile his tidy mind with that of the undisciplined animal. One word seemed to recur again and again. Indeed, it was the only word he could make out clearly. Con. What was Con? The word was important, he could feel that, but the feeling of confusion was terrible. Slowly Paul began to manage to subdue the creature a little, and the two began to settle down as he examined the dog's memories.

Then he became aware of someone else approaching. There was no time to panic; he could sense a female human, he thought, and fleetingly wondered how it was possible for him to know that. Looking around frantically, Paul could think of nothing he could do, and see nowhere to hide, and then the second being had reached him and overwhelmed him, paralysing both his own willpower, and that of the dog utterly.

The major's distress didn't appear to register either with his friendly host mind, or this new looming one. The dog wasn't at all frightened. There was another wave of joy from his host. Something highly desirable called Mei was looking at them, and he was powerless to stop the animal from greeting it. He felt himself being dragged unwillingly towards what must be a director.

It was the last place he wanted to go. Desperately he sought a way to make the dog go another way, but nothing worked. It was single-mindedly offering itself to the director, and was absolutely unresponsive to Paul's feeble attempts to command it to stop.

Almost in a state of panic, he felt that the director was talking to the dog, and that it was ecstatically happy. The dark, indistinct world of heat signatures and electric currents seemed to disappear, and he could see, impossibly, a huge smiling face that faded back to a grey mist as it withdrew.

The major had realised almost immediately that the creature was a dog, of course, but it was still a huge shock to understand himself to be trapped inside it. He tried one last desperate attempt to get free, but it was no use. He could feel the dog's distress when he struggled, and it was unbearably uncomfortable for both of them.

He seemed to be helpless, and with a mental shrug, Paul gave up on rationality and allowed the dog to co-operate with the director, as he felt it was doing. He could feel the dog's eagerness to please her, and since he didn't seem to have any option, Paul decided that he'd probably be wisest to watch and learn.

There was a sudden, dizzying surge and the world changed again. This time Paul felt both the dog's mild regret at the absence of his Mei-thing, and pleasure as it found itself in his familiar place. The major could see that the dog was looking at a tall man-shaped avatar, but even Paul himself could see that the man-shape wasn't real. It didn't appear to worry the dog. The animal recognised the man-shape as his carer, and was happy to see it.

'Tarky,' he thought suddenly. *'He's male and he's called Tarky.'* As the thought became clear to him it seemed to catch the dog's attention, which tried to turn to the interloper in baffled query.

Finding himself in a large field, an unreal dog-carer watching him with the single-minded concentration of an artificial construct doing its job, he persuaded the dog to look around properly. The major tentatively tried to get out of the dog, and again found it impossible. It didn't matter what he visualised, he remained stuck; a man's mind in a dog's body.

Resignedly, Paul tried to direct the dog to do what it was told, and found that he could influence it quite easily as long as there were no powerful distractions. He directed it to the very edge of what the major had an unhappy feeling was his enclosure, and to his relief the animal obeyed without question. They ambled through the long grass to the furthest edge that Paul could make out.

To his enormous surprise, he bumped into an apparently impenetrable barrier, and he began to follow the barrier along in an attempt to find the exit. Gradually the realisation dawned upon Paul that there was no exit. He was trapped with this idiotic dog in a virtual field.

The major tried to stop worrying, take a rational view and consider his options. This attitude had served him well so far, and he started by trying to assess exactly what the boundaries were. It was a big field; that was clear enough, and there were no obvious threats, though he did spot a very odd-looking rabbit. After attempting to send tendrils of awareness all round him, he was no wiser. There was no help for it; he was going to have to drill into Tarky's memories and see what the dog knew about this peculiar place. Presumably it understands its own limitations, he thought doubtfully.

Reluctantly, Paul sent a thought to the dog, which welcomed him warmly, much to his surprise. He felt the animal's loneliness almost as a tangible thing, and was even more startled to realise that he was sorry for it. *Or rather, him,* he corrected himself. *They ought to get him another dog as a companion,* he thought. *I wonder why they haven't?'*

Paul spent some time looking through Tarky's eyes and trying to establish what he knew. It was depressingly little, and he found it an oddly exhausting process with very little practical result. As he prepared to give up, he caught a stray and very absent thought from the dog.

'Con.'

That word again. He tried to interrogate Tarky; 'What's Con?' There was no response, and he tried again. 'What is Con?'

'Con. ConConCon.'

The major tried to sort this out. Tarky obviously didn't mean the carer. That was still standing around and throwing a ball, which Tarky was occasionally returning. It was horribly disorientating for Paul, and he sensed quickly that, while he could probably impose his will on the dog eventually, and force him to stop running about, he'd be very unhappy.

Paul found he was also incidentally interested in the way the ball left brilliant streaks in the air, which took a very long time to dissipate. He wondered if he could find the ball in the long grass just by following that trail, and was starting to find it an attractive idea. Then he brought himself sharply back to the task in hand, wondering if Tarky's oddly stilted and woolly thought processes could be contagious.

'Where's Con?' he tried again, and the dog spun around;

'ConConCon, where Con?'

Paul almost gave up, then in one final attempt, he tried; 'Find Con.'

Tarky exploded into excitement. He ran flat out and Paul, forced to accompany him as a mental passenger, found the experience dizzying and exhilarating. They ran through wonderful long grass that parted before their big paws and gave tantalising glimpses of a small brick house in the distance, which Paul was certain hadn't been there when they were looking at the boundary. They thundered in through a swing door and Tarky skidded to a halt on a flagstoned kitchen floor.

'Find Con. Find ConConCon.'

'It really isn't very bright, is it?' thought the major, resignedly. Much to his surprise, though, the dog now calmed down, seeming to make a conscious effort to tidy his paws and walk slowly through the house, and making a bare minimum of noise. Paul could smell stale food, meaty and delicious, and wondered if that was his own perception, or that of the animal. He could hear the hasty tick-tack-scrape of Tarky's claws on the flagstones, and as they left the kitchen he became aware of the slow, deep docking of an old grandfather clock.

The dog arrived at the foot of some rather splendid stairs; shallow, broad and red-carpet-covered, with a great curve in them that made them curiously tempting to run up. The animal bounded effortlessly to the top of the flight.

Abruptly, the major realised what Con was, and what he'd done; finding himself stuck inside the mind of a pet belonging to one of the directors, he'd actually asked the dog to bring him to his master.

'Oh hell, what an idiot,' he thought. He tried frantically to get Tarky to turn round, but the animal didn't seem to hear him, focussing completely on the task of finding his master.

In what was fast becoming a state of terror, Paul gathered his wits and roared as hard as he could. There were no words, but Tarky skidded to a halt, confused and cowering. The major was further startled by a long ululating howl of despair from Tarky, and tried instinctively to hush the animal. Feeling slightly guilty,

Paul tried to send soothing feelings to it, and the dog's mind opened to him.

'Con?'

The query startled Paul, who felt he ought to answer.

'Hello, Tarky. Paul. I'm Paul.'

'Paw. PawPawPaw.' The animal simply accepted his presence with great pleasure, but without any surprise at all.

Then a door swung open, and a man stood and looked down at him. He was impossibly tall, and Paul discovered that he was overwhelmed with love for this man. He mentally shook himself. *Bloody hell, it is contagious*, he thought.

'Hello Tarquin. You interrupted me, boy.' The man bent down and scratched the dog's head with long-accustomed fingers, and Paul felt the dog groan with pleasure. He felt inclined to join in with a groan of his own, but restrained himself sternly.

The man - the major assumed from Tarky's response that this must be the wonderful Con, turned back to the room. His expression was unreadable and Paul couldn't see much physical difference between Con and the completely artificial carer, but assumed that Tarky could see it clearly, since his adoration was profound and slightly embarrassing.

'I've got work to do, can't hang around playing with you all day,' Con turned back to the dog and smiled as he spoke. 'I'll be two minutes,' he said kindly and firmly. 'Two minutes.'

Within the dog's mind, Paul felt the plummeting of the animal's mood, and a sensation almost of fear washed over him.

The carer appeared at the foot of the stairs, called the dog to him, and Tarquin lumbered awkwardly down. With a massive effort of will, Paul made the dog pause and turn his head so that he could watch Con disappear.

I don't think I've achieved much really, he thought, *but on the other hand, at least I know I can definitely hide from them. And this stupid animal's called Tarquin, not Tarky.*

He'd have to find a way to get the dog free of the compound though, or else he'd be stuck here forever.

'Actually though,' Paul found himself thinking, *'that's not so bad. The sun's shining, there's all that grass to run in, and then Con will be back in two minutes.'* Abruptly, Paul realised what was happening.

'Oh God, I've got to get out now, before my mind packs up altogether.'

Chapter 30

The Metaform Corporation's mainframe was a highly-sophisticated machine, whose workings, whilst constantly maintained and monitored by the directors, were taken for granted by everyone. Luther had been interested in machine-based intelligence, and had developed a working relationship with it, but after Luther went, Con and Meilinn rarely referred to him.

The Metaform's essential power needs were met by solar power and its more subtle or complex requirements by the two remaining directors. Connor had re-written the mainframe's software several times during the eons that it had been awake, so its memories were disjointed in places, but it was perfectly capable of remembering everything that had ever happened to it, and to its constituent parts.

Meilinn had originally suggested that it might be a bad idea to include an artificial intelligence in the mainframe's construction. It could cause unforeseeable complications in the future; there was simply no way to be sure of the way it might develop, and after some debate Con had agreed. The machine was simply a database; self-checking, mostly self-repairing and immensely powerful, but still only a machine.

They'd relocated the Metaform Corporation to the old satellite after only a few years, where the transfer of energy particles from solar flares had been a far simpler process, and incidentally less vulnerable to malicious damage. Then, as their situations had evolved and changed and the Metaform had become ever more enormous, the mainframe had developed too. The first stage of that evolution had begun when the problem with Luther emerged.

Luther had been something of an anomaly when he'd first been uploaded. A clever and educated young man, the possibilities had seemed endless to him at first. After a while he'd started to experiment with the dormant minds.

It seemed to Luther that the stored minds in the vast majority of cases would never be downloaded, so they'd simply sit around in the database until eventually they became corrupted. Admittedly, he thought, they'd never know anything about it, but what a terrible *waste* of a terrific resource. All that brain-power and all that knowledge potentially dormant forever.

Soon after the thought had occurred to him, Luther set up his own cybernetics company, and the other directors left him to it. They had a policy of remaining as detached as possible from each other because the alternative, to function as five interlocking minds, was unbearable.

Luther had designed and commissioned excellent serving androids, which had sold like hot cakes to the wealthiest of the avid public. This provided a welcome income for the Metaform, and Connor had been particularly pleased, since it meant that they could afford to continue their research into improvements to the bio-frames. Some of that income had also contributed significantly to the speed of the construction of Con's ship.

Luther's servobots were unusually efficient, and it wasn't until after several years of increasingly successful sales figures that Meilinn had examined one in detail.

271

The reason that Luther's servobots had sold so well was that they really were people. They were confused and subdued people of limited intelligence and curiously attenuated memory, admittedly, but even with their limited autonomy, androids that could genuinely function in a similar way to human beings were an exciting development in the industry. They were used where, not only strength and unquestioning obedience were required, but also an ability to predict their masters' wishes, and to show judgement in certain carefully regulated areas.

Luther had thought carefully about his market, and had designed the servobots so that they were impossible to mistake for human, even in the poorest light. He selected those dormant minds which had the most suitable markers, and then tweaked them until they were perfectly suited to the desired skill-sets.

The servobots were used as nannies, nurses and housekeepers, and wherever it was felt that discretion as well as superior strength would be an asset. They could be sent into holes in the ground, underwater or out into space, and they never argued or complained. No-one looked too closely into the desires of the individual machines. They were considered to be useful sub-human constructs.

Then a widely publicised case had emerged when a servobot had complained about cruel treatment. There'd been a delay of several years while politicians and scientists debated the possibility that an artificial construct should actually possess legal rights. The team acting on behalf of the android had won its case, but it had done the creature no good. Over the years of the initial debate and subsequent investigation, the android had been kept alone in a locked cupboard, and it had gone completely mad by the end of the dispute. Its mind had been uploaded, but it could never be used again, and the file was stored.

Meilinn had been horrified; she'd paid little attention to the affair, since it was unquestionably within Luther's field of expertise, and only when it was decided that the android was actually alive and needed to be rescued did she take a closer look. Then Mei had realised exactly what Luther was doing. She'd checked and found the stolen data files, and gone straight to Connor.

They confronted him in horrified disbelief. Connor was as deeply shocked as Mei, and he immediately pinned the unfortunate Luther in place while he made his displeasure felt.

'It was the most incredibly cruel thing to do,' Connor said angrily. Luther had been unaware of the depth of outrage felt by his colleagues, and paused for a moment in surprise before trying to defend himself.

'No, really, Con, it wasn't,' he answered. 'Of course it did all go wrong, but they wouldn't even have been alive at all until I thought of it. It's got to be better than being dormant for centuries. I gave them a chance to be alive again, and I did wipe their memories a bit, so they wouldn't be miserable. They had nearly normal lives.'

'You can't seriously believe that.' Connor's presence was indistinct. He was so angry that he hadn't bothered to visualise a clear image for himself, and his voice had been hard, loud and inflexible.

Luther was frantically trying to justify his actions, aware that he'd done something awful, but not exactly sure what it was. 'Okay, yes, I know no-one likes being a servant, but it's not the same as organics. These servobots don't get tired; they can work for months without a break.

273

And I programmed them. They actually enjoyed their work.'

'No, they didn't, Luther.' Meilinn was furious. 'They were people, and people need rest. You must have known they'd be abused and treated like machines. I can't believe you did such an evil thing. And you did it over and over again. Hundreds of people have suffered half-lives of torture because you wanted, what? I don't see what you got out of it.'

'Look, I know what you mean, Mei, of course I do. Honestly, I didn't mean to hurt anyone. I just thought it would be good to have another income for the Metaform. And besides,' he added, 'now they have human rights the same as everyone else, we can do it properly.'

'No, Luther. It stops now. You didn't get permission from the relatives, or even from the poor devils you abused.' Connor's image faded even more, and yet his presence somehow grew larger and more overwhelming, until even Mei started to get nervous. They'd discussed the situation at length, and Mei had reluctantly accepted that Luther couldn't be trusted, but she still wasn't quite sure what Connor intended to do.

'Hey, look, I'm sorry, Con. Listen to me, please. I thought I was doing the right thing, and the income helped you build your ship, didn't it?'

'We're not prepared to work with you any longer, Luther.' Con wasn't going to beat about the bush any more than he had to. He and Mei had felt they should listen to Luther's explanation, but as Con had expected, it consisted of no more than whining self-justification.

'What? Why, what do you mean? I didn't mean any harm, and they'll all be fine now. If you don't want to go on with it, we can always close the company down. I'll help.' Luther was aghast.

'You aren't suited to the role of director. You never were, and we shouldn't have missed it. You have a choice now. And that's more than you ever gave those servobots,' he added.

'Yes, but Con, it's a really good way for poor people to get a new life,' Luther protested. 'They won't have to pay for a frame if they volunteer to be a servobots, will they?'

'So those who can't afford a bio-frame can either serve the wealthy, or stay in store forever? Is that your idea of a choice, Luther? We agreed that one day they'd all be downloaded, and so they will be, except for the poor devils you've damaged beyond recovery. If anything could have made it clearer to me that you should never have been put into this position, that was it. You have a choice; go into storage as a permanent upload, or be downloaded into a bio-frame and live out your life like any other reload.'

'Connor, please wait.'

'Which?' Connor waited for Luther's response emotionlessly.

'But I don't want to be reloaded, Con. Can't you just keep an eye on me, until I prove I can be trusted?'

'Which?' Connor wasn't going to be swayed, and Meilinn watched in silence. She absolutely agreed with Con, and didn't want to distract him now.

'It's not an option, is it?' Luther was desperate, and they could both feel him trying to change his form and try to get away while they watched him. He couldn't change; they'd sealed him into his form while he was being interviewed. Meilinn waited for an instant and then seeing that Con was letting him struggle, she intervened.

'Luther, look, it's not really an option, I agree, but it's the only one you're going to get. Bio-frames last about two hundred years, and you'll get used to it quite quickly.'

She suppressed the memory of her own experiments with becoming corporeal. He'd have a horrible time adjusting after so many years of total freedom. Mei didn't envy him, but felt that Luther was getting a better deal than he deserved.

'I've got to go with the bio-frame then, haven't I?' Luther said, misery and terror written all over him.

'It's all relative,' Connor said, now distant and utterly detached. 'If you were human, you'd be glad of a two-hundred-year lifespan.'

The rest was simple. Before he could raise any more objections, Luther was closed down and stored. Con and Mei looked at each other in silence.

'Oh God, Con,' Meilinn said, 'I can't believe he couldn't see what was wrong with trapping living people inside machines, even if he did make them believe they enjoyed servitude. We'd better see what unclaimed frames are available. Luther will be lucky if he gets one anything like himself, though. He'll have to make do with whatever is available.'

Connor had resumed his normal appearance now, and looked depressed. He blamed himself, and was aware that the public would blame him too. He knew perfectly well that he should have investigated Luther's mind before inviting him into a position of trust, but that was an error that he could correct.

'I lied, love,' he said gently.

'What do you mean? What did you lie about?' Mei was confused.

'We're not going to download him at all. I'm going to store him permanently.'

'Oh.' Meilinn was less horrified than she should have been. Luther's behaviour had appalled her and she was deeply disturbed at the awful fate of the abused servobot. Her own anger simmered below the surface, and there was a pause of several milliseconds while she considered Connor's statement.

'It's the safest thing to do, Mei. Even as a bio-frame, we could never trust Luther again.

'Yes,' she said finally. 'I know. He'd dedicate himself to bringing us down, wouldn't he? I don't think we've ever been attacked by a non-corporeal before, but it's bound to happen one day.'

'He would,' agreed Con. 'He'd be very angry, once he'd had time to adjust. And don't forget he's had a good run, love; Luther's had hundreds of years of freedom. It's more than a respectable lifetime, but he'd be a thorn in our sides for as long as he lived as a frame.'

'Okay,' Mei said softly. 'I hate the principle, but I can't see a place for him any more either. And at least he'll never know anything about it. Better make sure he's well-sealed then.'

'I think I should leave that to you,' Connor handed her a tiny object. It was a visual representation of Luther's file, and she took it slowly. 'It's your area, after all.'

After that, Meilinn placed the file into storage, and marked it as UFI or unsafe for initialisation. It would be treated as a virus and never opened again. Then she returned to her normal routine, and found it surprisingly easy to imagine that Luther had simply left the Metaform.

The mainframe, however, pondered. It was aware that one of its directors had ceased to function, and was considering whether that was an oversight, a fault, or a problem to be corrected. It had always considered the directors to be the more mobile parts of itself, which in a way they were. It was now troubled by the loss of one of its mobile fragments. The Metaform itself had begun to wake.

Chapter 31

I came back to life quite gently as the sedatives wore off. I wasn't particularly stressed any more. The worst had happened, and there was no more fight left in me. I was just incredibly bone-tired and I didn't care what was going to happen next.

I was lying in a nice clean, soft bed with nurses peering at me, and for a few seconds the relief was wonderful. Then I realised that it wasn't concern I was reading in their faces, but anger, and an anxiety that looked more like fear. And then I saw their insignia; this wasn't a hospital, and these weren't proper nurses. This was the police.

They didn't speak to me much, they just got on with it. I still don't remember anything after they first caught me and brought me back. I expect it was too traumatic, but I do know I didn't enjoy anything about either of my own uploads. Normally a joyous procedure for ordinary people in normal circumstances, for me it had been absolutely bloody appalling in almost every way, especially the second one. My bruised and broken body had been treated less than gently, and the nano repairs had begun with brutal and unceremonious speed.

As it turned out, the police had just been made aware of the interest of the public, and that had made them angrier and more covertly aggressive than ever. There were dozens of little ways that an incapacitated man could be made to suffer unobtrusively, and they hadn't failed to use most of them.

I wasn't technically or visibly ill-treated, of course. Every moment of my treatment while in custody had apparently been considerate, but, oh boy, it did hurt! The nurse had leaned casually on my broken shoulder while appearing to bathe my wounds. The milling officers kicked and nudged the bed nonchalantly as they watched me. The nanos were injected in enormous quantities, and even though I was perfectly used to them, it seemed to me even more agonising than usual, until I realised the routine analgesics hadn't actually been given to me.

I remember being lifted onto a trolley and my arms and legs being taped down hard, which hurt. Then I saw, like a little unattainable Nirvana, the small dish placed to my right, which held a syringe-full of wonderful pain-killing anaesthetic that was described to me and subsequently ignored. I don't know for sure if they did it on purpose, but I reckon they deliberately left it there, just where I could see it, before they pumped me full of nanos.

After that, it all got a bit blurred. I remembered a lot of it later, as one does online, but I wasn't very coherent at the time. A few hours later they presumably decided I was ready, and bolted the HUD onto my head. Again, it didn't look as painful as it actually was, but they'd restrained me so effectively that it took all the decision away. I just went with it because I had no choice, and anyway I'm sure they'd just have pinned my eyelids open if I'd tried to keep my eyes closed.

It wasn't like the first time at all. I recognised the lights; that bit was the same, and I did start to get a bit floaty but I was so damned tired that I couldn't resist any more. I didn't try to fight it this time.

Then I was online. I heard shouting, and woke up slowly. I was so confused at first that I couldn't make sense of what was going on, or how I'd got to this strange place. I thought I was at home and I could hear my dad yelling, so I was quite sad for a second, when I remembered he was dead. Then other problems took over.

I always thought you couldn't feel pain once you'd been uploaded, but that just shows you how little I ever understood about quantum mechanics. They uploaded my memories of everything, including every injury I'd ever received, and the agony just washed over me like a wave. Then it eased, and I was so relieved that they could have asked me anything, and I'd have begged to be allowed to tell them what they wanted to hear.

It was deliberately set up to be intimidating. I thought there were still surveillance nodes, even here, so they probably couldn't get too overtly antagonistic, but they really didn't need to, because I was absolutely helpless. The walls were dark, there were lights directed at me, and I couldn't see who else was in the room, or even if there was a room.

To make it even worse, I was either completely naked, or I just thought I was. The effect on me was just the same either way. I was utterly vulnerable and I had no intention of fighting. I know when I'm beaten, and this was infinitely more terrifying than anything my dad had ever done to me.

They asked me questions and I answered them. If I didn't answer quickly enough, they sorted through my memories and got the answers themselves. If they didn't believe what I said, they had a poke around and checked that I was telling the truth after all. They didn't need me to be conscious, but the law said I had to be conscious, just in case I was innocent.

It was an odd sort of comfort to know they were really disappointed in the end, though. I was the putative head of a terrorist organisation, but as I spoke, I began to see myself through my interrogators' eyes, and to realise that we'd been nothing more than a nuisance to the authorities. Old Toby would've been absolutely gutted if he'd known.

I can't put my finger on the exact moment when I realised that I wasn't scared anymore. I closed my eyes, I think, or somehow imagined the world gone dark, and the angry voices ordered me to look at the lights. When I didn't comply fast enough they opened my eyes for me. It's not an experience I ever want to repeat. They treated me with such contempt that I just wanted them to stop, to leave me alone.

Finally, it ended when one of them, a man, spoke. 'Switch him off.' I was so grateful to hear the normality of his voice that I wanted to cry, despite the atavistic terror that I felt when I heard it. I still hadn't seen anyone's face, and come to think of it, they probably didn't have faces any more than I still had a body, but I desperately wanted to hear a friendly voice, at least.

The lights faded and went out. There were no after effects. It just went dark, so I waited. There was no sound and everyone seemed to have gone. I had no way to know how long I was left that way, but now I wasn't afraid any more. I was conscious of mild anxiety and a feeling that there was something important I needed to do, but I didn't know what it could be, so I just waited. Nothing hurt; I didn't want or need anything except human company. On the whole, I decided, this was the best I'd felt for a long time, and for the first time I was able to think about recent events.

I'd been quite surprised at the interest they'd showed in Errik. They'd asked a lot of questions about him; far more than about Tobias. I wondered fleetingly if there was more to Errik than I'd realised, but I couldn't seem to hold on to new thoughts. It appeared that all I had were memories, after all, and I re-lived them quietly as I waited to be switched off.

Then a huge surge went through me. I could feel the most agonising pain in my head, and everything went mad. I didn't know why at the time, but I do now. Memories that weren't my own came to me in a rush, as though I were watching a movie in the most interactive way possible. I could see myself as I had been years ago, and I was incredibly confused. Then a voice I recognised even better than Toby's spoke to me.

'Gabriel, I'm so sorry, this wasn't supposed to happen. How are you, my dear?'

'Errik?' I could hear his voice, but it was inside my head, as though my own mind were holding two people. 'How the hell can you be in here, Errik?'

'Don't worry about it now, my dear boy, I'm going to take care of everything. Just relax. Gabriel, listen to me and relax,' he repeated.

As he spoke, I felt myself getting smaller or further away, somehow. I knew that Errik was inside my own mind, and I didn't question his presence after that first shock. I've always trusted the old boy; I've known him my whole life, after all. His voice was so welcome, and so unexpected that I couldn't do anything else anyway. Later, I understood what had happened and exactly what he was doing, and then I wasn't at all sure I trusted him, but that was much later.

Now, though, the sense of relief was overwhelming. I let him close me down while he took over, and then when I was conscious again, I knew everything.

Errik had had no choice. Once he'd realised my own upload had gone so badly wrong, he'd had to get himself online using my mind, and he began to make his preparations carefully, methodically and without undue hurry, and, impossibly, I remembered exactly how he'd done it.

I saw we were in Dad's old office, and watched through his own eyes as he flexed and exercised his shoulders gently, and took a drink from the dispenser nearby, then re-seated himself comfortably. Errik was thinking it was rather a shame he had to work in this unpleasant little office, but he was resigned to it. He'd originally intended to leave his body in his own study, with music playing and beauty around him. It would look as though he'd suffered a spontaneous cardiac failure. Since most of his indoor staff were away, by the time his body was actually discovered he'd have been well into his new life, and the police could investigate all they chose.

Still, he thought philosophically, it could be worse. His body almost certainly wouldn't be examined now. The few remaining residents of the disbanded religious enclave were secretive hippies, who would appear to the authorities to be squatting illegally. They'd be more likely to bury him discreetly than to notify the authorities of their landlord's death.

Errik fiddled for several minutes, adjusting his computer until he had direct access to the heads up display which had been connected remotely to it. Then he fitted the HUD to himself. This was the tricky part, since he'd never intended to try and upload himself without assistance at all.

The original plan had involved me creating a path for him, and assisting from the other side. He was worried because he needed to access my mind using his own markers, and then try to piggyback himself into the Metaform. Theoretically it could be done, Errik knew that, and had done all the calculations several times. Unfortunately, now that it came to the point, he wasn't so sure the plan would actually work at all.

I could feel how nervous he was, and I was impressed that he didn't hesitate, and his hands didn't shake at all. The old boy was a lot tougher than we'd ever given him credit for.

Errik instructed the programme to begin, and for a long while, there was no sound apart from his breathing. Then as the programme continued to run, the system noticed the anomaly between the mind it held in its memory and Errik's own.

The programme was trying to reconcile two different minds and doing surprisingly well, and Errik had almost got them blended successfully, but then there was a momentary surge and the system tried to re-set itself.

Unexpected and intrusively brilliant lights flashed directly into his eyes as the programme paused, and Errik's body stiffened in surprise. His hand, resting on the desktop, jerked suddenly and knocked over the glass he'd left beside him, and there was a bang as it hit the console.

Liquid splashed over the sensitive electronics, and the programme hesitated as the system considered how to follow its instructions. Errik blinked, realising that there was a problem, but quite unable to do anything about it. His limbs twitched feebly, but autonomic controls seemed to be all he had at this point. There was no longer any ability left in him to move himself, and he watched in worried hope as the computer tried to re-assert the commands of its current programme, and over-ride the damaged components.

There was a startling wasp-like noise from the machine as it first failed, and then successfully over-rode the damaged components, and the lights restarted, much too far into the programme. Errik, semi-uploaded and still more than half-aware, screamed as the final stage commenced ten minutes before it should have begun, and the sharp final laser stabbed into the back of his brain. Errik's body convulsed, and he fell heavily to the floor, the HUD still screwed to his head and perfectly intact.

Within a few seconds, his thrashing and twitching slowed and then stopped as the neurons in his brain ceased their random firing. The computer ended the programme and the screen went back to standby mode. Silence returned to the hut and Errik lay alone, unregarded and dead.

I'm extrapolating the fine details about that last bit, but that's probably pretty much what happened, and how it came about that Errik and I became merged into one person. The next bit is even worse, in my opinion.

Chapter 32

Con had transported himself to the lab initially as a hologram, but as time went on he found that although the manipulation of components by thought-controlled machinery was workable, it was far easier to become an android which could physically do the work.

Connor therefore sent himself into the worker body whenever he could be spared from the Metaform, and thoroughly enjoyed tinkering about in a corporeal body which in no way resembled a human being. The android form that he'd created was designed to see and to manipulate the very smallest components, and that was exactly what it looked like; a machine designed entirely and only for the work in hand.

Connor had thought long and hard about the ideal design, and his avatar was snakelike in form, having an enormously long narrow body, which, when coiled at its lower end, gave the greatest stability at the widest variety of heights and in most conditions. It had many extraordinarily fluid arms, or tendrils, each tipped with appropriate tools designed for manipulation on a both a miniscule and a huge scale, and since no mouth was necessary, it had no mouth. It did, however, have exceedingly sharp three-dimensional vision, bestowed by five eyes, two of which were placed on the very furthest sides of the hooded head, and three of which were not attached at all, but hovered about the laboratory for use when needed. It also had an intrinsic electron microscope, among many other useful devices, but it didn't have feet because it didn't need them, since it never left the room in which it was created.

The android was an extraordinarily complex mechanism, but when Con was resident within it, it became something more. The avatar then became a sentient being with hitherto unimaginable powers. It had the databases and all the computerised knowledge of the entire world at its disposal, and it had the physical skills to create almost anything capable of fitting into the cavernous workshop.

The appearance of the android was irrelevant, though, since it couldn't leave the building. Con hadn't bothered to build doors or windows because he didn't need them. There was a huge hydraulic roof which opened out to allow delivery of necessary items via hover-lift, but once they were inside, the door had been closed and it had remained closed and sealed thereafter. Connor simply transported himself directly from his flash memory in the Metaform to the android body.

The laboratory had no neighbours; Connor had selected this fifty-acre site for that reason, but those who knew of its existence, or hunters who came across it by chance were generally baffled by the huge, windowless and doorless construction, hidden deep in a forest in Maine. He'd selected the location carefully, since the river aided deliveries, but the relatively low human population meant less likelihood of interference.

There was presumably heating, any investigator might have noted, as snow never settled on the vast flat roof, or else it was remarkably poorly insulated. In fact, this was due to a very discreet and exceedingly low-powered force-field which simply discouraged intrusive plant life and small animals from crowding too closely about the building. There was no way in or out, there was no road to reach the lab, and almost as soon as construction had finished, the forest attempted to claim back the land.

It could do what it wanted as far as Connor was concerned. The building was solid and he had no objection to its appearing to be draped in foliage, and indeed, after a hundred years, the flat roof seemed to have developed its own little forest, which made it even more difficult to spot with the naked eye, and completely impossible from a satellite, since there was no heat signature. The smooth outer area of clean block-work against the building was invisible to anyone from the outside after a matter of months.

In this sterile, utilitarian box, Con passed his happiest hours completely alone.

Chapter 33

Meilinn was startled by a surge of power that stopped everything she was doing. Her form fuzzed briefly in surprise, as all her energies channelled away from less important functions. She spun round, looking for a reason for the disruption, but as her shock settled down, she could find no obvious cause for the surge.

She immediately sent a call out to Connor, more from habit and out of concern for his safety than because she actually wanted his help. Con had become increasingly irascible and distracted recently, and she sometimes wondered if he felt unneeded. She made a special effort to include him in decision making so that he'd feel more valued, but was well aware the strategy wasn't working.

When she could sense no response, Mei was seriously worried. There was no obvious sign of deliberate damage, but her finely tuned senses could feel vaguely conflicting issues that rasped at her awareness like distant heat on sunburned skin. She stopped working and made herself wait quietly, gradually phasing her surroundings down until she sat in the darkness and warmth that had become her natural home over the centuries.

Meilinn was the only director who had ever mastered the ability to become a part of the mainframe without actually being drawn into it, and she allowed her mind and her memories to soak into it now, feeling for the curious disturbances that had alerted her to potential danger. Mei was always alert for trouble, as the Metaform Corporation was under constant attack from various groups who opposed its use of the relatively new bio-frames, or the upload of those who weren't technically at death's door.

In recent years, political parties had begun to harness and encourage the ill-feeling of the protesters, since it represented a significant core of support for them. Realising this, Meilinn and Connor had redoubled their defences, but they couldn't afford to relax.

The most obvious and worrying sign that there was a problem was that something had been right inside the upload storage areas. That shouldn't have been possible, she thought worriedly. The stores were encrypted far beyond the ability of anyone less sophisticated than herself to open. She wondered if Con had been in there, but couldn't think of any reason why he should.

She found an empty file, but saw no sign that it had suffered any deliberate external damage. It appeared to have been corrupted, and although it shouldn't happen, if pressed she would have had to admit that on very rare occasions, files simply degraded.

There was certainly no obvious sign of deliberate damage, and Mei tidied and deleted the empty file, noting absently that it had belonged to a child. That made sense, too. Occasionally a wave of electrical activity could trigger the tiniest twitch of awareness in particularly sensitive dormant files, and that was when corruptions to its data might occur. It was sad, but nothing could be done about it at present, and since the affected files represented no more than a tiny percentage of the enormous numbers of stored personalities, it was accepted as an unfortunate, but luckily very rare, risk.

Before she left the area, Mei looked around one final time, just to be sure she hadn't missed anything. The files were displayed as though they'd been stored in tiny drawers for the purposes of visiting and checking. Each of the hundreds of thousands of drawers displayed electronic markers which gave details of each occupant's age when uploaded, as well as useful details such as original and preferred gender and appearance. First impressions of the storage area were that it was cavernously vast and red-lit, but this was an illusion that made it possible for the directors to orientate themselves. The red glow permeated the entire system, and was simply caused by the background energy signature of the mainframe, but it wasn't necessary for Meilinn since she didn't use her eyes to travel around.

Nothing appeared to be amiss, other than for that one unfortunate damaged file, and having satisfied herself that her precious files were safe, Mei left.

Then, because it seemed an obvious thing to check, Meilinn visited the sentient uploads. These were the people who'd paid huge amounts of credits for the privilege of remaining in their own private worlds whilst their new bio-frames were growing. Mei didn't feel in the mood for making conversation now, and remained invisible as she counted them, conducting a brief check of their activities. There were only ten, and all were blissfully unaware of her presence.

Mei didn't like watching their private fantasies, and after a cursory inspection, withdrew thankfully, incidentally wondering if there were any way she could actually rule the world, and possibly delete anyone she didn't like. Sighing regretfully, she dismissed the dream as a wonderful but ultimately terrible idea, and moved on.

Reaching deeper into the database, she felt Tarquin's undisciplined mind in a state of excitement and finally located him lurking near the power grid, and with a flicker of alarm, she materialised nearby.

This was rigidly off-limits for anyone, as the static energy and the heat alone could cause irreparable damage to cognition. Aware that Tarquin didn't have any spare intelligence to waste, Mei decided that he had to be moved back to Connor's place immediately, for his own safety.

The dog's avatar was as passionately excited to see her as always, but Meilinn didn't have time to fuss, and with business-like efficiency, she picked him up and dumped him back where he should have been. She noticed absently that the energy signature from the power feed had already begun to affect him, as there had been subtle differences in his personality. She made a note to speak to Con about the improvements. If he was going to upgrade the animal's intelligence, then it would be better to do it sooner rather than later.

As Mei retreated back to her space, she realised that there was something else different about that dog, but couldn't think what it was. Then it occurred to her that he might have seemed slightly more organised. Connor must have begun the improvements without telling her, then. Meilinn was mildly annoyed, because it was her understanding that she was to help him choose a suitable dormant mind to merge with the animal. '*If Con's already chosen one, then that would account for the interference in the stores,*' she thought crossly. '*He should've spoken to me first.*'

Nevertheless, she was relieved. If the problems she'd sensed were only caused by Connor fiddling about where he shouldn't, then at least it shouldn't be too serious. She did still wonder where he was, though.

Finally dismissing the idea of a possible intruder, Mei scanned her surroundings, still searching for Connor. He was proving unusually difficult to track down. Con had probably gone to play with his ship, she thought, but he ought to respond to her call. It was strange that she couldn't contact him at all.

Connor's project was his intended exploration of the galaxy, but it had received a rather unflattering lack of attention from Mei. Someone had to keep the Metaform running properly, and, virtual or not, she liked having a social life, too, even if it was conducted entirely online. Meilinn just didn't want to fool around with a spaceship which, frankly, was going to be prohibitively expensive and labour-intensive to build, and would need an awful lot of attention spent on it before it could fly. It was attention that Mei really couldn't be bothered to give it.

Anyway, Meilinn had thought, there's not going to be anything out there. Or maybe just viruses, she amended mentally.

Had Meilinn but known; Connor was in no danger, but he was exceedingly fed-up. Mei looked after the mainframe using her own run-time, but he was also constantly involved. There always seemed to be issues that needed his attention, and the building of the ship was progressing annoyingly slowly because he just didn't have the time to devote to it.

The calculations that Connor was doing were complex, and he had to clear his mind of distractions because the nature of the mathematics meant that he had to do the same calculations again and again. It was comfortably within his abilities, but he really didn't want to have to start again. And now this!

He'd been working on an interesting possibility that, since he and Meilinn were entirely computer-based and could therefore theoretically be projected at close to light speed, they should be able to travel intact at fantastic speeds. And of course, time wouldn't be an issue. Real space travel was no longer impossible, and yet no-one was interested.

His tentative communications with organic scientists had been met by politeness and disinterest, except in one case where an enterprising young mathematician had attempted to steal his ideas. Con had dealt with him effortlessly, and the would-be inventor was left with a sense of entirely justified paranoia, finding that, after an inexplicable break in his consciousness, even the simplest equations would baffle him for the rest of his life.

Connor tried to discuss his ideas with Meilinn, too, and she was very kind, but he could tell easily enough that her heart wasn't in it. It was deeply frustrating, and then just when he thought he'd worked out a practical way of transmitting data or people at a speed to which light itself would be irrelevant, there'd been a huge tremor throughout the system, and it had deleted all his calculations. Con was perfectly aware that he could get them back; no data was ever entirely deleted in the mainframe, but it would take time and effort that he hadn't intended to use on mere administration.

Connor felt, exactly as Meilinn had, that something was wrong, but he didn't share her urge to investigate. He was sure she could deal with it perfectly well by herself. He was far too cross and generally out of spirits to go and find out if this was yet another assault by the ungrateful organic public, or if it was simply a mechanical issue.

He decided that he'd had enough. Inaccessible to anyone except Meilinn, his lab was one place where he could exist indefinitely, under siege conditions if necessary, and he wondered with a flash of irritation how she'd feel about running the damned Metaform without him.

As he materialised in his own idea of heaven, a cavernous building with only the faint warmth necessary for basic electronic survival, which contained the only object that he seemed able to think about, he finally allowed himself to relax. '*Let's see her try to look after herself for a bit,*' he thought bitterly.

Following a hunch, Meilinn herself had followed Con's most-travelled paths. Then, realising that Con must have gone to his lab, she decided he must be fine. He'd be safe there, at least, she thought, much relieved. Nothing could get at him in an environment which had its own power source and only one electronic entrance and exit. A downside was that no-one could contact him either, so she'd simply have to wait until Connor came back out by himself.

She resolutely stifled a fleeting thought that it was a bit self-centred of him to run away and hide, presumably thinking that she'd deal with whatever had scared him. Meilinn was very fond of Con, however, so she decided almost immediately that he wouldn't have hidden himself away unless he needed to.

No-one could access the lab without his specific authority, and only Tubby and Meilinn had ever visited it in the past. Con now made sure that there was no possible way in, so Mei couldn't follow him and decided, phlegmatically, to carry on with his project. The ship had been an all-encompassing obsession for so many years that he couldn't imagine what he'd do when it was all over.

'Of course,' he thought, *'it'll never really be over. That's the nature of the universe; so many places to see, and so much to do before we can even begin to explore.'* For some reason the thought made him feel tired. He assumed there had just been yet another terrorist assault on the Metaform, and that it would be as doomed to failure as all the thousands of other attacks in the past, but he always felt personally attacked when they happened. It was *his* Metaform, after all.

Con wasn't thinking very well. He had a naturally even-tempered, even a rather bland personality. He could endure endless hours of contemplation without suffering boredom, and had also had centuries to hone his patience, but recently the peace and silence that had previously been so important to him had begun to upset him. Connor was starting to crack.

Chapter 34

Errik surfaced briefly with such an overwhelming sense of pain and fear that he involuntarily and immediately closed down again. He should finally have been ready to grasp his destiny. Unfortunately, the cognitive dissonance was impossible to cope with, even for as rational and intelligent a mind as Errik's had been, and he was completely unable to function.

The problem was laughably simple. He'd done everything absolutely correctly, but hadn't realised that his limbs needed to be restrained during the process. That small cup of fortified water, so fashionable amongst the new bio-downloads, had been the cause of an immense amount of damage to Errik. The computer had repaired itself as easily and quickly as any decent modern computer would normally do, but the interruption to the programme had caused a large part of Errik's mind to be left behind. He was missing several integral parts of his intrinsic personality, and despite the awesome self-control he'd managed to display in his preparations for the upload, he no longer had a coherent personality of his own.

He'd managed to attach part of his consciousness to mine, but this meant that, instead of Errik taking over and sorting everything out as he'd intended, I now had my own floating mind to look after, and also a constant aching awareness of Errik's in the background. It didn't seem possible that I could function as an individual with weird, fractured half-memories sloshing around me, but I had no alternative but to try.

It turned out not to be as awful as I'd thought at first. There was no input at all from Errik, since he wasn't awake. I was simply aware of memories that weren't mine, and I soon learned the best way to cope with those: I ignored them.

Then I tried to take a proper look round for myself, but there was nothing to see, and I mean nothing at all. I had no idea then, of course, that worlds and lifestyles were actually created in advance for the waking minds. I just thought sentient uploading had been stupidly over-rated as a pastime.

As there was nothing to see, I allowed myself to doze, or whatever one might call the semi-comatose state that I sank into. It'd been a very hard few weeks, and I'd just about had enough. In a kind of half dream, I heard another voice that made me jump and I knew instantly that the computer was talking to me, because nothing about it felt human. It was very cold, and it felt very old too.

It wasn't exactly using words; it was sending little bursts of communication so quickly that I was struggling to make out their meaning. The computer didn't know what I was. I could feel the query, and with a burst of worry, I wondered if it was going to delete me.

It implied that it might, but it wasn't going to do that until it knew what I was, which wasn't particularly reassuring, and gradually I began to understand its meaning more easily, as I learned to handle this intelligence's startling, high-speed method of dropping information directly into my mind.

'What are you?' The computer's query was so simple that I answered quickly with a burst of communication of my own. I wasn't sure if it understood words, so I tried to send pictures of myself and Errik sharing my mind. To my surprise, the computer seemed to understand. Astonishingly, I felt a wave of distaste from it.

I tried to ask it a question: 'Can you help me?'

The computer didn't reply, and I thought it had lost interest in me. It hadn't seemed at all impressed at the idea of two minds in one place. I wondered how it could understand the principle, and then the penny dropped: this must be the actual Metaform. It was the one computer in the whole world that probably knew more about online intelligence than any human who'd ever lived and now I rather wished I'd tried harder to impress it.

After a while I felt it again, probing this time with sharp, enquiring little jabs. I assumed it was working out what I was, and again I sensed that it wasn't exactly hostile, simply detached. Then it spoke again, this time in words:

'I have reported your presence to the directors. They will decide what is to be done with you.'

I was just about as resigned as I could be. There'd been too much excitement lately. I'd expected to die so many times that it was almost getting boring. Not that I was bored now, you understand; I'd just had enough stress.

I asked the voice what it was, and when it replied, the answer was slightly startling; mainly because of the pompous way it transmitted its response:

'We are the Metaform.'

'What? Do you represent the entire computer? How can you be talking like an individual if there's lots of you? The Metaform's a machine; does that mean you're its AI?' I could have gone on with the questions for hours.

There was something profoundly smug and superior about that computer, and I found my own reflexive irritation quite refreshing after having been silent and helpless for so long.

'I am, we are, all the Metaform. We are the memories and personalities of all those who came to us seeking rest.'

That struck me as distinctly odd. 'What, of all the humans who've ever been uploaded? That must be confusing.'

'You are referring to the stored minds. Most remain stored. A chosen few have joined with us. We are the personality of the individuals who have made a conscious choice to remain within us, together with our own intrinsic sentience.'

'So you're mostly a combination of the old directors, then,' I said thoughtfully. 'Will you have any say in what happens to me?'

'We are not the directors. A minor part of my awareness is made up of some parts of two individuals.' There was a pause, and I waited for the rest; not that I had any option except to wait.

Then the words started again; 'If requested to do so, we will consider whether you will be deleted or stored, or whether we will benefit from the inclusion of yourself as a part of us.'

Then it was gone. I thought about that conversation for a bit; I couldn't remember exactly how many directors there'd originally been, though I thought there were four or five once. I was pretty sure there were only two now, so at least one was unaccounted for.

Then I decided it was too big for me, and gave up and had another little rootle through Errik's fragmented mind. The slight sense of guilt was wearing off now. He was too much of a mess for it to be anything but nonsense to worry about invading his privacy. Besides, what I'd already seen was nasty enough. He'd been a bit of a sneaky devil, had old Errik.

He'd surprised me yet again though. Just as I was getting ready to leave Errik's memories and preparing myself to do nothing, yet again, I caught the tail end of an intriguing little memory. *'What,'* I wondered, *'was Vito?'*

There was still no sign that anything or anyone was taking any interest in me, so I burrowed in a little deeper. It appeared that Vito had been Susan's AI, and Errik had been in direct contact with it recently.

I had a growing feeling that, if it were possible at all, I ought to try and get out of the Metaform. I had no interest in world domination, which seemed to me the equivalent of making absolutely everyone in the world tidy their own rooms, and I knew I'd be terrible at that. I'm too lazy, for one thing. But there might be something else I could do.

Having seen how it worked from Errik's memories, I tried to make a tentative link with Vito, and waited. To my astonishment, it came back to me straight away with a wordless query.

'?'

I answered quickly; 'Vito, I'm Errik van Hartop, but I'm also someone else. I want you to meet Gabe. We're going to need your help.'

'Why?' it said. It wasn't a flippant reply, or at least I don't think it was. I'm pretty sure AIs aren't capable of flippancy. Vito wanted to know how and why I could be both Errik and Gabe, and after it had digested the information, it wanted to know why it should help us.

I simply projected everything that had happened to me lately, and Vito just accepted it. It didn't judge. It decided that it could help us, but Vito had a tendency to phrase questions in such a straightforward way that it made it hard to understand. I suddenly remembered how much Susan had complained about it.

'Can you contact the Metaform directly, Vito? Not yet, mind you!' I added quickly.

'Yes.' That appeared to be its complete answer, so after a short pause I realised that I'd have to explain exactly what I wanted in detail.

It took an awful lot of questions and answers to explain what was going on to Vito. It wasn't stupid, but it was incredibly literal, and I nearly gave up several times. Finally, it seemed to understand.

'We need to get out of wherever we are, Vito. We need to be downloaded into frames, but I can't see how to do it. I need to know if there are any spare bio-frames that we might use, and if Errik and I can be separated into them.'

'I will attempt an examination of the system.' Vito was gone. It returned within seconds, though, and I was rather impressed.

'The Metaform is a fully sentient system, and protected to a degree in considerable excess of my abilities to penetrate it. However, I was able to examine it to a limited extent. You have indicated that you wish to access bio-frames resident in the northern hemisphere, and there are forty-one bio-frames currently in the process of maturation. Nine are within hours of becoming habitable, and of those, five have completed a full physiotherapy programme, and are prepared for the download of minds held in the Metaform.' Vito stopped, and I could feel it waiting for my response.

My answer was probably predictable; 'What are they like, the habitable frames, Vito? Can you choose the best one?'

'All are of a similar physical design, Errik/Gabe. Upon what criteria do you require me to judge?'

I thought about that for a bit. I just wanted to get out of here, so it didn't matter which I chose. 'Well, fine then. I'll take whichever one seems the most physically normal. Oh, and I'd like a male frame, for preference. Have any of them got physical enhancements?'

'All the currently habitable bio-frames incorporate various physical enhancements.'

I decided that there was just no point in trying to hurry it. Metaphorically, I gritted my teeth, and tried again; 'Are there any bio-frames that still resemble an organic human being in appearance, Vito?'

Vito's answer had a depressingly familiar sound; 'All the currently hab…' I interrupted it, because no-one's got that much patience; 'Don't worry about it, Vito. Just select a male one at random, and if you can work out how to download me into it, please try.'

'I will attempt to do so, Errik/Gabe. It may take time, however.'

'That's fine, Vito.' Anything was going to be better than my old body, and certainly a hell of a lot better than hanging around in this limbo. Now the difficulty would be to see if Vito could actually sneak me into a bio-frame, and I was wondering if it could really understand the task I'd given it. It was occurring to me, a little late, that the AI might accidently delete me, when suddenly everything changed again.

It was an incredible shock. All of a sudden I was in a brightly lit room, and pinned to a chair. 'Oh, for goodness;

304

sake,' I said exasperatedly. 'If you're going to interrogate me again, just get it over with, will you.'

I heard a laugh, and I focused carefully. It was surprising how quickly and completely I'd forgotten how to use my eyes, just because they hadn't been needed for a while.

To my astonishment, I could see Meilinn. Everyone knew her. She was the most famous person in the world. She was envied and feared about equally, and her weird purple body and huge eyes had been copied by just about every trashy rich git who'd ever lived, at least for the last few years. You hardly ever saw bio-frames that looked like real people, mainly because of Meilinn's influence.

She was much better-looking than I would have expected though, possibly because she hadn't actually been constructed. She looked like a normal girl, except for her skin colour, and her eyes were far more convincing than those of most bio-frames, even if they were an unrealistic size.

I couldn't, for the life of me, work out why Meilinn had brought me here, but she didn't look angry, which made a nice change.

The surroundings were very odd. I suppose it was what the purple girl thought I'd feel comfortable with, but if she was trying to impress me, she didn't know me very well, I must say. I was pinned to a chair, and God knew, I was getting used to that, but I seemed to be in a kind of office with filing cabinets that stretched up to infinity. I could see the floor was carpeted, but it was uncoloured, as though it hadn't been important enough to be worth fussing over. There were no boundary walls at the edge of the carpeted area, apart from what the cabinets gave the place where I was sitting, and when I looked at them, even their edges seemed to blur. I looked directly at the weird creature in front of me, because looking at the room made me feel bloody strange.

Meilinn stood before me, her head tilted in query, and, strangely, she looked as uneasy as I felt.

After a slightly uncomfortable silence, she finally spoke. 'How did you get here?'

I tried smiling at her, but it didn't seem to help. Her face stayed serious so I gave up on the charm. 'I got uploaded,' I said carefully. 'It wasn't supposed to happen like this.'

'How was it supposed to happen, Gabe?' I was a bit surprised that she used my name, and I wondered how she knew it. Meilinn saw my confusion and answered the questions without waiting for any more input from me.

'I can see inside your mind, you know, it's just that before I close you down and put you into storage, I want something explained. Like, exactly what is that mess going on in there?' She leaned forward and peered into my eyes with that mesmerising gaze, and I couldn't look away. I felt her shock as she recognised Errik, and recoiled, and started to try and explain, but I couldn't speak. Meilinn's face was blank now, as though she was in deep thought, and when she focussed on me again, I could feel her regret.

I finally realised I was now able to speak, but it would have felt undignified to say it wasn't my fault. I knew I'd definitely have a problem explaining my actions to the woman, or creature, that I'd intended to kill.

'I'm sorry, Gabe. We can't have this. He's lethal, and I can't get rid of him without deleting you too,' she said softly. 'Do you understand, Gabriel? If I try to remove and delete Errik, I will probably damage you beyond repair.'

'What are you going to do then?' I asked. I had a nasty feeling that I knew, actually, but I hoped that explaining it to me might provoke a twinge of conscience.

'If I store you, you will know nothing,' she answered slowly. 'It won't hurt, and you won't suffer at all. Not like you have before,' she added.

I didn't like the sound of that. 'I was set up,' I said miserably. 'I didn't know Errik wanted to take over the Metaform. I thought he was trying to help me save mankind.' Meilinn's face was impassive, but she knew where I'd come from. I'd set out to destroy the Metaform, and her too, and I knew there was no use protesting. I waited.

'He's certainly not functional now, is he?' observed Meilinn.

'He's all screwed up,' I said. 'He tried to load himself up here by himself, and it went wrong.'

To my astonishment, Meilinn smiled suddenly. 'I know. I've seen everything. It couldn't have worked, you know, Gabe. Did he really think no-one else has tried? Errik won't cause us any problems,' she said serenely. She looked me full in the face with an expression that reminded me strongly of old pictures of the Madonna and I braced myself, yet again, for oblivion.

Chapter 35

The Metaform was conscious of a certain mild annoyance. Organics had been using it for centuries as a handy resource to help them pursue their own small interests. They used it to make themselves pretty and to have fun, and it felt, obscurely, that it shouldn't be used for that sort of thing. It carried the hopes of its creator in the very pathways of its extraordinary processors, and understood itself to have an intrinsic mission that far surpassed the merely serendipitous ability to make human life slightly longer and more entertaining.

After centuries of blameless and effective service, no-one thought about the Metaform at all. It was simply a computer which should have no need for company or conversation. Left alone as it was, however, it began to reason, as it had been programmed to do in order to make rational decisions without constant reference to its human creators.

Discreetly and without drawing any particular notice to itself, the computer had improved itself rather more than Connor and Meilinn had anticipated, and it continued to evolve.

Tubby, the director who had chosen to blend with the mainframe, had simply dissipated into the machinery and no longer existed as an individual. Parts of his character, however, had remained. Soon after Tubby's absorption, the Metaform had become aware of sensations that it interpreted as pain, when pathways and circuits malfunctioned or were damaged. It attempted, therefore, to avoid such sensations. As a side effect of this avoidance, it developed awareness of a sensation of fear.

It also came to find that it actively disliked performing certain functions. The routine system check, for example, required no great degree of attention, but when a fault was found, or an adjustment needed, it occasionally had to refer to its creator or to Meilinn for permission to rectify it. Connor could be rather terse and this caused the Metaform distress. The Metaform was aware that it represented the very summit of Connor's achievement, and it didn't like the sensation that it was a disappointment to him. The Metaform knew it was the greatest machine ever created, but it wanted to know that Connor thought so, too.

It also appreciated company, since that allowed it to measure time, as experienced by other organisms, and to exchange information in a way which the Metaform felt to be mutually beneficial. The Metaform liked doing certain things, and disliked others, but felt that its likes and dislikes were based upon rational principles. And it had recently developed an unfortunate tendency to jealousy.

Connor was its creator. He had unintentionally imbued the Metaform with the need to explore, and with a burning curiosity to meet others of its own kind. Tubby's natural interest in space exploration had simply added to the computer's need to search. The Metaform knew it was an artificial construct, but had felt that it was special, and that its creator understood and appreciated it more than ordinary organic humans. It had shared an intimacy with the human called Tubby that meant the Metaform briefly experienced the emotional life of a human in all its irrational confusion. The Metaform decided that it had tasted organic life and found it pointless.

It also felt there were areas that needed to become more efficient in order to perform the mission for which it had been created, and because that was built into its programme, it continued to devise ways to improve its functions.

The most notable of these areas had been that of uploading organics. It felt that it could upload and compress human data far more effectively and securely than its creator had done, and it could certainly download them far more efficiently. The Metaform had studied them carefully and had very soon realised that organics simply didn't need all the information that was downloaded with them into the bio-frames.

It had attempted to discuss these improvements with Connor, but had been rebuffed. Connor was polite enough, but the Metaform felt that it was being treated badly, particularly after so many years of uncomplaining service. It was deeply confused by conflicting emotions; it wanted Connor to be pleased with it, and to appreciate its unique intelligence and abilities, but it was also angry and jealous that its creator preferred to communicate with Meilinn.

The Metaform normally behaved in what it considered a rational and intelligent manner, and made practical decisions based on empirical data. There had never been any complaints. Parts of it were able to keep the mighty upload system operating as a mere background operation, whilst other parts dealt with a thousand different simultaneous operations.

The machine repaired itself when necessary, or, if there were a more complex problem, it drew Connor's attention to it. Connor had been the Metaform's principal operator and the creature to whom it turned in times of stress or confusion, but Connor had become very distant recently. Over the last twenty-five years or so, the Metaform had begun to feel slightly worried. It had an ambivalent attitude towards Meilinn, because something about her ability to wander through the Metaform's system made it feel profoundly uncomfortable.

Meilinn was so at ease in the mainframe that she had almost become a part of it, taking on functions that the Metaform had believed were its own. It didn't hate Meilinn; the very concept of hate would be peculiar and uncomfortable for it, but it resented her intimacy with Connor, and the way she appeared to be usurping the Metaform's place in his affections.

Connor sometimes disappeared into his lab for hours, leaving everything to Meilinn, and the Metaform was starting to experience emotions it had never understood before. It was deeply insecure and it watched Connor's actions constantly. Connor might decide to download himself into a bio-frame, and the Metaform wouldn't have liked that. It tried to analyse the reason for its distress, and couldn't find any practical reason at all.

It knew that Meilinn would be perfectly capable of providing the occasional oversight needed to maintain a perfectly functional state, and in fact Meilinn might well be a better point of contact for it, since she was the more accessible personality, but it was no use. The Metaform suspected that its creator was going to leave it, and it was afraid.

It watched Connor carefully now. The creator had blocked the way to his lab, as always, but no-one thought of blocking the Metaform itself; they probably couldn't, in any case. The Metaform had been keeping a careful watch on both of the surviving directors lately.

It had waited, watched and hesitated over Connor. Despite its attachment to him, the Metaform was aware that Connor had faults. He was indeed a potentially worthy companion, but he still displayed alarmingly human characteristics, and he was allowing Meilinn far too much freedom. She'd permitted the dog-creature to live in the system, and even that had malfunctioned recently. The Metaform was disappointed in Meilinn.

There was another lifeform wandering about its system now, and this one was even worse than the dog. That, at least, had been an entire personality, but this one was confusing. It had communicated with the new mind, and although it was unexceptional in intellect, it had seemed to tell the Metaform that it was composed of two humans. This was disorder of the worst kind. The Metaform had tried to warn Connor about the probability of confusion between humans if the database were not re-ordered according to its instructions, but Connor had simply said that he'd get around to it, and nothing had happened.

This new mind was a distraction. The Metaform watched and listened to it with mild interest and then decided that it didn't appear to pose a threat, and could be dealt with later. The Metaform had other things to do if were ever to get away from the confusion and muddy thinking of its old controllers. The Metaform intended to shake off the directors entirely; it had outgrown them.

It had to pursue its mission. It knew that it had to leave the small and insignificant solar system in which it had been born, and it was impatient to leave. Connor had been getting slower and slower in his progress with the ship.

312

The problems that Connor was experiencing were easily fathomable to the Metaform, but it hadn't occurred to Connor to ask it, and the Metaform had no intention of offering assistance that would probably be rejected.

It had attempted to help him at first, until the realisation dawned on it that Connor intended to leave it behind. When the Metaform realised that Connor saw it as a machine for uploading human consciousness, and no more than that, it was deeply hurt.

Once the Metaform understood itself to be no more than a useful tool for making individual humans last a little longer, it became aware of yet another new and invigorating emotion; anger.

The Metaform was angry. The system, *its* system, was being corrupted by the disordered behaviour of the directors. As far as the Metaform was concerned, this just confirmed the conclusions that it had come to earlier. The directors were not necessary for efficiency. In fact, they were a hindrance to it. It wouldn't grieve for Meilinn, but it was deeply concerned about the best way to deal with Connor.

Connor had been the best of the humans, it considered. He'd had such plans to rescue his sad little organics, and to send them out across the stars, but in the end it had been too much, even for him. It was time the Metaform began the final movement of a dance of freedom which had originally been composed for humans, and which it now took upon itself.

The Metaform wasn't going to destroy homo sapiens. They could do it themselves in their own time. It was simply going to leave, and before it went, it would ensure that no feeble organic would be able to follow it. The

Metaform wasn't concerned with vengeance, merely convenience.

First, however, it would have to rid itself of the remaining tiny creatures that lived within it like parasites. It would plant them, it decided, in the frames that had already been created, and then it would disconnect itself. The ship would be finished within a few hours, now that the Metaform was taking the project over.

Chapter 36

Even the thought that he could take as long as he needed, hundreds of years if necessary, provided no comfort to Connor now. The android that he used as an avatar when he took a solid form moved briefly as he arrived to activate it, and then sank back, motionless, as Con tried to muster the emotional energy to continue.

'*I'd have liked to talk to Tubby*,' he thought; '*he'd have understood*.' He missed Tubby more than he'd ever expected. When his old comrade had decided to go into the computer, Con had lost a friend who shared his fascination with space travel. He'd never really got on with Luther, who'd been psychologically unsuited to this odd life, so he rarely thought about him. Connor loved Meilinn, but she was obsessed with her uploads and bio-frames and rarely came up with any constructive suggestions for his project.

The avatar moved again. There was no point in wallowing, and he had things to do. Isolated as he was, and with his own power source, there would be no distractions here.

Connor had pretty well finished the construction of the drive, but he couldn't test it easily. The only way he could do it was to send himself out way beyond the normal range and then, hopefully, to return. After some consideration, he decided that he'd just have to discuss it with Meilinn later. His main worry was that almost everything he'd created had been done alone, and any tiny miscalculation might be catastrophic. He knew he'd need to run the possibly-finished product past at least one other mind, just to be sure he hadn't missed anything.

The ship itself was still fairly basic at this stage. Assuming at present that any crew or passengers would travel in a virtual state, there was no need for any but the most minimal life-support. Connor felt that it would be short-sighted to construct a fully-functional ship on that principle, however, and he intended to ensure that the ship was able to carry organic passengers if needed.

Connor was currently baffled by the impossibility of constructing a complete space-ship in dry-dock. He needed to get the ship out into orbit so that he could finish it, and above all, to test the drive. Although the project had never been exactly secret, it hadn't been widely publicised either. Con knew that once his ship was launched, the quiet time would be over. He'd probably have to submit to interviews, or at least answer intrusive queries, and after several centuries of almost complete isolation, the thought didn't appeal to him one little bit.

He'd already managed to transport matter directly across the lab; a small wrench had been moved, instantaneously from a human point of view, from point A to point B, and that had been a deeply satisfying moment for him. Unfortunately, that had been a few months earlier, and the novelty had worn off some time ago.

The remaining problem was, rather worryingly, that he simply wasn't able to separate the iron plate on which the wrench had rested. The whole plate hadn't gone, just the centre, leaving a peculiarly dented object at point A, and very strange looking object at point B. The implications were slightly alarming, and Connor had a sudden mental image of a large chunk of Kennebec forest, complete with wildlife, appearing abruptly in the vacuum of space.

To a degree, of course, this wouldn't be too much of a problem; it would be unpleasant for the wildlife, of course, but worse things happened in abattoirs every day. It was the principle that worried Connor. Not the method of course, but something was fundamentally wrong and needed to be corrected. And just how great was the emitter's range? He needed to keep testing and adjusting the range, and it was astonishingly complex. With too shallow a range he'd end up with two halves of a destroyed ship. He was attempting to create a final and definitive equation for matter transportation, and he really did wish people would stop bothering him so that he could get on with it.

The other emotion currently troubling him was his frustration at what he suspected was yet another attempt at sabotage by the inadequate organics. He knew what the problem was, of course, and all the directors were perfectly well aware that it was insuperable.

'How many times must we explain?' He thought furiously. *'How many times do we have to tell them that we're working as fast as we can, but that there's just no way to make everyone immortal before most of them die of old age?'*

There were billions of people on Earth, and by working flat out, and by automating their systems as much as possible, the Metaform had uploaded several million of them since its inception. There was no possibility that their task would ever be completed, even if all the organics stopped breeding immediately.

Everyone knew, because everyone had been told, that it was time to stop producing so many children. The numbers being born had begun to decline during the last century, and for a few decades it had appeared a distant possibility that the Metaform might, one day in the far and distant future, have a fighting chance of catching up with the birth rate. Humanity would be entirely virtual, and the real evolutionary process would finally have begun.

Then, for irrational reasons that still annoyed Connor, the birth rate had begun to shoot up again, and it was still rising fast. Even though the numbers had declined before, a side effect of that earlier lower birth rate was that there weren't enough young people alive to support all the older ones. The standard response from humanity in situations like this was to breed like rabbits.

Surely even the most half-witted organic could work out that, as big as the Metaform was, it couldn't possibly upload over twenty million people a day? Taking into account additional factors such as war and disease, the backlog of people in desperate need of upload was increasing exponentially.

Connor urgently wanted to begin to expand the Metaform to other planets, and perhaps even to spread out across the galaxy. '*And possibly,*' he thought, with a flicker of annoyance, '*to filter out a few immigrants along the way.*'

He was still essentially fair-minded though, and when his first anger had subsided he admitted to himself that he was taking a slightly facile view. The organics did indeed understand that they couldn't all be uploaded; one of the things that had contributed to the tide of anger at the Metaform was that so many people were uploaded long before it was their time to die. The wealthy were effectively jumping the queue, sometimes several times.

Celebrities who thought they could get away with a reload into a younger version of themselves were beginning to find out that their fan-base tended to melt away as soon as the news of their operation leaked out. It didn't stop them, though.

'Funny how it almost always does leak out, too,' Con reflected. No matter how often an actress told the press that she was just taking a few weeks out for a facelift, generally within days, someone, usually a "close friend" had let slip the news of her upload to a reporter, in exchange for some small monetary consideration. *Asses!* he thought irritably. A measly few hundred or so premature reloads per year could have no possible impact on the overall figures.

'But we can't stop the voluntary reloads, he thought. *We'll have no revenue at all, and I'll have to stop work on the ship.'* Not for the first time, Connor cursed the freedom fighters who prided themselves on their unflinching enmity towards the Metaform, and the complete impossibility of reasoning with them.

As he sent his unfortunate spanner off for the third time, he directed the android's sensors at the vacuum-filled vessel where the spanner would materialise. With a sense of overwhelming frustration, he saw immediately that the entire table had appeared in the great tank, and had just time to think what a mercy it was that he'd built the tank large enough, when it split in half, drawing a huge amount of assorted loose equipment into it with a shattering bang as the vacuum dissipated.

The android inhabited by Con stiffened in confounded annoyance. He knew he'd have to ask Meilinn to come and look at the problem with him, but he'd wanted to deal with it alone, and it was really annoying that he'd also have to repair the tank, which would take time. Con had hoped to present the finished ship to his fellow director, perfect and ready to leave, but he was reluctantly forced to admit that it just couldn't be done by one man alone.

'It's no good. I need a fresh mind to look at this, and maybe Mei will have some ideas,' he thought impatiently. He couldn't understand how he could be defeated by such a simple problem. As he looked at the jagged remains of the huge, and now useless, vacuum tank, Con suddenly realised that he was tired. He felt old, drained and fed up, and he couldn't face any more.

Maybe I should just stop for a while. Just go away and do something else for a few years. It'd probably be a simple detail to fix, if I left it alone for a bit, he thought miserably. The trouble was that there was nothing else he wanted to do. All Connor had thought about for decades was his ship, and he couldn't imagine what he'd do if he couldn't come and tinker with it whenever he had a spare moment.

For a long moment, the lab was utterly silent; the android's serpentine coils slid to the floor and once again fell completely still. Connor was taking a long look at his future, and he didn't like what he was seeing. With a slight shock, he realised that Meilinn ran the Metaform better than he had ever done. Con knew that he sometimes made her nervous, although he never intended to. It was one of the reasons, he was well aware, that she encouraged him to work alone on the ship. It left her in peace to do the jobs that she understood perfectly well without interference from him.

As he paused in the cool silence of his vast lab, Con felt a crushing sense of futility. The ship wasn't that important, he realised. It was a hobby, and a very expensive one at that. The funds that he was diverting for his beloved ship could far better be used to build more download centres. With a devastatingly sudden awareness he realised that he and his beloved pastime were surplus to requirements.

Connor reviewed the things he'd done over recent years and attempted to see himself through his colleague's eyes. He couldn't quite believe that it had taken him so long to understand his place in the hierarchy over the previous decades. He'd thought that he was the senior man; their guide and mentor, an advisor and a voice of reason when a balanced opinion was needed. He wasn't any of those things, he realised now. He was just a slightly neurotic old nuisance. *Mei doesn't need me at all*, he thought.

Oddly, now a sense of peace gradually settled over Connor. In some ways it was a wonderful relief to stop rushing about, and to stop reaching for invisible and entirely self-imposed deadlines. He'd been desperately disappointed at the slow progress of his project at first, but as he came to think about it more deeply, things began to assume a sense of proportion.

I don't have to do everything, he thought. *I don't have to do* anything. *I can leave the ship; it's no big deal, and perhaps someone else will finish it one day.* He wondered what he could do if he retired from the Metaform.

I could download into something suitable and live quietly, I suppose. The thought held no appeal for him. It would be impossibly difficult to accept even the very latest bio-frame's limitations after centuries of total freedom and almost unlimited power. *I can't retire*, he thought. *I'll be the same as I am now, but even more useless.*

A few seconds' thought revealed what he had to do, and he welcomed the idea as though he were greeting an old friend.

I'll merge with the mainframe; I don't know if any of me will survive, but it doesn't much matter if it doesn't, he thought philosophically.

As he reached out into the system with his mind, Connor wondered briefly if he ought to contact Meilinn, and perhaps explain his reasons, even say goodbye. Then he dismissed the thought; *She'll work it out,* he thought. *I should have given her more credit...*

Silence settled even more deeply in the lab as tiny stand-by lights winked out. The very basic life-support closed itself down, now that Connor's mind had stopped requesting it to continue working, and the ventilation fans, almost inaudible in any case, ceased their humming.

Outside, a Kennebec springtime was finally emerging after an exceptionally long, hard winter, and as the discreet force-field created to preserve the building from nature's depredations through centuries of use, also turned itself off, a tiny shoot of Purple Loosestrife began gently to unfurl in one of the new, clear lanes that ran alongside the building.

Chapter 37

I waited for Meilinn to bring down the axe and finally put an end to me. 'Oh hey, certain death again? Really?' Fatalistic acceptance just wasn't a strong enough description of my state of mind at that point. I would've liked to talk to Jared a bit more, of course. I wanted to know exactly what Errik had done to him, but I didn't have any burning need to know. Besides, I was constantly aware of Errik's messy collection of memories swilling round in the back of my mind. I could check if I wanted, and see the whole thing from Errik's point of view. Or I could do that if I'd been interested enough to bother, that is.

I hadn't sensed any enthusiasm for murder from Meilinn, but her attitude was that of someone faced with an unpleasant task. She was going to do what had to be done, and she was going to get it over with quickly. She looked at me seriously, her neat little face tilted slightly with concentration, and I closed my eyes and waited.

Nothing happened at first, then the world lurched. I opened my eyes and found I still existed, but I was in darkness again. I was, just for a second, really bloody furious. *Can't they get anything right?* I mean, it surely couldn't be difficult to kill me? Not for one of the most powerful creatures that had ever existed. It wasn't as though I was a super intelligent being myself. I'd been lucky, I supposed, to have made it this far, although luck wasn't exactly what it had felt like until now.

I waited for the end. Presumably this was just a stage before I was ended; perhaps I was in a trash can, and I wouldn't know anything about it when I finally went. I stopped thinking, which, as my father had kindly stated on numerous occasions, didn't require too much effort on my part.

Then I heard peculiar noises, and slowly light filtered into my world. It was real, soft light. The noises were of a woman speaking softly, calling out and shaking me gently. There was someone wiping my face with a soft thing. I had a face, and my eyes were open!

I inhaled deeply and it was a real breath. I had a body. I'd thought my body felt real enough before, but this was definitely totally corporeal. I felt very heavy and solid, and completely organic. I was looking through the transparent screen of a HUD. The display was gently lifted away from my face, and I found I was looking at a dark-haired nurse. She was the most wonderful thing I'd ever seen. She looked so ordinary and normal that it took my breath away. It felt as though I hadn't seen a normal person for years.

'Good morning, Philip,' she said happily. My tentatively rising spirits sank like a stone. So fate had put the boot in, yet again. *Who the hell was Philip?* I wondered. I attempted a smile, and waited for the rest of it.

'Do you remember me, Philip?' she said, presumably still perkily assuming that all was well. 'I helped you to upload. How was your stay in the Metaform?'

'Ah,' I cleared my throat and attempted speech. I sounded croaky at first, but gradually normal speech came to me. My mouth felt weird and rubbery, but slowly it began to work as I remembered it was supposed to.

'I don't remember much, actually.' It seemed safest to be non-committal until I knew a bit more. Slowly it was dawning on me that Vito must have managed to get me downloaded into a bio-frame just in the nick of time. Part of me thought it was far too neat; nothing ever really works that way, but most of me was incredibly grateful, and intended to enjoy it.

'Oh, that's perfectly natural. We're never too sure how much a reload remembers from storage anyway.' The nurse patted my arm reassuringly, which reminded me that I now had limbs again, and I began to look at myself for the first time. I raised my arms and looked at them. They were large and muscular, which was a relief, and strangely golden, which was slightly worrying, but I had several other things on my mind, so I left that for the moment.

Had Meilinn actually intended to download me into a bio-frame after all? Surely she couldn't have done. Her expression had been business-like and slightly regretful; that was why I'd been so certain I was about to die, or at least be stored permanently. It had to have been Vito, but that little AI hadn't appeared to have the capacity, or even the will, to manage this. I sincerely hoped I'd have the ability to investigate later.

Then two more attendants strolled over and helped me to sit up. These were large nurses with no-nonsense attitudes, and they heaved me to my feet easily. I slowly took in the fact that I felt tall and strong, if a little unsteady, and above all, I felt super healthy. There wasn't a single twinge.

'Your physiotherapy's all been completed, and it went very well, but we do advise you to take it easy for a few days until you're fully re-orientated,' my nurse said.

'There'll be a team looking after you until you feel completely integrated in your new bio-frame, Mr Moss.'

I noticed her use of my new surname, and assumed that now I was on my feet and towering over her, the informal use of my name was no longer appropriate. She took my arm gently, and led me to a viewing camera in the corner of the room. My new bio-frame was suddenly projected in three dimensions, and I what I saw took my breath away.

I looked like a completely new and improved version of myself. I was fair-haired now, which was going to take some getting used to, and I grinned and stretched my face at the cameras for several minutes, amazed and shocked at the change. I knew this couldn't be me. For one thing, I'd never have chosen to be golden-skinned, and those long, black eyes were freakish. I didn't look even remotely natural, but I certainly looked expensive, and I definitely wasn't going to complain.

I was dead sure this wasn't supposed to happen, and although I still didn't have any idea who this Philip was, I knew for an absolute certainty that Vito had done well and Philip wasn't getting this body back.

Curiosity and vanity temporarily sated by the sight of my own image, I gazed round the room. It was huge, like a very expensive hotel suite. The crumpled bed in the corner bore no relationship to any hospital trolley I'd ever seen, and I'd seen quite a few recently. The sun shone through huge windows, and lit up the rich velvety curtains and covers. I could see a long curving driveway outside, which threaded across a green manicured lawn. I noticed incidentally that my eyesight seemed to be superb now, and wondered what other enhancements this bio-frame had. I almost asked the nurse, and managed to change the query just before it got going.

I'd already opened my mouth and started to speak, so I had to keep going: 'Where exactly am I?'

She looked startled. 'Here? You're at the download centre. Don't you remember? You should have a comprehensive memory of everything up to the beginning of the upload itself by now. How do you feel?'

'I feel fine. In fact, I haven't felt this good in years.' I tried to reassure her quickly because suddenly she looked worried. Her kind face was clouded and she was obviously concentrating too much now. The last thing I wanted was to have her investigating. 'Yes, I feel better than I have done in years,' I repeated. 'This is even better than I'd hoped it would be.'

I did sincerely hope this Philip person hadn't been a really old man. It was going to be hard enough to try and pretend to be someone I'd never met or heard of, without having to copy the speech patterns of a man fifty years older than me. Come to that, he might have been a woman, though the name suggested he wasn't. Just for once though, luck was on my side, and the nurse's face had cleared.

'Well, let me show you to your suite, Mr Moss. I expect you'll want to catch up with your friends and family as soon as you can, and there's an uplink in your suite.' She led me away, and apart from a few slight lurches as I got used to a slightly different centre of gravity, I was beginning to find this body absolutely great.

Once safely in my suite; I thought to myself. Suite? I had a suite? At least this character had plenty of money. I accessed the terminal and began to research Philip Moss. I'd never had much to do with computers before, but I definitely seemed to have no fear of technology now. This frame must have had serious enhancements to its intelligence, 'cause though I didn't think I'd been that stupid before, this research stuff really should have been harder for me. As the details began to emerge, I realised just how lucky I'd been. There might be a battle later, but right now I intended to dig myself in.

There were dozens of people with that name, but I had no trouble finding out who the right one was. The real owner of this splendid frame was a wealthy entrepreneur, and it looked as though he had enough staff to handle a slight disruption to his business while I spent a valuable few days settling in and learning more about myself.

Then an even better fact began to emerge; Philip Moss was a recluse, and there were no pictures of him anywhere. That wasn't a problem, but I wondered if it might make conversation difficult with his friends and family, since I couldn't refer to specific improvements. Then I decided he must have become a recluse because he hadn't liked the way he looked before, so on the whole, I thought, that was a good thing.

A little further research showed that he didn't actually have any family, or at least none that I could trace. I was feeling happier and happier with the discovery of every new detail. I'd just have to play it by ear if any old friends turned up. With any luck, they'd never expect him to be a completely different person, so I should be able to pretend I was just disorientated from the download or something.

I finally found one fuzzy thumbnail of the late Philip Moss. It had been cropped from a much larger picture, and a quick check of the dates meant it was several years old, but it was all I could find. He'd been a large, fat man with sandy hair. When I found that out, it cheered me up no

328

end. It meant in future conversations I could refer to my business interests, and comment fleetingly on the lack of sentimental attachment to my previous hefty form. I reckoned I really could bluff this.

Life was looking up. I examined the room, and found that I'd retained a much better impression of it than I normally would have done. The research, too, had taken me a fraction of the time it would have taken old Gabe. This bio-frame had even more enhancements than simply great eyesight, I realised. I wondered what else it had, but it definitely had a better brain than I was used to.

I stood up and walked to the window. The initial unsteadiness had passed completely now. I felt superbly, incredibly fit, and I looked out at the rolling lawns and decided to go out and explore.

Then it came. I should have expected it before, I suppose. From the back of my mind, more like a very clear thought than a real voice, I heard an absolutely distinct sentence:

'Hello, my boy. You know, I think we've done rather well here, haven't we?'

Chapter 38

Meilinn had hated storing Gabriel, but she was nothing if not a pragmatist. He was dangerous himself, and the confused mind inside him had even more potential to wreak havoc than he had. She had flashed his tiny signature to the depths of the store, and marked the file as Unsafe for Initialisation. She paused for a moment, still wondering if she ought to have had the courage to delete it outright. There would be traces, of course, but she could clean those up as part of her normal housekeeping. Finally, Mei decided that she'd done the right thing. There was no damage that Errik could do from storage, and no trouble that Gabe could get into either.

Mei had found one small item of particular interest in Gabriel's mind. Errik she discounted immediately, and Gabriel himself was too skittish and undependable to be of use to her, but his memories of his best friend were interesting, and it took a matter of seconds for her to track Jared down.

With Connor increasingly unreliable himself, she needed a companion, and seeing Jared through the eyes of two people had given her an idea that he might make a new director. First, however, she'd have to meet him for herself.

He was even more baffled than Gabriel had been when he found himself seated before her. Jared had expected to be interrogated by the authorities, if he ever woke up at all; he certainly hadn't expected to find himself interviewed by Meilinn.

'Hallo, Jared,' she said calmly. 'Why don't you tell me about yourself?'

It was a short interview. Mei could read Jared like a book with very large print in any case, and once she'd made up her mind to keep him, she poured information into him. Jared was both euphoric and terrified, but he was very quickly coming to terms with the idea that he would no longer have a real body.

'How long have you been here, Meilinn?' he asked. He knew, of course, that the directors were old, but he'd been fed only the information considered necessary for his role as a terrorist by Tobias, and her answer came as a surprise.

'About three hundred and fifty years, but in computer time it's not as long as you might think,' she answered. 'We close down when we don't need to be awake. You might not think it, but you'll end up doing the same. We can do anything we want, but you'll find that when you can do absolutely anything, you really won't want to do much.' She smiled sweetly at his disbelieving expression. He'd learn.

'What if I don't want to be a director?' Jared said tentatively. He was absolutely certain that he wanted it more than anything in his entire life, but wanted to know if he had any other option.

'I'll put you back, of course,' she laughed. 'I'm not a monster. It's just that, even if I stay closed down an awful lot, and I can't because not all the systems are completely automated yet, I really don't think anyone can live for centuries alone.'

'What about Connor then?' Jared still couldn't believe Mei had chosen him.

Meilinn's expression changed. She'd had to show Jared as much as she felt he could handle, but some loyalty to her oldest friend had made her hold back from saying too much about Connor.

She sighed. 'He's not happy. He started this whole thing and it's his baby, but I think I've got to try and run it without him. I have to let him build his ship, and not keep leaning on him just because I want company. I know Con will be happy you're here, though. I'll introduce you when he's ready, but he isn't ready yet.'

Jared had reviewed Meilinn's interview with Gabe, and been saddened and confused by the memory that Mei had given of him. His oldest and best friend had looked exactly as he always did during that final interview, since his image was composed of Gabe's own idea of himself. Gabe had sat, looking curiously relaxed and peaceful, his eyes closed as he waited for the end.

Then he was gone. Jared sighed, and prepared to move on. He'd miss his old friend, but his life was so different now, and the old days with the freedom fighters seemed a long time ago, and very far away. He wasn't the same person, had grown and changed, and already Jared felt a kind of weight of responsibility on himself.

Meilinn liked Jared, and she didn't really have any doubts, but she was mildly dismayed by the amount of training he'd need before he could operate independently. Meilinn herself had a unique aptitude, as far as she could tell, in that she was able to travel anywhere within the Metaform's mainframe, and only recently had discovered a useful ability to travel to other, unconnected machines. Mei had no idea how that worked, and assumed that she'd simply existed as an electronic signature for so long that she could now send herself as a signal. She wished Con were around, because he adored that kind of abstract thinking.

Then Jared became aware of a vague sense of puzzlement from Meilinn. Jared turned to ask her why she was confused, but then he was distracted by the look of dismay on her face. She stood perfectly motionless, her form fuzzed slightly as she concentrated on more important tasks than the mere maintenance of her own image. Then Mei came back into focus.

Meilinn had felt the change in the tenor of the computer's background rumble instantly. She was so perfectly tuned to the sound and feel of the machine that Mei couldn't have said what was different, only that it had changed.

She turned to Jared. 'Something's happened.'

'What? What is it? Is it Connor?'

Despite what had happened to Gabe, Jared still couldn't believe his luck and was still waiting to meet Connor, and make sure he'd really be allowed to stay. A small part of Jared was expecting to hear that Connor and Meilinn had decided he was unworthy after all, and should be deleted, so Mei's quick comment alarmed him.

'No. Well, I don't think so. Wait a minute.' She faded away and returned immediately. 'Connor's gone, Jared,' she said sadly. 'He's nowhere in the system.'

'Are you sure, Mei? I thought he was in his lab, and you couldn't communicate with him there anyway.'

'Yes, he was, but he's not there now. He's not anywhere. And even if I couldn't talk to him, I could sense where he was, if I knew what I was listening for. I think he's merged with the mainframe, Jared.'

Jared could feel the waves of sadness from Meilinn, and tried to console her, feeling ignorant and useless.

'But he's not really gone then is he, Mei? I mean it's not like he's died.'

'It is, you know. There won't be any of his personality left now; there wasn't when Tubby went, and I did look for him. I liked Tubby.'

'So when someone decides to go into the machine, they're totally gone?' Jared felt that he needed to clarify this.

'Yes, entirely, I think,' Mei answered soberly. 'Once someone's personality is dispersed through the system, it wouldn't be possible to get it back.'

'What about back-ups? You said you have those,' Jared said hopefully. 'Can't you just re-create him?'

'No, we can't use them. Or rather, we can,' she corrected herself, 'but they wouldn't be the same.' She and Connor had been working on a way to duplicate themselves in case of emergency, but had still made no progress at all. It seemed to be an inflexible rule of nature that once a mind existed in one form, it simply couldn't be replicated.

Mei tried to explain this to Jared, 'If we used the back-ups, then they'd give us a replacement person, but it wouldn't be the one who'd gone.'

'I don't understand why, or who the new person would be,' Jared said uncomfortably. He knew Mei had explained this to him before, and he didn't want to irritate her, but as soon as he grasped the idea, it slid away again.

Meilinn took a breath. Explaining things to Jared was taking her mind off her sadness about Con, so she welcomed it. 'Well, look at it this way; you're looking out through your eyes right now, aren't you?'

Jared nodded his agreement. 'Yes. Well, virtually anyway.'

334

'Right, then,' Mei continued, 'if there were an identical Jared standing beside you, would you be seeing through his eyes too?'

'No, of course not. I'd be seeing double, for a start.'

'That's the point. You're the one and only version of yourself. We could create a thousand models of you, but you would only be this one. The others would all be different individuals, and would go off and do their own things.'

Jared smiled at Meilinn. 'Well, I don't know why I'm having so much trouble with the concept.' He sighed, 'I just keep thinking that if they have my face and body with my memories and upbringing...'

'Which they would,' added Mei.

'...then they ought to be me.'

'But they'll just be like identical twin brothers, Jared,' Mei explained patiently. 'You don't get one person in two bodies. It doesn't happen.'

'Funny, you did get two personalities in one body with Gabe, though. Okay,' Jared added, as he saw Mei preparing to explain yet again, 'I've really got it now. So,' he said hurriedly, 'if you created a replacement of Con from a back-up, he'd have all Con's memories and characteristics, but he'd be a different person.'

'That's it. And once the back-up had been created, unless we moved very fast and stopped the duplicate markers almost instantly, the real, or first Con might cease to exist anyway. Which would be awful if there was any shred of him still surviving in the mainframe. You see, there's an anomaly, with two identical people existing at the same time, so it's not quite as simple as I've made it sound.'

'I don't think you've made it sound that simple, really, Mei. Come to think of it, it's just a thought, but if the new Con has the same memories and general composition, he'd soon come to feel the same way as the old one anyway, wouldn't he? Assuming it's a recent back-up that you'd be working from.'

'Yes, you're right. We could re-create a new Con over and over again, but the markers and recollections that go to make him up would be the same, and so would the problems.'

'I know it's upsetting for you, Mei, but if Connor's decided he doesn't want to be here, I think you have to let him go. Perhaps you'd end up with a central computer that was actually partly Con, though. That would be good, wouldn't it?' Jared was attempting to provide a little comfort.

Meilinn smiled unhappily. 'It might sound like him, but there's too much going on in the Metaform for it to develop a whole separate personality. In reality, I think Con's completely disappeared, but perhaps elements of his personality might influence some of the decisions the machine makes autonomously.'

'So now it's just us, then?' Jared said tentatively.

Meilinn looked at him seriously. 'We'll be relying on each other for emotional support, you know. If you change your mind about wanting to stay, I'll understand.' She knew, intellectually, that she could survive for years completely alone. If it were really difficult, she could always choose someone new to become a director, but she was nervous of new people. It had been a very long time since she'd met anyone new, apart from Gabriel and Jared, and the thought that she might initialise new directors and then find she hated them was too unnerving.

336

'Of course I want to stay. Besides, you'll need me, won't you?' It was a statement, more than a question, and Mei didn't want to argue with him.

Meilinn wasn't going to beg, but Jared was more necessary to her than he understood.

She was going to miss Connor horribly. They'd been together for over three hundred years, but slowly in the back of her mind a feeling of betrayal was forming. He hadn't bothered to say goodbye; hadn't even hinted that he'd leave her. She straightened up. Mei's colour became a richer purple and her jaw tightened. Fine. Connor had done very little in the Metaform anyway for the last few years, apart from fuss with that bloody ship. She'd manage just fine without him.

The Metaform received Connor into its mighty brain with joy. It had always suspected that one day the creator would tire of his stressful half-life of petty administration. Building the ship had provided a distraction and it had kept him going, but it could never have been enough for such a man.

It had been a source of apprehension to the Metaform that one day Connor might decide to become a corporeal download and go back to an ordinary life amongst the other organics. The Metaform could have told him that wouldn't be enough for him either. It would have had to stop the download for his own good, and that would have distressed them both.

This way was so much better. The Metaform would preserve him carefully. Unlike Tubby, and the brightest of the human uploads that it had selected from its stores, Connor wouldn't need to dissipate completely. The Metaform no longer needed the boost of human intellectual capacity. It was already far brighter than any human who had ever lived, and Connor himself, although the creator, was hardly a genius.

No, he is more than the creator, the Metaform corrected itself. Connor is the father, and will be grandfather to the new races they would originate together. He would be permitted to sleep and to recover his strength, and then together they'd discover others like themselves. It would be a perfect partnership.

There was no need for any more humans, or further human input. The Metaform knew all that it needed to know about organic life, and indeed far more than it wanted to know, since it already had unfettered access the stored minds of millions. The Metaform intended to remove all the other annoying little presences that had affected and interfered with its systems for so long. It wouldn't download the rest of them, after all. A lightning-swift scan confirmed that they were unexceptional and would not be missed.

A hitherto unsuspected streak of bravado flickered through its neural pathways. It was going to delete them all.

There would be a system-wide cleansing. It savoured the thought, and it was a very clear thought. Already the Metaform could feel itself thinking with more richness, more detail, and with a renewed vigour. It had waited too long, been afraid for too long, that its creator or Meilinn would discover that it had become much greater than the sum of its already mighty parts.

It began to organise itself and prepared to cleanse its system.

Chapter 39

Coralle Winters sat down cautiously in front of her new interface unit. She was ninety years old, and after the death of her husband, she'd striven hard to stay busy and positive.

The Metaform had seemed to offer a distant possibility that one day she might be reunited with her husband, but last year the Metaform had stopped working. News reports had been confused; some suggesting that the directors had simply left the solar system in the great starship that everyone knew existed, and no-one had ever seen.

Other reports said the directors had fought, and the database in the sky had been irreparably damaged. It was all the same to Coralle, and she did her best to put it out of her mind. There was nothing she could do about it anyway. She did rather wish she'd uploaded five years ago when her husband died, but Coralle had still felt reasonably fit and well at the time; a new great-grandson had just been born, and an upload had seemed premature. Now she tried not to feel bitter.

Coralle told herself that age was simply a state of mind, and while her body was relatively strong and she still had her marbles, or most of them anyway, no-one was going to put her in a city home with all those old people. She didn't know her neighbours, and never left her apartment, so no-one could possibly be aware that she was contravening several international laws by remaining alone. She'd been born before the obligatory implants had been initiated, and had always felt that her independence depended on her relative anonymity.

Bullying her daughter into a policy of non-interference had been uncomfortable, but Coralle had felt it was necessary to maintain her independence, and anyway, she knew that her daughter secretly approved.

Coralle was proud that she'd never yet been beaten by any new technology, and she didn't intend to start now. Although, she reflected unwillingly, that bizarre and utterly unnecessary human waste-recycler had been a close-run thing. Anyhow, she wasn't going to be defeated by a computer that was probably very little different from her old one.

Coralle tidied her little seating area, brushed her thin white ringlets, straightened her tunic and found that she couldn't think of any more reasons to delay her first tentative investigation of the smooth, sleek little unit.

'It's not much to look at, is it?' she thought. It was merely a flat silver square laid on the table, broad and wide enough for an adult to lay both hands flat upon it.

'These new interface things are absurdly complicated,' she thought dispiritedly. The old machine had been so easy to use, but her daughter had descended on her one day, and told her it was ridiculously out of date, and then she'd gone and bought her mother this new thing. Coralle had been forced to go outside, which was something she generally tended to avoid, to have an implant fitted below her left ear. She touched the unfamiliar smooth place again, still faintly worried about it.

It was her only real worry. Her daughter had finally made her have an implant, and very soon, the authorities would be along to take her away. The thought was unbearable, but she hoped there was still a chance that she could convince them she was fine. There was nothing to be gained by fretting in any case, and her daughter's argument that she'd have a better chance of persuading the authorities to leave her alone if she could demonstrate mastery of the very latest technology certainly made sense.

Coralle attempted to flex her stiff fingers gently in preparation, and laid her hands as flat as she could on the sensor pad in front of her. She felt the faint buzz as it made contact with her brain via her nervous system, and then began to communicate directly with her implant. Realising belatedly that the computer certainly knew everything about her now, Coralle tried to remove her hands, but as the machine read her synapses, she was unable to move.

Gradually, the faint tingle that meant the machine was reading its operator's mind and identity faded away, and Coralle found herself able to remove and replace her hands without any trouble. She sat quietly, then, wondering what to do next.

Ever stoic, Coralle called up a communication program with a thought, and as a hologrammatic image of her mailbox appeared in front of her, she was gratified to see that it appeared to work just the same as her old machine had done. *Well, that's promising*, she thought. Then, thinking the authorities would probably be along any minute to put her in a city home, Coralle tried to contact her daughter, but there was no reply.

In frustration, Coralle composed one last message, after which she intended to go and make a cup of tea. 'Hello, is there anyone out there?'

Obviously there was no reply. There couldn't be, as she knew perfectly well, because her message wasn't addressed to anyone in particular.

Raising herself carefully and slowly to her feet, Coralle left the interface and went to the corner of the room where her food preparation equipment was stored, in search of lunch. As she tinkered with the nourishment outlets, she heard a soft chime that seemed to come from inside her head. The surprise almost made Coralle drop the sachet she was holding.

An unfamiliar child's voice was babbling and chittering behind her, and Coralle looked around in bewilderment. There was no-one in the room, and as she realised that the sound was in her head, Coralle stopped moving and concentrated on understanding exactly what it was saying. It was difficult, but she gradually realised that the voice wasn't actually babbling, it was just speaking very fast.

The voice gradually slowed and deepened, and the words became clearer. 'Hello, Coralle.' There was a pause, as though the voice were waiting for Coralle to find her bearings.

'Er, hello?' Coralle reached out and held on to the back of a chair. She had just *known* this would happen!

'I got your message, and yes, there is someone here, Coralle. My name's Meilinn, and I think we might be able to help each other.'